PREFACE

R.K Narayan is one of the most famous Indian English writers. His short stories delight us for much the same reason as his novels do. They give us sustained pleasure of short stories, and story telling has always been his forte. They create successfully the illusion of authentic social reality, and present a wide variety of people, all belonging to the little world of Malgudi. In them too is at work Narayan's unique comic vision of life which enables him to contemplate with his characteristic blend of humour and compassion the absurdities and pathos, fantasies and frustrations, illusions and ironies of everyday life. Narayan's stories belong to the native Indian soil and are redolent of its culture. They mainly depict the South Indian life and clearly express his view of the world and those who live in it. Simple but fascinating plot lively characterization, strict economy of narration and beautiful simplicity of language are some of the most outstanding features of his short stories. They serve as a good introduction to the foreigner who wants to acquire knowledge of Indian life. In his short stories, Narayan has depicted familiar situations and explored ways of life with which he was intimate. But the people here represent humanity at large and hence Narayan's stories have universal appeal. Some of Narayan's stories contain parallel characters.

It is indisputable that Narayan has a wide variety of themes. Though Narayan's novels have been studied from different angles, his short stories have been neglected by the critics. There are no full length studies of his short stories from the point of view of themes and techniques. This I hope will lead to a better understanding of R.K. Narayan as a writer.

(Ms. Disha Sharma)

ISBN 978-93-80190-16-7

First Edition : 2010

Published by :
R.D. Pandey
Satyam Publishing House
N-3/25, Mohan Garden, New Delhi-110059
Ph.: 011-25358642
E-mail : satyampub_2006@yahoo.com
Showroom : 4378/4B, 305, J.M.D. House,
Murarilal Street, Ansari Road,
Daryaganj, New Delhi-110002
Mob. 09868277749

Price Rs. 700.00

Composer :
Shri Krishna Computer Graphics
Delhi-110032

Printer :
Vishal Kaushik Printers
Delhi-110093

Short Stories
R.K. Narayan:
Themes and Techniques

Ms. Disha Sharma

SATYAM PUBLISHING HOUSE
New Delhi-110059

CONTENTS

CHAPTER – I
INTRODUCTION

A: Short Story as a literary genre

Telling stories and listening to them must be as old as language itself. Its popularity never waned but in modern times it has further increased. With the increasing speed of life in modern times, people find it less and less possible to read long novels. The short story is a convenient substitute, for it offers on a smaller scale and in a bricf manner the same pleasure that the novel does. The short story is an art form that defies definition and so there has been no completely satisfactory definition. However, there has been no dearth of definitions. These definitions differ regarding the exact nature of short story. No summary phrase encapsulates the diversity of all possible story types, lengths and approaches. Consequently, no one theory of short story form prevails. Ian Reid is of the opinion that it would be unsatisfactory to make word count the sole criterion. Genre is not arithmetically defined. (*Nair 14*) Edgar Allan Poe links brevity with intensity. He maintains that emotion or aesthetic arousal can be sustained only for brief periods. The story culminates in a moment of psychological reaction for the character and insight for the reader.

In 1842, Edgar Allan Poe had offered a definition of short story, which is still valid. He said it was "A short prose narrative requiring from a half-hour to one or two hours in its perusal." (*Hudson 337*) There is another definition of short story given by Sherwood Anderson, which highlights this point:

> The short story is the result of a sudden passion. It is an idea grasped whole as one would pick an apple in an orchard. All of my own short stories have been written in one sitting, many of them under strange enough circumstances.

> There are these glorious moments, these pregnant hours, and I remember such hours as a man remembers the first kiss got from women loved. (*Nair 14*)

Sean O' Faolin considers it "A more personal genre than the novel. It is kernel of the matter in hand, as the writer sees it. The writer need not be explicit". (*Nair 14*) H.G Wells has defined the short story as 'any piece of short fiction that could be read in half an hour'. (*Nair 14*) According to Brander Mathews, the short story 'deals with a single character, a single situation, a single emotion or a series of emotions called forth by a single situation'. (*Nair 15*) According to Somerset Maugham it is a piece of fiction dealing with a single incident, material or spiritual, that can be read at a sitting; it is original, it must sparkle, excite or impress and it must have unity of effect or impression." (*Nair 15*) A short story writer, must be concerned with a few heightened moments, perhaps only a single one, which he finds glorious and immortalizes.

All these definitions agree on certain vital characteristics though they differ in certain others. Some of them are too restricting and put the short story form into a rigid frame that inevitably hampers its freedom of movement, so that it does not include those, which do not conform to a rigid pattern. There is another definition of a recent definer of literary terms that it is -

> A relatively short narrative (under 10,000 words) which is designed to produce a single dominant effect and which contains the elements of drama. A short story concentrates on a single character in a situation at a single moment. Even if these conditions are not met, a short story still exhibits unity as its guiding principle.... Dramatic conflict- the collision of apposing forces- is at the heart of the story'. (*Dwivedi, 11*)

This is unmistakably a comprehensive definition of a short story. The traditional notions associated with the short story are: continuity and design, though it has to expand its scope in our own day to accommodate the truncation of ideas and the presentation of psycho-analysis, - the obvious result of a tension-ridden age enveloped in 'discontinuities' and 'disillusionments'. According to A. Walter Litz, the hallmarks of a well made story are: consistency of style, rationality of structure, steadiness in viewpoint. All definitions, however, agree upon one point, and that is 'the obvious distinctive element in the short story distinguishing it from every other art-its shortness'. Perhaps the most marked traits of short story are 'brevity, density and unity'. Short story generally depicts a single incident in a forcible way leaving a strong impression on the minds of the readers. It enables the readers to experience a kind of pleasure as they identify themselves with the characters of the play. Plot, structure and characterization are combine to create a short story. Sometimes the atmosphere, at other times incident or character take precedence over each other to play the major role in the story. Often it is an element of surprise which clinches the story as is demonstrated in the works of O' Henry.

Definitions of short story are generally elusive. The best definition of a good short story in most cases is the short story itself. The only proof of short story is its existence and its recognisability from among the many uninspiring things that pass as short stories. The short story, as its name implies, is defined by its shortness and its short element. A whole lifetime of experience might be condensed into the four, five, or ten pages if the writer is skilful. He might avoid a vision of life as being moral, metaphysical or mystical; he might also include it if he is able to. A short story does not allow any character within it to develop as to make itself full. Short stories are like poems, which seek to capture the mood implicit in a situation or sentiment. A short story strives for a unified emotional impact, which a novel might not attempt, thus distinguishing it in general from the novel.

The primary aim of a short story is to entertain the readers. Hence a short story must be interesting above everything else. It may convey some moral lesson, it may ridicule some human follies, it must all do this in an interesting manner. It must absorb the reader and make him forget the worries of his life for the time being. If it does not do so, it cannot be regarded as a good short story in spite of all the other excellent qualities that it may have. A short story is a story that can be read at a single sitting. Absolute economy of means is to be used and everything superfluous is to be strictly avoided. There is to be no word written of which the tendency direct or indirect is not to further the action of the story. Whatever may be its subject, the short story must leave us with the impression that even if nothing would have been lost at least nothing would have been gained by further elaboration. It must be complete without any suggestion of over-crowding. The attention must be focused throughout upon the single purpose.

As mentioned above the short story must have only one aim or purpose. It must also have singleness of effect. All the events, all the incidents, all the characters of the story must be invented to create that preconceived effect. The story must have one pivot of interest and by focusing the attention on the one point a powerful effect must be created on the reader. The satisfaction of the reader is the real test of the success. Owing to the exigencies of space a short story writer cannot portray a character in full. He can only exhibit some one aspect or at most of a salient feature of a character. The spot light is focused on some important aspect of character and it is thrown into prominent relief. Men and women are placed in such telling situations as are sufficient to develop the prominent trait of their characters. Here the novelist has an advantage over the short story writer. He has ample space at his disposal, and so can place his characters in as many situations as he likes and display different qualities of his characters. He can gradually develop the characters of his men and women and can lay their souls bare before us. All this is not possible in a short story. Besides, short story writer cannot introduce a dozen or even half-a dozen characters in the story, as it would result in over-crowding. None of the characters would then be effectively developed. This drawback has given rise to the one-man story. The plot hinges on the action of one man. All our attention is concentrated upon him and this result in a powerful impression and the story gains much in effect.

As in the novel and the drama, in the short story also the dialogues occupy a very prominent place. They add to the interest of the story and make it charming to read. In characterization, the dialogue counts for much. Every word of it is made to tell. We know much about the character of an individual by what he says and what others say about him. But the dialogue in a short story should be brief and to the point. Long speeches would be out of place and would be considered a serious defect. A suitable atmosphere is necessary for a short story. The atmosphere may be one of tragic gloom or of love and laughter or of suspense. But there should be consistency in the creation of this atmosphere of horror and mystery throughout. In a tragic story, the atmosphere must be one of gloom and a humorous or comic atmosphere would be out of place.

A short story is a kind of prose fiction but it may be written in both prose and poetry. In truth, the medium is not so important as the subject. A. J. Merson has rightly pointed out that 'Much of the popularity of the short story today is due to the diversity and unexpectedness of the subjects and that 'manner as well as matter further reveals the individuality of the writers'. Commenting on the wide range of the short story, H.E Bates has remarked that it can be anything from a prose- poem without plot or character to analysis of the most complex human emotions, and that it can deal with any subject, from the death of a horse, the loss of a clock, to a girl's first love affair. The theme may undoubtedly be ' anything' but it must be presented in such a manner that it carries the impression of being ' unified' and ' whole' in a limited sense. Edgar Allan Poe, has also laid great stress on 'a certain unique or single effect to be wrought out'. R. L. Stevenson insisted on the importance of an 'initial impulse' in the short story, which recalls the practice of Poe. At best, the short story writer must visualize the end in the beginning, and then alone he will be successful in communicating an 'impression' or 'idea', which is his primary concern.

The short story has its own significance and recognized place in literature. It must not be supposed that the short story is a novel on a reduced scale. It has a definite technique of its own, and has its own specific requirements of matter and treatment. Though immensely popular in modern times, the short story is not a modern product. It has been popular in every age and in every country from times immemorial. People, old young have always liked to be entertained, and the short story has been their most popular entertainment. The earliest forms of short story were the tales of adventure, dealing with the deeds of valour or of chivalry of some popular hero. Every country has got its own legends and mythology, and tales from them or their modifications have always been in wide circulation. Tales told in the *Ramayana, the Mahabharata, the Budhist, Jataka and Panchantras*, the *Aesop's fables*, the *Arabian Nights* and the *Decameron* testify to the popularity of the short story all over the world.

In the modern era, the short story has undergone a significant development. It exists with rare differences in attitudes toward life, which govern an author's sense of reality. The modern short story is a concentrated form, dependent for its success on feeling and suggestion. It developed almost simultaneously in France, Russia and the United States of America. From these Countries, it gradually spread into other regions of the world. For various reasons its efflorescence was delayed in England where it did not emerge as a distinct genre until the late nineteen eighties.

It is in France that the short story as a literary genre developed. The modern French short story is largely a creation of two persons– Prosper Merimee and Guy de Maupassant. The former fixed its form, the latter gave it perfection. Short stories of Merimee are triumphs of concentration, detachment and restraint. Like his friend Stendhal, he avoided all the tricks and devices of obvious romanticism – its misty eloquence and picturesque poses. His stories are all tragic or bitterly ironic tales of passion in which characters act under the stress of primitive emotions. There is even an element of cruelty in them. As a matter of fact, they might easily become melodramas but for the cold, dry, severe method of telling them, which is characteristic of Merimee. Besides two longer stories "Colomba" (1841) and "Carmen" (1845), Merimee wrote several shorter ones. All the stories show how, in the hand of a real master, the short story can have the unity of a lyric. Only with a few happy touches, he can make it run rapidly from one suspense to another whetting the curiosity of the reader all the time until it is raised to a climax. He applied his cool, clear-sighted intellect and serene sensitiveness to work on passionate problems at a time when his compeers regarded emotion, evident emotion, as everything. This dispassionate objectivity connects him to his great Russian contemporaries, Turgenev, on the one hand and Chekhov, on the other.

The literary career of Guy de Maupassant, the greatest short story writer of France, lasted only for ten years. He was such a prolific writer, that within this brief period, he wrote more than two hundred stories of diverse nature. Most of them are bitter and grimly ironic and deal with the futility and brutality of life. The few humorous stories that he wrote are not funny or even passably pleasant. He is at his best when he depicts middle class people or peasants of Normandy whom he knew so well. Most of his stories are frank to the point of broadness. However, they are told with great gusto and there is a masculine firmness in his style, which redeems them from much of their sordidness. As a story teller, Maupassant knows what to tell; he does not use a single word which is not necessary to produce the desired effect and avoids everything that he may do without; he does not care to explore the human kind or to play with ideas. He does not waste his time in superfluous comments or ornamental descriptions. To him the story is the only thing that matters, and so he holds fast to the essential facts of the story and never gets entangled in any discussion either of the reasons or of the meaning of those facts. None knows better than Maupassant how to bewitch the readers, how to interest, excite and surprise them in short, how to kindle their curiosity and satisfy it. Maupassant saw life through his senses alone, and almost alone with their help he described it. His senses were acute. Somerset Maugham and H.E. Bates are disciples of Maupassant by their own admission.

In Russia, the modern short story was introduced by Pushkin, developed by Gogol and perfected by Turgenev, Tolstoy and Chekhov. The greatest story of Gogol, "The overcoat", which was published in 1842, is one of the greatest short stories of all time. It begins a new chapter, not only in Russian, but also in world literature. It was Gogal who gave Russian Literature its first true modern short story, the artistically controlled narrative of personal life, releasing, in the very process of its unfoldment, overtones of the universal. It was he who made it the mirror of ordinary human life and by emancipating it from pompous encumbrances, took it back to the simpler days of folk tales.

The next great story teller of Russia, Turgenev, gave the modern short story its present shape. For it was probably he who created the dramatized structure. In his hand the old story of anecdote became transformed into modern story of character and feeling, with its sense of fate and folly, pity and wonder. All the distinctive traits of Turgenev as a writer of short stories appear in his early work, '*A Sportsman's sketches*'. It was begun in 1847 and published in 1852. As a storyteller, Turgenev avoids intricacies. He presents his simple stories – bare 'slices of life' – as simply as he can. Yet there is much art in his artlessness. He does not waste his time in useless preliminaries, but plunges straight in to the heart of the story. Only a few significant details serve for him the purpose of long descriptive passages and elaborate analysis of the character's minds. Plot is secondary to him, character and their emotional shades are his primary concern. Like Balzac, Tolstoy and Dickens, he absorbs and utilizes in his stories real persons – persons, intimately known to him.

As a writer of short story, Tolstoy was almost as great as Turgenev. But he is of lesser importance to us. For though Tolstoy is a phenomenon, an isolated splendour, an object of awe, wonder and admiration from afar, he is not a formative influence, at least, so far as English literature is concerned. The ideas of Tolstoy, rich that they are, have called forth responsive echoes in many a breast, but none has dared to imitate his methods.

Chekhov, the greatest Russian story-teller, had neither the massive genius nor the vast range of any of his illustrious predecessors; yet in his own sphere, as a portrayer of the humdrum life of the Russian intelligentsia, he has no parallel. In his sketches and longer tales, he brings forth petty officials, provincial clerks, shrewd tradesmen, dull school teachers, humble priests, and ignorant police officers. Even central character is the common man, a mediocre person devoid of any striking traits. Chekhov exposes his ridiculousness in anecdotal and farcical situations. He chose the path of objective depiction of life which intensifies the pathos in stories by getting rid of the elements of exaggeration, artificiality and melodramatic situations. Most of his stories are saturated with inner lyricism, expressed by the author's thoughts about brighter future, where life will acquire a new meaning. Chekhov showed his mastery in the creation of all the elements in composition of the plot, but his innovation is more evident in the endings of his stories. Chekhov's influence is felt in the works of many writers, from Katherine Mansfield down to Earnest Hemmingway or Katherine Ann Porter.

In America, Edgar Allan Poe was certainly the first writer of the tale of 'unity of effect'. By the time Poe came to write his stories, Washington Irving (1983-1859) had already established himself as the writer of short stories of some repute. The publication of Irving's Sketch Book in 1820 for the first time raised short story to the status of literature. Irving put more emphasis on the delineation of character than on action and theme. His story telling is leisurely. He takes time to describe the setting and the characters. Irving's common method of writing a tale is to rework an old story, often a folk legend of German origin. He, however transplants the story in American setting and makes his characters truly American. Many of his stories, especially 'Rip Van Winkle' and 'The Legend of the Sleepy Hollow' have achieved permanence and are often anthologized.

Another precursor of Poe in the genre is Hawthorne (1804-1864) who began to experiment with this form early in life. Because his stories were so different from those that were currently popular, recognition came to Hawthorne slowly. Literary fame was so slow in coming to him that he remarked that for many years he had been the obscurest man of letters. Although today, Hawthorne is better known as the author of *The Scarlet Letter* and other novels, had he died in his middle forties he should have been known as author of some finest tales in English. Hawthorne's first volume, *Twice Told Tales* most of which had been published in the annuals of the period, was published in 1837. It contains some of his finest stories. This was beginning of his recognition as a writer of talent.

The stories of Francis Bret Harte (1839--1902) also deeply influenced the English short story writers. Along with Mark Twain (1830–1910), he gave the English reader the new modes and broader criteria of humour. In many respects, he may be regarded as the prototype of Kipling. Both make interesting and unhesitating use of melodramatic devices; both derive comic and sensational effects from the unruly and the uncouth, and romance from the coarse and the vulgar. And in his use of local colour, Bret Harte is the literary ancestor, not only of Kipling, but also of a long line of short story writers including Katherine Mansfield.

Another great influence on the modern English short story came from Henry James (1843-1916). He was the first among the American writers to write impressionistic stories of situation illuminating a man's inner life and explaining, at the same time, his outward behaviour. He took up Poe's technique minus his sensationalism and polished it in to a high art at once subtle and intricate.

In Stevenson's stories, we find different elements as romance, mystery, adventure, exotic characters, picturesque scenes, murder and remorse. They are entertaining yarns, remarkable alike for their clarity and effective use of suspense. Purely anecdotic in character, they have no other aim than to amuse the reader. It is not for them to arrest a slipping mood or perpetuate an intense moment; they do not try to unravel the intricacies of a complex mind or illuminate the dark recesses of a mysterious heart. Deft manipulation of incidents and the immaculate art of narrating them are the main attraction of his stories. The only notable exception is the famous long short story 'The Strange Case of Dr Jekyll and Mr. Hyde' which is a study of dual personality and battle between a psychological document and a morality play without the dramatic form.

Thomas Hardy's method of story telling is rather primitive, though his stories are far more realistic. His language is sometimes cumbrous and style, too, ponderous for the delicate form of the short story. As in his novel, a pessimistic outlook runs through his tales also. His men and women are simple, innocent village folk, caught in the whirlpool of unkind circumstances beyond their control. His characters are more generic than individual, and the incidents are such as might have happened to anyone of the same type placed in similar circumstances. They are shaped and moulded by the local and natural environment in which they grow up by the topography of their native place and the beliefs, customs and traditions handed down to them from generation to generation. In the evolution of the form of short story also, Hardy's contribution is very little. As a matter of fact, most of his stories are miniature novels in form.

The stories of Rudyard Kipling may be broadly divided into two groups – Indian and British. The Indian stories are far larger in number and were until recently, supposed to be the more representative of their author and superior of the two. They show his keen power of observation, his capacity to understand though not very deeply, unfamiliar scenes and unaccustomed lives and his ability to make them real and lively. They are characterized by a sort of masculine energy rather than sweetness and grace. Many of them are sensational, even boisterous. But in the British stories of his maturer years we find a new sobriety, tenderness and grace – a quiet objectivity which was hitherto unknown. Some of these stories deal with the more private and sentimental aspects of personality and some with the occult and the supernatural.

While Kipling was acclaimed as the king of English story tellers, Conrad gave it a new charm. Being an expatriot, Conrad brought an exotic charm and alien grace to English fiction, together with an exquisite art, reminiscent of the finished products of Flaubert and Stendhal. And he gave it also a new technique that of oblique narration. As a device, of course, it was nothing new; what was new was the artistic use he put it to. By stepping down from the position of the omniscient author and entrusting the narration to a person who is himself involved in the action of the story, he not only gave it an added reality but endowed the characters with an extra dimension. The telling of a story from multiple point of view serves a very important purpose. It helps to establish the tentativeness of all patterns of significance and the baffling inscrutability of individual experience.

Other short story tellers are H.G. Wells, Arnold Bennett, John Galsworthy and Thomas Moore. But neither the careful art of Benett, not the originality of Wells nor the brilliant but less profound social criticism of Galsworthy and delicate method of Thomas Moore could push the short story in Britain further ahead. The originality of Wells is confined mainly to his subject matter, Bennett was not careful in his art. Galsworthy had a keen sense of character and situation but he could give it perfect expression within a brief compass. Moore is little read today, and this is mainly due to his method of story telling which though delicate and cautious, lacks warmth and ardour.

In the first quarter of the twentieth century, many great short story writers developed its field. James Joyce, E. M. Forster, Katherine Mansfield, Virginia Woolf and D.H. Lawrence are the major story tellers of this era. Somerset Maugham also gained popularity after the publication of his second volume *The Trembling of a Leaf*, all these writers are realistic who used the flash back interior monologue, symbolism and recurrent images in this genre. They incorporated in their stories actual incidents and characters.

The stories of James Joyce are called 'epiphanies' that is, they arrest the transcendental moments of sudden spiritual manifestation, when vulgarities rise above themselves and are transfigured, and common things assume uncommon proportions and exhibit the expansion of infinite things. He believed that the writer should always remain behind or beyond or above his handiwork. Consequently, his stories are scrupulously objective. He did not think of making stories more eventful than life with the use of surprise and coincidence. He aimed at exact production of the pattern of experiences. So his stories are based on actuality. However, we find there are some elements of romance and reality in some of his stories.

The short stories of Forster introduce us to his characteristic blend of poetry and realism. They also explore themes that are more amply developed in the novels, such themes as salvation, the past personal relations, getting in touch with nature, money, and the attack on conventional ideas of good form. There are four collections of short stories: '*The Celestial Omnibus*' (1911), '*The Eternal Moment*' (1928), '*Collected Short Stories*' (1947) – combining the earlier two collections – and the posthumous 'The life to come, and other stories (1972). In the introduction to '*Collected Short Stories*' Forster calls his tales 'fantasies'. They are certainly not to be judged by standards appropriate to realism.

Katherine Mansfield was, infact, the first among that little band of English writers who staked their whole future on the short story. She had no other aim in life than to shine as a short story writer. She was perhaps the first colonial writer to be accepted and naturalized in the domain of English writers. It stands to the credit of Katherine Mansfield that she could give it not only a form but also a new type of content, so that in her hand the short story gained a firm footing in England and was well on the way to catch up the rich continental standard. She gave it not only a new vitality but also a new character. The innovation of Katherine, for the first time in short story, led fiction within the mind, within the very process of consciousness. Her stories – at least the better ones among them-show rather than tell. She was a pioneer in the use of other literary devices also in that field, such as interior monologue or the objective correlative. It was she who started the device of unfolding a story through a series of characters from a 'multi-personal view point.

Virginia Woolf wants the short story to concentrate upon the inner life, the essence of reality. According to her, a complete story teller is one who can balance between two powers: the power of portraying the essence of life and the power of presenting everything in a story in an aesthetically effective manner. She more or less neglects the physical side of life- the eternal life of action, speech and passions characterized by violent expression of grief or boisterous outburst of laughter. She borrows concepts from visual arts and uses them in her discussion of the 'architectural quality', 'perspective' and 'form' in the short story. Some critics claimed that Woolf definitively abandoned the conventional short story.

However this is not absolutely correct for she never abandoned thoroughly the conventional short story, while her experiments in the genre depends upon the adaptation, often the sub-version, of existing forms and conventions. In fact, Woolfian story, continually revolves around conventional story types and never finally abandons the touches of its literary heritage. Her research of the 'plotless' story is made within well structured framework as for example in her stories 'Moments of Being', 'An Unwritten Novel' and 'The Lady in the Looking Glass'. In these stories, a single consciousness dominates each narrative, and a clear evaluative distance is maintained.

D. H. Lawrence's stories are embodiments of his intuitive experience of the mystery of being. They enshrine his immediate non-intellectual vision of life. Lawrence's primitive idealism and revolt against machine age, his belief in the blood and flesh, his instinctive awareness of the dark powers of unconscious impulse, and his search for central psychic forces in physical love all are distinctive traits of his stories. Throughout his short fiction, Lawrence peeps into the visible, endeavouring to penetrate through the action of the unconscious will to the elemental patterns of human behaviour. He explores, from the deepest zones of the individual's heart, which speaks the language of the unconscious self through the abstraction of the mundane affairs, man- woman relationship, mythical symbolism and the unending quest of the human beings is best represented by his dialectics, of mind and body.

As a master of short story, William Somerset Maugham was among the highest paid authors in the 1930s. He wrote with a sense of irony and wit. Often he expressed a cynical attitude towards life and his love of travelling found its way into his writing. His purpose was to entertain his readers. His keen eye for the minute detail of life is combined with his writing style in such a way to capture to keep reader's attention. His style is perfectly suited for short story writing. His facility of communicating all kinds of ideals is truly amazing. Thus, his stories feel like a light read, but they also often give the pause. Maugham is trying to pry deep into what makes people think and act the way they do. He wrote his stories a century go, and the mark of the time lies firmly upon some of them. It is clear that he was influenced by psychological insights and ideas that have penetrated intellectual circles of his time. These stories are about human nature and vivid images, such as those of the pacific and the industrial landscape of the rising American giant.

The Indian short story in English is virtually a product of this century: it was in 1898 that a collection of short stories by an Indian writer in English was first published. *Stories from Indian Christian Life* by Kamala Sathianadan was introduced then by a Madras publisher to a comparatively small reading public. When he started writing, the Indian short story writer in English took to the form not so much because he was interested in it as a literary form as because he knew that of all forms, it was the simplest and the most popular means of communicating a way of life; and he was interested in conveying, in a language understood by many, inside as well as outside India, the essential India which hc has understood and of which he wanted others to get a proper perspective. He found the short story in an almost perfectly finished form in his ancient classics, a form which exactly suited his purpose, for the purpose in those short stories was also the communication of an idea as clearly and as simply as possible, the diffusion of perpetual values and truths which when properly received, would stand the reader and listener in good stead. For these truths, the twentieth century Indian writer substituted the variegated and colourful picture of the India he knew and the essential fact of the underlying unity of the country, made possible by the unifying cultural bonds throughout its length and breadth, albeit its apparent diversities in language, habiliment and food habits.

The ancient Indian tale took broadly two forms – the fable, and the popular or the folk tale. The fable form is best exemplified in the tales of *Panchatantra* as well as in the *Jataka Tales*. These tales are epigrammatical in structure, ending with a significant utterance by one of the characters.Most of these are beast fables in which the characters are animals symbolizing human beings. With their concentration of approach, compactness of structure, and preoccupation with the daily realities of life, these fables are similar to the modern short story. The ancient Indian popular tale is an example of the typical oriental, a loosely constructed narrative of adventure and romance, in which the action is normally set against a background of the fantastic and the supernatural. *Kathasaritsagara* or the *Daskumarcharita* – are known for the successful description of human desire and aspirations in a highly imaginative way.

The purpose of the writer of these stories being moral edification mainly, philosophizing and introduction of pithy sayings and catchy verses bringing home some moral maxim or practical truth become common. This practice does not seem to have in any way affected the popularity of the tales – the evidence, indeed, is to the contrary. They add to the charm of the tales and are always welcome, and even sought after. The popular tales or the popular romances are not strictly religious in character; yet they do teach something – practical wisdom as how to achieve immediate gain in any given situation, often by sheer courage and perseverance. The didactic tale and the popular tale, however, have certain qualities in common. They impress one with their racy narration as well as their use of suspense, two virtues of any good story. Here is a sample from the Panchatantra:

> "Then with a sharp arrow he shot the boar, who in turn tore the hillman's stomach with a pointed fang that shone like the crescent moon, so that the man fell dead. The boar also, after killing the hunter, died in toment from the arrow wound". *(Venugopal, 4)*

The plot of a typical Panchatantra story shows how well the writer knew to whet the curiosity of the reader and preserve it till the end. The style of the *Panchatantra* in particular is direct, forceful and smooth-flowing. Its diction is simple and idiomatic and it avoids the ornate. The stories are spiced with innumerable witty statements, as the one below, giving them a perennial appeal:

> "If Fate has willed that I should die,
> are there no means save that soft eye?" (*Venugopal, 5*)

Supposed to have been a work written by one Vishnusharman who took upon himself the task of enlightening the children of a particular king in the art of living, the *Panchatantra* consists of five books, *The Loss of Friends, The Winning of Friends, Crows and Owls, Loss of Gains and Ill Considered Action.* The purpose of the work is best hinted at in this verse from its Introduction:

Whoever learns the work by heart?
Or through the story-teller's art
Becomes acquainted,
His life by sad defeat – although
The king of heaven be his foe-
Is never tainted. (*Venugopal, 5*)

Each of the five books is independent and has a framing story into which numerous stories are inserted. They are told, according to the need of the moment, by one or the other character in the main story. The first book, for example, tells the framing story of the broken friendship of Rusty the lion and Lively the bull, with some thirty stories inserted, told mainly by the two jackals, Victor and Cheek. The stories in the *Panchatantra* are thus related most intimately to our life in society. They do not advocate renunciation or a blind faith in divinity. Each story refers to some incident in which the fate of the characters takes us a step ahead in our grasping the meaning of niti – 'the harmonius development of the powers of man, a life in which security, prosperity, resolute action, and friendship and good learning are so combined as to produce joy.' (*Venugopal, 5*) The Panchatantra has also the basic requirements of a well-told story – an effective beginning, an interesting middle, and a perfectly logical conclusion.

Similar to the *Panchatantra* tales, but for their explicit didacticism are the *Jataka tales*. They have most of the virtues of the *Panchatantra*, especially the straight-forward and simple narration. They too picture human weakness as well as virtues but almost always with a moral tag: that only the good and noble and the virtuous are rewarded in the world and the evil and the ignoble have no chance of escape from paying the penalty for being so. Every story has Bodhisatta as a character who it is that will be instrumental in enlightening the one who has gone astray and who passes judgement on the wrong-doer. The stories, however, have not lost their appeal even today, for they portray human nature essentially. The explicit moral statement at the end may sound superfluous, but perhaps it was the most important aspect of the tale at the time of its creation.

Vastly different from the *Panchatantra* or the *Jataka Tales* in length and content but not in appeal are the popular tales of *Kathasaritsagara*. It is a colourful work consisting of innumerable stories of adventure. Conceived as originally devised by Lord Shiva to entertain his consort.

Yet, in terms of a portrayal of human dreams and ambitions, they have a firm grounding in reality. In these stories the grip of the author depends upon the curiosity of the reader. Curiosity, it is said, is the very essence of any successful narration, and from this point of view, the stories in the *Kathasaritsagara* never let the reader down. Incidents are cleverly manipulated to take the protagonists into more and more complicated situations. The final outcome, however, is never in doubt; either the gods take a hand or the hero will have been endowed with such superhuman powers (almost invariably he is a Vidyadhara born as a human being owing to a curse) that his success is assured.

Another virtue of the *Kathasaritsagara* is that its characters are not confined to any particular section of humanity: ranging from Gods from to the lowliest of human beings. Intrigue is an inevitable element in the story and almost every character exhibits an insatiable zest for life. The achievements of the character are very often assisted by supernatural agencies like a magic sword or a special boon by a goddess. In a scientifically and technologically advanced age like ours, much that needed supernatural interference may be substituted by real human achievements, but at the cost of the thrill provided by the authors of these romances. It is this high imaginative fecundity and the fact that basically the men and women they portray are as real as we are ourselves that have given the stories a perennial appeal. Also, while presenting the laiety in the emboxed stories, the writer deals with eternal themes.

The similes in the main stories are at times far removed from the familiar and have references to things in classical lore.

> "What could those Rakshasis do against one who swallowed the whole army of the Asuras, as Agastya swallowed the sea?" (*Venugopal, 7*)

This practice, however, does not hinder the Indian reader in his enjoyment of the stories, as these similes have actually become a part of his life. It is not uncommon for one to hear the beauty of a girl being compared to that of one or the other courtesan of king Devendra's court, or the patience of a woman to that of the Earth Goddess, ora woman's fidelity to that of Rama's wife Sita, or that of Satyavan's wife Savitri. Likewise, a beautiful garden is often compared to the heavenly garden Nandanavana, and a philanthropic soul to the divine tree Kalpavriksha, which can bestow on one anything. The writers of the popular romances did not very much bother to confine themselves to any harsh pattern of the short story; they frequently luxuriated in fanciful ideas and were perhaps preoccupied with methods of outdoing earlier writers in ornate expression. The *Kathasaritsagara*, perhaps being earlier than the other romances, is a rare exception to this temptation, despite its colossal size. But in the works like Dandin's *Daskumaracharita*, we have instances of occasional exercise in composition.

Taken in the bare outlines, and the basic feelings that motivate the action on the part of the various characters, the stories in the *Kathasaritsagara* as well as the *Daskumaracharita* are surprisingly down to earth. It is this fact that has mainly appealed to the writers of today, apart from their gripping narration. These romances bear evidence to the fact that the authors of yore did make a minute study of human nature and covered their pictures of men and women with romantically imagined outfits. Shorn of these romantic elements, these stories can be, and have been, as acknowledged by some of our present day writers themselves, models of the well-told short story.

Apart from these popular works, there have been other ancient works too in which the tale is frequently to be found: in various Upanishads, in the many Puranas like the *Bhagwata* or *Brahmanda*, in the epics *Ramayana* and the *Mahabharata*. Jainism has its tales and legends too. It has stories similar to the *Jataka tales* of

Buddhism, and has longer works such as the *Padmapurana* by Ravisena which tells the story of *Ramayana* with a few modifications, and the *Mahapurana* by Jinasena and Gunabhadra which also includes the story of *Ramayana* with a few changes though primarily dealing with the legendary biographies of the sixty three-great men of Jainism. As with the *Jataka Tales*, the Jain versions of the stories too take a didactic aim in the presentation of already popular stories.

The ancient tale form was later revived and preserved in the literature of the various Indian languages as part of bigger works. Most of these works were based on the models of the epics the *Ramayana* and the *Mahabharata.* As early as the eleventh century, poets like Pampa and Ranna had recreated the epics in Kannada, and were followed in the next two hundred years by Virashaiva poets notable among whom was Raghavanka who retold the story of king Harishchandra in verse. The fifteenth and sixteenth centuries witnessed religious movement gaining ascendance all over India and the ancient classics were revived again. Kumaravyasa and Lakshmisha retold the story of *Mahabharata* in Kannada in enchanting shatpadis, poets like Eknath and Mukteshwar retold the Puranas in Marathi, and Tulsidas brought out his now highly popular revered rendering of the Ramayana in Hindi, the Ramacharitamanas. All these works were mainly in poetry, but the ancient tale was preserved in them.

It was only in the 19th century, with the introduction of Macaulay's scheme of modern education, that literature in India came gradually into its own once again. By the time the century moved into its second half, English literature had its impact on Indian writing, prose works were attempted, and newer forms like the lyric, the novel, and the short story began to appear in Indian languages. By the turn of the century, short stories in the English language itself began to be written by the Indian writers. Though not much had been produced in the Indian languages themselves during the eighteenth century, the nineteenth century had seen the revival once again of the ancient Indian tale, now in fresher translations, and often in prose form too, as in Muddana's

Ramashwamedha, a 'novel' epic in Kannada. Also, the oral tradition of passing on the stories from epics and the fable cycles had never ceased and the Indian writer in English naturally turned to his own classical tales for inspiration when he decided to write short stories.

The fable form is not of course peculiar to the Indian tradition. The allegory in a fable as well as the representation of animals behaving as human beings has never failed to fascinate man. Without the embarrasing necessity of exaggerating unreasonably, types can be represented through beasts, especially as certain characteristics are universally attributed to certain animals and they are not normally thought of as being otherwise: the lion is majestic, the fox cunning, the wolf greedy, the monkey impish, the cow innocent and gullible, and the dog faithful. The fable has ever fascinated the Indian – and in ancient India the form had been developed to perfection – and evidence of its impact on our leading writers can be seen in more than one story: in the "Kanakapala" by Raja Rao, the "Five short fables" by Mulk Raj Anand, or the "Illumination" by Manjeri Isvaran. Even R. K. Narayan has a delightful story, "At the Portal", set in the fable framework. Our writers have normally found the fable form excellent for social satire. All the stories referred to above are examples of delightful satire. "Kanakpala" exposes the perennial jealousies and hatred among kinsfolk on account of wealth, and "Illumination", man's cruelty to animals; Anand's "Fables" are allegorical satires of the contemporary social scene. The Fable, it is indisputable, has always brought home a way of life or the transliteration of an idea, and the Indian writer has ever been quick to grasp this readily available and finished form of the story. If the satirical and allegorical elements in his short story may be traced back to the fable in the *Panchatantra*, the Indian writer's tendency to fill in his stories with continuous action, as in "The Barber's Trade Union" by Anand, or "The Roman Image" by Narayan, may be traced to the ancient Indian popular tale. The impact of the ancient Indian tale is also to be seen in the not so admirable features of our writer, such as his occasional leaning towards overt didacticism or his tendency to ramble, which had not been able to avoid consistently.

The Indian English short story is slightly less than a hundred years old. The earliest short story collections by Indian authors appeared in London in 1885: *Realities of Indian Life: Stories Collected from the Criminal Reports of India* by Shoshee Chunder Dutt and *The Times of Yore: Tales from Indian History* by Shoshee Chunder Dutt and Sourinder Mohan Tagore. Apart from P. V. Ramaswmi Raju who published two collections – *The Tales of sixty Mandarins* (London, 1886) and Indian Fables (London, 1887), there are only two short story writers with a collection each to their credit, until the turn of century: Khetrapal Chakravarti *Sarata and Hingana – Tales Descriptive of Indian Life*, Calcutta 1895 and Kamala Sattiandhan *Stories of Indian Christian Life* Madras 1898, B. R. Rajam Iyer's *Miscellaneous Stories* which appeared in The Prabuddha Bharata during 1896-98 are included in his *Rambles in the Vedanta* (1905). They are mostly a retelling of mythological and allegorical tales.

The first Indian English short story writer with a considerable output appeared with the dawn of the twentieth century. This was Comella Sorabji, the first woman advocate in Calcutta. Her four short story collections are: *Love and Life behind the purdah* (1901); *Sunbabies: Studies in the Child Life of India* (1904); *Between The Twilight: Being studies of Indian Women by one of themselves* (1908); and *Indian Tales of the Great Ones among Men, Women and Bird-People* (1916). These studies of mostly Hindu and occasionally Parsi Life in both princely and common circles are a mixed collection of stories, anecdotes and character-sketches. Among the notable short story collections of the period are: S. M. Natesa Sastri's *Indian Folk Tales* (1908); Dwijendra Nath Neogi's *Sacred Tales of India* (1916); A. Madhaviah's *Short Stories by Kusika* (1916) and Sunity Devee's *Bengal Decoits and Tigers* (1916) and *The Beautiful Moghul Princesses* (1918).

The Indian English short story came to maturity during the Gandhian age (1920-1947). First of all, we can take T. L. Natesan who wrote under the pen-name Sankar Ram. His main collections of short stories are: *The Children of Kaveri* (1926) and *Creatures All* (1933). Both the books appeared under the title *The Ways of*

Man (1968). These stories deal mostly with rustic life in Tamil Nadu. Most of the stories are artless, and some sentimental like "Blood is thicker than water", which presents a motherless boy persecuted by his step-mother. Many others rest upon fickle conventional motif like an estrangement between two near and dear ones, finally ending in reconciliation; and some animals stories like 'The Rajah's Lost Hunt' are almost artless. Sankar Ram's heavy- handed didacticism is writ large in crude titles such as 'When punishment is a Boon'. In most of his tales incident is more important than character. But Sankar Ram recaptures the village scene evocatively and his literal translation of rustic nicknames like 'barrel-nose Grandpa' and 'spider-leg' anticipates Raja Rao's effective use of this device in *Kanthapura*

Another leading novelist and short story writer of the period is A. S. P. Ayyar. He was a novelist and playwright. His three collections of short stories have been published. They are: *Indian After-Dinner Stories* (1927), *Sense in Sex and Other Stories* (1929) and *The Finger of Destiny and Other Stories* (1932), besides retelling ancient Indian legends in books like *Tales of Ind* (1944) and *Famous Tales of India* (1954). As in his plays, Ayyar's constant theme in his stories is social reform, and especially the condition of woman in traditional Hindu society, which a character describes as a 'woman-eating monster'. His women include young widows, who successfully remarry in the teeth of opposition; young girls married by their parents to old men for money; abandoned or persecuted wives; victims of the dowry system or of the absence of birth control, etc. His titles, like Sankar Ram's, are often stridently didactic:e.g 'Right to happiness' and 'The Ways of providence'. Ayyar's characters are mostly drawn in monochrome and both in conception and execution his stories are little more than anecdotage.

S. K. Chettur is another name in the history of Indian English short story. His collections of short stories are: *Muffled Drums and Other Stories* (1917), *The Cobras of Dhermashevi and Other Stories* (1937), *The Spell of Aphrodite and Other Stories* (1957) and *Mango Seed and Other Stories* (1974). These stories seem to be based on material collected during his official tours as a member of the Indian civil service. Village feuds, murders and local legends about serpents, ghosts and omen are his main themes of his stories. He seems to have a special fascination for fantasy and the supernatural as in 'The Spell of Aphrodite' in which Venus herself comes out of the ocean to lure an imaginative youth to his death. S. K. Chettur, however, hardly possesses the kind of imagination which can successfully accomplish 'a willing suspension of disbelief' in his readers. His narrative technique is far more mixed – especially in his later work. He uses a variety of narrative modes including the autobiographical methods, the device of the observer-narrator, and the epistolary method.

K. S. Venkataramani is another writer who made a contribution to Indian English short story with his two collections: *Paper Boats* (1921) and *Jatadharan and Other Stories* (1937). In his *Jatadharan and Other Stories* Venkataramani reveals himself a sensitive writer studying the various facts of the individual mind in its responses to the social conditions in whose midst it is normally thrown. He can depict a rather unhappy social situation with a touch of mild satire, as in his picture of the over populated little village Kakalani:

> The little village of Kakalani has an enviable reputation in the matter of population. The Bharadwajas and the Kusikas predominated, and each other in a matter which is after all the capital point of human endeavour and existence. They yearly added, true to the prolific instinct of the stock, with uneasing freshness and variety, to the gay group of little children that thronged the streets. (*Venugopal, 26*)

Although his narration is rather slow and discursive with intermittent deviations into edifying statements, Venkataramani is capable of holding the reader's attention with a realistic presentation of personal relationship as well as with his humorous touches:

> Lakshmi finished decisively, flinging the silver cut to lords, which bore a meekly as he the several dints of her temper. Ramanujam caught it nicely from the googly bowler. Thanks God, he had a quick and trained eye for all moving things,

> from the trains that fly at forty miles an hour to domestic furniture that spins eccentric circles. (*Venugopal*, 26)

The reference to trains flying at forty miles an hour is most apt in the context, for Ramanujam is a young station master recently transferred to an out of the way god-forsaken jungle point, precisely for which reason Lakshmi was furious. Venkataramani has a few memorable descriptions of his men and women too. Here is Lakshmi.

> Lakshmi was of medium stature, her body soft and all curves; it shone like burnished gold, and gave her a round face, perfect beauty. The high brow, the rising forehead, and the eagle nose and eyes, and the unfading luster of a high-class brahmin girl gave her a distinction and aristocratic bearing which was no ancestral gift. (*Venugopal*, 27)

The stories of Venkataramani also show an awareness of the social change being attempted by Gandhi, as is evident in his character of Jatadharan who becomes a teacher after a brilliant academic career, with a view to educating the illiterate rustics. Venkataramani also aims at exposing the more conspicuous social evils, as is seen in the story, "The Bride Waits". It depicts the anxious but futile efforts of Subramania Shastri to find a suitable bridegroom for his daughter, Pattu before she comes of age, facing the taunts of the people of his clan, and the wrath of his employers who transfer him to an unhealthy place as punishment for going on leave when they didn't want him to. True, his dialogue often rings artificial, inspired as it is by the flowery and ornate dialogues of our ancient classics. Yet in his depiction of the contemporary situation, and of the feeling heart, and above all, in his conscious attempts to translate the typically Indian idiom into the English idiom, he has contributed significantly to the development of the Indian short story in English.

Manjeri Isvaran though late, is slowly yet firmly gaining ground as a major Indian English short story writer. He has published ten volumes of short stories such as *The Naked Shingles* (1941), *Siva Ratri* (1943), *Angry Dust* (1944), *Rickshawallah* (1946), *Fancy Tales* (1947), *No Anklet Bells For Her* (1949), *Immersion* (1951),

Painted Tigers (1956) and *A Madras Admiral* (1959). Isvaran occupies a significant place among our pioneers. His keen interest in the form is revealed in his attempt to discuss the theory of the short story in some of his prefaces. In the preface to *A Madras Admiral*, he says, 'A Short Story can be a fable or a parable, real or fantasy, a true presentation or a parody, sentimental or satirical; serious in intent or a light-hearted diversion; it can be any of these, but to be memorable it must catch the eternal in the casual, invest a moment with the immensity of time'. He is a typical Indian writer who confined himself to the life of the low and middle classes in the erstwhile Madras state. In his tales, he observes fidelity to facts and his own experiences. He manages to write skillfully, from different angles, on a wide variety of subject – the ravaging result of the great war and the Indian National movement (as to be seen in "Between two Flags"), the naivete of children (as in "Kolu"), the love affairs of a confirmed thief or a motor driver (as to be had in "The Motor-man"), the uninhibited exhibition of love leading to sensual gestures and sexy word duel (as to be found in "Mango Lane"), the rape of the volatile Jagada by the Crafty Cartman (as in "Immersion"). But of all the subjects, Isvaran seems to excel in the sympathetic revelation of female psyche, ranging from housewife to a school-going girl, a mother-in-law to a daughter-in-law, from a young widow to a granny. In depicting the womankind, Isvaran is close to earth and keenly alive. But he does not succeed so well when he comes to deal with children and their delicate psychology. An Isvaran story usually begins leisurely but ends up with some authorial comments or philosophical reflections. What is tormenting, however, is the truth that he starts casting his views and reviews in the midst of a story. But for this weakness, he is a truly powerful story teller, who is equally at home in narrations and dialogues. His total commitment to India, especially to the life around Madras, is unquestionable. Isvaran is not an experimenter with English idioms, as Anand or Raja Rao is.

Raja Rao is another famous writer of short story in Indian English. He is soberer and more serious in evoking a proper atmosphere for the flowering of Indian thought and tradition. He writes mostly on social and political scenes around him with a natural case and philosophical resignation. He is not so prolific a writer of shorter fiction as Mulk Raj Anand or R.K. Narayan. He has contributed to Indian English short story with his two collections known as *The Cow of Barricades and Other Stories* (1947) and *The Policeman and the Rose* (1978). The long gap between the publication dates of the collections of short stories is quite in keeping with the temper of the author, for we know that he had taken a long rest in the fictional world after the release of his *Kanthapura* in 1938. Raja Rao goes to the folk tales and the epic legends to evolve a form of his own with all the simplicity and credulity as a myth-maker. He has published a dozen stories, and these stories display considerable thematic and formal variety. The true story of Kanakapala, Protector of God is a retelling of an ancient legend about a snake-motif handed by various Indian English writers, but Raja Rao succeeds best because he rightly tells the traditional tale in the traditional manner.

Raja Rao often writes on such subjects like the popular myths, national upsurge, and rural characters. His story "Narsinga" for example, brings to the fore an orphaned village boy filled up with Gandhism. He may not have a wide range of themes like Anand, Narayan, and Isvaran but he commands greater depth and philosophical probings in his works. His later short stories like "The Policeman and the Rose" and "A Fable" confirm the statement. If "Javni" in the first collection is the charming tale of an untouchable woman widowed and disdained by all and earning only a rupee per month for her livelihood, the short stories of a later day probe deeper into the metaphysical longings of man. True, the first collection remains incomparable in the presentation of social problems and national stirrings. The story "Akkayya" is a memorable presentation of the traditional Hindu widow and her dull and cheerless life. Like "Narsinga", the story "The Cow of Barricades" powerfully evokes the picture of the suffering motherland (symbolized by the cow Gauri) under the tyrannical rule of the red Englishmen. The stories "Kanakapala", "Companions" highlight the popular snake myth, while "The Little Gram Shop" and "A Client" focus our attention on the cunning banias exploiting the innocent people and themselves wallowing in wealth and prosperity. As a short story writer, the real charm of Raja Rao lies in his profundity of vision and in his deep-rooted Indianness. He appeals to us for his onrushing narrative technique – as though the tale has gushed forth from a dark, deep cavern – and his masterly handling of the English language.

Mulk Raj Anand published seven collections of short stories. *The Lost Child and Other Stories* (1934), *The Barber's Trade Union and Other Stories* (1944), *The Tractor and the Corn Goddess and Other Stories* (1947), *Reflection on the Golden Bed and Other Stories* (1953), *The Power of Darkness and Other Stories* (1959), *Lajwanti and Other Stories* (1966), and *Between Tears and Laughter* (1973). Anand has also retold traditional Indian tales in his Indian Fairy Tales (1946) and More Indian Fairy Tales (1961). A representative selection is selected short stories of Mulk Raj Anand edited by M.K. Naik (New Delhi, 1977); The Selected stories Moscow (1955) is now out of print. Anand's aims and method are explained at length in his prefaces. In the preface to *Indian Fairy Tales*, he observes: 'Although I have taken in much new psychological technique into my writing of the short story, I have always tried to approximate to the technique of the folk tale and the influence of these fairy stories has always been very deep on my deep fiction' (*Naik* 180). In his Preface to *Selected Stories*, he adds, 'While accepting the form of the folk tale, specially in its fabulous character, I took in the individual and group psychology of the European conte and tried to synthesize the two styles.

Anand's short stories are wide-ranging in mood and tone. First, there are stories of 'lyric awareness' (to use his own phrase) like the "The Lost Child" a parable in which the traumatic experience of a child separated from its parents in a country fair symbolizes a universal human plight; and 'Birth' which presents a young, simple, peasant woman in an advanced state of pregnancy. She feels assured that the goddess Kali is by her side as she finds the birth-pangs starting, when she is on her side way to work, alone and nervous. In contrast to these imaginative tales, there are starkly realistic studies of men and women crushed by overwhelming forces. Among these are "Lajwanti", the story of a helpless rustic girl persecuted by her in-laws; and "Old Bapu" and "The Cobbler and the Machine" – sketches of two unfortunate outcastes. Another prominent group is that of stories of strong social awareness revealing Anand's acute understanding of the complex social forces at work in modern India. "The Power of Darkness" and "The Tractor and the Corn Goddess" demonstrate the inevitable clash between tradition and modernity in our country today; and feudalism and capitalism are pilloried in "A Kashmir Idyll" and "The Price of Bananas" respectively. Stories such as "A Pair of Mustachios", "The Barber's Trade Union" and "The Liar" provide pure fun seasoned with farce, while subtle studies in psychology like "The Tamarind Tree" and "The Thief" strike a different note altogether.

The range and variety of Anand's short stories are evinced not only in mood, tone and spirit but also in locale and characters, form and style. While both the village and the city get almost equal representation, the men, women and children that move through these narratives come from different strata of society. The forms Anand draws upon are the fable, the parable, the folk-tale, the bardic narrative and sometimes even the well-made story; and his style can be in turn lyrical and satirical, light-hearted and indignant. As in his novel, he makes an almost aggressive use of a great variety of Indianisms. His chief weaknesses are an occasional failure of sensibility which can make him lachrymose and crude and a tendency to write in a verbose – and sometimes even slipshod – manner. In his finest stories like "The Lost Child", however, there is an admirable control of both the material and the expression.

Khuswant Singh is another significant name in the field of Indian English short story. He has published four volumes of collections: *The Mark of Vishnu and Other Stories* (1950), *The Voice of God and Other Stories* (1957), *A Bride for Sahib and Other Stories* (1967), and *Black Jasmine* (1971). These four volumes greatly consolidated the position of Khushwant Singh as a short-story writer of outstanding merits, – a writer who moves from this genre to fiction in due course, and not *vice versa* (as in case of many other authors). He and Attia Hosain are perhaps the two writers who began their creative career with short story, – Hosain having produced *Phonex Fled and Other Stories* (1953). Khushwant Singh comes down heavily on what is repugnant, repulsive, and hypocritical. Thus, "The Mark of Vishnu" launches a scathing attack on blind belief which impels Ganga Ram, a pious and devoted Brahmin, to worship and feed with milk the black cobra which eventually bites him to death. "The Voice of God" highlights the inherent evils of a democratic system of Government in which elections play a dominant role, but these elections are often won by hardcore criminals like Ganda Singh at the cost of deserving candidates like Baba Ram Singh. How hard-hitting is the irony of Mr. Singh when he remarks – 'The people had spoken. The voice of the people is the voice of God'. Another title-story, "A Bride for the Sahib", is a tragic tale of the schism between an Oxonian and his docile Indian wife, Kalyani Das. Some of the humorous and fantastic stories of Mr. Singh are: "Posthumous", "My Own My Native Land", and "Rats and Cats in the House of Culture." Obviously, Mr. Singh's forte is irony and comic sense. V. A. Sahane has rightly pointed out that "The predominant quality of Khushwant Singh as a short-story writer is his comic spirit, informed by the sense of incongruity and by the bewildering phenomena of contradictions in life". (Shahane, 67)

Another remarkable name in the field of Indian English short story is that of Ruth Prawer Jhabvala, who is a Polish by parentage, a German by birth, an English-woman by education, and an Indian by marriage. In a way, English is her mother tongue, and she writes her novels and short stories in it with utter sincerity and command. Her portrayal of Indian life is sensibly executed, with the added advantage of a somewhat detached observer. So long she has written four volumes of short stories, namely *Like Birds, Like Fishes & Other Stories* (1956), *How I Became Holy Mother & Other Stories* (1964), *A Stronger Climate* (1968), and *An Experience of India* (1972). Besides these collections of short stories, she has written nine novels. From these volume of short stories, it is clear that Jhabvala gets totally depressed and disillusioned in India, which she calls a country of 'heat and dust', of slow movement and activity, of indolence and laziness. Her *A Stronger Climate* is a pointer to this fact. Even *An Experience of India* is cast in the same gloomy mood and in the same attitude of helplessness.

K. A. Abbas is a well-known name in the film industry, but he has also created a place for himself in the niche of Indian-English short story by dint of his five collections. Abbas seems to be impatient with the present-day social set-up, which is dominated by poverty, ignorance, inefficiency, hypocrisy, selfishness, and unemployment. He is no less disturbed by the prevailing political problems like those of partition, bloodshed and refugee influx. His two volumes, *Blood and Stones & Other Stories* (1947) and *Cages of Freedom and Other Stories* (1952), treat these political issues, whereas his works like *Rice and Other Stories* (1947) and *One Thousand Nights on a Bed of Stones & Other Stories* (1957) highlight some of the glaring social evils, in whose portrayal he sometimes becomes enraged and furious and at others sentimental and melodramatic. His technique of narration is definitely coloured with strong urge for the visual cinematic effects, and as such he offers us a series of striking and memorable flashes of events and scenes. The overall impression that Abbas creates through his short stories is one of harsh realism vehemently attacking the odd and the incongruous with the fond expectations of a zealous socialist who believes in setting things right in the last run, though sometimes he loses his grip over the medium of his art and slips into slipshod generalizations.

Another famous writer of short stories in English is G.D. Khosala, who gives us a peep into the multifaceted personality of Mother India through his wide-ranging themes. His characters are both types and individuals, and he portrays them with sensivity and objectivity. All walks of people – from rickshaw-pullers to businessmen, from film heroines to defiant loving ladies: all find a berth in his creative world. With his four volumes – *The Price of a Wife* (1958), *The horoscope cannot Lie & Other Stories* (1961), *Grim Fairy Tales and Other Facts and Fancies* (1966), and *A Way of Loving & Other Stories* (1973) – steeped in humour and realism, Khosala has undoubtedly earned an abiding place for himself in literature. Through them he hits hard at the social evils like untouchability and ill-matched marriage. His stories, though they have logical conclusions, sometimes become too long and hence a bit dull. But his wit and humour come to his rescue and prove to be his saving grace.

Nagarajan made contribution to Indian English short story with his single volume, *Cold Rice* (1945). Nergis Dalal also contributed with her single volume, *The Nude* (1977) which is now out of print. Rabindra Nath Tagore is another important writer of twentieth century. He did not write any story originally in English. He wrote all his stories in Bengali then translated them himself or through others into English. Some of his popular stories are: "The Cabuliwallah", "Subha", "Master Mashai", "The Post Master", or "The Castaway". Some Indian English poets have also experimented with the short story form, and Margaret Chatterjee, K. N. Daruwalla and Shiv K. Kumar are significant names in this regard. Apparently, they have written their stories in a leisurely mood to relieve themselves of the burden of a nerve- tingling, delicate and tense genre. Some others like Bhabani Bhattacharya, Chaman Nahal, Anita Desai, and Arun Joshi have produced a single volume each and possibly deserted the genre for good in favour of the novel. Bhabani Bhattacharya's *Steel Hawk and Other Stories* (1968) is as satirical in tone and social in theme as some of his novels. Ruskin Bond and Manoj Das are no doubt, the redeeming figures for Indian English short story. In addition to the above-mentioned established writers, we have some other memorable literary personalities of yesteryears. They are, Bunny Reuben, G.K. Chettur and Ramesh Shrivastva. They have contributed in their own way to the growth and expansion of this genre.

B: R. K. Narayan: Life and Works

Most educated people have read or heard of R.K. Narayan but few of them recognize Rasipuram Krishnaswamiyer Narayanswamiyer, which is the full name of R. K. Narayan. Narayan was born in Madras on 10th October 1906 at his maternal grandmother's home. His maternal grandmother kept Narayan with herself when his family shifted to Mysore. Narayan's grandmother's name was Parvati. She was an extremely hard working woman. She was specially fond of gardening. Narayan went to school in Madras under the care and tutelage of not only his maternal grandmother but also his maternal uncle Seshachalam. He may have also received a special gift from his grandmother: humour. Narayan's father was (in government education service) a head master in Mysore. Narayan left Madras in 1922, at the age of sixteen, when he finally rejoined his parents and the family in Mysore. He failed two years in a row in the Mysore university entrance examination (first in English then in Tamil). In 1926, he passed the university enterance examination and began his studies at Maharaja College, Mysore. It took him four years to graduate, a year longer than usual. At last, he completed his graduation along with his younger brother in 1930. At the age of twenty-four R.K. Narayan tried a number of professions. He worked in the Mysore secretariat for sometime but found his work tedious. Then he became a teacher, but the vocation did not suit him. Thereafter he was a correspondent of *Madras Justice* and a sub-editor. At last he left all work and took to creative writing. When his father lost his dear friend, Narayan wrote ten pages on friendship in flamboyant poetic-prose. In the beginning many of his writings were rejected outright which naturally had a dampening effect on the young author. R.K. Narayan described this episode in his *My Days: A Memoir*:

> I offered samples of my writing to every kind of editor and publisher in the city of Madras. The general criticism was that my stories lacked "plot". There was no appreciation of my literary values, and I had nothing else to Offer. Malgudi was inescapable as the sky over-head. (*Atma Ram, xviii*)

Narayan was determined to live on writing alone but his earnings were very scanty. In his first year of writing, he earned nine rupees and twelve annas; the second year a story was sold for 18 rupees, in the third a children's tale fetched 30 rupees. When Narayan wrote his first novel *Swami and Friends* he did not find a reader. Then a college friend came forward to go through the manuscript, he read and certified it as readable, which was very encouraging for R. K. Narayan. This boy later became a constant critic and adviser of R. K. Narayan:

> Years ago when I wrote my first novel, *Swami and friends*, and found none to read it, a very young-college friend came forward to go through the manuscript; he read and certified it as readable which was very encouraging. (*Atma Ram, xviii*)

Later, Graham Greene was impressed by Narayan's fiction. He wrote "introduction" For *The Bachelor of Arts* and *The Finacial Expert*, and also persuaded a leading publisher to bring out his first four novels.

In 1933, Narayan sighted a young beautiful, tall and slim girl Rajam, drawing water at a street tap and he fell headlong in love with her. He described this episode in his autobiography:

> In July 1933, I had gone to Coimbatore, escorting my elder sister, and then stayed on in her house. One day, I saw a girl drawing water from the street tap and immediately fell in love with her. I could not talk to her. I learned later that she had not even noticed me passing and repassing in front of her while she waited to fill the brass vessels. I could not really stand and stare; whatever impression I had of her would be through a side-glance while passing the tap. I suffered from a continual melting vision. The only thing I was certain of was that I loved her, and I suffered the agonies of the restraint imposed by the social conditions in which I lived. (*Atma Ram, xviii*)

Rajam's father turned out to be a local headmaster, the families were known to each other and the requirements of class, community and caste were all correct. Rajam's father loved books and was interested in literary matters and was glad to talk to Narayan about such subjects. But Narayan crashed through all conventions by outrageously announcing directly to the father that he wanted to marry his daughter. But their horoscopes did not match. Narayan said:

> My horoscope had the Seventh House occupied by mars,

> the Seventh House being the one that indicated matrimonial aspects. The astrological texts plainly stated that Mars in the Seventh House indicated nothing but disaster unless the partner's horoscope also contained the same flaw, a case in which two wrongs make one right. (*William Walsh, 19*)

The infatuated lover bribed his pundit who compared the horoscopes and declared them all right. The wedding took place in 1934. In a letter to Graham Greene in 1936 Narayan said, "I married a girl from Heaven three years ago...." (Rao, 18) At the time of his marriage, Narayan was twenty-eight and Rajam seventeenth; Narayan was five-foot four, Rajam an inch or two taller. Their daughter Hema, their only child was born in 1936. Rajam helped her husband in creative writing.

To support his family Narayan became a reporter, gathering news for a Madras paper called The Justice. The paper was dedicated to the rights of non-Brahmins dominating in public life, government service, and education. The newspaper proprietors had no objection to a Brahmin reporter – indeed they relished the idea of having a Brahmin on the staff who supported the non-Brahmin cause – and Narayan spent his days hunting out news from the bazaar and market-place, the law courts, police station, the municipal building, doing his best to make at least ten inches of news a day before lunch. He rushed home and typed his findings – hardly scoops – on his ancient portable Remington, and got them off to the Post Office before 2.20. Murders were his standby, he says, and he became a familiar figure in the mortuary. He always took care in his reports to sprinkle the word 'allegedly' generously. He was intimate with police officers, detectives and informers, and came into the closest contact with an immense variety of men and manners. It was work that he might have continued indefinitely except that once, when his payment was held up for three months, he wrote to the editor to protest:

> I am a writer in contact with many newspapers and periodicals in America and England, who make their payments on precise dates; I am not used to delays in payments ...

> To which the editor replied, "If you are eminent as you claim to be, you should not mind a slight delay on our part; if, on the other hand, you could realize that after all you are a correspondent eking out your income with such contributions as we choose to publish, your tone is unwarranted by your circumstances." I resented the tone of their reply, and decided to give up this work as soon as I could afford it. (Walsh, 20-21)

This experience of reporting was of inestimable benefit to him in supplying material for fiction and in deepening acquaintance with human character, relationship, oddity and suffering. In every corner he found a character that he could fit into a story. Narayan sent his first novel, *Swami and Friends*, to his friend Purna, who was at Oxford where Graham Greene was living. Purna approached Greene, Greene recommended it to Hamish Hamilton, and Narayan's career as a novelist was lanuched. It was well reviewed but there were no sales, and Hamish Hamilton rejected the option on his next novel, The *Bachelor of Arts*, which was published by Nelson, again with the help of Graham Greene, thereby fulfilling a fantasy Narayan had entertained many years before when a Nelson representative called on his father to sell school books and was asked by Narayan: 'If I write a book, will you ask your company to publish it? "Undoubtedly", he said and gave me his card.'

Narayan's father died in February 1937, living, Narayan tells, to the last day of the month 'as if to satisfy a technical need, and died leaving us to draw his pension for the full month. The family, that is extended family, had hardly anything else to live on, since father of Narayan had no belief in savings and very little property. The elder brother opened a small grocery shop called National Provision Store, and he shared the household expenses with Narayan who had a scrappy, fitful income from various sources. He was also by now the father of a small, adored daughter. He arranged with his landlord who lived some distance away in Bangalore, to collect the rent in June and December when his exiguous royalties would come in. He was getting a few short stories published in India and elsewhere, and he forced himself to write a humorous article at ten rupees a time for the weekly *Merry Magazine*, a very painful experience for someone of Narayan's sensibility. He began and completed his third novel. *The Dark Room*, in which woman is the victim and man her constant oppressor.

In Narayan's life 1939 turned out to be the disaster year. After only five years of rapturous marriage, Rajam caught typhoid and on June 6, 1939, around midnight, passed away. He has described his married life, his wife's death and the recovery he made through spiritual experience in detail in *The English Teacher* published in 1944, a watershed in his writing in which there is very little fiction. The commercial failure of Narayan's first three novels (*Swami and Friends*, *The Bachelor of Arts*, and *The Dark Room*) which Narayan equated with professional failure joined hands with his personal loss.

Gradually, Narayan got both popularity and money from his novels and other writings. He did not wary again.

His daughter was married in 1956 and Narayan, for all the expense of building his own house had saved enough to celebrate the marriage in the grandest Hindu manner according to the scriptures. In 1956, too he began his travels and became and habitual globe-trotter, and even when travelling he tried to keep to fifteen hundred to two thousand words a day as his literary stint. His novel Guide was actually written in the United States during his travels. It attained such popularity that the Indian film producer Dev Anand wanted to acquire the right of it for a film. Narayan's first collection of short stories, *Malgudi Days*, came out in November 1942.

After he fell ill in 1990, Narayan moved to Madras to be close to his daughter's family. He wrote in 1996, "Visiting my granddaughter and her child is my sole occupation these days, six to eight every evening" (Rao, 24). This grand-daughter, Smt Bhuvaneswari, now manages Narayan's estate. Narayan grew old gracefully. He had accepted life; old age and death were just stages in the journey. He mused on death. Anthony Spaeth of the *Time* magazine reported: "I don't believe that death really is death", he says today. "It is a continuation of personality in a different medium. What we lose is the physical structure, but there is something else that keeps the physical structure moving and thinking and acting. It's like casting off your old clothes and getting new ones" (Rao, 24). When his daughter Hema, his only child, died in 1994 at the age of 58 Narayan remarked to his friend, N. Ram: "We are all in the queue. She has jumped the queue" (Rao, 24).

R. K. Narayan has received a number of literary awards and distinctions: National Prize of Indian Literary Academy in 1958. His novel *The Guide* won for him Sahitya Akademi Award in 1960. The Government of India conferred on him the title Padma Bhushan in 1964. The National School of independent award came to him in 1965. He was awarded in 1980 the A.C. Benson Medal by the Royal Society of Literature. He received the English Speaking Union Book Award; he was made a Fellow of American Academy and Institute of Arts and Letters in 1982. In 1989, he was made a member of Rajya Sabha. He received Sahitya Akademi's fellowship (their highest honour) in 1996, joining 'immortals of Indian Literature'. He was reported short-listed for the Nobel Prize. Narayan has been translated into many languages of the world and – important for Indian writing in English – translated into Indian languages as well. A couple of days before his death, he asked for a notebook – most probably for composing another short story. For a man who lived a life of uncommon discipline all his life, the end came rather abruptly. Within three days of admission in a hospital, Narayan's condition grew critical and on 14 May 2001, he passed away.

R. K. Narayan, one of the most famous Indian English writers, the well-known author of *Mr. Sampath* and *The Guide*, is popular in the western world more for his novels than for his short stories or for other forms of literature that he has tried. Narayan has published twelve novels and three novellas in his life-time. A chronological survey of Narayan's novels and novella is given below–

Swami and Friends is the very first novel of R.K. Narayan. It was published in 1935. It is the story of a young schoolboy, Swaminathan, who seeks excitement in the company of friends This novel is remarkable for the study of child psychology. R. K.

Narayan has produced some brilliant descriptions of childhood experiences both in his novels and short stories.

Bachelor of Arts the second novel of R.K. Narayan, takes up the theme of a young man's search for a place in the society. The search is, however complicated by the various ups and downs in his life – the havoc caused by his frustration and disappointment in love, his subsequent renunciation of society and search for meaning in the garb of an ascetic, his realizations of the deception of it all, his return to his home and parents, his taking up the agency of a newspaper as a source of his livelihood and then his marriage and complete absorption in the householder's life. Thus the name of the novel appears to be an ironic comment on the inability of a university degree to equip a man to face the challenges of life. The hero of the novel, Chandran, is really swami grown up, and now a college student. The college life of those days is perfectly delineated, There is a good bit of Narayan in this novel, especially in the episode of Chandran's falling in love with a girl, whose horoscope unfortunately does not match his.

Dark Room is the next novel of R.K. Narayan. It is the story of a Hindu woman Savitri who is neglected by her husband because of his infatuation with another, and who decided unsuccessfully to run away from home. Savitri returns to his husband's home because of an all-pervading fear of loneliness and object misery. Savitri's quest for identity or at least of her independent, individual entity begins in the dark room of her husband's house, which for her, is a way of protest against her husband's tyrannical behaviour. But no light of love or understanding penetrates this dark room, and it becomes emblematic of darkness that decends into Savitri's heart as a result of the unmending and unbending ways of her erring husband. She seeks release from this darkness in an attempted embrace of death, but the dark river is no less menacing than the darkness back at home. When she saves from drawning by wandering repairer of locks and umbrella, she seeks independent existence and rejects all charity. But her search for work brings her to a temple which too has a dark room where she must sleep. Savitri's return to her husband and children may thus be constructed to mean a return to reality, while her endeavour to discover the meaning of her life away from the social context of her family was just a bed dream or a delusion. The fact that the world outside her husbsnd's home is equally dark and dismal and doesn't have to offer her any new opportunity of self-realization makes it obvious that under the given socio-economic structure the dark room of her husband's house is, after all, preferable to the dark room of death and renunciation.

The English Teacher the fourth novel of R.K. Narayan, appeared in 1945 seven years after his third one and that too because an occult and esoteric experience had helped him to overcome the traumatic shock of his wife's death. The material for his novel came from the innermost depths of his own being and so it contains some of the most personal and autobiographical writing that ever appeared in his novels. Writing about in his memoirs, entitled *My Days*, he says more than any other book, The English Teacher is autobiographical in content, very little part of it being fiction. The English Teacher of the novel, Krishna is a fictional character in the fictional city of Malgudi; he goes through the same experience Narayan had gone through, and he calls his wife Sushila, and the child is Leela instead of Hema. The toll that typhoid took and all the desolation that followed, with a child to look after, and the psysic adjustments, are based on his own experience. The novel falls in two parts – one is domestic life and other half is 'spiritual'. *The English Teacher* is essentially a love story with lyrical beauty in its portrayal of the conjugal life of a young couple, and the deep agony of separation, by death a loved one. It is at the same time, "an attempt to look steadily at death and see if there is anything beyond", (*Girla, 28*) Krishna's final act of giving his job as lecturer and his ultimate mystical contact with his wife's soul may appear again as improbable and incredible to a critical and matter of fact mind. But, in its context, it is surprisingly authentic in an occult cum-spiritual sense. At least with a willing suspension of disbelief, we are made aware of an unknown plane of being. As for Krishna "Life has taught him a little, but death has taught him more, and has reason to be grateful to life and death". (*Girla, 29*) This deeply autobiographical novel completes a trilogy – the other two being *Swami and Friends* and *The Bachelor of Arts*. The three novels, taken together form an Odyssey of growth in the Malgudi world of education. Swami, the schoolboy, Chandran, the college student, and Krishna the English teacher at Albert Mission College fit in at the proper places.

Mr. Sampath is R. K. Narayan's fifth novel; it was published in 1949. It was inspired partly by his experience with his printer during the brief life of Indian thought, and partly by his brief sortie into the film world – he wrote some scripts for the Gemini Studio in Madras. Mr. Sampath was the harbinger of the great reputation he was to make as writer, not only in the English-speaking world but also in other countries, in languages ranging from Hebrew to Japanese. As in the of Mr. Sampath, almost all his fiction is based on a person or an incident which he was familiar. By the time Narayan came to write his fifth novel, he was in his forties, and had obviously reached a point where his fascination for certain aspects of Hindu religious and philosophical tradition had grown into a full-fledged conviction of their truth and relevances, particularly with reference to an individual's persistent quest for identity and self-knowledge. By the time Narayan had also perfected the typical structural pattern of events. The protagonist, in this pattern, is initially engaged fruitfully in the pursuit of some aspect of social reality. But gradually he find himself drawn into a range of activities that appear to belong to the region of the unknown and the 'illusory'. After realizing the futility of this 'illusory' world, or after gaining fresh insights into the nature of really from his encounters with this world, he returns to the world of his former activity. The novel thus ends with an acceptance of the world, as it exists, because the new knowledge gained by the protagonist help him overcome his reservations about the actual world.

The *Financial Expert* is next novel of R.K. Narayan. It was first published in 1952 and turned out to be a major literary event of the year. Richard Church commented, "*The Financial Expert* is likely to survive as one of the most original pieces of fiction published this year" (Gilra, 34). The basic theme of the novel is clear from the title *The Financial Expert*. Passion for money is a theme which has been treated by writers. In Financial Expert R. K. Narayan has also taken up this theme of universal interest. It shows how uncontrolled lust for money is harmful for personal relationship and how it destroys all peace and happiness of life. *The Financial Expert* is the story of the career of man who is obsessed by money. Margayya, a resident of Malgudi is a financial expert. In the beginning he is an ordinary man. He sits under a banyan tree and act as a middle man between villagers and bank. He shows the path to the villagers to solve their money problems. One day a new secretary of the bank takes all his loan forms, which he has been keeping illegally. However, Margayya thinks that the new secretary has behaved in this way simply because he is a poor man. Margayya's insult by the new secretary of the bank is a turning point in his life. A man who has no money is hated even by his wife. Now Margayya decides to collect money with single minded devotion. Now his one-point programme is to get more and more wealth.

Pursuit of money makes him take the help of religion and superstitions. He performs forty days worship of Laxmi. At last the goddess Laxmi smiles at him. He get a pornographic book "Bed Life", from Dr. Pal who becomes his friend. He gets the book published. The book sells like hot cakes. He suddenly becomes rich. His passion for money is insatiable. He has already collected great wealth but the real jump comes in his life when he gets the help of his friend Dr. Pal. He starts an investment scheme and gives very high rate of interest to the people who deposit their money with him. The money of all the rich people regard him as financial expert. He has reached the height of financial success. However, his financial success does not bring any piece to him. For him money is everything. He has no time for his wife and son. His wife feels very sad. He spoils his son Balu by too much love. His son Balu falls in bad company. Moreover his passion for money also prones to be short lived. Dr. Pal brings about his downfall. His dream of collecting money tumbled down like a house of cards. This greed and avarice and passion for money is the theme of

Financial Expert. Money is a good servant but a bad master. When man becomes money maniac, it destroys peace, happiness and harmonious human relationship.

Waiting for the Mahatma is seventh novel of R.K. Narayan. It was first published in 1955. It is Narayan's only fictional attempt to take notice of the freedom struggle that had gone on in the country. By the time he wrote the novel, the country had been free for ten years, and one assumes that he had an irresistible desire to bring Mahatma Gandhi into one of his stories. In the novel, the Mahatma plays an important role in the romance of Bharati, a dedicated young follower of his and Shriram, a feckless but young rich man. Some readers were critical of the novel, feeling that Mahatma would not have been made a fictional character, but the story is really about the transformation of Shriram from a lackadaisical youth into a stronger person, thinks both to his brief association with the Mahatma, and his profound love for Bharti. Actually, the minor characters – Shriram's grandmother, Kanni, the shopkeeper, the chairman of the town council and others – are interestingly drawn, but while not a failure, the book does not command the same attention from his faithful readers as others do. The fragile foundation of this novel's theme – a youngman's infatuation for a girl landing him in the midst of strange experience and ultimately restoring him to his original self – is a repetition of the pattern of his earlier novels, but conviction and credibility are the prime casualties in the novel's recording of the human motivation and in its gra of the nature of political pressures working during India's national struggle for freedom. It would appear that the author's own ideological myopia might partly account for this lack of authenticity in the novel.

The Guide is the eighth novel of R.K. Narayan. It was first published in 1958. It won for Narayan a Sahitya Akademi Award in 1960, proved to be a great, popular success. Dev Anand, the matinee idol of Hindi cinema, made a film on it, which again proved to be a quite a box-office draw. And the university professors found it of sufficient literary merit to recommend it for study by the undergraduate and post-graduate students. Literary critics also showered rich encomiums on it and praised it as the most creditable achievement of Narayan's art so far. This novel translated into the leading languages of Europe and India. It is most widely read of Narayan's novels. In this novel Narayan tells the story of Raju, a railway guide, whom circumstances, after a period of good fortune when he acted as the agent of a dancer, put in prison for criminal misappropriation. When he comes out after his term, he settles down under a tree near a temple in a village. The simple villagers take him to be a holy man despite his telling them the story of his life in crime, and continue to pay daily tribute to him. When a drought occurs, they look to him to produce rain. One has to read the novel oneself to see how brilliantly Narayan achieves an ambiguous ending, which quite satisfactory just the same. Told on two levels which closely mesh, this is probably Narayan's most polished work of fiction.

The Man-Eater of Malgudi is ninth novel of R. K. Narayan. It was first published in 1961. This outstanding work of fiction is regarded by many critics as Narayan's greatest novel as yet. Rosanne Archer (in the New York Herald Tribune) opines, "In *The Man Eater of Malgudi* he is often if not always, at his very best: sure, dexterous and penetrating." Anthony west (in The New Yorker) regards this novel as "one of his most successful efforts. *The Man Eater of Malgudi* is a delightful, funny, and deeply thoughtful book." Girla, 57) While views may vary in regard to the relative merit of his novels, there can hardly be any doubt regarding the excellence of this novel as a creation of sheer fecundity of comic art and vision of a born story teller. In this novel, R. K. Narayan explores the problem of evil, which he sees as the expression of man's arrogant rationality and of his urge for power over others and which he considers to be self-destructive. In contrast to this he tends to approve of religious ritual as something good and holy and the observance of customs and tradition as something meritorious, leading ultimately to man's salvation. Vasu, a taxidermist, is projected in this novel as a symbol of evil, while Natraj, the printer, is shown as upholding the values of a cherished tradition and culture. The intricate complex love-hate relationship between the two forms the dynamics of action in this successful and thrilling novel. The novel is written in the first person and it narrates the events as seen through the eyes of its protagonist.

The Sweet-Vendor or *The Vendor of Sweets* is tenth novel of R. K. Narayan. It was first published in 1967 by The Bodley Head Ltd., London. This novel has quite adoring theme – for Narayan. The novel takes up his favourite theme once again: the theme of man's quest of identity and self-renewal, which is portrayed in this novel through its protagonist Jagan, who is a sweet-vendor by profession, but a Gandhite and follower of the Gita in his thinking and conduct. His entire outlook is conditioned by Gandhian thinking, with all its contradictions and unadorned impulses. He is a man of high philosophy and ideals. He is very proud of his son Mali who has gone to abroad. One can imagine Jagan's mental travail when Mali returns, accompanied by a Korean wife. Soon enough Jagan realizes that they are not even married. This is a classical story of the generation gap, made the more palpable as father and son are sure of the correctness of their attitudes. Neither will give in, but Narayan resolves the whole tangle in his own amiable fashion, making each give in a little to the other.

The Painter of Signs is eleventh novel of R. K. Narayan. After a gap of nearly a decade which produced stories, essays, memoirs and retold versions of mythological tales and an epic, came from Narayan's pen a major work of fiction. *The Painter of Signs* was first published in 1976 by the Viking Press in America and by The Macmillan in Canada. The thematic content of the novel is centrally based on the population-problem, and the national programme of family planning. In this novel, Narayan explores the theme of man's quest for identity through its protagonist, Raman, who is a painter of signs, and his bitter-sweet experience of love disenchantment with Daisy, an ardent worker at the family planning centre in Malgudi. Raman is a self-styled rationalist, who wishes to establish the age of reason in the world. Daisy, on the other hand, is a champion of woman's rights, who asserts woman's independent entity and advocates the norms of small families to solve India's population problem. She carried a sense of intense conviction to her work, which makes her sacrifice everything in her life. Her missionary zeal and total commitment to her profession are imbued with a steely purposiveness which helps her tide over the moments of personal weakness when she surrenders herself temporarily to the demands of physical love. For Raman, the entire experience of involvement with Daisy, proves to be something of an unreal, though enchanting, dream, after which he feels he is back in the solid world of reality to which he had belonged before his encounter with Daisy. *The Painter of Signs* has the most topical and contemporary of the themes and settings in Narayan's fiction. The Malgudi world, as portrayed in this novel, presents quite an interesting and intrigue blend of modernity and tradition, contemporaneity and convention, reason and superstition.

A Tiger for Malgudi is novella of R. K. Narayan. Six years after *The Painter of Signs*, it was published in 1983. The hero of this slender novella is a tiger, who is trapped by circus owner. The harassed beast kills him accidentally, terrorizes malgudi until a sage adopts him as a disciple. A tiger for Malgudi charts the extraordinary spiritual transformation of a ferocious tiger, 'an unmitigated animal', into a spiritual adept. The hero is no ordinary run-of-the-mill beast; he is a tiger 'almost human in understanding' who is trapped by a man: I had let myself into ultimate slavery'. The hermit assures the crowd: 'inside he is no different from you and me.' He progresses further: 'my tiger is godly…' The guru talks to him every evening 'on life and existence and death…' and God, 'the Great Spirit pervading every creature, every rock and tree and the sky and the stars; a source of power and strength.' Finally he is able to 'calm his turbulent soul.' The tiger develops into a contemplative animal under the guidance of the yogi. The spiritual progress of the tiger seems to have been charted from the novelist's own personal memories of the post-Rajam ordeal. 'There were the stages of knowing attained through suffering.… I can hardly describe that kind of suffering, an emptiness, a helplessness, and a hopelessness behind the bars.' But Hindu humanism comprehends one's karma: "That's the natural law of life, as inevitable as the ripening of a mango in its season or the fall of a withered leaf.

A stage comes when the tiger can appreciate the higher stages: '... My sight became clearer; if I lifted my gaze to the horizon, the sun shining on the land filled me with joy; the leaves of the mighty banyan trees sparkling like gems, the bamboos swaying their golden stems with their filigreed leaves- I felt I could ask for nothing more in life.' After The Vender of Sweets, we have in this novel finally sanyasa in total spirit and spirit and content: time to 'shed purpose of every kind'; and move from time to timelessness. A masterly idea, this certainly is: and the introduction by the author carries the normal Narayan clarity. As it is, however, the narrative is uniquely digressive; with a shuffling, wayward point of view. Besides the early part is no more than kindergarten stuff. We notice in this novella a listlessness we do not associate with Narayan at all. It is like coffee decoction hurriedly strained through a cloth.

Talkative Man is next novella of R.K. Narayan. It was published in 1986. It is the tale of Dr. Rann, a compulsive womaniser. He is also yet another rough in the post-independence gallery. From the havoc he creates, it is the return of Vasu as a demonic woman-eater. We have another predator here: Rann is 'like a feline coming upon its unsuspecting prey.' After Vasu with his 'black halo', we have a 'lecherous demon...irresistible to women'. The portrait of a lady-killer who works on unsuspecting women 'as if playing on a musical instrument...' He is also 'the wolf of the fairy tales'. Narayan has been attracted by the concept of the Talkative Man, we remember, almost since the beginning of his creative career. *The Talkative M*an is a bachelor, hence eligible to talk wryly of the much-married Rann. He is like Narada- who more voluble than the sage of ancient epics, Narada, who is synonymous in the popular mind with 'trouble-maker. 'I'd choke if I didn't talk. The talkative Man himself belongs to a vanishing breed, the declining upper-class Brahmin gentry of Kabir Street. He identifies himself: 'I belonged to the Kabir Street aristocracy, which was well known for its lofty, patronizing hospitality, cost what it may.' Sambu, the Talkative Man's neighbour is another specimen: Sambu 'spent more and more of his time reading'. But confesses the narrator, 'This sort of existence did not appeal to me. This novella, narrated by the

Talkative Man himself in the first person, is filtered through his sensibility; Narayan's lively wit directs it with great economy.

The World of Nagaraj is another novel of R.K. Narayan. It was published in 1990. It is the most recent of Narayan's full-length novels. It has a serious theme in that it deals with both the generation gap and family dissensions. Nagaraj is conservative and well-to-do. Respected by the denizens of Malgudi, childless, living with his mother and wife, his great ambition in life is to write a book on the sage Narada. This never really gets off the ground, but he derives a lot of gentle pleasure from talking about the book, tracking down sources of information, and generally doing research for a book which he cannot admit to himself, he will never finish. His placid life is suddenly disrupted when Tim, the rebellious son of his older brother, suddenly appears to stay with him. Nagaraj's brother is furious, his wife is embarrassed, and Nagaraj is in a quandary as he loves Tim, but also has the greatest respect for his older brother whom he dare not offend. On the level, the novel is about the present young generation the value of which mystify a conservative Hindu like Nagaraj, yet he cannot bring himself to abandon Tim, who, however difficult, has come to him for refuge. On another level, the attitudes moulded by hundreds of generations, the expectations of the joint family, and the deep traditional respect he has for his older brother leave Nagaraj in a welter of conflicting emotions.

Grandmother's Tale is the most recent book of R.K. Narayan. It was published in 1993. This novella was the last book of R.K. Narayan. This is the story of his great-grandmother as he heard it from his grandmother. His great-grandmother was a spirited young woman, who deserted by her young husband at an early age, went after him all by herself, picking up clues here and there, and finally found him in distant Poona. She also succeeded in bringing him back with her. Narayan says that 'this is mainly a story writer's version of a hearsay biography of a great-grandmother. She was seven when she got married, her husband being just ten years old.' One would not decry Narayan if one were to suggest that *The Grandmother's Tale* belongs with the recently popular genre of 'faction', that is fiction based on facts. Narayan himself gives sufficient indication in the narrative that it may be so. Whatever it is, it is an absolutely delightful period-piece with a heroine who is tough and tender at the same time. An interesting feature of the novella is that it is the only one of his works of fiction not to have Malgudi as its locale. *Grandmother's Tale* tells us the story of a determined young woman who goes searching for her husband missing for years; she succeeds in her mission, with unexpected consequences. The heroine of this novella Bala develops into another complex rajasic character, selfish, scheming, determined, ruthless and unfortunate. Surma the second wife, does not suspect that Bala is her co-wife leading her into a trap. Suddenly at a moment convenient to herself, Bala discloses her identity to Surma and demands that she completely cut herself off from her husband. She blackmails the junior wife: otherwise, she will drown herself in the 'next available tank'. Bala is 'dominating, devious, and aggressive': belongs properly to the post- Independence world of Narayan's novels. Once she gets back her husband, she becomes docile'. When Bala and her husband manage to reach their village after decades, the whole place is completely changed; with two exceptions: two landmarks have withstood the hand of time. 'Only the river was there and the temple stood solidly as ever'.

Besides these novels and novellas Narayan has non-fiction work which is as follows –

Gods, Demons and Others was published by Viking Press of New York in 1964. It was first substantial evidence of the development of his interest in Indian myths, epics and legends. Probably the interest in Indian culture he had perceived in the west also promoted it. Narayan took the stories in *Gods, Demons and Others* from various epics, Puranas and literary classics. The introduction itself suggests a change in stance from the 1938 interview with his elder uncle. In Gods, Demons and Others, from the second section onwards, this short story presents himself now and then like a Sutradhar or a chorus and the mediates between the epic poet and reader. The protagonists of these tales perceive 'interrelatedness of things', even as Narayan's heroes seek to do all along, especially in the early phase; they too strive for 'four-square understanding' of life; and life invariably includes death. Concept Narayan had been interested in appear her: wife as; love mocking death; and sublimation. The higher concerns are the essence of this volume of stories retold. *Gods, Demons and Others* is mire than a curtain-raiser for Narayan's epics retold. The mythological fascination is reflected in some of Narayan's novels to come, such as the Bhasmasura myth in *The Man-Eater of Malgudi*. *Gods, Demons and Others* is not just magic realism – antedating by aeons the rage of the moment-but magic itself. Though the stories are retold primarily for foreigners, our urban educated will benefit from Narayan's enterprise. Here is Hindu wisdom at its best. Ted Hughes pays a rich tribute: 'These are far and away the best retellings of Indian tales that I've read, and I've read some hundreds.

Narayan has also retold the Indian classics, the *Ramayana* and *Mahabharata* as well as narrated tales from Hindu myths and legends. These are told with a novelist's skill, and may well serve as introduction to the great books, especially for foreigners. The writing is easy and limpid and the narratives flow effortlessly. Being a perfectionist who left nothing to chance in his writing, he worked with scholars in the preparation of these works. He has also written a number of short stories, some of which are included in this selection and discussed elsewhere. He wrote two travelogues on Mysore, both commissioned by the government.

Narayana's *Mahabharata* reads even better than his Ramayana. He focuses on certain fascinating episodes in the epic; such as Drona's story; as also the lac house episode. Narayan gives the episode of the game of dice due importance; and the drama of the catechising Yaksha which sums up the human values the epic embodies.

What is one's highest duty?'

To regain from injury. (*Ranga Rao, 43-44*)

Narayan's *Mahabharata* highlights for us the great women characters, such as Kunthi and Draupadi. They are heroic women, and more than a match to their menfolk; as is Gandhari. These women shine effortlessly in what comes naturally to epics and epic societies: debates: as in the debate between Yudhistira and Draupadi. We get more than a complex characterisation of the original epic: for example, Dhritarashtra, the uneasy relationship between Dhritarashtra and Vidura is quietly foregrounded. Narayan is there to note when Yudhistira, a model pacifist for most of us, turns out to be a formidable warrior! Balancing the picture, Bhima comes up with pacifist inclination. Narayan was a very private person. To give us a composite portrait of the man, the post-Rajam R.K. Narayan, we have, besides the short pieces of his non-fiction, two books: *My Dateless Diary* and *My Days, the memoir*.

The novelist was among the most home-bound of writers, until he was past fifty when the Rockefeller Foundation did a service to their own land and people by sponsoring Narayan's tour of the United States. The visit through-going itincrary only a person of Narayan's vitalities could have undertaken and accomplishes – the tour yielded *My Dateless Diary*. No tourist brochure could have done more to present Americans as essential humans.

The Emerald Route is not the best example of Narayan's writing. With the charm of Laxman's decorations, though, Narayan does a bit of India here almost as he does the USA in My Dateless Diary. There is a big defference, however; in his American diary, the people of the USA take centre-stage: people and more people, the American. In *the Emerald Route* it is the culture and the landscape that is the subject; as he declares, 'scenes, histories, and the cultural heritage, and whatever seemed to me worthwhile in each place...' The American travelogue is a personal document; in *the Emerald Route*, Narayan 'tried to be impersonal.' The book all the same, is a mix bag. The earlier version, Mysore, was a more unified book.

My Days is the story of Narayan's nurture. This memoir presents the archetypal story of a self-launched artist; we are also privileged to witness here the making of an Indian novelist in English. Especially evocative are the early pages recreating his childhood; the novelist relieves the spirit of *Swami and Friends* again: amazingly, after over six decades. The trial, the humiliations too have not lost their sharp edge even in Narayan's cool recall of success. "My father occasionally enquired of me, 'What are you attempting on that road-roller?'(my typewriter)." This was Narayan's first type-writer: 'a monstrous type-writer... It had separate keys for capital and lower cases; and its carriage moved with a big boom....the entire staircase rocked and boomed when I was at work...' As a bonus to us, evident throughout *My Days*, is the comic novelist's interest in people: confirming the image in *My dateless Diary*. The book lights up with the manners comedy. About the man who received him while going through his oil massage, Narayan says: '...no man in his senses would let himself be seen by a visitor in that messy state....' How many funny characters Narayan's eye discovers! And with the prodigality of true talent, Narayan does not use any of them in his fiction: a variety and range of human types recollected with a delight anything but diminished in the writer's recall. Naturally, the most closely observed of all is Narayan himself – remembered with a steady clarity and often with amusement and sobriety of success. Towards the end of his career, the prose pieces wrote grew even shorter. The best of these essays and causeries are found in three volumes: *A Writer's Nightmare*, *Story Teller's World*, and *Salt and Sawdust*: *Stories and Table talk*.

R. K. Narayan is not only the most popular and prolific novelist but also the most prolific short story writer. Much unlike Anand or Raja Rao apparently, R.K. Narayan approaches the Indian scene with no serious angle of study. He is more akin to Isvaran in that he has an uncanny eye for detail, both of them create memorable stories out of casual roadside events and characters. But he is much different from Isvaran too, for while Isvaran attempts to see in casual events some deeper meaning and significance. He takes life for whatever it is worth, present those familiar scenes with amuse or delight him, rarely bothering to touch its deeper and darker aspects. Brought up in the journalistic tradition, he is ever on the look out for a 'story' in whatever he sees or whatever he meets. Consequently, his stories bristle with innumerable familiar Indian faces. This feature of short stories, coupled with the fact that he delineates his characters with a comic touch, through a language normally lively and engaging has gained for him a popularity rarely enjoyed by the other Indian short story writers in English. But for the way in which his story normally commences, where he takes the reader right into the scene of action with no time lost. Narayan used in his short stories the tradition of the ancient Indian method of narration. He borrows from our ancient technique the idea of narrator too: in quite a few of his stories, the incidents are narrated by the character whom he calls 'The Talkative Man', who is the modern prototype of Bodhisattva of the *Jataka Tales,* present in a dozen diverse places in a dozen diverse forms. Narayan's stories are uniformly compact and are told in his usual seemingly artless style. Abrupt starting, happy ending and the presence of omniscient narrator some of ancient Indian techniques found in his stories. Like the other major short story writers, Narayan also comes under the influence of western masters. The techniques of Narayan's stories are clearly influenced by those of foreign masters that he is interested in. He adopts his form and style from the west. Many of his stories have the expected kick, sting or swing in the end.

As Dr. C. V. Venugopal says "...They rather end the O' Henry way, with a sudden reversal of situation... a feature decidedly a strong point of the journalistic tradition." (M.K. Bhatnagar, 208) In his stories like "A Horse and Two Goats" and "Annamalai" Narayan truly evokes memories of great Russian master Chekhov. Many of his stories are built round the principle of simple irony of circumstances, leading to shock of discovery or surprise or reversal at the end. He steers clear of a message or doctrine to his readers. He analyses individual feelings, and emotions and actions to explore hidden human conflicts. Nowhere in his novels or short stories does he preach or pontificate. The short stories of R.K. Narayan are remarkable more for their workmanlikeness and finish than for the quality of the reading of life they offer; and one of the chief reason for this is the limited role played by irony in them, though a persisted ironic note is, by and large, their distinguishing feature. Apart from his eleven novels, a volume of fifty-five sketches conveying his travel impression,

Narayan has written about 200 short stories; those have been collected and published in seven volumes. They are as follows–

(i) *Malgudi Days 1942*, (ii) *Dodu and Other Stories 1943*, (iii) *Cyclone and Other Stories 1944*, (iv) *An Astrologer's Day and Other Stories 1947*, (v) *Lawley Road and Other Stories 1956*, (vi) *A Horse and Two Goats 1970*, (vii) *Under the Banyan Tree and Other Stories 1985*.

Some of his stories appeared in leading newspapers, Magazines and journals like 'The Hindu', 'Indian Thought', 'The Reporter', 'In Vague' and others and their length and technique testifying to their newspaper provenance. They present the fictional documentation of Narayan's life as a reporter. The stories published in 'The Hindu' were meant largely for the reader who could read and comprehend English. Any man with a vocabulary of about 5,000 words can easily comprehend Narayan's works. All these stories belong to the native Indian soil and are redolent of its culture. Though his stories mainly depict the south Indian life, they clearly express Narayan's view of the world and those who live in it. Simple but fascinating plot, lively characterization, gentle irony coupled with humour, strict economy of narration and beautiful simplicity of language are some of the most prominent features of his short stories. They have a good introduction to the foreigner who wants to gain knowledge of Indian life. Narayan did not mention the date of publication of these collections. *An Astrologer's Day and Other Stories* was first published by Eyre and Spottiswoode, London in 1947 and then Narayan's own publishing institute, the Indian Thought Publications, Mysore. *Lawley Road and Other Stories* has been brought out by Hind Pocket Books (P.) Ltd., Delhi 32. The Other collections have been published by Narayan himself. And since they are published in India, people in foreign countries know very little about the first three volumes.

Unlike Anand and Raja Rao, he is neither a committed writer nor a spiritualist. His delicate mixture of gentle irony and humour, warmth and sympathy, quiet realism and fantasy keep him poles apart from Anand's militant humanism and robust earthiness. Narayan takes life for whatever it is worth and presents familiar scenes which amuse or delight him. He never touches the deeper and darker aspects of life. Wide range of characters, a rare touch of irony and humour, lively and engaging language are some of the main features of short stories which brought him a popularity rarely enjoyed by the other short story writers in English. R.K. Narayan occupies a prominent place as a writer of short stories in a lighter vein and style. Without allowing his stories to be loose in structure, he ends most of them on a happy note. Narayan usually fixes his stare on those aspects of an incident or a character which are appealing to him. He is a fine painter of the ludicrous and the humorous in his stories.

CHAPTER – II
MALGUDI DAYS

Malgudi Days is the first collection of short stories of R.K. Narayan. It was published in 1942. Among the nineteen stories in this collection, two stories "Old Bones" and "Neighbour's Help" are laced with supernatural elements. This volume includes such memorable stories as "The Gold Belt". "The White Flower", "An End of Troubles" and "Under the Banyan Tree". Some of the stories may be viewed as social criticism. Narayan looks with a satiric eye on various aspects of traditional south Indian Society, particularly the dowry system and the powerful impact of astrology and other forms of superstition on it.

One of the finest stories in the collection, "The Mute companions." centers on the ubiquitous Indian monkey, a source of meager income for poor people and a source of delight for children. Adopting the Omniscient point of view yet without moralising or judging, Narayan portrays the life of Sami the dumb beggar, whose "very existence depended on the behaviour of the monkey". Having taught the monkey several tricks, Sami is able for a time to subsist on the earnings of the clever creature, who is his "only companion." This brief story is an excellent specimen of Narayan's art, revealing his ability to portray a segment of society that typically goes unnoticed. The story emphasizes the passiveness characteristic of the poor Indian, his acceptance of his Karma, or fate. Narayan's gentle social criticism too, emerges: "Usually he [Sami] avoided those big places where people were haughty, aloof, and inaccessible, and kept formidable dogs and servants". (76) As in many of his stories, Narayan in "The mute Companions" blends humour and sadness.

Malgudi Days it should be noted, is also the title of a later collection, published in the United States in 1982. Eight of the thirty two stories in this collection "Naga", "Selvi", "Second Opinion", "Cat Within", "The Edge" "God and the cobbler", "Hungry Child" and "Emden" were previously uncollected; the remaining stories were selected from Narayan's two earlier volumes, An Astrologer's Day and *Lawley Road.*

"Naga" describes the plight of a boy more than ten years old whose father, a snake charmer, has abandoned him, leaving him eighty paise in small change and a snake too enfeebled by age to impress the street crowds. In the beginning of the story the boy tells the snake: No one wants to see you, no one has respect for you, and no one is afraid of you, and do you know what that means? I starve, that is all. (145).

In this story the boy and his father earn their livelihood by showing the dance of the snake, people were afraid but enthralled. At the end of the performance people gave them coins and rice and sometimes an old shirt. They packed up and repeated the performance at the next street or at the market, and when they collected enough food and money they returned to their hut. Their hut was beside the park wall, in the shades of a big tamarind tree. The man cooked the rice & fed his son & they slept. The boy had followed his father ever since he could walk and when he gained the age of ten his father let him handle Naga. His father often said:

> We must not fail to give Naga two eggs a week. When he grows old, he will grow shorter each day; someday he will grow wings and fly off, and do you know that at that time he will spit out the poison in his fangs in the form of a brilliant jewel, and if you possessed it you could become a king? (146)

One day when the boy had stayed beside the hut out of laziness he noticed a small monkey leaping amidst the branches of the tamarind tree and looked it with open mouthed wonder, not even noticing his father arrive home. His father gave him a packet of sweets and told him that the sweets had been given him by the people of the big house where some festival was going on. His father also told him that Naga understood all his speech and danced wonderfully.

One day when the little monkey was tempted down with a piece of sweet, his father caught him cleverly. The man trained him to perform before the crowd. They gave him the name Rama. Rama became famous among school children. They traveled widely, performing at all market fairs, and earned sufficient money to entertain in an occasional tiffin at a restaurant. The boy's father left him in the evening, saying that he has a stomach ache, he will get some medicine for it and come back. He returned tottering late at night. The boy felt terrified of his drunk father. He would lie on his mat pretending to be asleep. Father kicked him and said: "Get up, lazy swine, sleeping when your father slaving for you all day comes home for speech with you. You are not my son but a bastard." But the boy would not stir (149).

One night the boy actually fell asleep. When he woke up in the morning, he found his father gone. The monkey was not there too. He knew that they must have gone off together. He called his father several times. He then peeped into the hut and found the round basket undisturbed in its corner. He became happy to find eighty paise in small change on the lid of the basket left by his father. He lifted the lid of the basket to make sure that the snake at least was there. He felt hungry and thought proper to buy his breakfast with the coins left on the basket lid. He was frightened if his father should abruptly come back, he would slap him for taking money. He put the coins back on the lid and sat at the gate of the hut. He reached for a little cloth bag which was full of variety of nuts & fried pulses to feed the monkey. The boy opened the bag, looked the contents & put a handful into his mouth and chewed. A woman asked why he was not out yet. He replied that his father was not there and he did not know where he was gone. The woman put down her basket and sat by his side and asked if he was hungry. He said that he had money. She patted his head and said: "Ah, poor child! I knew your mother. She was a good girl. That she should have left you adrift like this and gone heavenward."(151)

Although the boy had no memory of his mother yet at the mention of her tears came down his cheeks. The woman abruptly asked the boy what he was going to do. The boy answered that he did not know. He asked the woman to wait till his father returned. The woman told him that his father had gone with a strumpet. The boy asked, "What about the monkey? "Won't it come back?" she had no answer to this question. Meanwhile, a man was selling rice cakes on a wooden tray at the end of the lane. The woman called him and ordered to give the boy two idlies. After satisfying herself that the boy had eaten well, she went away.

The boy found that he could play the pipe, handle the snake and feed it also in the same manner as his father used to so he started going out with the snake. He earned sufficient each day. On account of his age the snake became slow moving. When a number of days passed without any earnings, he decided to get rid himself of the snake, throw away the gourd pipes & do something else to earn a livelihood. The boy could not afford to find eggs & milk for the snake so the better way was to get rid of him. He carried the snake basket along to an alone place where a snake could move about in peace without getting killed at sight. In the lonely part of Nallappa's grove there were many mounds and anthills. He left the snake there and began to run at full speed in the apposite direction. The boy stopped at a distance, hid himself behind a tree & looked. The snake was approaching the slope of the anthill. The boy had no doubt that Naga would find the hole on its top, slip itself and disappears from his life forever. But the snake turned round & came along in his direction again. When the snake saw the basket, he slithered back into it. Naga was finally replaced in his corner at the hut beside the park wall. The boy said to the snake:

> If you don't grow wings soon enough, I hope you will be hit on the head with a bamboo staff, as it normally happens to any cobra. Know this: I will not be guarding you forever. I'll be away at the railway station, and if you come out of the basket and adventure about, it will be your end. No one can blame me afterward. (154)

The story brings out effectively the pathos in the life of the little boy. Contrasted with the cruel behaviour of the father is the humane relationship between the boy and the snake.

"Selvi" is next story of the collection. It is traditionally story. The author begins the story with mediation of third person narrator. In this story Selvi, the protagonist is a well-known singer. The story moves round Selvi and her husband Mohan. Mohan is a typical Indian husband who cannot bear her to talk to any person. She does whatever her husband says. Selvi had been wedded to Mohan for over two decades and had never spoken to anyone in his presence. The author gives description of the physical appearance of Selvi in these words:

> Her eyebrows, which flourished wildly, were trimmed and arched. For her complexion, by no means fair, but just on the borderline, he discovered the correct skin cream and talcum which imparted to her brow and cheeks a shade confounding classification. (155)

Mohan did not want to encourage the use of cosmetics because he had been a follower of Mahatma Gandhi and spent many years in prison. He wore only cloth spun by hand and avoided all luxury; there could be no question of his seeking modern artificial aids to increase the personality of his wife.

When Selvi came on the stage, she looked radiant, rather than dark brown or fair. People could not guess what colour her skin was. There were thousands of fans of Selvi. Varma was one of them who had a desire to meet her. But she was never left alone even for a moment with anyone. Mohan found money to buy the house when Selvi received a fee for lending her voice to a film-star, who only moved her lips, synchronizing with Selvi's singing, and achieved much glory for her performance in a film. But Mohan closed all film offers. He said: "I'll establish Selvi as a unique phenomenon on her own, not as a voice for some fat cosmetic dummy" (157). He rejected various film offers for no other reason.

There was a place, "Boardless" where Selvi's admirers assembled and talked. Varma overheared conversation from his pedestal at the cash counter, especially when the subject was Selvi. One day they were talking about Selvi's early life. Varma heard their conversation and came to know that Selvi had been brought up by her mother in a back row of Vinayak Mudali Street. She learnt music from her mother. At that time Mohan had a photo studio on market road. Once Selvi's mother brought her to be photographed for a school magazine after she had won the first prize in a music competition. Mohan visited them casually as a kind of well-wisher of the family. At the Boardless no one knew how or when Selvi and Mohan were married. Mohan bought Lawley Terrace, and after freshening up its walls with lime wash and paints, on an auspicious day engaged Gaffur's taxi and took Selvi and the family to the Terrace.

Selvi's mother, brother and sister were excited to come in the house but Selvi showed no reaction. Mohan desperately asked her how she liked the place. At which Selvi said that it looked big. At the end of the guided tour Mohan described the history of the house. Selvi listened, without any show of interest. Her mind was elsewhere. She was dressed and ready for the concert at the appointed time in the evening. That day she did not want to know or questioned where she was to sing or what fee they were getting. When Mohan asked her to pack and get ready, she became ready not even questioning where they were going.

She sat in a reserved seat in the train. She was ready to leave when Mohan said to get off at the next stop. She was undemanding, unenquiring, uncomplaining. She was lost in her thought without noticing anything or anyone. Selvi became famous in quarter century. R.K. Narayan describes this in these words:

> In the course of a quarter-century, she had become a national figure; traveled widely in and out of the country. They named her the Goddess of Melody. When her name was announced, the hall, any hall filled up to capacity and people fought for seats. When she appeared on the dais, the audience was thrilled as if vouchsafed a vision, and she was accorded a thundering ovation. When she settled down, gently cleared her throat and hummed softly to help the accompanists tune their instruments, a silence fell among the audience." (159)

During a concert Mohan occupied the centre seat in the first row of auditorium and stared at Selvi. Though his eye were on her, his mind would be busy doing complicated arithmetic with reference to monetary problems. Selvi got out of the defilement of Vinayak Mudali Street. She separated from her mother, brother and sister. As time went on Selvi saw less and less of them. At the beginning a car would be sent to fetch them, once a week. But Selvi's public engagement increased, and her mother, sister and brother gradually disappeared from her life. Selvi tried to speak to Mohan once or twice about her mother but he became angry at the mention of them and said: "They must be all right. I'll arrange to get them – but where is the time for it? When we are able to spend at least three days at home, we will get them here." (161)

Selvi's mother and others generally came by train or car and left again within twenty four hours. When Selvi and Mohan had the time and if Selvi timidly talked about her mother, Mohan spoke angrily: "I know, I know, I'll send Mani to Vinayak Street – but some other time. We have asked the Governor to lunch tomorrow and they will expect you to sing, informally of course, for just thirty minutes." (161)

After this Selvi never talked about her mother. But she became very sad at this. Mohan knew that Selvi would not bother him about her mother anymore. He felt triumphant. He congratulated himself on the way he was tackling her. Thus month and year passed.

One day the news of her mother's demise reached her. That day they were in Calcutta. When she heard it, she refused to come out of her room, and wished all her engagement cancelled. Mohan went to her room to entice her, but quickly came out when he found her tear-drenched face and disordered hair. All through the train journey, she kept quiet and didn't speak a word, although Mohan did his best to engage her in talk. She was generally not talkative. On the thirty six hour journey she never spoke a word or looked in Mohan's direction. When they reached home, Mohan hurriedly arranged to take her down to Vinayak Mudali Street. Selvi's sister could not come from Singapore, and her brother's whereabouts were unknown. A neighbour explained the circumstances of the old lady's death and how they had taken charge of the body. Mohan interrupted his narration and sent him away. Selvi told Mohan that he might go back to the Terrace if he liked. She was staying there. Mohan had not expected her to talk to him in that way. When Mohan said that he would send back the car when she wanted it, Selvi replied that there is no need of it because she is staying there as she did before. Mohan objected how she could in that street. She ignored his objection and said: "My mother was my guru; here she taught me music, lived and died . . . ." I'll also live and die here; what was good for her is good for me too . . . ." (163)

Mohan wandered, waited for a moment hoping for a change of mood. After waiting restlessly Mohan rose to go and asked Selvi, "anything you want to be sent down?" (163). Selvi replied that she needed nothing. Mohan saw that she had worn an old sari and had no make up or jewellery, it was left at the Terrace. He asked, "you mean to say, you'll need nothing" (163). He asked, you have the series of at Bhopal, shall I tell them to change the dates" (163). It was the first time when he was consulting her on such problems. She simply replied, "Do what you like" (163). He asked again what she meant by that. She did not give answer to this question.

When he pressed her she said to leave her alone. He came again after a week. She neither welcomed him nor asked him to go. He advised her to use the car but she refused. After four weeks when he came again to visit her, he found a big crowd in her house, overflowing into the street. Selvi sat at the back of the small hall, holding her thambura, and was singing to the audience as if it were an auditorium. A violinist and a drummer accompanied her. Mohan thought that she was wasting her art. She asked Mohan to sit down. He sat in a corner, heard for a moment and came out. He visited her many times and found people around her all hours of the day, waiting for her music. News about her free music sessions spread, people gathered there in cars, bicycles and on foot. Varma of the Boardless brought a packet of sweet and handed it to Selvi quietly and went away.

Mohan thought he might find her alone at night. At eleven O' clock one night he left his car in Market Road and went on foot to Vinayak Mudali Street. He called Selvi in soft tone:

"My dear it's me, I have to talk to you urgently. Please open the door, please."

Selvi opened a window shutter and said:

"Go away, it's not proper to come here at this hour...."

Mohan turned back with a lump of his throat, swearing half-aloud, "Ungrateful wretch . . . ." (165)

In this story Mohan is presented as a selfish and self-centered man. For him money is more important than any other thing. In a way the story reminds us of R. K. Narayan's novel *The Guide*. In that novel Raju who was behind making Rosie, the famous dancer also tried to control her life in the same way. Rosie became fed up with Raju's commercial attitude as Selvi is with Mohan's in this short story.

"Second Opinion" is another story of the collection. It is the longest story of the collection. It reaffirms Narayan's or at least his protagonists' belief in the variously understood 'Philosophy of detachment'. The story is told by Sambu, the protagonist, in the first person. It opens on a note of stealth, when Sambu enters his house "like a hunter stalking in a jungle" (66). The imagery of primitive jungle with its thief-like hunter assumes further significance when the narrator describes the cobwebs hanging like festoons in his room and lizards "ambushing little creatures that crawled about, urging them on their evolutionary path"(166). And what kind of evolutionary path is charted out by Sambu's imagination for these little creatures? – "Every gnat at death was reborn a better creature, and ultimately, after a series of lives, became an ape and a human being, who merged ultimately in a supreme indivisible godhood" (166). Thus hoping that one day these gnats will attain godhood, he refuses to have anyone use spray or duster to clean the cobwebs.

The philosophical meaning of this primitive setting is soon manifested by Sambu when he says: The moment I shut the door of my cubicle, I was lord of my own universe-which seemed to me boundless, although enclosing a space of only eight feet by ten. (166).

This supreme individualism of Sambu, blossoming in his primitive retreat away from social obligations and commitments, is an expression of his philosophy of detachment. Till he can reach his safe retreat, he has to walk stealthily like a hunter in the jungle. But the moment he is in his ivory tower, and the moment he shuts the door of his cubicle, signifying his insulation from all social contact, he feels that he has become an emperor of his boundless universe, which though limited in physical space, is limitless in metaphysical space. It is obvious here that individualism as a creed is a product of the primitive jungle law ("each one for himself, and the devil take the hindmost") and that the philosophy of detachment is a parasitical offshoot of this narrow and selfish individualism.

The fact that, Sambu is a conscious and determined practitioner of this philosophy of detachment is made explicit when sambu is shown reflecting "how difficult it was to practice one's philosophy of detachment" (167). He thinks approvingly of Siddhartha who "did wisely in sneaking away at midnight when others were asleep, to seek illumination" (167-168). He says to himself that in his own way he too was seeking illumination, but regrets that he "continued to remain in bondage" (168). And what are the instruments of this bondage? –

> The common roof, the married state (ultimately, of course), every kind of inheritance and every bit of possession acted as a deadly tentacle. Following this realization the first thing I abandoned was furniture and, in a manner of speaking also the common roof of the main house, since my cubicle was detached. (168)

The implications of Sambu's philosophy of detachment now become clearer. He should not stay under a common roof, that is, he should not share life with anybody else, not even with his mother, because it is a deadly tentacle. He should refuse "every kind" of inheritance (Does it mean that he should he should disown his parents too, and refuse to accept that they had any role in his making, genetic or physical?), because that too is a deadly tentacle. And, finally, he should avoid "every bit" of possession because that also is a deadly tentacle. One wonders, however, why he depends on the visitors to the Boardless to provide him with free coffee. It is also not clear what sort of illumination he is seeking.

The primitive jungle, with its philosophy of detachment, also grows in the back of Sambu's house. The river Sarayu, which once used to provide a place for community gathering, has now been sealed off by the "thorns and wild vegetation choking the path" (168). In its passage to 'modernity' the town of Malgudi is now dotted with wells which, according to Sambu's mother, have rendered people lazy and made them neglect the river. To Sambu, however, with his mind always making forays into the realm of metaphysical speculation, the water of the wells is no different from that of the river, it being "a big connected water sheet, just as you say Brahman is all-pervading in this form and that in the universe" (169). It is quite amazing to discover that Sambu, with his primitive philosophy of detachment, should still consider himself a rationalist and a modernist. Talking of the polarity of ideas and beliefs between his mother and himself, he says:

> In those days I had nothing much to do except sit down, leaning on the pillar, and attempt to enlighten my mother's mind on modern ways. But she was impervious to my theories. We were poles apart. Not only on the river, but on every question, she held a view which, as a rational being, I could never accept. (169)

It would appear here that Sambu's mother, with her commitment to the value of togetherness, solidarity and social intercourse symbolized by the river, is naturally opposed to the narrow, individualistic values represented by Sambu. Moreover, Sambu's professed rationalism is nothing but a pose to hide the irrationality of his own beliefs and practices.

Sambu can afford to make a show of his philosophy of detachment from the activities of life because he can manage to subsist on other people's labour. From the description that he gives of his father's property it becomes clear that he owns paddy fields in the fields which are, of course, cultivated by hired labour. His father has also obviously made money from the business of lending. Describing the occupation of his father he says, "....... all his hours were spent in adding, subtracting and multiplying figures" (169). It appears that he thinks of his father as a sort of mechanical calculator for whom the 'squat wrought-iron safe' containing cash and documents seemed to have become a part of his personality. Thus the father is relegated to the status of a thing by his son, possibly because the latter can take airs for having read the books of philosophy and religion – Christianity, Upanishads, Plato and Socrates – that he found in possession of his father. It is indeed ironical that the father had nothing to do with the intellectual contents of the library because "it had been hypothecated to him by some poor academic soul who could never redeem it" (170). Moreover, Sambu himself has never gone beyond matriculation and it is amazing that he should find himself at home with the books that need profound intellectual powers for their comprehension. It is also curious that this prophet of detachment is not so much concerned with what the books certain as he is with the "weight, feet and scent of every volume" (170). May be, he can discover the meaning of Upanishads just by smelling them or having a feel of their build and weight.

A very appropriate symbol of Sambu's philosophy of detachment can be seen in the 'loft', a wide wooden panel below the ceiling in the central hall of the house in which he lives. Describing this loft he says: "From a proper distance, aimed correctly, you could fling anything into it, to its oblivion" (170). Thus it appears to be the objective correlative of the philosophy of detachment which is built on a kind of oblivion.

Sambu wants to lead a life as if he were also a discarded object in the loft. He always retreats from everything that demands his attention to the daily needs of life. The main reason of his dislike of his mother is that she is always in a state of anxiety over one thing or another while he just wants to shut himself in his room. And for what purpose does he want to do so? –

> I wanted peace of mind to go through the book in hand, life of Ramakrishna, passages from Max Muller, Plato's Republic – it was a privilege to be able to be a participant of their thoughts. I felt thrilled to be battling with their state-

> ments and wresting a meaning out of them. Whatever they might have meant they all seemed to hold forth the glory of the soul, which made me survey myself top to toe and say: "Sambu, who are you? You are not the creature with a prickly stubble on the chin, scar on the knee-cap, with the toenail splitting and turning blue . . . You are actually made of finer stuff. I imagined myself able to steer through the traffic of constellations in the firmament, in the interstellar spaces, and the milky way: it enabled me to overlook the drab walls around and the uninspiring spectacles outside the window opening on Kabir Street. Into this, shattering my vision, would come hard knocks on my door (172).

It is obvious from this statement that Sambu is an inveterate escapist who shirks all his social responsibilities and duties only to sponge on other people's hospitality. Besides the enclosed world of his own room which ironically enough provides him the backdrop for his soaring visions of interstellar journey, the other favourite haunts of Sambu are "the town library, market place, college sports ground, and more than any other place, The boardless Hotel, to pass the time in agreeable company." (173)

Sambu, the parasitical hunter, finds himself one evening turned into a 'hunted' one when he finds his mother talking to some stranger in the hall because of which he can neither go to his room nor can he go back to The Boardless. He is quite surprised to hear his mother speak highly of him to the stranger. He immediately feels that he ought to have a second opinion about his mother's opinion of him. He finds his mother feeling very proud of her diligent son about whom she says, "I don't think even an M. A. has read so much!" (174) It turns out that a gentleman has brought a matrimonial proposal for Sambu. Sambu's mother describes him in these words – "The richest man in our village – a hundred acres of paddy, coconut garden – from the coconut garden alone his income would be a lakh of rupees, and from cattle . . . they are distantly related to us. (177)

She further tells Sambu that "The girl has studied up to B. A. and is to be married in June" (177). Moreover the horoscopes have already been found matching very well.

Sambu, the arch-escapist that he is, does not want to be involved in any kind of alliance. The only thought in his mind is how to get away and escape from it all. He refuses point-blank to be coerced into marriage or involved in any other kind of responsibility. In her own ironical way his mother tries to puncture his superior and learned airs when she tells him: "With all that reading you couldn't even get a B.A..! While every slip of a girl is a graduate today" (179).

Sambu finds it difficult to face his mother's volleys and grabbing his kurta and the upper cloth he abruptly leaves the house. His characteristic avoidance of any kind of involvement or identification is brought out again when he says about these clothes that he "generally avoided this dress as it made one look like a political leader" (179). It is obvious here that he doesn't wish to be identified as any particular person with some specific profession.

Sambu is barely out of one trap when he finds himself in another. He meets on the way his family doctor Kishen of M.M.C. who calls him into his clinic. The doctor is an interesting character whose views on prescription and medicines are very rational and show his progressive and committed outlook. About prescriptions he says: "Every prescription must be a special composition to suit the individual, how can mass produced tablets help" (180). About the new drugs advertised as infallible, he says that these are "of value only to the manufacturers all those big companies and multinationals, not to the ailing population of our country" (180). After some such preliminary observations he drops the bombshell of a question on Sambu when he asks him, "Why don't you give me a cheque?" (181). Sambu is taken back at this demand because he is completely unaware of its context. The doctor then explains to him how he has been paying visits to his ailing mother and how the amount is due for these visits and medicines. He asks Sambu if his mother has never spoken to him about this. Sambu replies that he has been wondering why his mother has been insisting on his marrying some girl. The doctor tells him that his mother feels strongly that there must be a successor to her when she leaves the scene. Sambu is really baffled to hear all this and when the doctor notices a puzzled expression on his face, he asks Sambu, "Has she not discussed her condition with you?" (182). Sambu is stunned when he is told by the doctor that his mother is in a leave taking-mood. For Sambu it was inconceivable that a person like his mother who seemed to have her feet firmly planted on earth could over think of leaving this universe. Sambu is really shocked to realize that his mother may not live long. The doctor tries to console Sambu by preaching to him the philosophy of detachment.

Further conversation between Sambu and the doctor reveals what a self-centred person the former is. The doctor wonders why Sambu's mother has not been taking to him and calls him an undutiful fellow. Sambu is only able to provide a lame excuse when he says: "I have to see people and do things. One has to live one's own life, you know!" (183). Sambu is keen to know the nature of his mother's ailment. The doctor is vague on this point and is only able to say that "she is subject to some kind of fainting which comes on suddenly . . . it must be some kind of cardiac catch . . . due to normal degenerative process" (183). Sambu also learns from the doctor that she already knows about her ailment. The doctor also tells that she has a lot of philosophy and that he should spend some time with her. Sambu is troubled in his conscience when he realizes that he had not paid "any attention to my (his) mother, to her need or her wants or her condition, and had taken her to be made of some indestructible stuff" (184). He is shaken when the doctor tells him that "the only thing that bothers her now is that you will be left alone, she told me that if only you could be induced to marry . . ." (184).

Sambu now realizes the truth of entire situation, feels guilty and is filled with self-loathing for his self-centred existence. Before he leaves, the doctor repeats to him his old advice about taking a 'second opinion' if he likes. Sambu assures himself that he ought to be filled now with a sense of self-sacrifice and martyrdom for the sake of his mother. He prepares himself to plunge into this frightful marriage which he hates, but he says that "I had to do a thing I hated to please a dying mother . . . One had to do unpleasant things for another person's sake. Did not Rama agree to exile himself for fourteen years to please Dasaratha?" (185).

Sambu has a fine lunch served to him by his mother, after which he retires to his room. He doesn't find anything wrong with his mother. He is happy to feel that she doesn't give any indication of her illness. "She seemed all right and I felt relieved" (186). After a nap in the afternoon, Sambu began to feel bored and wanted to be out, to his accustomed haunts – The public Library, Town-Hall, the riverside and Nallappa's Grove and finally The Boardless. Before leaving he tells his mother very calmly and casually: "If you like, you may tell that man with the tuft who has brought the matrimonial proposal" (187).

Sambu remains disturbed throughout the evening and is listless even at the Boardless. After this he plods through the sands of Sarayu and walks down the bank listening to the rustling of leaves overhead and the sound of running water. He feels revived with the quality of the hour. But no amount of distraction can solve his problem which haunts him with its nagging presence. Verbalizing his thoughts, he says: "I should welcome neither marriage nor my mother's death. They impaled me on the horns of dilemma; I understood now what it meant. I felt hemmed in, with all exits blocked-like a rat cornered who must either walk into the trap or get bashed" (188). The imagery used here by Sambu to define his predicament is reminiscent of existential jargon to describe the human entrapment. It looks as if Sambu had been trapped in a situation from which there was no possible escape route, just then he chances to hear one passerby telling the other, "I'd not rely on any single opinion before deciding the issue" (188). This casual dropping of the phrase 'second opinion' is a godsend and suddenly opens a door for him. He decides to take a 'second opinion' on his mother's condition from Doctor Natwar, a cardiologist and neuro-surgeon.

A ray of hope suddenly dawns on Sambu's mental horizon and he only hopes that his mother has taken no action on his impulsive request in the morning concerning the matrimonial proposal. Next day he goes to Doctor Kishen and again seeks his permission to take a 'second opinion' about his mother's condition. The Doctor readily agrees and even gives him a letter for Doctor Natwar.

At Doctor Natwar's modern clinic, fitted with electronic and other gadgets for medical examination, his mother undergoes various kinds of tests. Observing her Sambu says, "She looked pleased to be the centre of so much attention and to be put through so many gadgets" (190). At the same time Sambu feels his fate hanging in a balance because on the doctor's word depended his future freedom. Sambu takes a great sigh of relief when Doctor Natwar tells him that there is nothing wrong with his mother. Even after this he can't resist the impulse to ask the Doctor, "How long will she live?" The Doctor's reply is really classic. He says: "Who can answer that question? . . . . I would not be surprised if she outlived you and me" (190). This firm assurance about his mother's condition puts him into his element again and he begins to think to himself: "Why could I not tell her straightway that the time had come for us to dismiss her tufted cousin and his daughter from our thoughts" (191). He is baffled by his mother's curiosity to see him wedded which appears to him nothing short of monomania. Sambu is really puzzled by his mother's deep interest in his personal affairs. He therefore, expresses his wonder at the whole thing: "I couldn't understand what pleasure she derived in destroying my independence and emasculating me into a householder running up to buy vegetables at the bidding of the wife or changing babies' napkins" (191).

Sambu's self centred individualism gets a proper focus here. He is afraid of losing his parasitical independence if he marries and imagines himself becoming a henpecked husband doing all the feminine chores. Marriage, which may put a man's masculinity to test, is thought of by Sambu as something 'emasculating'. Sambu is obviously not enough of a man to face his manly duties and seeks refuge behind the irresponsible cult of unattached individualism. Sambu's mother is thrilled to receive a letter from her 'tufted cousin' as Sambu calls him. She cannot understand, however, Sambu's disrespectful attitude to her cousin. She even admonishes him for having kept the taxi to bring him home from the bus stand. As if to impress Sambu with the fabulous wealth of the tufted man, she says to him: "They are such big people, you have no notion how wealthy and influential they are, nothing that they cannot command, if you went there, they could command big cars for your use, you have no idea" (192).

Sambu, however, with his own notions of an independent existence, simply refuses to be impressed by all this. He is no mood to go to receive the visitor. He tells his mother in a disrespectful tone: "That tufted man is welcome to find his way here, eat the feast you provide and depart. He will not see me at the bus stand or here . . ." Sambu displays almost an inhuman unconcern with the whole thing. He actually sets out to leave the house, when his mother suddenly blocks his way, imploring tearfully:

> You need not marry the girl or look at her, only I beg you to go up receive that man. After all he is coming on my invitation, we owe him that as a family friend, otherwise it'll be an insult and they'll talk of it in our village for a hundred years. I'd sooner be dead than have them say that a wretched widow could not even receive a guest after inviting him. Don't ruin our family reputation (192-193).

The mother thus displays her commitment to certain human decencies and social values of which Sambu is devoid. He claims to hate himself for causing pain to his mother, but he is not prepared to do anything to allay it. With a last desperate effort she reminds Sambu of his social obligations and tells him:

> Meet him, bring him home, eat with him, talk to him and then leave if you like. I'll see that he doesn't mention his daughter, you don't have to bother about the marriage. Do what you like, become a sanyasi or a sinner, I won't interfere. This is the last time. I'll not try to advise you as along as I breathe; this is a vow, though let me confess my dream of seeing grand children in this home is . . . ." (193).

She breaks down and is unable to complete the sentence. The story ends when Sambu promises that he will go to the bus stand and bring the visitor home. The conflicting approach of Sambu and his mother to life, society and human relationships do not so much reflect the polarity of generations as two distinct philosophies of life. The mother's is based on an awareness of togetherness and human solidarity with due regard for social relationships and obligations, while Sambu's is marked by a self-centred and narrow individualism which wishes to enjoy the luxury of detachment by parasitically feeding on the goodwill and hospitality of others. Thus one feels impelled to have a second opinion on the question of relationship between individual and society and the concomitant philosophies of detachment and attachment.

"Cat within" is another story of the collection. This story is about a man who has a shop in which he sells sweets, pencils and ribbons to children. At night locking up the shop he sleeps across the door. Once at midnight a cat entered inside the shop chasing the mouse. The cat thrust its head in a brass jug. The mouth of the jug was not narrow enough to suffocate the cat or wide enough to allow it to withdraw its head, the cat began to jump and run around hitting its head on every wall. The shopkeeper was sleeping; he was awakened by the noise in the shop. He peeped through a hole into the dark room, but hurriedly withdrew his head and cried 'Thief! Thief'. Hearing the cry of the shopkeeper, his tenants woke up and gathered a big crowd around him. They peeped through the hole and trembled to hear the metallic noise inside. They declared that some devilish creature was inside, and suggested to call up the exorcist. The exorcist earned fifty rupees a day without leaving his cubicle; a circle of clients always wait his door. His client were said to come from even distant Pondichery and Ceylon and Singapore. Narayan narrated his physical appearance and said he never came out of his house without appropriate make up. R.K. Narayan describes this in the following words:

> The exorcist never emerged from his habitation without the appropriate make up for his role – his hair matted and coiled up high, his untrimmed beard combed down to flutter in the wind, his forehead splashed with sacred ash, vermillion and sandal paste, and a rosary of rare plum-sized beads from the Himalayan slopes around his throat. (195)

He always kept an ancient palm-leaf book in which everyone's life was engraved in mysterious couplets. He read out the couplets in a sing song manner. No one except the exorcist could comprehend the meaning of the verse composed in old Tamil a thousand years ago. To every person he said these words: "In your life you did certain acts which are recoiling on you now" (195).

In the night the shop man went to call the exorcist. He told him that a jug had come to life and moved up and down, hitting everything. To hear this the exorcist said:

> Oh it's the jug-spirit, is it! It always enters and animates an empty jug. That's why our ancients have decreed that no empty vessel should be kept with its mouth open to the sky but always only upside down. These spirits try to panic you with frightening sounds. If you are afraid, it might hit your skull. But I can deal with it" (196).

The story goes on to describe the activities of the exorcist that night. He is also afraid of entering that dark room from where the strange sound is coming. Once he ventures into it but comes out very soon when he knocks against empty tins and thus is frightened by the noise he himself has created. But he is a very smart person and soon starts behaving in the way he used to with his customers. He pretends to be talking to the spirit inside that room. Soon he asks his shopkeeper landlord if he has ever cheated someone.

What goes on between the exorcist and the shopkeeper tells us about both these characters. It seems that the shopkeeper had in the past acquired some property through foul means. At the end the cat escapes from the shop and then the shopkeeper realizes that it was only a cat. The exorcist however insists that it may be a spirit in the form of a cat.

The story is a typical example of Narayan's humour. It describes an interesting situation and makes humorous observations on the life and thoughts of the common Indians. He describes in this story how simple Indians believe in ghost. The description of the exorcist in this short story reminds us of the astrologer in the short story "An Astrologer's Day".

The short story "The Edge" is remarkable in the sense that it reflects a particular feature of India's socio-political situation at a particular time – something which Narayan does not usually do. The story was obviously written during the period of emergency in the mid- 1970s. at that time the family planning programme of the government of India – was going in full swing. Unfortunately, the medical officers and the other employees engaged in this work adopted both fair and foul means to achieve their target. People, particularly from the lower section of society were lured by the promise of money and gift to undergo family planning operations. This is what happens to Ranga the central character in the story.

This story presents the character Ranga who sharpens knives and scissors. His family is very small with only three persons – his wife, his daughter and Ranga himself. He came in town to earn his livelihood by sharpening knives and scissors. His wife and daughter lived in the village, so Ranga's mind was occupied with thoughts of his wife and daughter. In the beginning of the story R.K. Narayan introducing Ranga in the following words: In such a blissful state, clad in a dhoti, khaki shirt and turban, he was a familiar figure in the street of Malgudi as he slowly passed in front of homes, offering his service in a high-pitched, sonorous cry, "knives and scissors sharpened" (203).

When people said to him that they had nothing to grind he cleverly said: "If you do not sharpen your articles now, you may not have another chance, since I am going away on a pilgrimage" (204). Ranga's customers liked his jokes and appreciated his work. Ranga guaranteed his work for sixty days.

Earlier, Ranga worked in his village itself. He used to sit beside the shop of the Ironsmith and get his customers there only. His wife, however, was not happy with this arrangement. In the company of the village blacksmith Ranga had started drinking. When he went home, he had to face the ill-temper of his wife. One day, he had taken more drink than normal. His wife became furious, beat him with broom, pushed him out and closed the door. After this incident he decided to avoid the blacksmith. He noticed an improvement in his wife's temperament. He wanted to educate his daughter against the will of his wife. His wife persisted that girl's schooling should be stopped. To earn money to educate his daughter Ranga had started living in Malgudi. He used to visit his family in the village at regular intervals.

Once when he was returning from his village to Malgudi, he had to wait for a long time for any transport. Then he noticed a coming vehicle at the turn of the road. It was a yellow car of propagandist of birth control. The man who was bearing a blue bush-shirt asked him where he was going. Ranga replied "Town". At this the man opened the door and asked him to come in the car and said that he would drop him there. Ranga was very happy to be seated at the front seat. The man in blue bush-shirt asked him if he wanted to earn thirty rupees. He said that if he obeyed his instructions, he would get thirty rupees and a transistor radio. He took him to the lonely part of the camp. Ranga was pleased enough at prospect of getting thirty rupees. But he was slightly suspicious and confused. He imagined what he would do with the money and the transistor radio. He thought: "He could give the money to his daughter to keep or spend as she liked, without any interference from her mother. He could also give her the radio. She was educated and would know how to operate it" (211).

Thinking this Ranga closed his eyes and fell into a drowse. The man in blue bush-shirt woke him and took him to another part of the camp. Inside a large tent a man was seated at a desk. He was the chief of the man in blue bush-shirt. The man instructed Ranga not to speak till he spoke to him. He ordered him to be respectful because he was his officer. After giving these instructions he went away and was not to be seen again. Ranga felt terrified in the presence of the officer. When the officer asked him if he was married, he explained his domestic problems. He told him about the ill-temper of his present wife, who was in fact his second one. He had to marry that woman under the pressure of his relatives. When the officer asked how many children he had, he said that his first wife would have ten if God had given her long life. He described in detail his wife's sickness and death. The officer asked again, "How many children?"

He told him that six died before they were a year old, by the Goddess's grace only one left. The officer noted number of children "seven". He took the sheet of paper and ordered him to sign there. Ranga was perplexed and said: "Oh! If I had learnt to read and write . . . ." (213). Then the officer ordered him to press the thumb on the sheet of paper. Ranga was thinking that the time has come of receiving the reward. That time some people seized him and carried him into a room where a doctor and his assistant were waiting at a table for operating him. One man held his head and two other held his feet. They put off his clothes and wrapped him in a white sheet. He felt ashamed to be wrapped like this. He remembered his butcher friend reading from a news paper that the government was opening camps all over the country where men and women were operated upon so that they could have no children. When the doctor was about to operate him, he got himself free and ran away across the fields crying, "No I won't be cut up . . . . (214).

The short story, "God and the Cobbler" is the story of a cobbler and a hippie. In the seventies hippies from American were quite a common sight. They were young men and women who had left their country in search of spiritual happiness and peace. In this story Narayan depicts one such hippie. The hippie comes to the cobbler to get his sandal mended.

The cobbler compared the hippie with God Shiva. His outward appearance was similar to God Shiva as he described: "With those matted locks falling on his nap, looks like God Shiva, only the cobra coiling around his neck missing" (215). Seeing his leather sandals, thick with patches, he guessed that the hippie was coming from the Himalayas, habitation of Shiva. The cobbler put off the sandals from his feet to examine. When the cobbler was stitching his sandals, the hippie sat down on the sheet of papers provided for him. He was very happy to see that he had lowered himself on to the head of a colourful film star. He has seen at Gaya a repentant who had a long needle thrust through his cheeks. It interfered with his tongue. He was under a pledge of silence. He had watched at Allahabad during Kumbha Mela millions praying and dipping at the confluence of the rivers Jamuna and Ganges. The hippie wanted to be composed and complete in itself like the cobbler.

One day he had sat with the beggars holding out their hands for alms on the temple steps. Some of them were of a strong constitution, some were crippled blind or half-witted, but all of them were looking hungry. At the evening time, worshippers passing the entrance of the temple threw coins into the alms bowls. It was a matter of luck in whose bowl a particular coin fell. There was general understanding among the beggars to leave another alone to face his fate. Being in a good mood that evening, the priest had distributed to the beggars rice sweetened with jaggery, remainers of offerings to the Gods. That evening the hippie had slept at the entrance of the temple.

At the morning, he saw the cobbler with a gunnysack over his shoulder and settled down under the limb of the margosa. He wanted to talk to the cobbler. The hippie offered him a beedi. The cobbler hesitated to accept it, at which the hippie said: "Go on you will like it, its good, the parrot brand . . . ." (219). The hippie drew matches from his bag. Both of them smoked for a moment in silence. After some time the hippie began a conversation. He asked the cobbler, "Do you believe in God?", which surprised the cobbler. Perhaps he was testing the cobbler by asking this question. The cobbler said:

> And [God] He can't sleep, either. Our pundit in this temple said in his lecture that do not wink their eyelids or sleep. How can they? In the winking of an eyelid, so many bad things might happen. The planets might leave their courses and bump into one another, the sky might pour down fire and brimstone or all the demons might be let loose and devour humanity. Oh, the cataclysm!" (19-20).

The hippie trembled at the sight of disaster. The cobbler replied, "I ask God every day and keep asking every hour. But when He is a little free, He will hear me, till then, I have to bear it" (220). At this the hippie asked "Bear what?" The cobbler answered that he begged the God to take him away. The hippie asked, why he is not happy to be alive. Then the cobbler described his financial problems that he has to earn at least five rupees everyday, sufficient to purchase some corn or rice before going home. But it is not adequate for two meals. Betel leaves are two for a paisa, and his wife must chew even if she had no food to eat. He said that God punished him in this life. In his last birth he must have been a money lender extorting money from the poor. The hippie asked him, "What do you want to be in your next birth?" The cobbler was feeling that he might be talking to a god or his agent. He replied that he does not want birth in this world. The hippie asked, "What have you done?" a suspicion again came in the cobbler's mind that he might be talking to a God. The hippie said: "When you drink, you may not remember all that you do" (221). The cobbler said that now his limbs were weak but when he was young he had burned an enemy's hut at night while his children were asleep. The quarrel took place. That man took away his money, menace to molest his wife. She lost her eye in the conflict when he beat her up on suspicion. They had a lot of money, and a rupee could purchase three bottles of toddy in those days. He had a son, but after his death, he changed. He lived with his grandson. The hippie rose to go, and slipped his feet in the sandals. He gave the cobbler five paise and the silver figure of Durga. The cobbler returned it saying that it would protect him.

This story is one of those stories of R.K. Narayan in which he has presented strange encounters between strangers.

In the short story, "Hungry Child" also R.K. Narayan takes up the clue from an earlier novel *The Painter of Signs*. The central character of that novel, Raman is also the central character of this story. In that novel Raman who was a signboard painter had fallen in love with Daisy, a Family Planning worker. Their marriage was settled but could not take place because at the last moment Daisy decided against it. In this short story Narayan takes up the character of Raman who is now some years old but a still bachelor. All this, however forms only the background of the story. The story is about a lost child in a fair whom Raman meets.

The story begins with a description of an exhibition that was held in Malgudi. It was called Expo 77-78, the year which probably suggests the year of the composition of the short story. Narayan gives a description of the fair in his typical style:

> At the Expo, as they claimed, you could get anything from a pin to an automobile, although the only automobile in sight was a 1930 Ford displayed under a festoon of coloured

> bulbs and offered as a prize to anyone with a certain lucky number on his ticket. Special buses leaving the market road disgorged masses of humanity at the Expo archway all day Loudspeakers mounted on poles every few yards saturated the air with an amalgam of commercial messages and film-songs, against the unceasing din of the crowd. The organizers had succeeded in creating an incredible world of noise, glare, dust and litter (223).

Raman was enjoying wandering through the fair. It was then that he heard a public announcement through the loudspeaker. It announced that a boy of five named Gopu was found by the organizers lost in the fair and was brought to the central office. His parents were requested to take the child away. On a whim Raman decided to take a look at the child. When he went to the central office, the organizers mistook him for the father of the child. So they asked him to take the boy away. Raman took the boy along. What follows is a hilarious account of the interaction between Raman and that child. R. K. Narayan is a keen observer of the child psychology. In this story we find an example of this. The boy was hungry and Raman had to feed him with several things. The boy was a naughty one. Describing his antics the writer writes:

> The boy exhibited, when he had a chance, signs of mischief: he toppled flower pots, tore off posters, performed an occasional somersault wherever he found a little free space, splashed water from fountains, particularly on passing children; he also wrenched himself free and dashed forward to trip up any other boy of his age or tug at the pigtail of a girl; he picked up pebbles and aimed them at lightbulbs. Raman held him in check no doubt, but secretly enjoyed his antics. Raman felt nervous while standing in a queue with the boy since no one could foresee what he would do at the back of a person ahead. Raman admired the little fellow's devilry and versality, but held him in check, more to prevent his being thrashed by others. He told himself, "Normal high spirits, it shall be canalized when he is put in school. In our country we don't know how to handle

children without impairing their Development" (230).

"Emden" is last story of the collection. The story opened with the celebration of the eightieth birthday of Rao. Rao is protagonist in the story. His age is between ninety and one hundred and five. His family is very large. In his family there are seventy five members. He couldn't remember the name of most of the children at home or didn't know how many were living under his roof. Rao had bought a piece of land beyond Vinayak Street which was developed into a residential colony and was named Ratnapuri. Rao's earlier years were spent in Kabir Street. When he decided to live in style, he sold his old house and shifted to Ratnapuri. His first wife's children were eight of different ages. His second wife had born him four daughters. His uncle used to cast and read the stars for the entire family. He told him that Rao had Mars in the seventh house. Therefore, he had to lose his wives. After the third marriage and more children he became sure of the ill-will of Mars.

> The eightieth birthday had great significance in his domestic career. At this age faculties became dim. Rao himself said this in the story: "If I see less or hear less, so much the better. Nothing lost. My legs are still strong enough to take me about, and I can bath and wash without help . . . I enjoy my food and digest it" (234)

When the hall clock struck four, he got ready to go out on a walk. When he crossed the hall, someone or other advised him to be careful and carry a torch. Before 6:30 he returned his home. He never used his torch which he carried in his shirt pocket. When he would feel nervous in crossing the market gate Jayraj, the photo framer always called him from his little shop "Grand Master, shall I help you across" (236). Rao would ignore his offer and passed on. He had no time for people like Jayraj. When Rao went away Jayraj commented to his customer:

> At his age! Moves through the crowd as if he were in the prime of youth. Must be at least a hundred and ten! See his recklessness. It is not good to let him out like this. His people are indifferent. Not safe these days. With all these lorries, bicycles and auto- rickshaws he'll come to grief

someday, I am sure . . . ." (232).

At this the customer who was waiting for his picture to be framed asked him who he was. Perhaps he was new comer in the town.

Then Jayraj told him that they called him Emden. Emden was a German warship that shelled Madras in 1916; ever since, the term indicates anyone who is formidable and ruthless. They were frightened of him when they were boys. When he had on the road on his bicycle in his khaki uniform. They considered him to be a police inspector from his dress. They were unaware that he wore the uniform of the Excise Department. He behaved like the police. When Jayraj was a boy he used to linger about the market gangs. If Emden saw them he ordered him to go home. Once he caught them urinating against the wall at Adam's street as they always did. He caught four of them and carried them before the headmaster and said: What are you doing, Headmaster? Is this the way you train them? Or do you want them to turn out to be guttersnipes? Why don't you keep an eye on them and provide a latrine in your school? (237).

The headmaster was terrified with him. His business was merely to stop the taverns selling drinks. He collected fifteen thousand rupees in a month. He used to take bribe so he was dismissed from his service. Later he had taken the voluntarily retirement. He had great hunger for the female tribe like nurses and school mistresses and chased them.

Rao used to keep his important papers in an almirah that he kept locked and the key concealed under a lining paper in another cupboard. The key of this second cupboard also was concealed somewhere so that none could reach to these two cupboards which comprised all the clues to his life and his documents, title deeds, diaries and a will.

That day he finished reading the newspaper in ten minutes. He rose from the chair and quietly bolted the door. He opened the cupboard and stared at the papers. All the records of his official career were on the top shelf. The papers were tied in dusty & yellow paper. He had not touched anything for fear of dusting his fingers and catching a cold. He wanted someone to destroy the papers, but whom could he trust. He did not want that anyone read his memorandum. Then he saw a packet containing receipts bills and various diaries. He always purchased the same brand of diary called "Matchless". The diary had a button so that no one could easily open its pages and read its contents. There was a heap of thirty old diaries. He dragged one from the heap and wiped it with a towl. He went to his chair and turned over the pages. The diary was fifty-one years old. He found difficulty in reading his own hand writing. He watched at the calendar, the date was twentieth of March. He wanted to know what he did on that date. On the same day before fifty-one years the page comprised only four lines. They were as following:

> "To lenient with S. she deserves to be taught a lesson . . . ." This triggered a memory, and he could almost hear the echo of his own shouting at somebody, and the next few lines indicated the course of action: "Thrashed her soundly for her own good and left will not see her again . . . . How can I accept the responsibility? She must have an affair-after all a D. G. wish I had looked her in before leaving". (240).

He was surprised as to who she was. He had known nobody with a name beginning with S. He remembered her outline loving and jasmine- smelling. He was sure that the note referred to that woman and not to another one. He could not remember the house, but he had known that there was a coconut palm and a well in the street in front of the house. Suddenly he remembered that the name of the street was Gokulam. Rao rose and locked away the diary and concealed the key. He decided to visit with that S. He came out of the house. Mani from his cycle shop advised him to walk slowly because road was dug up everywhere. Rao slowed down his pace after Mani's advice.

At Jagan's sweets he temporary stopped. He packed up jilebi for three rupees. When Rao was hesitating in crossing the road. The shopman called him from his shop if he wanted anything. He felt angry why they couldn't leave him alone. Then a young shop assistant came out to take his order. Rao asked him mentioning the cross street, "Where does it lead". The boy replied, "To the next street". The boy asked him what he could get him. Rao was irritated from this question. He embraced the packet of sweets. The boy was selling something. He asked if he had sandalwood soap. Rao recollected that S. She was fond of it. Its fragrance reminded some old memories. The boy gave it to Rao with cheerfulness. He asked Rao "anything else sir?" Rao replied no, he might go.

Rao took many turns but couldn't find Gokulam Street. Then he saw a cobbler on the roadside. He asked him the way of Gokulam Street. After telling him the way he began again his stitching. Although there was no coconut tree, yet he was sure that it was somewhere there that he used to come, but everything was changed. New generation was totally forgetful of the past. When Rao was returning home the packet of jilebi fell from his grip, and the brown dog picked it up. Rao watched him helplessly and began again his journey to home. The story ended with these words of Rao: "Who knows, S. is perhaps in this incarnation . . . ." (244).

The character of Jayraj and Jagan appear in earlier works also. Jayraj is in the short story "Uncle" as well and Jagan is the leading character in the novel, *The Vendor of Sweets*.

CHAPTER – III
AN ASTROLOGER'S DAY AND OTHER STORIES

The central story, "An Astrologer's Day" after which this collection of short stories is named, presents an interesting encounter of wits. This is the story of a road side astrologer who saves his life through his presence of mind. In its turn and twist, its humour and its racy narrative this story is a typical Narayan story. The story begins with a description of the astrologer. The Astrologer "had not in the least intended to be an astrologer when he began life" (2). It was a life forced upon him, for once in the village when he was a silly youngster he left a person for dead in a well and fled for life to the city. He became an astrologer there as he was trained for nothing else. One day as he was about to move after the day's business, a stranger came to him and requested him to foretell whether he would get at the person, who tried to kill him to take a revenge. The astrologer refused as it was getting late and he was in a hurry to go home. When his credibility was challenged by the stranger, the astrologer asked for more money which was agreed upon subsequently. As the other person lit a cheroot, the astrologer caught the glimpse of his face by the match light" (4). The astrologer felt very uncomfortable and tried desperately to free himself. After a good deal of haggling, the astrologer took courage and said:

"You were left for dead. Am I right?"

"Ah, tell me more."

"A knife has passed through you once", said the Astrologer.

"Good fellow!" He bared his chest to show the scar, "What else?"

"And then you were pushed into a well nearby in the field. You were left for dead."

> "I should have been dead if some passer-by had not chanced to peep into the well," exclaimed the other, overwhelmed by enthusiasm. "When shall I get at him?" he asked, clenching his fist.
>
> "In the next world," answered the astrologer. "He died four months ago in a far-off town. You will never see any more of him." The other groaned on hearing it (5).

The story ends with a brief conservation between the Astrologer and his wife. The Astrologer after dinner, sitting on the pyol, told her:

> "Do you know a great load is gone from me today? I thought I had the blood of a man on my hands all these years. That was the reason why I ran away from home, settled here, and married you. He is alive."
>
> She gasped. "You tried to kill!"
>
> "Yes in our village, when I was a silly youngster. We drank, gambled and quarrelled badly one day – why think of it now? Time to sleep," he said, yawning, and stretched himself on the pyol.(6-7).

The story ends with the shock of discovery that what the astrologer had read and advised was from his own experience and that he is the man who had knifed his client in his native village. This is an example of irony of circumstance which Narayan deftly unfolds to his readers after a lot of suspense. There irony of both astrologer's reading of the past and his advice to his client is brought home. There is a bit of humour in the story when the astrologer and Gurunayak try to make a fool of each other. The astrologer tries to charge more money for reading Gurunayak's past, and on the other hand, Gurunayak wants to know his future at less money. At last, Gurunayak makes a fool of the astrologer by giving him less money than he had promised to give. Narayan keeps it secret till the end that the astrologer was himself the person who knifed that man. We know the truth at the end of the story when he talks to his wife.

In the beginning of the story, Narayan tells the reader time of the starting Astrologer's business and about his professional equipments:

> Punctually at midday he opened his bag and spread out his professional equipment, which consisted of a dozen cowrie shells, a square piece of cloth with obscure mystic charts on it, a notebook and a bundle of palmyra writing (3).

There is full detail about the astrologer as to where he sits, what dress he wears and about his physical appearance. The story starts from the place where astrologer transacted his business and ends at the home of the astrologer with the conversation between his wife and him. The action moves round Gurunayak and the astrologer. Wife of the astrologer comes in the story only briefly Narayan has given a brilliant physical description of the astrologer:

> His forehead was resplendent with sacred ash and vermillian, and his eyes sparkled with a sharp abnormal gleam which was really an outcome of a continual searching look for customers, but which his simple clients took to be a prophetic light and felt comforted. The power of his eyes was considerably enhanced by their position – placed as they were between the painted forehead and the dark whisker which streamed down his cheeks: even half-wit's eyes would sparkle in such a setting. To crown the effect he wound a saffron coloured turban around his head. This colour scheme never failed. (3)

Narayan has adopted the technique of third person narration to tell this story. P.D. Westbrook (1968) criticizes the story for its element of unconvincing coincidence. He does not seem to have properly understood the importance of coincidence in a story. As Brooks and Warren argue:

> Coincidences do occur in real life, sometimes quite startling ones, and in one sense every story is based on a coincidence namely, that the particular events happen to meet, for example. But since fiction is concerned with a logic of character and action, coincidence is so far as it is purely illogical, has little place. Truth can afford to be stranger than fiction, because truth is "true" is acceptable on its own merits – but the happenings of fiction must justify themselves in terms of logical connection with other elements in

fiction and in terms of meaningfulness. (Amur, 112-113)

It is quite logical that the stranger, a gullible rustic in search of his assailant to take revenge may call upon an astrologer and request him to foretell if he would be successful in his mission or not. Even educated people in India approach astrologers to know their future. The use of coincidence gives substance to the story. The story can be read as a metaphor. The astrologer "knew no more of what was going to happen to himself next minute" (2). Moreover he was forced to take up this job which needed "a working analysis of mankind's troubles: marriage money and the tangles of human ties, long practice had sharpened his perception" (3). He took to astrology to hide his identity with whiskers which streamed down his cheeks, and the saffron coloured turban he wound around his head prevented him from being recognized by others. The author has succeeded in achieving the aim of objectivity by incorporating the crisp conversation between the astrologer and the stranger, and the man and his wife.

"Our friend piqued." The remark is addressed to a hypothetical spectator, a device whereby Narayan is able to maintain the indirection or objectivity. This is guise under which the omniscient narrator speaks, substitute for the intuitions and the speculative commentary of the first person. The story is praised for its dialogue between the astrologer and the stranger in the beginning, and the Astrologer and his wife at the end. The dialogues reveal the character and motivation of the protagonist and further the dramatic action of the story.

A final shock of surprise is the main point of stories of R.K. Narayan. This is the case with "The Missing Mail" also. The focus is on the protagonist Thanappa, the postman. The story is told by the omniscient narrator. The story moves round a marriage problem in which Thanappa plays an indirect but very important role. In the beginning of the story Narayan has given the brief description of the work of Thanappa:

> Though his beat covered Vinayak Mudali Street and its four parallel roads, it took him nearly six hours before he finished his round and returned to the head office in Mar-

ket Road to deliver accounts (8).

Ramanujam is a clerk in the Revenue Division Office and lives at no, 10, Vinayak Mudali Street. Thanappa, the postman had carried letters to that address for over a generation now. Thanappa's earliest association with Ramanujam and his family is very old. Ramanujam is the father of a daughter whose name is Kamakshi. He is worried for his daughter's marriage, and his father-in law thinks that he is not sufficiently active in finding a husband for his daughter. The main problem in the marriage of Kamakshi is money. The bridegroom's party demands too much dowry, and Ramanujam cannot afford a big dowry. Ramanujam is very disappointed and says to Thanappa: "I don't think there is a son-in-law for me anywhere . . . ." (10) At this Thanappa says to him not to speak inauspicious words. Then Thanappa tells Ramanujam that there is a boy in Delhi earning two hundred rupees. The parents of the boy ready for the marriage and marriage is fixed on the twentieth of May. At last, the wedding takes place. The author has given the description of the place where marriage is held:

> It was four hours past the Muhurtam on the day of the wedding. A quiet had descended on the gathering. The young smart bridegroom from Delhi was seated in a chair under the pandal. Fragrance of sandal and flower, and holy smoke hung about the air. People were sitting around the bridegroom talking (12).

At the end of the story comes in surprise. Thanappa, the postman had kept secret the news of Ramanujam's uncle's death. He did not deliver a letter and a telegram to Ramanujam. Had it been otherwise, the marriage which was fixed for certain urgent reason, would not have taken place. Thanappa knows very well that the marriage of Ramanujam's daughter must not be postponed under any circumstances. It is only after Kamakshi's marriage that Ramanujam learnt about the sad demise of his uncle. After the marriage, Thanappa hands Ramanujam the telegram and confesses:

> "Yes, sir, and the telegram followed next day – that is, on the day of the marriage. It was unhappy to see it . . . . 'But what has happened has happened,' I said to myself, and

kept it away, fearing that it might interfere with the wedding." (13)

He is also ready to undergo punishment for this, and mumbles: "You can complain if you like, sir. They will dismiss me. It is a serious offence" (6). It moves round Thanappa, Ramanujam and his family. There are four characters in the entire story – Thanappa, the postman, Ramanujam, wife of Ramanujam and Kamakshi, daughter of Ramanujam. Thanappa is a practical man and he is an altruistic postman. The author has presented him as a well- wisher of Ramanujam and his family. He keeps secret the news of the death of Ramanujam's uncle only for good purpose. He knows that if he would hand over the telegram to Ramanujam, the marriage of Kamakshi might be postponed. He does not want any obstacle in Kamakshi's marriage. Another character in the story is Ramanujam. The author has described his mental condition very well. It is quite possible that being a father of a young daughter he is worried about her marriage. Kamakshi comes on the scene for a short time. But the whole story moves round her marriage. The wife of Ramanujam comes into two scenes only. Narayan has not given the description of physical appearance of the characters, except few words about Kamakshi and his bridegroom. The story starts at Vinayak Mudali Street and ends in house of Ramanujam. Narayan's mastery over language is depicted in the brevity, in the conciseness of his descriptions of the situations – depicted in the story. The structure of the story follows the sequential progression of time but ends with the technique of ironic reversal or ironic twist creating the surprising ending. This is a coincidence that Ramanujam's uncle died on May the nineteenth, one day earlier than Kamakshi's marriage. This is an example of irony. Narayan conceals the news of Ramanujam's uncle's death and at the end of the story he surprises the readers unfolding the truth. Narayan adopts the technique of third-person narrator to tell this story. Here the narrator is somebody outside the story. The third person narrator allows for plenty of flexibility for authorial comments. Narayan introduces dramatic elements into the story by having a lot of dialogues.

"The Doctor's Word" is another story of this collection. The story describes the importance of faith. Faith can create miracles. This is proved by the story where a critically ill person survives a severe heart attack because a doctor famous for never mincing his words tells him that he is going to be well. This is a story of Dr. Raman and his dearest friend Gopal. The story begins with a description of Dr. Raman: "People came to him when the patient was on his last legs. Dr. Raman often burst Out, "Why couldn't you come a day earlier?" (14)

Dr. Raman is a gifted doctor and his fee is more than that of other doctors. So people come to him when the patient is on his last stage. He is not a mere doctor expressing an opinion but a judge pronouncing a verdict. The patient's life hung on his words. Dr. Raman and Gopal had known each other for forty years, starting with their kindergarten days. They could not meet as much as they wanted, each being busy in his own family and profession. Often on a Sunday they used to meet each other. Gopal had not called Dr. Raman in for over three months but Dr. Raman had not noticed this thing. He only remembered this when he saw Gopal's son sitting on a bench in the consulting hall one morning. Dr. Raman was so busy in attending his patients that he could not talk to Gopal's son for over an hour. That day he was very busy because it was an operation day and he was not free till three in the afternoon. When Gopal's son told him that his mother had sent him because father was ill, Dr. Raman went straight from the clinic to his friend's house, in Lawley Extension. Gopal was suffering from heart attack. After an operation at about eight in the evening, Gopal opened his eyes and stirred slightly in bed, Dr. Raman said to his assistant: "If the pulse keeps up till eight in the morning, it will go on for the next forty years but I doubt very much if we shall see anything of it at all after two night" (16).

Dr. Raman was unsure about recovery of Gopal. At about eleven in the morning, Gopal opened his eyes and smiled at his friend Dr. Raman. He showed slight improvement, he was able to take in a little food. A great feeling of relief and joy went through the household. Gopal felt that he was about to die so he wanted to sign his will before he died. He asked Dr. Raman to sign the will as a witness. Dr. Raman was in confusion that he should tell the truth or not. It was a perplexing situation for him. He had never concealed the truth from the patient. Gopal was not merely a patient he was also an old friend. If he asked him to sign the will, it would mean that he also did not expect him to survive. This would take away the slightest chance that he had of recovery. Dr. Raman said to himself, "If my word can save his life, he shall not die" (17). At last, he decided to tell a soothing lie. He said to Gopal with deliberate emphasis, "Don't worry about the will now. You are going to live. Your heart is absolutely sound" (18). The Doctor's word had a great impact on the patient: A new glow suffused the patient's face as he heard it. He asked in a tone of relief, "Do you say so? If it comes from your lips it must be true . . ." (18)

In this way, Dr. Raman told a lie to his friend by giving him the hope of survival. This created a great confidence in the mind of his friend, and he eventually recovered. Dr. Raman himself got surprised and said to his assistant: How he has survived this attack will be a puzzle to me all my life. (18)

This story had been praised for its well-made plot. The structure of the story followed the sequential progression of time, but ended with the technique of ironic reversal or ironic twist creating the surprise ending. Gopal's recovery from illness is an example of irony. There are five characters in the story – Dr. Raman, Gopal, Gopal's son, wife of Gopal and Dr. Raman's assistant. Dr. Raman is an idealist doctor. He is very straightforward and truthful in dealing with his patients. The author presents him as an eminent doctor, a stickler for truth, a conscientious and determined fighter against death. His main motif was to save his bosom friend Gopal from illness. He never believed that agreeable words ever saved lives. The moment of trial, however came in this great doctor's life when his dearest friend Gopal waited for death sentence from his lips. On the other hand, Gopal is a very faithful and sincere friend. The author has not given the description of physical appearance of any character. The focus is on Gopal's illness. The dialogues are apt and forceful. The story is told by the third person omniscient narrator. The author gripped the attention of the reader at the very end of the story. The story has taken place at the Gopal's house in Lawley Extension.

The next story in the collection is "Gateman's Gift" It is the story of a man, Govind Singh. He is a illiterate ex-gateman. Now he is retired and gets pension every month. Being a retired man he has a lot of time. In this state, he makes a new discovery and makes fascinating models out of clay and dust. The discovery comes suddenly when one day a child in the neighbourhood comes to him with its little doll. He not only repairs it but also gives it a new look. This discovery pleases him so that he decides to proceed with this work. He gets a plentiful pliant clay and sawdust for his work. He makes a miniature universe, all the colures of life was there, all the forms and creatures, the entire villages and towns are there, as well as all the persons he had seen passing before his office when he was sentry there. It is a wonderful reflection of the world. He keeps his models in his cousin's shop and they attract big crowds everyday and sell very quickly. Govind Singh feels ecstasy when he sees admiring crowds gather around his handiwork.

On a pension day, Govind carries to his office a street scene, which is his best model. He hands it over the counter to the accountant with the request to give it to the General Manager. It disturbs the routine of office working for nearly half an hour. On the next pension day, he carries another model of the playing children and hands it over to the counter. He asks the counter clerk if the manager liked the last one. When the clerk replies in the affirmative Govind asks him to give the model to the General Manager and passes it over the counter. Thus on every pension day he carries a model and his reward is the accountant's reply of his question. At last, he makes his masterpiece. A model of the front part of his office with himself with his post, a car at the entrance and the chief getting down. This composite model is so realistic that he is reminded his office days. He hands it over to the accountant on his pension day. It is a matter of excitement for the people of the office. People admire Govind Singh after seeing the model. Govind is fearful to think that Manager will be angry for the disturbance of the routine of office working. He receives his pension and goes to his home. After one week, one day when he is sitting on the pyol, the postman comes to him with a registered letter. He becomes upset to take the letter and does not want to open it because he thinks that his pension is stopped. He has received only two letters in his lifetime and each letter put him in trouble. Govind Singh thinks that only lawyers send registered letters. This is his first registered letter. Instead of opening it, he says to everyone whom he meets to tell him what is inside the letter without opening it. Every person gives him the same answer to open the letter and see it. But he is horrified at this suggestion. Then the ex-compounder who lives in the next street advises him to take the help of ex-ray institute. Govind Singh reaches x-ray institute at Race Course Road. He asks the assistant if he can know what is inside the letter. When the assistant takes the letter in his hand and asks to open it, Govind Singh cries, 'No, no'. There is a lot of terror in his eyes. At this behaviour of Govind Singh, the assistant puts his hand on his shoulder and says, "You get well first, and then come back. I tell you – you are not all right" (23). At the time of returning home, he thinks over it, why they are all behaving like this, as if he is a mad man. He reaches home in a terrified condition. His hair is covered with street dust; his body is splashed with mud. His wife who is grinding chilli in the backyard looks up and asks, "What is this?" but he does not give any answer and only laughs. He walks down the market road, with a feeling that he is the sole occupant of this globe; his madness has given him a sense of limitless freedom, strength and buoyancy. It is a long desire in him to throw a stone at the lamp. Now he feels in his joyous and free condition, that he is free from the trammels of convention and need not push back any inclination. The shattering noise of glass is as music to his ears. A policeman puts his hand on his shoulder and asks him why he has done it. Govind Singh seems angry and replies that he likes to do so. The policeman carries him to the police station. On the way to the police station Singh meets the accountant of the office. When the accountant sees the letter in his hand, he recognizes it although it is mud-stained and crumbles. The accountant asks Govind why he has not opened the letter. He tears open the envelope and takes out of it a letter and read aloud:

> The General Manager greatly appreciates the very artistic models you have sent, and he is pleased to sanction a reward of 100 rupees and hopes it will be encouragement for you to keep up this interesting hobby" (25-26).

The accountant translates to him word for word and the enclosure, a cheque for one hundred rupees, he hands to him. A big crowd assembles to see this scene. Singh presses the letter to his eyes. He asks the accountant: "Tell me sir, am I mad or not." "You look quite well, you aren't mad", said accountant. Singh fall at his feet and said with tears choking his voice, "You are a god, sir, to say that I am not mad. I am so happy to hear it." (26) On the next pension day, he turns up neat end clean as ever at the office accountant. As they handed him the envelope they asked, "What toys are you making now?" At this Govind Singh replies, "Nothing sir. Never again. It is no occupation for a sane man . . . ." (26). After receiving his pension, he goes out of the office. With these words the story ends.

Narayan adopted the technique of third person omniscient narrator. The plot of the story is compact and dense. There is no looseness anywhere. The story moves round Govind Singh. He is a simple hearted man. He does not follow the advice of the people to open the registered letter that he has received and to read the contents. The presumption that it is from lawyer unhinges his mind. Besides Govind Singh, there are minor characters also. They are – wife of Govind Singh, the accountant, assistant of the x-ray institute and ex-compounder. These characters come on the scene for a short time. The author has not given the description of the physical appearance of any character. It has a psychological story, which tells us about the psychology of a simple-minded illiterate person who does not want any complication in his life. Each word is used to show Govind Singh's state of mind. The story shows Narayan's close and minute observation of life and its unpredictable twist and turn. The situation is unusual but the author's treatment makes it authentic and credible.

"The Roman Image" is one of the most interesting of R.K. Narayan's stories. The yarn in this story is spun around an image with 'an arm, an eye, the nose, and the mouth missing (38) accidentally discovered by the talkative man in the river Sarayu. This grotesque is identified by the learn doctor (the archaeologist) as the image of Tiberius II, a Roman Emperor. The joke here is that it is neither a Roman image, nor has Tiberius II ever existed, it is that of a dwarpalaka of a nearby village temple. The comic irony of the story is that the identity of the image is revealed by an unlettered rustic. Thus both the learned archaeologist and his assistant are made fool of. The narrator is the talkative man. He tells us of his own experience 'years ago' when he was an assistant of a famous archaeologist. In the beginning of the story he tells the readers:

> Once I was an archaeologist's assistant. I wandered up and down the country Probing, exploring, and digging, in search of antiquities, a most interesting occupation, although cynics sometimes called us "grave digger" I enjoyed the work immensely (31).

He informs the readers that he got himself appointed an archaeologist's assistant. The archaeologist:

> Was a famous person called doctor something or other. He was a superb, timeless being, who lived a thousand years behind the times, and he wanted neither food nor roof nor riches if only he was allowed to gaze on undisturbed at an old coin or chip of a burial urn (31).

During their search they were camping at Siral – a village sixty miles away from the town. The Sarayu River wound its way along the northern boundary of the village. One day after a good day's work while assisting the doctor to clean up and study a piece of stained glass picked up in a field outside the village, he constantly shook his head and said:

> This is easily the most important piece of work which has come under my notice. This bit of glass you see is not an ordinary archaeological stuff, but a very important link. This piece of glass is really Florentian, which went out of vogue in A.D.5. How did this come here? It is not found any-where else in the world. If the identity of this is established

properly we may ultimately have a great deal to say about the early Roman Empire and this part of India (38).

With these thoughts in his mind, he dived deep into the water and suddenly his hand struck against a hard object in the sandy bed. He came to the surface with the object, a stone image. Without drying himself, he handed over the image to the doctor whose reactions were: "This takes us to an entirely new set of possibility" (33). The archaeologist keenly examined it: "This is a Roman statue. How it came to be found in these parts is an historical fact we have to wrest from evidence. It is going to give an entirely new turn to Indian history" (33). On the basis of their recent findings, it was decided to publish a monumental work covering over a thousand pages of demy size, full of photographs and sketches. The assistant pored over books for months in libraries, and was about to give finishing touches to what might become a monumental contribution to the country's history. It was then that the assistant in need of some vital information visited the spot where they had unearthed the image, and in a casual conversation with a man of the locality, learned that the image had nothing Roman about it. It was just an ordinary Dwarpalaka of a Mari temple situated nearby. As for its antiquity, he was the very man who had commissioned it for the temple. The shocking news was delivered to the doctor who ordered him: "Drown it. After all you picked it up from the water – that piece of nonsense" (38). He also asked him to "Throw all that rubbish into the fire before we are declared mad" (37). The archaeologist's dream, "to have a monopoly of the earliest known civilization and place it where he chose" (37), was shattered.

The sudden denouement has indeed all the ingredients of a conclusive impact not only on the work of the archaeologist, but on the story itself and reminds us of O, Henry's technique of surprise at the end. O, Henry achieved this effect by employing an omniscient narrator who reserves some vital information and releases it at end of narrative, thereby producing a surprise. Narayan has achieved this effect by employing the first person narrator. It is quite like him not to give the archaeologist a precise identity because in this story he presents himself as a shade more important than his matter. And it is also a familiar trick of his to distance all his experience and anecdotes in time to a remote period in the past, so that, it should be obvious, the truth of what he says cannot be verified at all. The charm of the story is in the skill with which the talkative man persuades his listeners to the point of believing in the plausibility of the image being Roman, and the ease with which he reserves it. He is infact a master of art of manipulating and controlling the listeners' response to his tales. Some of which are tall tales like the present one. His technique in general is to begin with the familiar world of facts, then move on the plane of the improbable or fantastic or both, and finally return to the world of actuality he started from. This pattern may be noticed in all his stories. He begins "The Roman Image" with a seemingly factual account of himself and his master, and of the neighbourhood of Malgudi which is their field of activity. He builds up carefully the image of the learned doctor as an eminent though some what eccentric archaeologist whose obsessive ambition has been to discover something more ancient than Mohenjodaro and such other places. Thus, the narrator tricks his listeners from the beginning to expect from the archaeologist momentous discoveries. The learned man himself is seen to be so full of Roman thoughts long before he happens upon the statue that it seems only natural that he should regard it as a Roman image which would 'give an entirely new turn to Indian history' (33). The discovery of the image itself is described with such excitement and seeming naivety that its comic implications and the sheer absurdity of the fantastic claims made for it are not suspect, such is the hold the narrator has on them, that the movement of the yarn has been all along from the sublime to the ridiculous.

The Talkative Man does not end his story with the discovery of the identity of the image, but goes on to explain at some length how the image found itself in the river. One might well ask whether the story does not logically end at this point? Is not the rest a mere padding? If the story had ended at the point of sudden reversal, it would have to course made the end dramatic. But it would not have been true to the character of the talkative man, the protagonist-narrator. Moreover, having presented himself as one who had caught something of his master's archaeological enthusiasm, to be true to his profession, he could not but go into the other details concerning the changing fortunes of the image. However, the somewhat rambling account of the drunken priest could have been shortened with advantage. The talkative man concludes the story by saying that having made a fool of himself he flung the image into the sea. By seeming not to mind being made a fool of and enjoy a joke at his own expense, he succeeds in winning and retaining his listeners' sympathy. His strategy of confusion establishes his credibility with them. When Narayan thought of writing this story his initial intention was perhaps to poke fun at archaeologist and antiquarians, professional as well as amateur. But in the creative process, the comic possibilities of the material seem to have so swayed his imagination that the narrowly satirical intention is almost completely transcended resulting in a delightful talkative man yarn.

The story is satire on the research which is futile, a waste of time, money and energy. The narrator creates an atmosphere of curiosity with an ascending degree of emotional attachment to the events. Narayan could have achieved unity of effect by avoiding the description spread over two and a half pages on the responsibility of telling the reader how the temple image come to be associated with the river bed. The narration is deceptively simple since it is ironic in tone. Narayan always speaks with his tongue in his cheek, intending not to criticize but to show things as they are, achieving thereby brilliant effects. The story is long in length. There are only three characters in the entire story. The archaeologist, the talkative man and the villager. The focus is on the temple image.

"The Blind Dog" is next story of the collection. It is a simple story about a dog and a blind beggar. The story moves round both of them. In the beginning of the story the author introduces the dog:

> It was not a very impressive or high-class dog; it was one of those common place dogs one sees everywhere – colour of white and dust, tail mutilated at a young age by God knows whom, born in the street, and bred on the leavings

> and garbage of the marketplace. He has spotty eyes and undistinguished carriage and needless pugnacity. Before he was two years old he had earned the scars of a hundred fights on his body (27).

When the dog wants to rest on hot afternoon, he lies under the culvert at the eastern gate of the market. In the evening, he goes to his daily rounds, to spend time idly in the surrounding streets and lanes busy himself in an irregular fight, picks up edibles on the road side and returns back at the Market Gate by nightfall. This is his daily routine. After three years a change comes in his life when a blind beggar appears at the Market Gate. An old woman leads him up there early in the morning, gets him seated at the gate, and comes up again at midday with some food, collects his coins and takes him home at night. The dog is sleeping near the beggar. He is excited by the smell of food. He gets up, comes out of his shelter and stands before the blind man, wagging his tail and gazing hopefully at the bowl. The blind man moves his arm about and asks, "Who is there?" At this, the dog comes to him and licked his hand. The beggar throws a handful of food that the dog eats thankfully. He sits up beside the blind man and watches him receiving alms morning to evening. In a little time, observing him the dog understands that the passersby must give a coin and whoever goes away without dropping a coin he is chased by the dog. He tugs the cloth of the people by his teeth and pulls them back to the blind man at the gate and lets them go only after something is dropped in his bowl. There is a village urchin who likes to tease the blind man by calling him names and by trying to pick up the coins in his bowl. The blind man helplessly shouts and moves his stick. On Thursday, this boy comes there carrying on his head a basket loaded with cucumber or plantain. Every Thursday afternoon it is a crisis in the blind man's life. There are some people who usually assembled under the same arch. They are – a seller of bright coloured and but doubtful perfumes with his wares mounted on a wheeled platform a man who spread out cheap storybooks on a gunnysack, a man with coloured ribbons on an elaborate frame. On Thursday when the village urchin comes to the blind man, he moves his hand towards the bowl. The dog springs on him and bites the boy's wrist. The boy releases his hand and runs for his life. The dog chases him out of the market. The perfume vendor is surprised at the dog's affection for the blind man. One evening at the usual time when the blind man waits for a woman and is worried because the evening grows into night. Then a neighbour comes to him and says, "Sami don't wait for the old woman. She will not come again. She died this afternoon." (28) The blind man loses the only home he had, and the only person who cared for him in this world. The ribbon vendor suggests the blind man to tie the dog. He gives the ribbon to blind man at free of cost.

Life of the dog takes a new turn now. He takes the place of the old woman in the life of blind beggar. Hè loses his freedom thoroughly. His world is confined to the limits of the white cord. He forgets his old life. When he sees other dogs, friend or foes, by force of instinct he springs up, tugging the cord, and this constantly earn him a kick from his master. At this the old man rebukes the dog. In a few days the dog learns to discipline his instinct and impulse. He stops to take notice of other dogs, even if they come up and grumble at his side. All the day the blind man is on his legs, led by the dog with his stick in one hand and the dog-lead in the other. After the old woman's death the blind man moves out of his home- a corner in a chaultry veranda a few yards off the market. He goes early in the morning and finds that he can threefold his income by moving about instead of staying in one place. He moves down the Choultry Street, and wherever he hears people's voice he stops and spread out his hand for alms. The blind man gives a tug when he wants to stop the dog, and shouts like a bullock-driver, when he wants him to move on. The dog protects his feet from going into pit, or stumping against steps or stones, and takes him up inch by inch on safe ground steps. To see this scene people gives coins and help him. Children assemble around him and give him things to eat. A dog is indispensably an active creature who punctuates his hectic rounds with well-defined period of rest. The dog has lost all his rest. He rests only when the old man sits down somewhere. At night the old man sleeps with the string around his finger. The blind beggar starts to treat the dog badly. He hits the dog cruelly with his stick. The ribbon-seller, the novel vendor and the perfumer observed it one evening when their business was slow; they held a conference among themselves. The ribbon seller says that it rends his heart to see that poor dog slaving. The blind beggar earns more than he needs. He becomes a very devil for money. While the blind man is passing in front of the eastern gate, the dog sees a piece of bone lying on the way and he attempts to pick it up. The lead becomes tight and hurts the blind man's hand. He tugs the cord and kicks till the dog roars. The perfumer applies the scissors and cuts the string. The dog dashes and picks up the bone. The other half of the string remains in the blind man's hand. He cries, "Tiger! Tiger! Where are you?" (30). At this the perfumer says to the blind beggar, "you heartless devil! You will never get him again, he has his freedom" (30). The dog goes off at top speed. The dog becomes very happy to free his eyes sparkling with joy. He returns to his favourite resort and hangs about the butcher's shop, the tea-stall and the bakery. The ribbon vendor and his two friends stand at the market Gate and enjoy the scene immensely. The blind man struggles to find his way, waving his stick; he feels as if he is hanging in mid-air. He mourns, "Oh, where is my dog! Where is my dog? Won't someone give him back to me? (31). He says that he will murder the dog when he will get at it again. He tries to cross road, comes near being run over by a dozen vehicles at different points, tumbles and struggles and catches breath with open air. The blind beggar finds his way back to his corner in the chaultry veranda with the help of someone. He is half-faint with the stress of his journey. The blind man is not seen for twenty days and nor is the dog seen anywhere. The ribbon vendor and his friends comment among themselves: "The dog must be loafing over the whole earth, free and happy. The beggar is perhaps gone forever. Then they see the beggar again coming up the pavement led by the dog. They cry, "Look! Look! "He has again got at it and tied it up." (31) The ribbon seller runs up and asks where they have all these days. The blind man told that he was imprisoned in his corner all these days. He tells them that last night at midnight when he slept in bed, the dog came and licked his face. He felt like murdering him, but forgave the dog. He watches his time idly as long as he can pick up some rubbish to eat on the market gate, but real hunger has driven him back to the beggar. The blind man says that he will not leave him again because he has a steel chain this time. There is a dead despairing look in the dog's eyes once again. The blind man cries like an ox-driver to go on. He pulls the chain strokes with the stick, and the dog moves away on slow steps. They stand listening to the tap- tap going away. The story ends with these words: "Death alone can help that dog", cried the ribbon- vendor, looking after it with a sigh." What can we do with a creature who returns to his doom with such a free heart?" (31).

The story is a rather simplistic presentation of canine affection, which offers no variation on a commonplace theme. The protagonist is dog. What is striking about the story is forceful description of the selfish nature of man. The blind beggar represents an ugly side of human nature. Initially his helplessness arouses our sympathy, but his cruelty towards the dog, born out of his greed takes away our sympathy for his blindness. Narayan's typical comic vision is present in this story as well.

"Attila" presents another dog story, offers no finer aspect of a dog, who accidentally catches the man with whom it was friendly and the man is traced as a thief. They named him Attila after long debate. The main reason for buying him was a series of house breakings and thefts in the neighbourhood, and householders decided to put more trust in a dog than in the police. They searched and found this dog. They purchased it at the cost of seventy five rupees. The puppy was only a couple of months old. His complexion was black and white. A variety of people entered the gates of the house everyday like mendicants, bill collectors, postmen, tradesmen and family friends. Attila received all of them warmly. When he heard the sound of the gate he became alert and looking towards the gate. Gradually he became change, when he heard the sound of the gate barely moved. He only looked in that direction and moved his tail. The householders did not like this attitude very much. Someone suggested changing his name to blind worm. The mother of the family said that they could employ two watchmen for the price of rice and meat Attila consumed. They complained that somebody came every morning and stole all the flowers in the garden and Attila would do nothing about it. The youngest of the family always defended Attila and told his mother that Attila did not sleep at night. He has often seen him going round the house and watching all night. The mother advised to lock him up in a room at night otherwise he might call in a burglar and show him round. The young man was extremely irritated at this. He considered it to be the most uncharitable cynicism, but the dog justified it that very night.

Ranga lived in a hut three miles away from the town. He was a gang coolie who often employed in road repairing. Occasionally at night he enjoyed the thrill and profit of breaking houses. At one O' clock that night Ranga removed the bars of a window on the eastern side of the house and went in. He searched all the trunks and almirahs in the house and make neat bundle of all the jewellery and other valuables he could pick up. When he was starting to go out, Ranga saw Attila standing below looking up expectantly. Ranga thought his end had come. He hoped the dog to bark, but Attila did not do this. He waited for a while, and became tired of waiting, stood up and put his forepaws on the lap of the burglar. Ranga became sure that the dog would not bark. He pointed the dog towards the backyard. There was a cat. Attila ran in the direction indicated. As soon as the dog left him Ranga ran for the gate. But the dog saw him running, in one spring he was at the gate, and followed him. Attila's greatest ambition in life was to wander in the streets freely. He liked his new friend so much that he wouldn't leave him alone for a moment. Ranga requested him to leave him alone for a moment.

Attila's absence created a sensation in the bungalow. The eldest son of the house was going towards the market one day. He saw Attila going behind someone on the road. He called Attila who always suspected that his new friend was waiting for the slightest chance to leave him, galloped behind Ranga. The young man again called Attila he turned his head for a second and ran faster. Ranga doubled his pace. Attila decided to adhere to him at any cost. As a result he ran so fast that he overtook Ranga and awkwardly blocked his way, and Ranga fell down. As he rolled on the ground a piece of jewellery dropped from his hand. The young man recognized it as belonging to his sister and caught Ranga. A crowd gathered and the police came on the scene. Attila became the hero of the day. The mother of the family softened towards him. She said Attila was a very cunning detective. Narayan's description about Attila's physical appearance is plausible: "He had square jaws, red eyes, a pug nose and a massive head" (85). In this story Narayan presents Attila as a faithful dog.

"Fellow Feeling" is another story of the collection. In this story, a typical scene in a crowded train compartment is turned into a hilarious situation. Rajam Iyer picks up the quarrel with a brawny fellow-passenger but outwits him in a casual and clever manner, playing on his bravado:

> "You stand there and it will be over in a fraction of a second" "Fraction of a second? What will you do?"
> Oh nothing very complicated", replied Rajam Iyer nonchantly, "nothing very complicated. I will slap your right cheek and at the same time tug your left ear, and your mouth, which is now under your nose, will suddenly find itself under your left ear, and what is more, stay there. I assure you, you won't feel any pain."
> "I must admit you have a tolerably good face and round figure. But imagine yourself going about the streets with your mouth under your left ear . . . ." (36-37)

This is the only story by Narayan in which caste is allowed to operate freely, uninhibited at the verbal level. The story concerns Rajam Iyer, who is travelling on the Madras-Bangalore express and is annoyed by the rudeness displayed by a fellow passenger; he tries to make him behave himself. At this point the following conversation ensues:

> "Just try and be more courteous, it is your duty."
> "You are a Brahmin, I see. Learn, sir, that your days are over. Don't think you can bully us as you have been bully-

> ing us all these years."
> "What has it to do with your beastly conduct to this gentleman?"
> The newcomer assumed a tone of mock humility and said, "Shall I take the dust from your feet, O Holy Brahmin? O Brahmin, Brahmin."
> "Your days are over, my dear sir, learn that. I should like to see you trying a bit of bossing on us."
> "Whose master is who?" asked Rajam Iyer philosophically. The new comer went on with no obvious relevance: "The cost of mutton has gone up out of all proportion . . . yes, and why? "Because Brahmin have begun to eat meat and they pay high prices to get it secretly . . . ." I have with my own eyes seen Brahmin, pukkah Brahmins with sacred threads on their bodies, carrying fish under their arms, of course wrapped up in a towel. (33-34).

The fact that Rajam Iyer, the Brahmin, triumphs in the end over the muscularly built non-Brahmin may not be irrelevant for a discussion of Narayan's attitude to caste, though even here it is (as it normally is with him) ambivalent when Rajam Iyer boasts that he has driven the bully away, Narayan tells us that a few of the passengers looked sceptically at him. The story shows how sometime violence becomes necessary to deal with undesirable people.

"The Watchman" is next story of the collection. It is a story of a watchman and a girl who comes to the tank to commit suicide. But the watchman prevents her from it. The author begins the story with these words:

> There was still a faint splash of red on the western horizon. The watchman stood on the tank bund and took a final survey. All the people who had come for evening walks had returned to their homes. Not a soul anywhere – except that obstinate angler, at the northern end, who sat with his feet in water, sadly gazing on his rod. It was no use bothering about him: he would sit there till midnight, hoping for a catch. (39)

The Watchman is satisfied of his final survey. When he is about to go, he sees, about a hundred yards away a shadowy figure in the water. He thinks for a moment that it may be a ghost. He goes to examine. He observes that it is a woman's form. She goes to the last step and puts something on it – perhaps a letter. She then goes into knee deep water, and stands there. She joins her hand together in prayer. He asks her to come out of the water. She looks up from the water. He lits his lamp. The light falls upon the young girl's face; her eyes are wet with tears. He feels pity upon her, and says her to sit down. The girl hides her face in her hands and begins to weep. He feels sorry and asks her why she doesn't go home. At this the girl replies that she has no home in this world. He asks her if she grew up without a home all these years. She tells him that her mother died when she was five years old. He says, "Your father married again and you grew up under the care of your step-mother" (40).

He asks her if her step-mother persecutes her. She replies, No, she is very generous to her. She has been looking after her ever since her father died a few years before. She has a little money on hand left by her father, and she spends it on the girl. When the watchman says her to go home, she replies why she should be a burden to her step-mother. She does not want to live on anybody's charity. He suggests her to wait till her mother finds her a husband. The girl does not want to marry. She wants to study and become a doctor and earn her livelihood. She often heard her step-mother talking far into the night to his eldest son, worrying about her future, and about her marriage. she knows very well that her step-mother cannot afford to keep her in college very long now because it costs about twenty rupees a month. He wondered at twenty rupees because it is his month's salary and says, "How can anybody spend so much for books! (41) The girl further says that she was hoping that she would get a scholarship, but other have got it is not she. Her name is not there in the list. He sees at her in surprise, but understands very little of this entire situation. The girl says if his mother will come to know that she did not get scholarship, she will try to arrange her marriage. She also tells him that someone is coming to see at her tomorrow. He suggests her to marry him. She cries that she does not want to marry, she wants to study. Seeing the girl suffer he remembers his own sorrows in life, how in those times, in his little village home a epidemic of cholera laid out his father, mother and brother on the same day, and he was the only survivor. He came out of his ancestral home through the deception of his father's kinsmen, and wandered as an orphan, suffering hunger and privation. He says: "Everyone has his own miseries", If people try to kill themselves for each one of them, I don't know how often they would have to drown" (41). He remembers incidents and sorrows of his past and says that she is young and doesn't know what sorrow is. He tells the girl that he prayed to all the gods in the world for a son. His wife gave him eight children. But only one daughter lives now, and none of them saw the eleventh year. He says to the girl to go home but she repeats that she has no home. The girl is so obstinate that he picks up his lantern and stick and gets up to go. He puts her letter down where he found it. He leaves the girl alone saying this, no one can blame him. Next morning he sees that the letter is where he had dropped it on the previous night. He takes it hoping that it might tell the fate of the girl after he had left her. He thinks that the girl had committed a suicide. For this he blames himself for leaving her alone. He says himself, "I am responsible for at least one suicide in this tank (42).

After some years, one evening when he stands on the bund and takes a final survey before going home, he sees a car coming on the road below. A man, a woman and three children get down from the car and climbed the bund. When they approach the watchman the figure and face of the woman seems familiar to him. Though the woman is changed by years, ornaments and dress, he recognizes the face he had seen by the lantern light. He is excited and has numerous questions to ask. He salutes her respectfully, and hopes that she would stop and speak to him. But she only gives him an indifferent glance and passes on. He goes home saying that probably she was someone else. With these words the story ends.

The story is short in length. There are only two characters in the story – the watchman and the girl. R.K. Narayan did not give the name of the both of the characters. The watchman is protagonist of the story and the name of the story is after him. He is an altruistic man. He becomes upset to hear the problem of the girl. On the other side, prevents the girl from committing a suicide. He is not sure that the girl has committed a suicide and considers himself guilty. He does not know the truth. We feel pity for the girl. But after marriage her attitude towards the watchman changes, and she does not talk to him. Her bad conduct takes away our pity from her. It may be possible that she could not recognize him. This is a story of incident because in this story the author has described the incident in the life of the girl and the watchman. This story brings out Narayan's message on how "to bear the slings and arrows of outrageous fortune."

"The performing child" is next story of the collection. This story is about a girl Kutti. In the beginning of the story Kutti sees a dream:

> There was a green railway engine just large enough to accommodate her. She got into it all over the garden. Near the jasmine plant she stopped it for a while, and put her hand out of the window and plucked flowers, and then the engine took her under the red flowers of a creeper hanging over a wall at the street end and then she drove all by herself to the Zoo and all the monkeys there wanted to ride. Of course there was no room for all of them. She had just enough space for herself and the bald doll. She applied some oil and began to have such long tresses that braided them and put jasmine into them; and she clothed the doll in a green frock and the doll said how nice it was. Of course there were bags and bags of sweets scattered all over the floor of the engine. . . she was just pick up a handful of chocolates when mother's voice called, "Kutti! Kutti get up." And Kutti came out of the dream. "Get up, it is eight O' clock." (111).

Kutti asks her mother the reason of disturbing her. She says her to let her sleep again. She wants to travel a little more in that engine. Her mother tells her that cinema man will be coming and she must be ready. If they like her dancing they will give her so much money that she can buy ten dolls and engines. Kutti thinks that her mother will take all the money, and she won't be able to buy anything. Her mother makes promise that she will give all the money, but only on the condition that she will dance and sing as she did in her school the other day.

Two persons related to the film had seen Kutti's dance and song in her school and they are coming to see her. This is a good fortune for the family. Kutti's father is a school master earning fifty rupees a month and with it he has to pay for Kutti's education, pay off instalments of a co-operative debt that he has taken for his sister's marriage, and also run the household. For two years there is a major worry for the family and now relief is coming in most unexpected manner; the debt can be payed off, the piece of jewellery that is pledged with a banker can be released and mother can live with prestige. She often asks her husband how much he is going to demand and suggests taking ten thousand rupees. At nine O' clock the film persons arrive. One of them is elderly and wears diamond rings on his fingers, and the other is smart and wears a tweed suit and rimless glasses. They spend a few minutes in Kutti's house then the smart man says to call up the child. Kutti comes into the hall. She wears a chequered silk skirt, and a green jacket. Her hair plaited and has flowers. The elderly man gives her a packet of chocolates and asks does she like cinemas child. She replies that she does not like them because there is so dark. The smart man sees her gestures and movement critically. He suggests her to change into frock and hair unties. But Kutti refuses to change the dress. The smart man says her to sing the piece of song that she sang in her school the other day, and dance. Kutti refuses to sing saying that she has forgotten it. The elderly man fumbles in his pocket and gives another piece of chocolate. Kutti looks at her father, he says to go and sing. Her mother says from an inner room to accept the chocolates. At last Kutti sings and dances. She sings an invitation to Lord Krishna. The smart man takes her in his arms and kisses her. He says her companion: "This is a marvellous child, just the kid for the picture. I shall refuse to go on with your picture unless you take in this, understand." (114)

They go away saying that they will come back at four O' clock to take the kid to the studio for a test. They liked Kutti very much. They hope that she will be famous very soon. The entire day Kutti's father and mother would think and talk of nothing but their child. Her father says that he will give up this dirty work and do else. After this picture Kutti will be in demand everywhere. He also says that he will buy a house for her in the extension. Kutti's mother says her husband not to fail to give her the engine and the bald doll. Kutti is dressed and ready at three O' Clock. When her mother wants to wear her frock and her hair free, she becomes angry and refuses to wear the frock. Her mother calms her. After this she goes to play in the backyard. Her mother instructs her to take care and not to make herself dirty. At four O' clock when the film people arrived Kutti's father went to the backyard to bring her. Kutti was neither in the backyard nor in the next house. The Smart man waited for fifteen minutes and then says whenever they find the child, they will bring her in the studio. Kutti's mother and father begin to search for Kutti. Her mother wanders up and down the street; her father went to her school. After an hour they become disappoint. They have looked into every corner of house, and enquired in every possible place. They thought that anybody kidnapped the child. Kutti's father goes out to talk with his friends in the police station. After Kutti's father's departure her mother looks again into every corner of every room. At last she notices slight movement of a linen basket in an ante-room. When she opens the lid finds Kutti inside the basket. Seeing Kutti in that condition she becomes hopeless and mourns. She cries for help. Someone takes pity on her and admits Kutti in the hospital. The doctor tells her that she has only fainted. She will be all right. Within an hour she sits up and becomes quite well. On the way to home Kutti's mother asks reason of going into the basket. Kutti enquired about the cinema men whether they have gone or not. She says if they come to her home again she will go back to the basket. The story ends with her mother's assurance that they will not trouble her hereafter.

The story is short in length. There are five characters in the story – Kutti, her mother, father and two cinema men. Except Kutti R.K. Narayan has not given the name of any character. Kutti is the main character of the story. She is idealist character of R.K. Narayan. She does not change her dress and hair style at the suggestion of the smart man. She keeps fix her decision. She hates cinema men. There are also two minor characters in the story – a person who helps Kutti's mother and doctor. They played minor but important role in the story. The story is a fine example of child psychology. For a child money and fame do not mean anything. What it needs is the protection of the family

"Father's Help" is another story of the collection. It is basically a child story. It is about a school boy Swaminathan who carries a letter of complaint to the Head Master of his school. The content of the letter includes something adverse against the nature and character of Mr. Samuel, Swaminathan's class teacher. On that very day, Swaminathan behaves abnormally in the class and is punished by Mr. Samuel. It is deliberate on the part of Swaminathan to drag his class teacher into trouble. At the end of the school hour, Swaminathan rushes to the Head Master to hand over the letter. But his hopes are dashed into pieces when he learns that the Head Master is on leave and the letter has to be handed over to Mr. Samuel, his assistant. When inquired by his father he says "I will give this to the Head Master as soon as he is back . . ." Father snatches it from his hand, tore it up and thrust it into the wastepaper basket under his table" (62).

The story moves round swami, who thinks of every available excuse not to go to school. The gentle ironic humorous tone comes through in the conversation Swami has first with his mother and then with his father. In this story Narayan uses a combination of irony and humour. There is not much description of scenes – each word is used to mainly show Swami's state of mind and how he thinks and what results from his action. Narayan's mastery over language is depicted in the brevity, in the conciseness of his description of the situations depicted in the story. Narayan has not given physical description of the characters, except for a few lines about Samuel, the teacher with his "dark face, his small red- streaked eyes, his thin lines of moustache, his unshaven cheek and chin, his yellow coat" (58). Narayan has not wasted words on the description of Swami's home or on the school, while is just a yellow building. He concretizes the school by giving it a name the Albert Mission School. The story starts at home, moves to the school and ends at home. Though the scene of action shifts twice, the place at the beginning and at the end remains the same – Swami's home. There are four characters in the story – Swami's mother, father, his teacher Samuel and Swami himself. The protagonist is Swami as the story shows. Narayan uses framework of Swami's childhood and the crisis that has arisen is due to Swami's reluctance to go to school.

The story begins at 9 in the morning when Swami wails, that he has a headache. At 9:30, when he should have been in the prayer hall at school, Swami is still at home, where his father finds him. Inspite of all his excuses, Swami lands half an hour late at school at 10 in the morning. The teacher Samuel, on Monday takes his first class, and also the last class which begins at 3:45 and ends at 4:30 p.m. Swami during this last hour plans to irritate his teacher. He succeeds to such an extent as to get caned eight times. He thus justifies to himself the taking of his father's letter of complaint to his head master. The first twist comes when Swami learns that the headmaster is on leave and the assistant Head Master is none other than Samuel. The ironic twist on which the story ends is when Swami returns home with the letter still with him. His father refuses to believe that the Headmaster is on leave, calls Swami a coward, tears up the letter and turns his anger on Swami. His father believed him when he bluffed and made up tales about Samuel. But ironically when he told the truth, his father got annoyed and the story ends with the father's statement: "Don't come to me for help even if Samuel throttles you. You deserve your Samuel." (62) The story echoes R.K. Narayan's first novel *Swami and Friends*. The character Swami is taken from this novel.

Another story of the collection is "Crime and Punishment". It is the story of a poor teacher, ambitious parents and a naughty child with a below- average ability. For only thirty rupees a month, the teacher patiently puts up with the lectures on child psychology delivered almost everyday by the educated parents. The story begins with the question asked by teacher to the boy, "What is sixteen and three multiplied?" The boy answered twenty four. The boy repeated again twenty four. The teacher controlled himself and as a last chance he asked again "How much?" When the boy stubbornly gave the same answer, he couldn't control over himself and slapped on boy's cheek. The boy stared at him a moment and began to weep. The teacher begged the boy not to weep. The boy threatened that he would tell his parents about it. According to the parents the boy was a little angel. He was their only child; they had plenty of affection and sufficient money. They built a nursery, purchased him costly toys, filled up portrait furniture sets, gave him a small pedal motor car to go about in all over the garden. They filled up his cupboard with all sorts of sweets and biscuits. On thirty rupees a month they appointed the teacher for their son. The teacher had to teach all three hours every evening, of which first half an hour he had to listen to the psychology theories of the parents. The father had written a thesis on infant psychology for his M.A., and the lady had studied a great deal of it for her B.A. They lectured to him everyday on their theories. He had to pretend that he agreed with them, while his own view was that he was in the grip of a little gorilla.

The teacher did not know how to control the boy. The boy did not stop weeping. He told the boy that he must not cry for those trifling matters. He must be like a soldier. The boy replied that a soldier would shoot with a gun if he was hit. At this the teacher laughed artificially. This eased the situation something. The teacher ordered him to go and wash his face. But the boy disobeyed and commanded to close the lesson. The teacher was terrified. The boy threatened that he would go and tell his mother. He said to look him put the engine on its rails. The teacher said what if his father came in. The boy suggested him to tell him that it was an engine lesson. He opened his cupboard took out his train set, and began to collecting the track. He wound the engine, put it down and it went round & round. He declared the teacher station master. The teacher refuses to become a station master. The boy's cheek was still red, and it was paining. The boy said if he is not ready to become a station master, he will show his cheek to his mother. The teacher became ready to be a station master. He asked the boy what he will have to do. The boy directed him when the train came to his station he had to blow the whistle and said the engine driver to stop the train. The teacher became tired of thirty minutes game, he was unhappy with his pupil. Fortunately for him the engine also refused to move. The boy handed it to the teacher and said to repair it. He replied that he knew nothing about it. The boy said steadily he must go. The teacher felt hopeless. He was completely non-mechanical. The teacher said that he could not repair it. Then the boy immediately demanded to tell him a story. The teacher said that he had not done a sum though it was eight thirty. The boy replied he didn't care for sums and demanded again to tell him a story. The teacher refused to tell the story. The boy called his father. When the teacher asked him the reason of calling his father. He answered that he had something important to tell him. The teacher told the story of a bison and a tiger, "Ali Baba and Forty thieves" and "Aladdin's lamp". The boy listened the stories rapturously. He desired to hear the story of the bison again. The boy said again to tell his parents. He rose and started running towards the house, and the teacher chased him. The boy was so fast for him that he couldn't catch him. He made the teacher run round the garden thrice. He looked beaten. The boy took pity on him and stopped near the rose bush. When he went up and tried to hold his hand the boy ran fast. It was a hopeless pursuit for the teacher but the boy enjoyed it immensely. At that time Father and Mother came out from the house and asked the reason of their running. The teacher was still panting badly and couldn't speak. He had already made up his mind to confess and take the result, rather than stand the blackmail by this boy. They inquired the boy why they had been running in the garden at that hour. The boy looked mischievously at the teacher. The teacher cleared his throat and said that he would explain. He was trying to find out words for his sentence. The father inquired him about the preparation for his test in arithmetic. On hearing the word test the boy's face fell. He requested the teacher by his look and gestures behind his parents not to betray him. The teacher replied, "Only please let him mug up the 6th table a little more . . . . He is all right. He will pull through" (173). The boy relaxed. The teacher saw his grateful face and felt confident that the boy would not give him up now. He said: "Good night sir; we finished our lessons early, and I was just playing about with the child . . . Something to keep up his spirits, you know." (174) Here the story ends.

The child and teacher relationship is favourite subject with R.K. Narayan. Not only in his short stories but also in many of his novels we come across it. For example, in the novel *The Financial Expert* we find a similar situation. In that novel Balu, the son of Margayya who is a wealthy man and also the secretary of a school, behaves in a similar manner with his teacher who comes to teach him at home. He also blackmails the teacher in a similar way and makes him accept his wayward behaviour.

"The Tiger's Claw" is another story of the collection. It is basically Talkative Man story. It is best of his stories because in telling it he is most fully in his elements. It is told by the third person narrator, and the narrator is the talkative man. It is very interesting from the point view of plot and character. The story, which also shapes itself into a tall tale, is all about his supposed encounter with a tiger, alone and bare handed, in a remote village. A maneater, which has been successfully killed, is brought in a procession and the acquaintance of the talkative man gazes at it lost in wonder. Pretending to be provoked by them, although he does not always need a pretext or provocation for his stories, he sets out to narrate the story of his adventure. The tiger held a reign of terror for five years in the villages around Mempi forest. The Talkative Man's work was as agent of a soil fertilizer company so twenty five days in the month, he had to be on the road, visiting secluded places and corners of the country to popularize the stuff. One such journey brought him to the village Koppal. It was not really a village but just a clearing with about forty houses and two streets, surrounded by the jungle on all sides. Its centre of civilization was its railway station. The author gives a brief description of the station master and station. Station master was a wizened man wearing a green turban, and with red and green flags always wrapped under his arms. After this he tells the readers about the station:

> It was not a building but an old railway carriage, which having served its term of life was deprived of its wheels and planted beside the railway lines. It had one or two windows through which the station master issued tickets, and spoke to those occasional passengers who turned up in this wilderness. A convolvulus creeper was trained over its entrance. No better use could be found for an ex-carriage. (40)

One November morning a train brought him to this station. The Station master became excited at seeing him. He had seen so few travellers arriving that it gave him endless pleasure to see a new face. He asked him to be his guest. He took him to his house – a stone building consisting of just one room, a kitchen and a backyard. The train would be at five on the next morning. After dinner at the station master's house he felt that the time had come for him to leave. The station Master's house was very small so the narrator wished to sleep at the station master's office at the station. A heavy table, a chair and a stool filled most of the space in there. He pushed them aside and made a little space for himself in a corner. He had at least eight hours before him. He felt deserted. It was very hot and he couldn't sleep. He rose and opened the door slightly to let in a little air. He put the chair across the road and went to his bed. He fell asleep and began to dream. He was standing on the top of a hill and looking the valley below. He saw catlike creatures moving across the slope. He was so lost in this scene that he didn't notice them. He saw that they were not catlike in size but full grown tigers. He ran to the only shelter the station room. Here the dream ended. He opened his eyes and saw that a tiger was trying to push himself in. It was a perplexing situation.

He was not sure whether the dream was continuing or whether he was awake. At first he thought that it was station master. But when the tiger came near him he got frightened. The tiger was surprised by the noise of furnitures. Wild animals are less frightened of human beings than furnitures like chair and table. He seized the chair like a shield, and the tiger went back a step or two. The railways chose the heaviest wood for their furniture, that saved him. The tiger could do nothing more than put himself high on the roof of the table and bend down his paws. He tried to strike him down but he prevented him with the chair and stool. After struggling to save himself, he applied knife on tiger's paw which was lying on the table nearby. The tiger again tried to come in. The narrator employed the long knife and cut off a digit with the claw on it. It was the end of a fight between the tiger and the narrator. He cut out three claws. He became as bloodthirsty as the tiger.

At about five in the morning the station master and the porter arrived. When they entered inside the room, the tiger left the narrator and turned on them. Both of them ran at top speed. The station master went to his house and closed the door. The porter climbed up a tree.

At 5:30 the train arrived. The tiger became afraid of the sound of the engine and went to jungle. His encounter with the tiger, contrary to one's expectations is said to have taken place in an old discarded railway carriage, used as the station master's office, where he is lodged for the night of the anecdote by his host, the station master himself. To render this highly improbable and utterly fanciful fight plausible, the talkative man prefaces the anecdote with many matter of fact but significant detail regarding his visit to the remote village, which is actually "A clearing with about forty houses and streets, hemmed in by the jungle on all sides" (68). In such a place as this an encounter with a tiger does not at all seem improbable.

Next, as the talkative Man gives a brief but vivid account of the actual place of the encounter, the different humming and rustling sounds disturbing the stillness of the night, his own sense of being forlorn, and of his lapsing into a dream about full- grown tigers, he creates masterfully an atmosphere appropriate to inducing the illusion of a real fight with a real prowling tiger. Then he goes on to give a precise account of the move made and fighting strategy adopted by either party. He creates the fight so tellingly, combining successfully in his account its drama, excitement suspense and humour, that one finds himself suspending his disbelief in the truth of the encounter. Further even the patent absurdities of the supposed fight are made to appear probable. The tiger and the narrator playing a kind of cat and mouse game inside the carriage, his resisting the tiger by building a sort of stockade with the stout wooden table and stool available there, his flourishing the chair at the tiger in the circus fashion – in fact, what we have here is a parody of the circus fight – and his using the station master's knife to cut off some digits of the tiger's claw, all these are made to seem perfectly credible by the vividness and precision of the narration. So that when he makes the astonishing claim that the man- eater paraded now is the same as he had fought with earlier, and adduces as proof its missing toes, his listeners are readily taken in. The Talkative Man tells the story so absorbingly and with such gusto that till the penultimate moment they do not realize that they have been fooled by him. Even when the truth about the missing claw is known – "that some forest tribes, if they catch a tiger cub, cut off its claws for some talisman, and let it go" (74). One cannot help admiring his resourcefulness since; obviously, he must have made up that fib immediately after he noticed the missing toes in the man-eater's paw. The O. Henry-like finish of the story is inevitable.

"Iswaran" is a remarkable story with a poignantly sad ending. It is a story of a boy, Iswaran, who has earned the reputation of having aged in intermediate class. He is in fact a tortured unhappy soul. He has been failed several times in this class. When he first time failed his parents sympathized with him, the second time he also got their sympathies, but after this, they became more critical and unmerciful, and after repeated failure they lost all interest in his examination. His parents often told him to give up his study and to do something useful. He always requested his parents to give him one last chance. The whole town was excited with the expectation of the results in the evening. The boys wandered about the street in groups, and on the bank of Sarayu they sat in groups. Some boys assembled at the gate of the senate house staring anxiously at the wall behind which a meeting was going on. Not only the boys but also their parents were worried about their results. Nobody was worried for Iswaran because his result was famous and known to everyone in advance. Iswaran said his father in a humorous way that he has passed this time because he did study quite hard. At this his father replied that he was the greatest optimist in India. His mother asked why he didn't go and wait along with the other boys to look up his results. Iswaran answered that there was no need of it; if he passed they would bring home the news. He had not seen his results last year and spent his time in a cinema. He saw two shows continuously.

He changed his dress, combed his hair with deliberate care because he knew everybody looked on him as a kind of an outcast for failing so often. He knew behind him the entire family and the town were laughing. He felt that they remarked among themselves that washing, combing his hair and putting on a well-ironed coat were luxuries far above his state. He was a failure and had no right to such care. He responded their attitude by behaving like a desperado. He moved his arms, strode up and down, boasted and shouted and went to cinema. All his happy-go-lucky exterior was only a mask. "Under it is a creature hopelessly seared by failure, desperately longing and praying for success" (40). On the day of the result he was inwardly, in a trembling suspense. He said to his mother not to wait him for dinner that night because he would eat something in a hotel. He sat through both the shows at the Palace Talkies. He went in the most obscure corner of the hall. There was not a single student in the entire theatre. All the students of the town were near the Senate House, waiting for their results. Iswaran felt very unhappy to be the only student in the whole theatre. Fate seemed to separate him from his fellow beings in every respect.

Soon the lights went out and the show started. It was a Tamil film with all the known gods in it. He soon lost himself in the politics and struggles of gods and goddesses. Soon the heroine of the story sat on the low branch of a tree in heaven and would not move out of the place. She sat there singing a song for half an hour. This scene tired Iswaran and all his pains and dejection returned there. He requested the heroine to move on. It seemed she heard his appeal the lady moved off, and brighter things followed like a battle, a great flood, someone dropping headlong from cloud, and someone coming from the bed of an ocean, a rain of fire, a rain of flowers, people dying, people rising from graves and so on. All sorts of thrills happened on that white screen. For sometime the film stopped. The cry of the salesman selling soda, the non- stop comments of the spectators; all this disturbance helped Iswaran to forget the senate house and student life for a few hours. The show ended at ten O' clock in the night. A crowd was waiting at the gate for the night show. Iswaran walked across to Anand Bhavan – a restaurant apposite the Palace Talkies. The owner of the restaurant was a friend of Iswaran. He asked about his result. Iswaran replied that he did not write any examination that year. His friend said that he thought that he paid his examination fees. Iswaran laughed and said he was right, he had passed his intermediate. When his friend asked about his future plan Iswaran replied that he would go to a higher class. After taking dinner in the restaurant he went to the Palace Talkies.

He again purchased a ticket and went to see the picture. All discord, struggles, and stratagem of gods were repeated before him. He was once again lost in it. When he saw on the screen some young men of his age singing and playing in the water he said: "Well might you do it, boys. I suppose you have no examination where you are . . . ." (48) Then the leading lady sat on the branch of the tree and began to sing, here Iswaran lost interest in the picture. He saw several happy groups of the boys. He knew that all of them had seen their results and had come to celebrate their success. He thought that they would look at him with feeling that he had no business to seek the pleasure of a picture. He looked at the screen, there was nothing to gladden him. The heroine was still there, and he knew she would definitely stay there for the next twenty minutes singing her masterpiece. He came out of the theatre.

He felt extreme disgust for himself after seeing those successful boys. He thought that he was not fit to live. The idea of suicide came in his mind. He wanted to go to a world where there were young men free from examination. This solution gave him feeling of relief. He went to the hotel. The hotel man was about to go to bed. He demanded him a piece of paper and pencil. He wrote a message for his father, folded the slip and put it carefully in the inner pocket of his coat.

After returning the pencil he came out of the hotel. On the way to the river he talked himself that the water of Sarayu would end all his miseries. He thought that he should leave the letter in his coat pocket and remember to leave his coat on the river step. On the river he removed his coat quickly and went down the steps. He said to address the god, if he could not pass an examination even with a tenth attempt, what was the use of his living and disgracing the world. His feet were in water. He looked at university building. Before dying he thought of going to the Senate House to see his results. He came out of the water and went to the Senate House leaving his coat behind. He entered the Senate House with a fearless heart. The Senate was deserted not a sound was everywhere. The entire building was in darkness, except the staircase landing where a large bulb was burning. The notice board was hanging on the wall. By the light of the bulb he examined the numbers. He looked through the numbers of students who had passed in third class. His own number was 501. The successful number before him was 498, and after that 703. He hoped that somehow his number would have found a place in the list of successful students. After staring at the notice board he found that his number was nowhere. He looked at the notice board again. He stared at the top column of the results. He looked at the first classes number and admired the students who have got first-class. After this he saw second classes number. It was in two lines starting with 98. There were about fifteen. He looked at each number going on to the next. He came to 350 after that 400, and after that 501 and then 600. He looked at the number again and again. At last he became sure that he had obtained second class. Thinking that he would sit in B.A. class next month, he was very happy. He said that he would flay him alive who called him a fool. He felt dizzy. Years of strain and suspense were suddenly relaxed, and he could hardly bear the force of this release. The madness of the moment overpowered him and imagining himself 'the sole occupant of the world and its overload (50). He rode his imaginary horse to the Sarayu and into it.

Next afternoon his body found about a quarter of a mile down the course of the river. Some persons picked up the coat left on the step and searched in the inner pocket the slip of paper with the inscription: "My dear father: by the time you see this letter. I shall be at the bottom of Sarayu. I don't want to live, don't worry about me. You have other sons who are not such dunces as I am."

Here the story ends. The story is a powerful expression of the psychology of failure. The ironic double twist at the end seems to interest the author more than the psychology of the protagonist. The story takes an uncommon situation, and succeeds in making the end dramatic. The story is comparable to "A Breach of Promise", which appeared in Lawley Road: about it, Narayan told Ved Mehta, "That was almost my first tale . . . It is very truthful – autobiographical, you know. It concerns a student, myself, who fails a lot of examinations." (Gilra, 83) Unlike Iswaran, "A Breach of Promise" has, however, a happy conclusion.

"The Evening Gift" is another story of the collection. It is about a man Sankar and his drunkard master. Here is a typically effective Narayan beginning:

> "He had a most curious occupation in life. Having failed in every effort, he had to accept it with gratitude and enthusiasm; he received a thirty rupees a month for it. He lived on fifteen rupees in a cheap hotel, where he was given a sort of bunk in the loft, with rafters touching his head." (96)

He saves fifteen rupees for paying of the family loan in the village that he had taken for his sister's marriage. He earns one or two rupees by filling money order forms and postcards for illiterate villagers, whom he meets on the post office veranda. But his chief work is very peculiar. His business is to prevent his drunkard master from drink after nine in the evening, and take him home. A rich man wanted someone to prevent his drink after nine in the evening and take him home. Sankar's bodily structure qualified him for this work. His master says him not to hesitate to use force on him if necessary. But he had never done this. Sankar within five minutes always succeeded in wresting the gentleman from his cups and pushing him into his car. On the next morning he asks him the time of their returning home. His master says to go and come back in the evening. After finishing his morning work Sankar goes to his garret, returns to work at six O' clock. Sankar and his master go to oriental café. That day Sankar was in a dejected state, he felt sick of his vocation. He became bored in the company of a drunkard. He decided to give up his job and go back to the village. He received a letter from his village. His family needed a hundred rupees. It was the last date for mortgage instalment otherwise they would lose their house in the village. The house was their last possession in the world. He thought if it went, his mother, brother and little sister would be without a roof over their heads. He cursed himself for being the eldest son of a troubled family. At about ten to nine the last ounce of drink would be poured out, and Sankar sat down apposite his master instead of going out to the veranda. This was a kind of warning bell. His master asked the reason of sitting there, and ordered him to go to the veranda. He replied that he liked that place so he sat there. The drunkard said it was not time for him come in yet. Sankar answered it has become ten minute more. When the clock struck nine, he put his hand on his master's shoulder and said to finish his drink and get up. At this master became angry and abused him. He ordered him to go out of his service. He offered him his four month's salary and asked him to go. A conflict was in Sankar's mind that he should accept the salary or not. Finally he decided to take the money and said thanks to his master.

Next morning Sankar went out for shopping. He purchased bits of silk for his younger sister, a pair of spectacles for his mother and a few painted tin toys for the child at home. He went to the hotel and paid all his bills. When he left his garret he had a feeling of sadness. He reached the bus stand at about eleven in the day.

The bus was ready to start. He took his seat. He thought that he would be home at six in the evening. It will be surprise for his mother. He would talk all night and tell them about the drunkard. He came out of this day- dreaming. A police man came to him, put his hand on his shoulder, asked him to get down from the bus and follow him. The inspector brought him to the police station where he asked many questions, searched his pocket and took away all his money. The inspector examined the hundred rupee note. Both of them go to the drunkard's house. He was sitting in a chair on the veranda, with a very tired look on his face. He moved the chair and said to address Sankar in a voice full of sorrow: "I never knew you were this sort, Sankar. You robbed me when I was not aware of it. If you'd asked me I'd have given you any amount you wanted. Did you have to tie me up and throw me down?" (100) He showed the injury by blow on his arm. Sankar explained all that had happened in the evening. Neither police inspector nor his master believed him. The inspector found about one hundred and ten rupees and some change. When the inspector inquired about the money Sankar replied that he had bought some toys and clothes. The drunkard said that he could have asked him for money instead of robbing him by force. He asked Sankar if he knew where they found him. He told him next day they took him home. He said inspite of leaving him unconscious he will, however, withdraw the complain. He said do unto others as he would be done by is his motto. He said Sankar not to come before him. He said inspector to give him the seized amount the next day. Sankar starved for two days and wandered about the street without a place for his head and trunk. At last, wandering near the post office one day, he got a few money orders and postcards to write, which earned him a rupee. With it he ate a meal, and took the bus for his village and back to all the ancient never-ending troubles of his family life.

The story deals with the ironies of life. It is also a reflection on the behaviour of drunkard. It is the irony of fate that though Sankar loses his job so that he might help his family, he fails to do so and his sacrifice becomes useless. His master represents a typical drunkard. Like all drunkards he cannot remember the things that happened to him when he was drunk.

"A Snake in the Grass" is next story of the collection. It is a snake story. On a warm afternoon when the dwellers of the bungalow are at their short sleep, a cyclist rings his bell at the gate and declares that a big cobra has got into their compound. He says that it crossed his wheel. He points to its track under the gate, and begins his journey. In the family there is a mother and her four sons. All of them assembled at the gate in great commotion. The old servant Dasa is sleeping in the store. They move him out of his sleep and tell him of the arrival of the cobra. He says that there is no cobra. They swear at him and force him to take an interest in the cobra. They say if the cobra is not found before evening, they will turn him out from service. They also say that his neglect of the garden and the lawns is responsible for all these fearful things coming in. They see accusingly at Dasa, and say that he is the laziest servant on earth. Dasa replies that he has been asking for grass-cutter for months. In monotony they order him to manage with the available things and not to make demand.

That time an old beggar asks for alms at the gate. They say her not to trouble when they are engaged in a snake hunt. The old woman becomes happy on hearing this. She says that they are lucky. It is God Subramanya who has come to visit them. She forbids killing the snake. Mother becomes agree with her and says: "You are right. I forgot all about the promised Abhishekam. This is a reminder." (94) She gives her a coin, who promises her to send a snake charmer as she goes. After some time an old man seems at the gate and declares himself as a snake-charmer. They collect around him. He tells them of his life and activities and his power over snakes. They ask him with praise how he does catch the snakes. He says "Thus" pouncing upon a hypothetical snake on the ground. They mention the direction in which the cobra has gone and says him to go ahead. He seems helpless and could not find the snake. He says if they show him the snake, he will catch at once. He says them to call him when they see the snake again. He gives his name and address and goes. At five in the afternoon, they throw their sticks and instruments old repair to the veranda to rest. They have turned up every stone in the garden and cut down every grass blade and shrub, so that the smallest insect coming into the garden should have no cover. They are loudly discussing the various measures they would take to protect themselves against crawling animals in the future. Dasa appears before them carrying a water pot whose mouth is sealed with a slab of stone. He puts the pot down and says: I have caught it in this. I saw him peeping out of it . . . . I saw him before he could see me." (95) He describes the strategy he had employed to catch and seal up the snake in the pot. They stand at the safe distance and stare on the pot. He feels victor and says not to call him idler hereafter. Mother admires him on his sharpness wants to place some milk in the pot as a kind of religious duty. Dasa picks up the pot carefully and walks off saying that he would leave the pot with its contents with the snake-charmer living nearby. He becomes the hero of the day. They look at him in great admiration and decide to reward him.

The youngest son sees out of a hole in the compound wall a cobra emerging. It glides along towards the gate, stop for moment to see at the assembling people. It creeps under the gate and vanishes along a drain. When they come out of the shock they ask, it means there are two snakes. The college boy says in low tone: "I wish I had taken the risk and knocked the water-pot from Dasa's hands. We might have known what it contained" (95). Here is the end of the story. This story is very short in length. The beginning of the story is remarkable. There are various characters in the story such as mother and his four sons, their servant Dasa, a cyclist, old woman beggar, and snake-charmer. R.K. Narayan has given the name to only their servant Dasa. There is no description of any character. The focus is on the snake.

"The Snake Song" is another snake story of the collection. In this story the narrator takes his listeners into the world of classical Karnatak music, and spins out a story on the popular mythical notions about the mysterious powers of music over the snake. Using the pretext of a conversation on the state of south Indian music, he strikes the pose of one who is a little more knowledgeable in music than all others, and goes on to elaborate one of his experiences 'years and years ago' when he was learning to play on the flute under a master musician in a remote village. The real interest of the story hinges on two strange encounters of his on a certain night: first with an unseen sadhu who curses him that his music is at end for having refused him both food and music; next, soon after the mendicant's departure, with a black cobra which is apparently drawn to the place by the compelling power of his music. The latter is the more startling and mysterious and forms the climax of the story.

As always the talkative man builds up the climax steadily. He takes particular care to impress on his listeners his rapturous involvement in his own music as preparation for his encounter, first with the mendicant, and a little later with the snake. To render probable to his listeners the sudden dramatic appearance of the black hooded serpent, supposedly drawn to the place by his flute, he conjures up with shrewd calculation an impressive vision of the snake song in punnagavarali (a raga believed to be very dear to snakes) he happened to be playing at time of the snake's arrival. He describes vividly and imaginatively the verbal text of the song which celebrates the manifold significance of the cobra in myth and legend, and thus propitiates it. Thus he builds up the mood receptive to the mysterious arrival of the snake, as though in answer to his song. The snake strangely turns out to be a demanding creature. It enjoys listening to the snake song but lets out a hiss of angry disapproval whenever the narrator renders a different song. Therefore he has to play the same song repeatedly until he falls prostrate exhausted before the snake. The snake's demand for the snake's song only is the talkative man's mischievous improvement on the popular myth about the snake's love of music. Of course it goes undetected by his listeners. He ends the story by saying that since the encounter has been anxiously looking for the sadhu or that the curse might be undone and he resumes his music. The question, how do the curse and nocturnal encounter with the cobra qualify him to claim for himself better knowledge of music than others, remains unanswered. But the Talkative Man so engrosses his listeners in the mystery of the curse and the snake and wins their sympathy for himself that the question regarding his musical credentials does not occur to them at all. Nor does it occur to them that he may have pulled their legs by yarn.

Another story of the collection is "An Accident". It is a ghost story. Here the narrator is the talkative man. In this story a car which for no conceivable reason suddenly stalls is set right by a fellow who turns up from nowhere, gives out his name as Arul Doss, and is later identified with a driver of the same name who had died in a car accident a month earlier at that very place. The story is told by a first person narrator. While returning from the temple the narrator has been held up till nearly nine O' clock. He drives the car down the hill, turns to his left, and goes a few yards further skirting the base of the hill when the engine sighs and bustles, the entire car jerked and stops. The hill appeared him, jackals lamented in the dark. He got down, went round the car, opened the bonnet and stared in. He knew nothing about the car's inside. After doing every possible effort to start the car he put it to the nearest workshop. He was hoping that some motorist would along and help him. The time passed there was not a single person. The narrator describes the atmosphere of the story as: "The wind rattled the side screen, and unseen insects hummed and whirred about" (104). The narrator feels that he is only human being on the strange planet.

He thought if the car did not start he would abandon it and walk home. Then he saw a shadowy figure at his side. He was surprised. He asked when he came and who he was. He replied that he had come there a moment ago. The narrator said that he did not hear sound of his coming. He asked his name. He told his name Arul Doss, he was a motor driver. It seemed unbelievable that the gods had taken so seriously his threat to leave up the car, and send mechanic along. He asked the driver from where he was coming. He replied he was usually there. He was a motor driver, the car broke into pieces and he had been without a car since. The narrator requested for help to start the car. The driver opened the bonnet and examined the engine. He put his head into the car, and pulled out the screw from the switchboard. He came out and announced his diagnosis: "Loose contact jet trouble". The narrator said that he had examined it. The driver replied that it was a bad place and worse things happened there. He asked what he means by bad. The driver answered that things happened there to a car that people could not understand. The driver told him that hardly a month old car Austin Sedan was destroyed in an accident on that place. He also said that he remembered the accident till then. Before a few months an Austin coming down from the hill after nightfall collied against a stone and was broken into pieces. The narrator requested him to move the car on the road. He offered him two rupees for the service. After a quarter of an hour he started the engine. The driver suggested him to change the piston rings as soon as possible. He opened the door and came out of the car. He told him that he had been a driver for twenty-five years, and it pained him when he saw a car suffer. For only twenty five years he served only two masters. With the first master he lived only four years and with the other for over twenty years. He loved car, and if he saw anyone make slightest scratch on a mudguard he slapped his cheek though he might be an emperor's son. He would willfully dash and smashed an Austin, which was only a month old. His master thought that he was drunk at the time of accident but he swore that he was not drunk. He had occasionally taken a drink, but he was not drunk that day. He requested the narrator to meet his master and tell him that he was not drunk and the accident occurred because of the evil nature of the place. The narrator wanted to give him two rupees, but he refused to take the money. He said that there was no use of it, he needed his good will. The car behaved so well that he was filled with great admiration for the mechanic, and he decided to meet his master the next day. He went to the owner of the wrecked Austin and conveyed to him the driver's message. The owner of the Austin said, undoubtedly all that was true, but he was puzzled because Arul's skull was jammed when he picked him up and carried his remains in a basket and buried him. He said him not to say in his apposition, the driver was drunk. He caught him several times and warned him. He knew all along that he would come to a bad end.

The story deals with the dead man. There are only three characters in the story – the narrator, the driver Arul Doss and his master. The author did not give much description about the characters. The focus is on the driver Arul Doss, and he is the main character of the story. The narrator is the Talkative Man and protagonist of the story. He could not know whether the driver is a drunkard or not. His master told him that he was drunk at the time of accident. On the other hand the driver said that he was not drunk and an accident occurred due to the evil nature of the place. So we can say that there is suspense in the story.

"Old Man of the Temple" is another ghost story. In this story to effect the required suspension of disbelief in his listeners, the narrator prefaces his anecdote with these words: "It was some years ago that this happened. I don't know if you can make anything of it. If you do. I shall be glad to hear what you have to say; but personally I don't understand it at all. It has always mystified me" (156). This seeming confession of his bewilderment disarms even the most sceptical of his listeners. Then he goes on to narrate with seeming matter-of-factness but sure calculation the circumstances leading to his accidental meeting with the Old Man of the Temple – or rather his ghost. He knows that the success of this story and of all such stories depends on building up a suitable atmosphere as well as manipulation of the movement to and from the natural and the supernatural. First he tells us about his driver Doss and lays particular stress on his 'perfect judgement, good sense, and sobriety', (156) and his absolute reliability as a driver so that his seeing the old man's ghost cannot be dismissed as the hallucination of a superstitious man. Then he builds up with verbal economy the atmosphere appropriate to his sudden and incredible meeting with the ghost:

> It was about eleven when he passed the village Koppal . . . . It was the dark half of the month and the surrounding country was swallowed up in the night. The village street was deserted. Everyone had gone to sleep; hardly any light was to be seen. The stars overhead sparkled brightly. Sitting in the back seat and listening to the continuous noise of

> the running wheels, I was half lulled into a drowse. All of a sudden doss swerved the car and shouted: "You old fool! Do you want to kill yourself?" (156-57)

Description here is kept to the essential minimum. The stillness of the night, the enveloping darkness relieved only by the distant starlight, and the monotonous noise of the wheel dulling one's mental powers are all well brought out in the above passage and contribute to creating on urgent sense of an unearthly atmosphere, in which unbelievable things such as this tale narrates may happen.

Significantly it is Doss who first sees the old man coming out of the road-side temple, which to the narrator's eyes appears to be just an old ruin. It was indeed a ruin. When Doss next says that the old man is sitting next to him in the car and wants a lift, the narrator suspects that Doss has had 'a drop of drink'. But soon to his despair, Doss assumes a hunched up position, trembles like an old man and speaks in a thin piping voice, as though he has become a different person altogether. From the ensuing conversation between himself and the spirit that possesses Doss, the Talkative Man not only gathers all about the old man, who belongs to the previous century, but persuades him successfully to join his dead wife, instead of haunting the village. The narrator sustains the tone and tempo of the narrative so well without any let up that he gives his audience little time to raise doubts or ask questions regarding the credibility of the anecdote. This story is narrated by the Talkative Man, this is his own experience of life. As a successful Talkative Man story this ranks next to "The Tiger's Claw".

"Old Bones" tells another absorbing story of a spirit possessing a human being for a short while. The anecdote is even more incredible than the one in "Old Man of the Temple". The experience recalled is close to a nightmare. It seems so very real to the narrator even long after it happened, that he does not find any need to offer an apology or explanation for the truth of it. So proceeds straight away to tell it. In other words his strategy in this story to make it a brisk and straight-forward narrative with sustained tempo so as to convey something of the compelling power of his experience. He begins the story with a brief description of the old deserted dak bungalow tucked away in a casuarina grove, where he was held up for a night, its old caretaker 'a parched old man who looked like a lost soul; who refuses to sleep in the bungalow come what may, and of his young nephew's discomfort and nervousness at the prospect of spending a night in the bungalow all by themselves. This description, almost matter of fact, sets the stage for the poltergeist phenomenon which appears after the midnight hour, and rouses the mood appropriate to the weird account of the murder of a certain Murugesan by the caretaker. The Talkative Man's account of the altercation, both verbal and physical, between himself and the spirit possessing his young nephew, which is the most incredible part of the episode, is also brief and precise. He takes care to avoid all melodrama while presenting the unavoidable details of the murder of murugesan and the unceremonious disposal of his bones, as revealed to him by the dead man's spirit. Thus he not only holds his listener's attention but convinces them of the probability of the episode. But the lame excuse he offers at the end of the story for not reporting to the police against the old caretaker, characteristic as it is of him, may rouse some suspicion that this story may be one of his yarns. This is one of the interesting Talkative Man story. This is very skillfully narrated by the Talkative Man.

In all of these stories "An Accident", "Old Man of the Temple", and "Old Bones" which deal with the supernatural, the Talkative Man makes no attempt to fool his listeners. He seems in earnest. The rather abrupt beginning of these stories, which gives them a certain dramatic suddenness and compelling power, is somewhat reminiscent of the way Coleridge's Ancient Mariner holds the attention of his listener, the wedding guest. But the Talkative Man has no burden of guilt on his conscience, and is interested in mere story-telling. As a seasoned narrator he can anticipate the likely reaction of his listeners to such improbable stories, and therefore adopts a suitable narrative strategy to render them plausible

"Such Perfection" is quite different from any other story. In this story a sculptor Soma who makes a too perfect image of Nataraja later ascribes the devastation of this imperfect world to this very image. When Narayan describes some unusual things he straight-forwardly describes the protagonist. Same is the case with this story. In this story he directly tells about soma, the protagonist of the story. The beginning of the story as follows:

> A sense of great relief filled Soma as he realized that his five years of labour were coming to an end. He had turned out scores of images in his life time, but he had never done any work to equal this. He often said to himself that long after the Deluge had swept the earth this Nataraja would still be standing on his pedestal. (53)

No one had seen the image yet. Soma closed himself in the room and bolted all the doors and windows. His labour has come to an end. He sat, wiped the sweat of his face and surveyed his handiwork with great satisfaction. When he saw the image he was agitated by the power of this image. He fell flat before it. He requested the image to dwell permanently in the temple and bless all human beings. Soma was lost in this vision. A voice said Soma not to take the image out of the room because it was too perfect. Soma shivered with fear. He saw a figure bending in a dark corner of the room. It was a man. Soma came forward and seized him by throat and asked the reason of coming there. The man twisted his body in pain and replied that he had come in admiration for him. He told him that he always loved his work. He had waited for five years. Soma asked him how he came in. he told him that he came in with another key when he was eating inside. Soma grinded his teeth and said to strangle him before God and offer him as sacrifice. He said that even with a sacrifice he could not take the image out because it was so perfect that it was not for mortals. Soma replied that he worked privately only for this perfection. The man lay flat before the image and prayed to God to give the strength to bear His presence.

The man spoke to the people and the secret became disclosed. A kind of fear caught the people of the village. On a favourable day, Soma went to the temple priest and asked to consecrate Nataraja, and made a place for him in the temple. The priest said to see the image first. He went to the sculptor's house, stared on the image and said: "This perfection this God is not for mortal eyes. He will blind us. At the first chant of prayer before him, he will dance . . . and we shall be wiped out . . . ." (53). Soma became unhappy to hear this, then the priest suggested him to break a little toe or some other part of the image and it will be safe. The leading citizen of the village came over and said that they could not give the place to his image in their temple. They said that they had to think of the safety of all the people in the village. Soma shouted that he didn't care to bring Nataraja to their temple. He tells that he will make a temple for him where He is at present. It will become the greatest temple on earth. Next day he drew the boundary wall of the room and built a large door, opening on the street. Soma called the tom beater and said to declare in all nearby villages that the Nataraja would be sanctified at the full moon. He promised to give him a silver coin for his work. If a huge crowd turned up, he will present him with a lace shawl.

At the full moon Men, women and children came from the surrounded villages. There was barely an inch of space vacant anywhere. The streets were filled with people. Vendors of sweets, toys and flowers shouted their wares, moving about in the crowd. Pipers and drummers, groups of persons singing a song of praise to God, children shouting in joy, this created a noise. Fragrance of flowers and incense hang over the place. This is how Narayan describes the inauguration of the image in the temple:

> A great flame of the camphor was waved in front of the image, and bronze bells Rang. A silence fell upon the crowd. Every eye was fixed upon the image. In the flame of the circling camphor Nataraja's eyes lit up. His limbs moved, his anklets jingled. The crowd was awe-stricken. The God pressed one foot on earth and raised other in dance. He destroyed the universe under his heel, and smeared the ashes over his body, and the same God rattled the drum in his hand and by its rhythm set life in motion again . . . . Creation, Dossolution and God attained a meaning now; this image brought it out . . . the bells rang louder every second. The crowd stood stunned by this vision vouch-safed to them. (54)

But this vision is overwhelmed by an appalling storm, by thunderbolts, houses collapsing, fires descending, winds screaming, floods and disaster still Soma cannot bear to mutilate the image. But just as he prepares to commit suicide a great wind dashes the statue of Nataraja to the ground where the image lies unhurt except for a little toe severed by a falling splinter: "God himself had done this to save us!" people cried. (53) The image was sanctified with due ceremonies at the temple on the next full moon. Wealth honours were showered on Soma. He lived to be ninety-five but he never touched his mallet and chisel again. The main theme of the story is consecrated of the image at the temple. Narayan has beautifully described the scene of great flood and deluge. Here is the example of cataclysm:

> The moon's disc gradually dimmed. The wind gathered force, clouds blotted out the moon; people looked up and saw only pitch like darkness above. Lighting flashed, thunder roared and fire poured down the sky. It was a thunderbolt striking a haystack and setting it ablaze. Its glare illuminated the whole village. People ran about in panic, searching for shelter. The population of ten villages crammed in that village. Another thunderbolt hit a house. Women and children shrieked and wailed the fires descended with a tremendous hiss as a mighty rain came down. It rained as it had never rained before. The two lakes, over which the village road ran, filled, swelled and joined over the road. Water flowed along the streets. The winds creamed and shook the trees and homes. "This is the end of the world! Wailed the people through the storm (54).

This description of the "end of the world" is quite inadequate – only the end of a poor paragraph which lacks powerful imagination and appropriate linguistic resources. A comparative study between Narayan's descriptions of the present phenomenon with that of Manjeri Isvaran's in his story "The Dance of Shiva" in which an English Man visualizes the great God's dance of destruction in a dream:

> He woke up to see a gigantic figure towering to the skies

> with eyes like fiery globes, its forehead burst upon in the middle like a smoldering planet, and pillars of flame shot forth and a wilderness of alms with lethal weapons . . . . a dread combustion roared, with the thunder of a billion rockets exploding; everything was an endless, immeasurable furnace into which the hounds of hurricane swept and swirled. (177)

This description of Isvaran, no doubt stirs the imagination of his readers, but Narayan's description falls in its effect. The story also presents a traditional Indian belief that no art can hope to reproduce the define form. So not to invite the divine wrath the artists' used to flaw flawless works of art

"A Career" is next story of the collection. Here the narrator is Talkative Man. He narrated his own life story. Before many years he had a shop in Lawley Extension. The name of his shop was "The National provision Store". He went from house to house to secure orders. He had examined every pantry in the Extension and filled up the gap. When the bell rang for the midday interval at the Extension Elementary school, children gathered into his shop to take sweets, ribbons and fancy stationery. He had taken the small house in Kabir Street on a rent of five rupees, which was far more than a mile from his shop. He left at seven in the morning and returned at nine in the evening, after clearing the every day's accounts. Thus a year and a half passed. One day a young man came at his shop. He seemed about twenty, very fair and bright. He wore a spotless dhoti and shirt. The narrator asked him what he could do for him. He respectfully replied that he needed his help. He would do whatever work he might give him in return for a little food, shelter and kindness. There was something in young boy's personality that appealed to him. He told him that he belonged to a family of wealthy landholders in a village Trichinopoly. His mother had died some years ago. His father took a mistress who ill-treated him. Consequently he ran away from home. The narrator took him to his house. When he returned home in the evening, he found that he had become the favourite of his family. His life had deeply moved his wife. He went into the kitchen, and prepared delicious food for the narrator and his family. When he ate he attended to the school children who came into the shop. Within a month he became an expert in shop work. As a result of Ramu's presence his business increased nearly ten fold. He had plenty of rest then. He left the shop completely in his hands. He went home for food at midday. After that he slept till three in the afternoon. And then he returned to the shop, but stayed there only till five O' clock. He had gone to an open space nearby to play badminton with some friends. He came to the shop again at seven in the evening.

Once or twice the narrator and his wife had tried to fix up a monthly pay for Ramu. They felt that they should not exploit Ramu's friendliness. But when the subject was mentioned Ramu became angry. Thus five years had passed. He lived with them through all their joys and sorrows. His business had prospered excessively. He was living in a bigger house in the same street. He had taken shop building on a long lease. He had an immense stock of all kinds of provisions and goods. He had extended his business. He had purchased large quantities of butter in all the nearby villages and sold them to butter and ghee merchants in Madras. This business had given large profits. He had kept him running between the villages and Madras. The shop was entirely in Ramu's hands. At Madras he used to stop with a merchant in George Town. Once work had kept him there a little longer than he had expected. On evening when he was starting out to post a letter for Ramu, a telegraph messenger gave him an envelope. He had torn the cover and read: "Father dying of cholera. Must go at once. Return immediately Ramu". (46)

The next morning at five O' clock he had got down at Malgudi. He met Ramu at the station. He was going to Trichinopoly by the same train. The train stopped for a few minutes. He has consoled him to see his condition. He could not ask about the shop. He himself said that he had handed the keys and all the accounts of cash to his wife. He assured him that he will come back next day by the night train, if his father got better. When the narrator opened the shop he found that the shop was empty. Except few bags of rice and some bars of cheap soap, all the racks and containers were empty. He had picked up the books and examined them. The entries were all in a mess. Filling up again the stock was more necessary. He had made out a list and went to the market. When he went to Sadik Sait, his whole sale supplier, he came to know that his account with him stood at 3,500. He was very shocked to hear this. He went back to the shop, and once again examined the books. Next day when he went to collect all his bills, people said that they had paid their bills completely a fortnight before. His wife told him that in his absence he had been coming home nearly at twelve every night. He gave the reason that accounts kept him late. When the narrator's wife inquired about the business every day, he said not to worry about it, he would manage it. An old man of Lawley Extension inquired about Ramu. He told the narrator about the people from Hyderabad who lived next door to him. He also told him that there was a pretty girl with them. Ramu was taking her out every evening in a taxi. He closed the shop at six in the evening. Those people had gone back to Hyderabad a few days before.

Later on he made inquiries and came to know that Ramu had got stitched four tweed suits, eighteen silk shirts and other clothes worth about a hundred rupees, purchased leather suitcases, four pairs of pump shoes, two pairs of velvet slippers, a wrist watch, two rings, a broach, silk saris, blouse pieces and etc. He learnt from Ramu's relative that his father was healthy and hearty, and there was no mention of cholera. His whereabouts were unknown. Someone told him that he saw Ramu in some music festival in Hyderabad. However he was not sure about it. The narrator sold his shop and everything to pay off his creditors, and left Malgudi. He became bankrupt with his wife and four children. He wandered from place to place, living on the mercy of friends, relatives and unknown people. Further the narrator told another story about Ramu. After four years he came across a coffee-estate owner in Mempi Hills, who gave him a fresh start. He did very well indeed in coffee trade. One day he was panting up the steps of Triupathi Hills. He had a vow to fulfil at the temple. Among the group of beggars he heard the familiar voice but he could not recognize him. This was Ramu. He became changed. His face was dark, scarred and pitted. His eyes were fixed in a stare. He should have passed him without noticing if he had not called out for alms. His voice was still unchanged. When the narrator inquired about his identity, he refused to tell anything about himself. The narrator often said if he met Ramu he would break his bones. But to see him in miserable condition he felt unhappy, and dropped a coin on his upraised palm and passed on. He inquired about Ramu from another beggar sitting by his side. He gave him an anna coin. He said that he had no arms and Ramu had no eyes, so they found each other helpful. He also told him that Ramu was not a professional beggar like him but a Sanyasi. He had come there two years ago. He had once much money in Hyderabad, Delhi, Benares, or somewhere. Small pox had taken away his sight. His wife a bad sort left him. He was troubled with the world. Some pilgrims coming from the north brought him there. The beggar forbade him to tell him that he had spoken all that because he became wild if those days were mentioned.

He went back to Ramu, stood before him and looked him for a while. He felt that god has punished him enough. He wanted to ask him about his beloved and his money but he checked himself. He felt that the greatest kindness he could do him was to leave him alone. He silently put a rupee on spreading palm, and went away. That was the last he saw of him. When he returned after four days on that way, he was not to be seen. Perhaps he went to another place with his armless companion

The story presents the Talkative Man as an average human being in his weakness as well as his virtues. The anecdote in this story reveals that he can be as credulous and gullible as his listeners. The story takes the expected turn when he finds himself grossly cheated by his assistant Ramu, to whom he had given shelter out of sympathy. When he meets him by chance ten years later and finds him to have become a blind beggar, his earlier desire to take revenge on him is overcome by compassion. On the other hand Ramu is a frustrated servant fall in love with a girl from Hyderabad. He squanders his master's money and ruins his credulous master completely. God had given him plenty of punishment for his evil work by taking away his sight. The second twist follows when the shopkeeper in a fit of pity for the man places a rupee on his outstretched palm, thus adding a touch of irony to the shock of discovery.

"Forty-five a month" tells the story of a poor clerk working for years and years on forty rupees a month. He resolves one day to take up his little girl to the cinema, which he can do only if he leaves his office on the stroke of 5, not keep working there till 7 or 8 at night as has become his habit. When Shanta asks her father to take her to the cinema, he was about to go to his office. The writer writes:

> Venkat Rao, Shanta's father, was about to start for his office that morning when a jutka passed along the street distributing cinema handbills. Shanta dashed to the street and picked up a handbill. She held it up and asked, "Father, will you take me to the cinema today?" He felt unhappy at the question. Here was the child growing up without having any of the amenities and the simple pleasures of life. He had hardly taken her to the cinema. He had no time for the child. While children of her age in other houses had all the dolls, dresses and outings that they wanted, this child was growing up all alone and like a barbarian more or less. He felt furious with his office. For forty rupees a month they seemed to have purchased him outright. (76)

He said Shanta firmly that he will take her to the cinema that evening. He also said her to ready at five. If she was not ready he would be very angry with her. Shanta could not remain in her class any longer. She was restless to know the time. At three O' clock he got her teacher's permission to leave the class. Picking up her books, she ran out of the class with a cry of joy. When she reached home her mother asked the reason of coming so early. Shanta inquired about her father. She would not take her coffee and tiffin but insisted on being dress first. She opened the trunk and persisted on wearing the thinnest frock and knickers, while her mother wanted to dress her in a long skirt and thick coat for the evening. After argument with his mother shanta put on her favourite pink frock, braided her hair and flaunted green ribbon on her pigtail. She became ready at four O' clock and waited her father. After some time standing in the street she asked her mother why father has not come till then. Her mother replied he is perhaps stopped in the office. She went back to the gate and stood looking out. Her mother called her inside but she did not go. She stood at the gate and a wild idea came in her mind to go to her father's office to call him, but she did not know where her father's office. She had seen her father take the turn at the end of the street everyday. She went to call up her father without telling her mother. She had taken two turns and did not know where she was. She thought how she would reach home. Then a servant employed in the next house was passing along, she asked him if he would take her to her house. She followed him and was soon back in her house.

When at five he asks his manager for permission to leave till some small discrepancy in the account has been reconciled. At 5:30 he writes out an indignant letter of resignation, seals it and hands it over to the manager who receives it mechanically, puts it aside and tells him that he is being recommended for an increment in his salary, of five rupees per month. Overpowered by this windfall he takes back his letter pretending that it was an application for casual leave, forgets all about the promise to his child, and return to his desk to trace the error in the unreconciled accounts. Shanta who has been waiting for her father from 3 O' clock cannot keep her eyes open till he returns home at 9, and falls asleep in her "pink frock, hair combed and face powdered, dressed and ready to be taken out." (79) But of course once she has fallen asleep, the cinema is out of question. Venkat Rao looked shanta for a while and mourned: "I don't know if it is going to be possible for me to take her out at all. You see they are giving me an increment." (79)

The story is a pathetic one. It shows how a poor man, in his effort to make both the ends meet, is unable to enjoy even the ordinary pleasures of life. It shows Narayan's deep understanding of human nature when he describes Venkat Rao's behaviour after he hears about his increment. Shanta's not taking of her dress is quite touching.

The next story of the collection is "Dasi the Bridegroom". It is a touching tale of an ugly and mentally retarded young man Dasi. He has a physical strength of a bull. He falls a victim to a heartless joke of the people that Bamini Bai, charming film star from Madras was his wife and she had arrived in town. What he gets from her is a slap in the face. On being teased and tortured by children calling him "Bridegroom", he ultimately breaks down, explodes in a fury of anger and ends in a mental hospital. In the beginning of the story Narayan has directly introduced Dasi, the protagonist of the story. He has given enough information about his physical appearance. The beginning of the story is as following:

> His name was Dasi. In all the extension there was none like him – an uncouth fellow with a narrow tapering head, bulging eyes, and fat neck; below the neck he had an immense body, all muscle. God had not endowed him with very fluent speech. He gurgled and lisped like an infant. His age was mystery. It might be anything between twenty and fifty. (148)

After giving description about his physical appearance Narayan has given further detail about his background where he lives. He lived in a house in the last street. Nobody knew how he was related to the master of the house. Some person said he was a young brother and some said he was a foundling brought up by the gentleman. In return for the food and protection, he served the family in his own way. He drew water from the well from dawn till midday, chopped wood and dug the garden. There was particular a group in a house nicknamed Mantapam. In the front porch of the house all the old men were gather. To them Dasi was a source of great joy.

One day Bamini Bai – a film star from Madras came to the Extension. She took her residence in the little cottage which was in the third street. Very soon the extension dwellers knew all about her. She was going to stay in Malgudi for a considerable time training herself under a famous musician of the town. She had her old mother staying with her. The extension inmates had also a complete knowledge of her activities. She left home early in the morning returned at midday, slept till three O' clock, went out on a walk along the Trunk Road at five O, clock and so on. At the Mantapam the people told Dasi one day that his wife had arrived. They showed him the house of Bamini Bai that was in the next street. Dasi went there. It was about one O' clock in the afternoon. The film star was not to be seen. Dasi stood on the road looking at the house for sometime. He returned to the Mantapam. They welcomed him with warm heart. They asked him about his wife. He replied that he did not see her because the door was closed. One of them suggested him to go to Trichy Road and wait. She went out everyday at five O' clock and he would see her. He went to the Trunk Road and waited there. He sat under a tree on a roadside. It was not even two O' clock, and he had to wait till nearly six. A few cars passed raising dust, bullock carts with jingling bells, and villagers were moving about the highway, but Dasi saw nothing and noticed nothing. He sat looking down the road. And after all she came along. He had never seen anything like her in all his life. The scene of beauty and youth dazzled him. He sprang on to his feet and ran home at full speed. He lay down on his mat in the store. He was so much lost in his thought that he would not get up when they called him for dinner. His master came to the store and shook him up and asked him what the matter with him was. He replied, "My marriage . . . she is there. She is all right. (153) His master ordered him to go and eat and to do his work.

Next afternoon Dasi was again at the Trunk Road. This became his daily habit. Day by day his courage increased. At last came a day when he could gaze at her. But her mind was busy with other thoughts and didn't notice him. He waited till she returned that way; he followed her, his face lit up with joy. She opened the gate of her cottage and stepped in. He hesitated a moment and followed her in. He stood under the electric lamp in the hall. The mother came out of the kitchen and asked about Dasi. Dasi looked at her and smiled, at that the old lady was frightened. She cried and asked his daughter about Dasi. Bamini Bai came out of her room and asked Dasi who he was. With great difficulty Dasi replied, "Wife . . . wife you are the wife. . ." (153) At this Bamini Bai asked what he was saying. He repeated again that she was his wife and moved nearer. She became angry and slapped his face. And then she and her mother created such a cry that all the neighbour and passers-by came in. Somebody called a police-sub-inspector. Dasi was brought to the police station. The member of the Mantapam used their influence and had released late in the night. His body had received numerous blows from all kinds of people in the evening; but he hardly felt or remembered any of them. His soul resisted against the memory of the slap he had received in the face. When they called him to eat, he refused to get up. His master went to him and ordered him to go and eat, and forbade him to go out of the house hereafter.

Next day Dasi had the misfortunately to go out of his house just when the children of the Elementary School were streaming out at midday interval. They had heard all about the incident of the previous evening. They then surrounded him and teased him by calling him “Bridegroom”. He turned and looked at them; there were tears in his eyes. He requested them to go and not to trouble him. A boy said that the bridegroom is crying because his wife beat him yesterday. On hearing this Dasi became angry he lifted the boy by his collar and moved him into the crowd. He moved his arms and knocked down the people who tried to get near him. He entered into the school and broke chairs and tables. He hit four teachers who tried to stop him. He ran out of the school and assaulted everyone he met. He crashed into the shop and threw things. He leapt about like a panther from place to place. Gates were quickly shut and bolted. A group of persons tried to run behind Dasi, while a majority preferred to take cover. Soon the police came and Dasi was ultimately overpowered.

He was kept that night in the police lock up and sent to the mental hospital next day. He was not very easy to manage at first. He was kept in a cell for some weeks. He requested and look down the road. The doctor promised him but as a reward for good behaviour. Dasi improved his behaviour. He was then sent to the main gate where he stood for a whole hour looking down the road for the coming of his wife.

The next story of the collection is "Out of Business". It is a story of a man Rama Rao who works in a gramophone company as the Malgudi Agent, loses his job because the owner of the company meets death due to a crash. Rao's financial condition deteriorates and his family is thrown into utter poverty. This stringency forces him to make an attempt for suicide. He lies across the railway lines, but fortunately is saved due to the late running of the train.

The story opens with the detail of Rama Rao's work. He had put into that agency the little money he had herited, as security within five years his business brought him enough money, to help him keep his wife and children in good comfort. He built a small bungalow in the extension and was thinking of buying an old car for his use. One day Gramophone Company collapsed on account of owner's death. The owner was driving down hill when his car flew off sideways and came to three hundred feet below the road. It was thought that he had committed suicide because the previous night his wife had eloped with his cashier. Rama Rao found himself in the streets. At first he could barely understand the full significance of this collapse. There was a little money in the bank and he had some stock on hand. But the stock became empty; he had hardly a few hundred rupees. When he applied for the refund of his security, there was none to receive his application. The money in the bank was spent. Rama Rao's wife became thrifty. She sent away the cook and the servant, withdrew the children from a fashionable nursery school and admitted them to a free primary school. And they let out their bungalow and went to a very small house behind the market.

Rama Rao sent out a dozen applications a day for employment. But he could not find a job. At the extension Rama Rao's wife had friendly neighbours, a women's club and everything to keep her happy. But now she barely had the heart or the need to change in the evenings, she spent all her time cooking in the kitchen. The house in the extension children had played with a dozen other children, it was possible to have numerous friends. But here they had no friends and could play only in the backyard of the house.

Rama Rao spent sleepless nights. All the cash in hand was gone. Their only source of income was the small house rent they were getting for their house in the extension. They were worried to think what would happen to them if their tenant suddenly left. Rama Rao came across a journal in the jubilee Reading Room called the captain. It consisted of four pages, and all of them were devoted to crossword puzzles. It offered every week a first prize of four thousand rupees.

Next day his mind was free from family cares. He was thinking intensely of his answers: whether it would be Tallow or Follow. Whether Bad or Mad or Sad would be most suitable for a clue. Every week he invested a little money and sent his answers, and every week he waited the results with eagerness. On the day the solution was due, he wandered about newsagent's shop to have a look into the latest issue of the captain without paying it. He became sad when he came to know the prize winners. There was not his name among the winners. It took three hours for Rama Rao to recover from this shock. At home he did not speak to anyone. His mind was busy in thought. He quarreled with his wife if she refused to give him his rupee a week for puzzles. One day the good journal announced a special offer of eight thousand rupees. It excited Rama Rao's imagination He studied the puzzle. There was only four doubtful corners in it, and might have to send in at least four entries. A huge expenditure was involved. He demanded five rupees from his wife at which she became speechless. Five rupees were nearly a week's food for the family. He felt disturbed for a while but he turned his attention to think whether Hope or Dope or Rope would be apt.

After sending away the solutions by registered post he built castles in the air. He imagined he would send away tenants, take his wife and children to the bungalow in the extension and leave all the money in his wife's hands to manage. He himself would take a hundred and go away to Madras to seek his fortune there. By the time the money in his wife's hand was spent, he would have found some profitable work in Madras. On the day of the results Rama Rao opened The Captain, and gazed the correct solution. His mistakes were various. There was no chance of getting back even a few anna. He was dejected till the evening. All the losses, disappointments and frustration of his life came on him with a new force. In the evening instead of going home he turned along the railway station. He decided to commit suicide. He thought he was not fit for living. He lay across the lines. The iron was still hot. Rama Rao felt very happy as he knew that in less than ten minutes the train from Trichinopoly would be arriving. But there was no sign of train. He became tired of lying down there. He rose and went back to the station. There was a big crowd on the platform. He inquired someone about the train. He told him: "A goods train has derailed three stations off, and the way is blocked. They have sent up a relief. All the trains will be at least three hours late today . . . ." (84). Rama Rao showed gratitude for God to save his life. He returned home and found his wife waiting anxiously for him. His children had gone to sleep. When he sat down to eat she said:

> Our tenants in the extension bungalow came in the evening to ask if you would sell the house. They are ready to offer good cash for it immediately". She added quietly, "I think we may sell the house" (84).

Now he is satisfied to find his financial problems temporarily solved. Obviously this kind of sudden solution surprises and amuses Narayan's readers. In this story R. K. Narayan has described the ups and downs of Rama Rao's life. This story tells us "Life is struggle: face it. It is successfully narrated by the third person narrator.

"The Axe" is the story about an old gardener Velan. When he was eighteen he left home. The reason was that his father slapped his face one day for coming late with the midday meal, and he did this in the presence of others in the field. Velan left his village at once and came to the town. An old man employed him as a gardener. The master walked about bending on a staff. The lady of the house spent most of her time in chair on the veranda, gazing at the garden with dull eyes. Velan himself was much changed. Now he had to depend more and more upon his assistant to keep the garden in shape. He had lost his parents, his wife and eight children out of fourteen. He had managed to recover his ancestral property which was now being looked after by his sons-in-law and sons. He went to the village for Pongal, new years and Deepavali, and came back with one or the other of his grand children. Velan was perfectly happy and satisfied. He wanted nothing more of life. His master became ill and one mid night he passed away. Velan thought what was to happen to the garden and to him. The sons were no good. They stayed for a year more, quarreled among themselves and went away to live in another house. After a year some other family came in as tenants. These people had no regard for a garden. They walked on flower beds, children climbed the fruit trees and plucked unripe fruits and dug pits on the garden paths. But Velan had no courage to protest. They misbehaved with Velan. They ordered him and lectured him how to grow a garden. His life became intolerable. He much hated the whole business and often thought of leaving his work and returning to his village. But this was an unendurable idea; he could not live away from his plants. Fortunately the tenants left. The house was locked up for a few years. Occasionally one of the sons of the late owner came round and inspected the garden. Gradually this was stopped. They left the keys of the house with Velan. One day a prospective tenant came down to see the house and went away after remarking: "It was in ruins plaster was falling off in flakes, paint on doors and windows remained only in a few small patches and white ants were eating away all the cupboard and shelves . . . . (91). After a year another tenant came and then another and then a third. But no one remained more than a few months. And the house obtained the reputation of being haunted.

The owner left the practice of coming and seeing the house. Velan was very nearly the master of the house because the keys were with him. He was growing old. Although he did his best, grass grew on the paths, weeds and creepers strangled the flowering plants in the front part of the garden. The owner leased out the entire of the fruit garden for three years. Velan was old and he had no energy to put out up a new thatch. So he shifted his residence to the front veranda of the house. Often he opened the house and swept and scrubbed the floor. But gradually he gave up this practice. He was so old that he couldn't do these things. Many years passed without any change. The house was known as the "ghost house". Then change occurred in his life. He lost his job when the ownership changed. The new owner was determined not to afford space for gardening. One day, one of the sons of his old master came and asked Velan to go back home because the house had been sold to a company. Moreover, the company was not interested in maintaining a garden. He was given the fifteen days notice to leave the place. After two days of the notice he heard the sound of an axe, and found four men engaged in hacking the old margosa tree; he expressed his reaction because he had planted the tree and loved it as a child. He requested the tree cutters to stop till his departure. Hurriedly he left the place before the tree was demolished.

In this story the attachment of Velan to the tree is beyond description. He loves the trees so much that he cannot see it demolished. He requests the tree cutters not to cut the tree in his presence and leaves the place immediately. We find a verisimilitude in "The Cherry Orchard" of Chekhov, but Narayan has avoided the challenge of his tragic theme in this story.

"Engine Trouble" is another story of the Talkative Man. In the story the Talkative Man tries to make a story out of the fantastic idea of winning a road engine for a prize, and its consequences. In fact he makes a comic adaptation and elaboration of the familiar proverb about gifting an elephant to poor man. It gives him an opportunity to satirize incidentally municipalities and municipal administration. The Talkative Man begins the story with the information that some years ago a showman had come to his town.

The show was held in Gaiety Land. Gymkhana Grounds was extremely bright with banners and streamers and coloured lamps. From all over the district people came to see the show. Within a week they collected nearly five hundred rupees a day. Gaiety Land provided all kinds of fun and gambling and sideshows. For a couple of annas in each booth everyone could watch anything from parrot to crack motor cyclists looping the loop in the dome of death.

Moreover, there were lotteries and shooting galleries where for an anna everyone always stood a chance of acquiring a variety of articles like pincushions, sewing machines, cameras or even a road engine. On the evening they drew ticket number 1005, and the narrator became the owner of the road engine. He forbade asking him how a road engine came to be included among the prizes. He looked deafened. People assembled and stare at him as if he were some strange animal. He asked the showman if he would help him to transport the engine. But he only mentioned at a notice which showed that all winners should remove the prizes immediately on drawing by their own attempt. They agreed to keep the engine on the Gymkhana Ground till the end of their season, and then he would have to make his own arrangement to take it out. His friends and well-wishers congratulated him on his winning a road engine. He was not a very rich man so he became happy to win this engine and thought that his troubles were coming to an end. But he was ignorant of his future troubles.

When the showman took down his booths and packed up, he received a notice from the municipality to attend his road engine. When he went there next day the ground was deserted, none was there. The showman went leaving the engine where it stood. The Talkative Man left it alone for a few days, not knowing what to do with it. He again received a notice from the municipality to move the engine immediately from the municipality grounds, otherwise they would charge rent for the occupation of the Gymkhana grounds. After deep thought he agreed to pay the rent and paid ten rupees a month for the next three months. Someone suggested him that the secretary of the local cosmopolitan club might be interested in buying this engine. But when approached him he laughed and asked what he could do with a road engine. Next someone advised him to see the municipal chairman. He might purchase it for the municipality. But he also did not buy it. The narrator was becoming a bankrupt maintaining this engine in the Gymkhana grounds. The municipality was pressing him to remove the engine from the grounds. He met with the priest of the local temple and managed to gain his sympathy. The priest offered him the services of his temple elephant. He also engaged fifty coolies who demanded eight annas per head, and the temple elephant cost him seven rupees a day and he had to give it one feed. He took the help of one Joseph, a dismissed bus driver who said although he knew nothing of road rollers he could nevertheless steer one if it somehow kept in motion. The temple elephant was engaged to move the engine, and consequently a compound wall was demolished and the elephant got injured, involving further expenses. The owner of the compound wall slapped the narrator's face. The police came on the scene and took him to the police station. When he was released from the lock up, he found further consequences waiting him. He had to build several yards of compound wall and pay wages of fifty men who ran away, Joseph's fee for steering the engine over the wall; cost of medicine for treating the knee of the temple elephant, which had received some injuries while kicking down the wall; last but not least the demand to move the engine out of its present station. Just as the owner of the engine was deciding to leave everything and flee from Malgudi, an earthquake occurred, shifting the road engine into a disused well belonging to his creditor. The engine fitted the well like a cork. The owner of the well says:

> You have done me a service. It was the dirtiest water on earth in that well and the municipality was sending a notice to close it, week after week. I was dreading the cost of closing, but your engine fits it like a cork. Just leave it there. (73)

The owner of the well offered to withdraw all complaints against him and build that broken wall. The narrator mentioned a few other expenses that the engine had brought on him. He agreed to pay for all that. Thus the earthquake solves the problem of the owner of the engine. Both plot and theme are very simple here: the road engine, a heavy inanimate object, attaches itself to the man and works on his living, human individuality until the balance is restored. The success of the story depends very much upon our granting the initial improbability of a road engine being offered as a prize. Of course the narrator shrewdly anticipates his listeners' objections and tried to explain it thus: Don't ask me how a road engine came to be included among the prizes. It is more I can tell you". (67) But this trick of confession does not work, as it certainly does in "Old Man of the Temple". The Talkative Man of course diverts his listeners by a detailed account of the comic pathetic consequences of winning the elephantine prize. It is certainly amusing to see him being driven from pillar to post, and pushed about by different people, all because of an unromantic thing like the road engine. Yet the narrative is somewhat strained. The story lacks a central focus, a central organizing experience, and rambles along, though engagingly enough. The narrator gives an improbable end to an improbable story. In trying to be inventive he overreaches himself in this yarn. This story reminds one of the famous Tight Corner of E.V. Lucas.

"All Avoidable Talk" deals the character Shastri who works in jewelers shop as an accountant. There is a friend of Shastri near his house who has a great knowledge of stars. His friend gave out free prophecies, and many things he said came true. His friend tells him the previous evening that he sees his worst period is coming to an end, he advises him to avoid all avoidable talk the next day. Shastri follows his friend's advice. At the time of dinner he sits silent, he replies to his wife's questions with a brief yes or no. while starting for his office it was his habit to stand in passage ask for a little betel-nut and leave. But that day he stood on the entrance waiting to see if anyone would serve him. He went to office without chewing betel leaves. There was big crowd in the tram. Somebody stood on his toe but he bore it patiently without uttering a single word. When the tram conductor pushed him aside and spoke rudely for standing in the way, he kept quiet. At the office he reached only two minutes late but his employer behaved as if he had been two hours late. He stood before him mute listening patiently. He began routine of office life. The attendant wiped and rearranged the showcases. Customers started coming in to buy and sell gold trinkets and jewellery. A customer came to him and asked, "Look here, can this diamond be taken out and reset in platinum?" (89)

Shastri replied that he knew nothing about it. The customer complained to the owner of the shop. He called Shastri to come there. Shastri replied "Yes Sir" without lifting up his head. He was busy in looking at the figures in the pages. There were three more lines to be added to complete the page. If he was interrupted, he would have to begin from the top of the gigantic folio all over again. When his master again called him, there was still one more line to go in. When he went to his master he asked the reason for not coming at the time of calling. He replied that he was totaling up so he couldn't come. His master inquired why he was rude to the customer. He answered curtly he wasn't. His master warned him to be humble to all his customers otherwise he might get out of the shop. He only said that he didn't know about platinum. His master said that everyone in the shop must be able to answer about any department; otherwise he didn't want him in his service. The customer went throwing at him triumphant and scornful look. His boss went to his home. Others in the office also went. Only shastri and watchman remained in the office. Shastri switched on the light and worked till nine. He thought he had been insulted by strangers and his master at the presence of everyone. He thought he had served for twenty years for less than fifty rupees a month. He decided not to dine without extracting an apology from boss. Otherwise he would give up his job. A tram for Rayapetta stopped near him but he let it go. He seeked out the bus for Kilpauk and got into it. Instead of going to his house he went to his master's residence. It was nearly ten when he reached at the gates of his master's bungalow Amber Garden. When he inquired about his master from the watchman, the watchman told him that he has just had his dinner and was sitting in the front room. Shastri felt uncomfortable as he remembered the advice of his friend. He stood in the hall. His boss was sitting in a sofa with a sheet of newspaper before him. He thought it was better to tackle him in the office. It was difficult to talk to a boss in his home. When he was thinking whether he should talk or not, his master saw him standing meekly. His master thought that he had come to his house to ask his pardon. He said that he had enough sense to feel sorry for his own conduct. He warned him if he found him rude to others, he would dismiss him at once. He told him that the man who was coming for platinum setting was a madman. He says it doesn't matter whether mad or sane, whoever it may be, it is his business to answer politely whether it be about platinum, silver or rag. Everyone in his office should know about every other department. He said that he would dismiss him for his speech and conduct, but it is his principle to forgive a man who faithfully repents. Shastri shows his gratitude to his master. He goes home with a feeling of triumph over his stars.

"Fruition at Forty" is next story of the collection. It is about a man Rama Rao who wanted to surprise his family by giving gifts instead of receiving at his fortieth birthday. He selected three or four bits of printed silk cloth. When his hand went into his pocket to bring out the purse for paying his bill, he found that the purse was not in its place. It was stolen by some pickpocket. The author begins the story with these words:

> Rama Rao obtained his officer's permission to absent himself on the following day. "Happy returns", exclaimed his officer. "Honestly, I did not think you were forty!" (166)

In the way to the bus stand Rama Rao stopped for a minute to see himself in a huge mirror. He said himself that he doesn't look forty and passed on. When he left home he had not known that it was eve of his birthday. While drafting an office note he realized that the 14th of April was ahead. At parry's corner he struggled into a bus and hung on to a strap. The conductor had tried to push him out; somebody pushed him aside and scowled at him. Rama Rao got down when the bus stopped at central station. He went to Moore market for shopping. None at home knew of his birthday. He wanted to surprise them with gifts like printed silk pieces coloured ribbons, building blocks, and sweets. It would be a novelty, giving gifts instead of receiving. He must also buy vegetable and provisions for a feast. It was going to be a family party. If the children were unwilling to go to school he would not force them. He went round the Moore Market corridor for a survey. He said himself shall buy vegetables last. He went into a cloth shop and wished to be shown printed silk and chose three or four bits. When the bill was made he fumbled his pocket to pay his bill, the purse was not its place. He returned the package, and came out of Moore

Market. He sat down on the park bench and tried to remember when he had last taken out his purse. He said himself that some pickpocket has stolen it in the bus. He thought some pickpocket has deprived him of his fortieth birthday. He felt angry with the perverse fortune which destroyed all one's plans.

People said forty was man's best age. Everyone attend maturity of mind and body. A man's habit were fixed his prejudices and favours were solidified once for all, all his human relationships were well defined and would be free from shocks and surprise. Rama Rao dwelt on these fruitions of forty and was fitted with disbeliefs. What he has achieved, he asks himself. He has four children, the eldest reads in a college. The wife has all the jewellery she had asked for. Although he has become the head of his section in the office yet he lives only in a rented house. The wedding of his daughter and the career of his son will have to be tackled by him within five years. He asks himself if he is good for it. He was filled with terror at being forty, at the duties that were definitely expected of him because he was imagined to have reached maturity. He thought and was surprised if he had really changed. He cast his mind back and remembered the earliest birthday when his father had gifted him a glittering lace cap; then there was his twentieth birthday soon after his B.A. He remembered when he had determined never to marry and never to take up any employment until they offered him three hundred rupees for a start, some job which would put him on a swivel chair behind a glass door. And then his thirtieth birthday, he was held with panic as he realized that he was a father of three. He then believed that things would somehow be clear-cut and settled at forty. He thought what it was going to be like at fifty or sixty. Things would remain just the same. Rama Rao did not feel that the person who was happy with the gift of a lace cap was in any way different from the one who felt thrill when the office imparted an increment. Person who felt the home tutor's spiteful grip felt the same emotion when the officer called him up in a bad temperament. He abruptly felt that he had not been growing and changing. It was deception of his appearance caused by a change of dark hair into grey hair, and by the bearing of longer clothes. This realization brought to his mind a deep relief, and destroyed all idea of years. A birthday had no more importance and fixedness than lines marked in the air with one's fingers. He decided not to mention to anyone at home that it was his birthday.

When he was going back home his mind was still worried about the purse. The purse contained twenty rupees and receipts. He decided not to tell anything to his wife about his purse because if she heard of the loss she would get positively mad. Last time when he couldn't count for five rupees after a shopping expedition she totally broke down. So he would keep her mind free and happy and that would be the birthday gift for her. The purse was a gift to an unknown pickpocket. He went home late. Next morning when he reached to his office as usual his chief asked, "Your birthday is over" He replied "Yes, sir, over earlier than I expected" (169). The officer said, "Very good, I was hoping you would turn up for at least half a day, a lot of things to do. Rama Rao replied going to his desk "I know that, sir" (169). With these words the story ends. The story is simply a commonplace reflection of an office clerk on his fortieth birthday.

CHAPTER – IV
LAWLEY ROAD AND OTHER STORIES

In *Lawley Road,* as in most of his fiction Narayan is concerned more with character than with plot. He notes that he discovers "a story when a personality passes through a crisis of spirit or circumstances," but some stories present flashes of significant moments in characters lived without any dramatic circumstances; others simply show "a pattern of existence brought to view". Many of the pieces in this collection have a reportorial quality – there are sketches and vignettes, character studies and anecdotes. The collection comprised twenty-eight stories in which fourteen are reprinted from previous collections. The title story is delightful. Named after a typical thoroughfare in the fictitious city of Malgudi, the story recounts how Kabir Lane is named as Lawley Road. The narrator is one of Narayan's most engaging recurring characters, whom the people of Malgudi have nicknamed "The Talkative Man" or TM for short, who lends distance and historicity to the story. In another strong story "The Martyr's Corner" the focus is on a humble seller of bondas dosais , and chapatis rather than on the violent action. It is the character of the vendor – his dreary and drab life and his attitude toward existence – that holds the interest of the reader.

"Lawley Road" is the opening and also the title story of the collection. In this story, depicting the unbounded enthusiasm of a municipal council to do his best to commemorate the day of our independence, Narayan narrates his varied activities. The council decided to "nationalize" the names of all streets and parks, in honour of nation's independence. They find no difficulty in renaming the coronation park – whose coronation God alone knew as Hamara Hindustan

> Park. But when it comes to renaming the streets, tempers rise and the councilors all but come to blows. Mahatma Gandhi Road was the most sought after name – with eight councilors after it. Nehru Road and Netaji Subhash Road come close seconds with six each; and a point is reached when, just to avoid a possible skirmish, it is decided to give the same name to different streets. The consequence is anybody's guess – ". . . letters went where they were not wanted, people were not able to say where they lived or direct others there. The town became a wilderness with all its landmarks gone." (9)

The chairman was satisfied with his work but not for a long time. He wanted fresh fields of action. At the corner of Lawley Extension and market there was a statue of Sir Fredrick Lawley. The Extension had been named after him. Now it was changed to Ganghi Nagar, and it seemed impossible to keep Lawley's statue there any longer. The council with one opinion decided to remove it. The Municipality called for tenders. A dozen contractors sent their estimate, the lowest was fifty thousand rupees for removing and brought the statue to the municipal office. The chairman ruminated over it and asked the narrator to take it himself. He said that he would give him the statue free of cost if he didn't charge anything for removing it. The narrator calculated the entire affair as a pure investment which is clear from the following words:

> Suppose it cost me five thousand rupees to dislodge and move the statue (I knew the contractors were overestimating), and I sold it as metal for six thousand . . . . about three tons of metal might fetch anything. Or I could probably sell it to the British Museum or Westminster Abbey. I saw myself throwing up the upcountry job. (10)

He borrowed money from his father-in-law and hired a team of fifty coolies to break the pedestal. They tried to break it for ten days, but the statue didn't move. The narrator feared that he might become bankrupt in two weeks. Then he received permission from the D.M. to gain a few sticks of dynamite, cordoned off the area and lighted the fuse. At last the statue was removed from the pedestal without injuring any limb. The Municipal council thanked the narrator for his service. He published this news in his paper, making it a ten-inch story about the statue. After a week the chairman came to narrator's house and informed him that the government had ordered them to reinstate the statue because people of historical society were protesting against the removal of the statue. The narrator demanded his expenses in removing & bringing the statue.

After six months the Government demanded a report from the Municipality on the question of the statue. The narrator asked the chairman to take his house as a national trust. He was ready to give his house for a reasonable price. At last the chairman purchased his house and changed it into a park. The Municipal Council had decided to change Kabir Lane into Lawley Road.

The story seems at first to be a mere variation of "Engine Trouble". Instead of road engine we have here an equally improbable object, a huge statue of molten lead, which the narrator gets free of cost from the Malgudi Municipality. The two stories have more or less the same pattern of development, and rely on fantasy for much of their effect. And in both there is a good deal of satire. Perhaps "Lawley Road" is the most satirical of the Talkative Man's stories and rouses good humoured laughter at many of the lapses, commissions and omissions of Municipal Councillors and petty local politicians. But the Talkative Man is too good a man to be a pungent and indignant satirist. As a short story "Lawley Road" is much better organized. The statue of Sir Fredrick Lawley is no mere curiosity like the road engine, but becomes the centre of attention for all Malgudians whose strong patriotic passions are roused by it. Therefore "Lawley Road" is much more convincing than "Engine Trouble", through based on an equally improbable situation.

"Trail of the Green Blazer" is the story of a pickpocket Raju who earns his living by picking the pocket of the people. Raju likes the bulging purse. He picks the purse of a man and takes away the cash from it, and before he tries to throw the purse away he finds a toy balloon inside it. His heart is filled with filial affection and pity for the motherless child which is clear from these lines:

> Raju almost sobbed at the thought of the disappointed child – the motherless boy. There was no one to comfort him. Perhaps this ruffian would beat him if he cried too long. The Green Blazer did not look like one who knew the language of children. Raju was filled with pity at the thought of the young child – perhaps of the same age as his second son. Suppose his wife were dead . . . (personally it might make things easier for him, he need not conceal his cash under the roof); he overcame this thought as an unworthy side issue. If his wife would die it would make him very sad indeed and tax all his ingenuity to keep his young ones quiet . . . . That motherless boy must have his balloon at any cost, Raju decided. But how? He peeped over the parapet across the intervening space at the far-off crowd. The balloon could not be handed back. The thing to do would be to put it back into the empty purse and slip it into the other's pocket. (17-18)

At last Raju decided to put the purse back in the blazer's pocket while attempting to put back money in the pocket, he was caught red handed. Even before the Magistrate Raju kept saying, that he was only trying to put back the purse. Everyone laughed at it. It became a stock jock in the police world. Raju's wife came to seem him in jail and said, that he had brought shame on them and wept.

After imprisonment of eighteen months when Raju came out. He could not decide what he should do with himself. He said: "If ever I pick up something again, I shall make sure I don't have to put it back." For now he believed God had gifted the likes of him with only one-way deftness. Those fingers were not meant to put anything back. (19)

The short story is a good example of Narayan's use of irony. Life is full of contradiction and this is what the story conveys to us in a typical Narayan's way. The pickpocket was successful so far he was a professional devoid of human sentiments. As soon as he became sentimental he was caught.

"The Martyr's Corner" is one of those stories of Narayan which end on a serious note. It also deals with the little ironies of life, but the irony in this story takes away all happiness from the life of the hero of this story. The story is about a street vendor who used to sell edible items in the evening. He did his business at the turning between Market Road and the lane leading to the chemist's shop. It was his fixed place. He did his business only for two hours from eight to ten in the evening. He sold all his goods in these two hours and departed. Those who saw him were surprised at his success. Some where even jealous that he earned so much in so little a time. Describing his business the writer remarks:

> At about 8:15 in the evening he arrived with a load of stuff. He looked as if he had four arms, so many things he carried about him. His equipment was the big tray balanced on his head, with its assortment of edibles, a stool stuck in the crook of his arm, a lamp in another hand, a couple of portable legs for mounting his tray. He lit the lamp, a lantern which consumed six pies' worth of kerosene everyday, and kept it near at hand, since he did not like to depend only upon electricity, having to guard a lot of loose cash and a variety of miscellaneous articles. When he set up his tray with the little lamp illuminating his display, even a confirmed dyspeptic could not pass by without throwing a look at it. A heap of bondas, which seemed puffed and big but melted in one's mouth; dosais, white, round and limp, looking like layers of muslin; chappatis so thin that you could lift fifty of them on a little finger; duck's eggs, hard boiled, resembling a heap of ivory balls; and perpetually boiling coffee on a stove. He had a separate aluminum pot in which he kept chutney, which went gratis with almost every item. (20-21)

His customer liked him. They could not expect to get such tasty food at such a low cost. They came mostly from the working class. Another group of customers was that of the people who came out of the cinema hall everyday. So life was going on smoothly and happily for the street vendor. This however did not continue forever the writer remarks:

> Rama's life could probably be considered a most satisfac-

> tory one, without agitation or heartburn of any kind. Why could it not go on forever, endlessly, till the universe itself cooled off and perished, when by any standard he could be proved to have led a life of pure effort? No one was hurt by his activity and money-making, and not many people could be said to have died of taking his stuff; there were no more casualties through his catering than, say, through the indifferent municipal administration. But such security is unattainable in human existence. The gods grow jealous of too much contentment anywhere, and they show their displeasure all of a sudden. (23-24)

One night when he arrived at his usual spot, he found some disturbance there. He came to know that people had gathered there to protest against the murder of a political worker. Soon the situation became violent the police arrived at the scene. To control the violent mob the police used ladhis and tear gas, and finally opened fire. Many people died. This changed the life of Rama, the street vendor. For some days he could not go there to sell his goods and when he went there he found that he could not do his business there. His spot was declared The Martyr's Corner. A statue was be installed there.

With the loss of his place Rama also lost his usual customers. He could not repeat his success at another place. Soon his business was ruined. He had to take up a job in a restaurant. The story ends with these words:

> For twenty rupees a month he waited eight hours a day at the tables. People came and went, the radio music from somewhere frayed his nerves, but he stuck on; he had to. When some customer ordered him about too rudely, he said, "Gently brother. I was once a hotel-owner myself." And with that piece of reminiscence he attained great satisfaction. (26)

"Wife's Holiday" presents Kannan, the gambler, as a deceiving guardian who taking advantage of his wife and child's temporary absence smashes the little money box and takes away all the coins. He returns home losing all the money meets his family and apprehends the consequences. The absence of irony in the ending makes the story pointless. Narayan begins the story with these words:

> Kannan sat at the door of his hut and watched the village go its way. Sami the oil-monger was coming up the street driving his ox before him. He remarked while passing, "This is your idling day, is it? Why don't you come to the Mantapam this afternoon?" Some more people passed, but Kannan hardly noticed anyone. The oil-monger's words had thrown him into a dream. The Mantapam was an ancient pillared structure, with all its masonry cracking and crumbling down on the tank bund. It served as a clubhouse for Kannan and his friends, who gathered there on an afternoon and pursued the game of dice with considerable intensity and fury. Kannan loved not only the game but also the muddy smell of the place, the sky seen through the cracking arches and the far-off hillocks. He hummed a little tune to himself at the thought of Mantapam. (38)

Kannan was very happy at his wife's absence and celebrated her absence remaining at home and thought: If she were here, would she let me rest like this?" He would have to be climbing coconut trees, clearing their tops of beetles and other pests, plucking down coconuts, haggling with miserly tree-owners, and earning his rupee a day. (38) Kannan searched money everywhere but he could not found even an anna. Then he found a cigarette tin in a corner of the box. He shook it. It jingled with coins. It was his small son's saving bank. He recollected how his son had found it from the rubbish dump behind the traveller's bungalow. His son had played with it whole day in the street, filling it with dust and emptying it. Then Kannan had advised him to make a money-box of it.

At last Kannan decided to take the money from it. But before taking money he asked himself: "Am I right in taking my youngster's money?" "Why not?" whispered a voice within seductively. "Son and father are the same Moreover, you are going to double or treble the amount, and then you can put it all back into the box.

That way it is really a benefit you are conferring on the son by opening the little box. (41) He took away all the money in the box by breaking the box. At Mantapam within a short time he lost all his money. When he was coming homeward as he turned into his lane, he saw that his wife was coming. He stood deafened and surprised:

> "May it be a dream!" he muttered to himself. She came nearer and said, "A bus came this way and I returned home." She was going towards the door. He watched her in a sort of dull panic. Her box with all its contents scattered, the god's picture on the floor, the battered red tin – she would see them all at once the moment she stepped in. The situation was hopeless. He opened the door mechanically. "Why do you look like that?" she asked, going in. His son held a couple of coins up to him. "Uncle gave me these. Put them into the box." A groan of misery escaped Kannan. "Why do you do that, father?" the boy asked. Kannan held up his thumb and mumbled, "Nothing I have crushed my thumb." He followed them in, resigning himself to face an oncoming storm. (42)

"A Shadow" is very simple story of a boy Sambu and his mother. Sambu's father was an actor. He had died six months ago. His father's one film was remained unreleased so the producers decided to release it after six months of his death. Narayan opens the story with Sambu's demanding money to see the film:

> Sambu demanded, "You must give me four annas to see the film tomorrow." His mother was horrified. How could this boy! She had been dreading for six months past the arrival of the film. How could people bear to see him on the screen when they knew he was no more? She had had a vague hope that the producers might not release the picture out of consideration for her feelings. And when a procession appeared in the street with tom tom and band, with young boys carrying placards and huge coloured portraits of her husband. She resolved to go out of town for a while; but it was a desperate and unpractical resolve. Now the

> picture had arrived. Her husband was going to speak, move and sing, for at least six hours a day in that theatre three streets off. (79)

Sambu was very happy and requested his mother to see the film. But she refused. Next day, in his class room he asked his friend but he also refused saying that he hated Tamil pictures. Consequently he had to go alone. He sat in four anna class, and was curiously waiting for the beginning of the film. It was the story of Kumari, a young girl who refused to marry at fourteen but desired to study in a university and earn an independent living, and was abandoned by her strict father and forgiven in the end. In the film Sambu's father's actions and activities resembled to his real life. The writer describes this in this way:

> The hall darkened. Sambu sat through the trailers and slide advertisements without enthusiasm. Finally, his father came on the screen. He was wearing just the dhoti and shirt he used to wear at home; he was sitting at his table just as he used to sit at home. And then a little girl came up, and he patted her on the head and spoke to her exactly as he used to speak to Sambu. And then father taught the girl arithmetic. She had a slate on her knee and he dictated to her: "A cartman wants two annas per mile. Rama has three annas on hand. How far will the cartman carry him?" The girl chewed her slate pencil and blinked. Father was showing signs of impatience. "Go on, Kumari," Sambu muttered. "Say something, otherwise you will receive a slap presently. I know him better than you do." Kumari, however, was a better arithmetician than Sambu. She gave the right answer. Father was delighted. How he would jump about in sheer delight whenever Sambu solved a sum correctly! Sambu was reminded of a particular occasion when by sheer fluke he blundered through a puzzle about a cistern with a leak and a tap above it. How father jumped out of his chair when he heard Sambu declare that it would take three hours for the cistern to fill again. (80-81)

When the film ended Sambu stared at the hole in the projection room as if his father had disappeared into it. He missed his father very much. At nine O' clock he reached his home. His mother was waiting for her at the door. Throughout the dinner he told the story of the film to his mother. She listened him without uttering a single word. Sambu asked the reason of his silence. At which she replied she had nothing to say. She asked Sambu if he would like to go and see the picture again the next day. He answered yes, if possible everyday as long as the picture was shown. He asked if she would give him four annas every day. When Sambu desired to see both the shows everyday his mother denied him. He asked her mother to see the picture but she refused again. More than one week Sambu saw both the shows but he felt depressed at end of every show because everyday, it was a parting for him. He also wanted to see the night show but his mother was very much worried about his lessons. He thought that lesson could wait, but not father. He felt jealous those who were seeing the picture at night.

Last day Sambu's mother could not refuse and agreed to see the film. They went to the night show. She felt great relief when slide advertisements and trailer pieces ended. When the picture started, her heart beat fast. A scene came in which her husband was talking to his wife on the screen, playing with his child. She felt that the whole thing was punishment for her. She closed her eyes many times, but the picture attracted her. It had the attraction of a thing which was painful. After this another scene came:

> In which he reclined in a chair reading a newspaper. How he would sit absorbed in a newspaper! In their years of married life, how often had she quarrelled with him for it! Even on the last day he had sat thus after dinner, in his canvas chair, with the newspaper before him; she had lost her temper at the sight of it and said, "You and your newspaper! I could as well as go and sleep off the rest of the day," and left his company. When she saw him later he had fallen back in his chair with the sheets of newspaper over his face . . . . (82)

This was a troubling scene for Sambu's mother. She could not control herself and sobbed. On the other side Sambu was enjoying the film. Then he heard a burst of sobbing in the women's class. Sambu stood on a bench to see. When he saw his mother lying on the floor, he jumped over the barrier and mourned. Then someone told him that she was only fainted. His mother was brought out. The people returned to their seat and the show continued. Sambu's mother opened her eyes, sat up and asked to go. Sambu brought a jutka and sat her into it. As he was climbing into it, from the darkened hall a familiar voice said, "Kumari will you go out or shall I throw you out?" (83) Sambu's heart became heavy and began to weep. He was affected both by his mother's breakdown and by the feeling that was the final parting from his father because they were changing the picture next day.

A few of Narayan's stories can be described as stories of character, in which the study of the protagonist's psychology is the chief point. But in the limited number of stories the author has not taken full advantage of the opportunities offered by the protagonist. "A Willing Slave" is a fine example of it. It is the story of an Ayah, the old servant who takes care of the young Radha. In the beginning of the story the author introduces Ayah in the following words:

> No one in the house knew her name; no one for a moment thought that she had any other than Ayah. None of the children ever knew when she had first come into the family, the eldest being just six months old when she entered service; now he was seventeen and studied in a college. There were five children after him, and the last was four years old. (84)

Besides Ayah in the house there were one cook, two men servants, a maid servant, a gardener and his assistant. She was not interested in their conversation, and informed her mistress whatever she heard. Because of this habit of Ayah, the gardener lost his job for his opinion of his master. She was a time-keeper and those who came late for work could not escape her notice. She also kept an eye on the home tutor who came in the mornings and taught children arithmetic and English. She remained around him all the time because she had doubt that he would torture the children. She considered all teachers as her enemies and all schools as prison houses. If he spoke loudly, she stopped him by saying these words: "Don't you try any of your tricks on these angels. These are no ordinary children. If you do anything, my master will lock you up in jail. Be careful." (85)

Her other works were to see that baker's boy didn't cycle on the lawn, the newspaper man didn't drop the paper into the nursery and the servant didn't drowse in the afternoon. When everyone in the house was out, she closed and bolted the doors, sat down on the front porch and kept watch the house. All these were her secondary duties. Her main job was to take care of four years old Radha. For this Ayah got two meals a day, fifteen rupees a month and three saris a year, this kept her active for over twelve hours in the day. Very often Ayah frightened Radha by telling her about the "Old Fellow", the Ayah's husband, who was interested in carrying away his wife:

> When the story was over, Radha said, "I don't like to sleep. Let us play something." Ayah asked, "Do you want the Old Fellow in?" The mention of the Old Fellow worked wonders, and child after child was kept in terror of him. He was supposed to be locked up in a disused dog kennel in the compound. He was always shouting for the Ayah. He was ever ready to break the door open and carry her away. The Ayah always referred to him in scathing language: I have beaten that scoundrel into pulp. Very bad fellow, disgusting monkey. He won't leave me in peace even for a moment. If you don't sleep, how can I find the time to go and kick him back into his house. (88)

One day, the "Old Fellow" actually arrived to fetch the Ayah, and Radha ran away in fear and bolted the door inside. Ayah felt proud of his slave, and became ready to go with him. When the hour of the Ayah's departure came, she requested Radha to come out of her prison, but she refused to come out, and asked:

> **"Is the Old Fellow carrying you off?"**
> **"Yes, dear bad fellow."**
> **"Who left the door of the dog house open?"**
> **"No one. He broke it open."**

> **"What does he want?"**
> **"He wants to carry me off," said the Ayah.**
> "I won't come out till he is gone. All right. Go, go before he comes here for you." The Ayah acted on this advice after waiting at the kitchen door for nearly half an hour. (131)

"In Mother and Son" Ramu, an unemployed and unmarried youth quarreled with his mother at the mention of his marriage. His mother wanted to get his marriage with his brother's daughter but Ramu wanted to marry a girl like Rezia, whom he had seen in two or three Hindi films. Ramu's mother longed to get Ramu's marriage soon because she was getting old and might die any moment then who would cook Ramu's food and look after him. When Ramu didn't agree to marriage, she spoke angrily: "This is the last time I am speaking about this. Hereafter I will leave you alone. Even if I see you drowning. I will never ask why you are drowning. Do you understand?" (146)

Ramu's mother spoke nonstop when Ramu was taking dinner. He ate his food in silence. After dinner he went out and didn't return at night. His mother with her usual fears and anxieties apprehends that he has gone and drowned himself in the water:

> She did not dare to contemplate what he might have done with himself. Gradually she came to believe that her words during the meal had driven him to suicide. She sat up and wept. She was working herself up to a hysterical pitch. When she closed her eyes to press out the gathering tears, the vision of her son's body floating in Kukanahalli Tank came before her. His striped shirt and mill dhoti were sodden and clung close to his body. His sandals were left on one of the tank steps. His face was bloated beyond all recognition. She screamed aloud and jumped down from the pyol. She ran along the whole length of Old Agrahar Street. It was deserted. Electric lights twinkled here and there. Far away a tonga was rattling on, the tonga driver's song faintly disturbing the silence; the blast of a night constable's whistle came to her ears, and she stopped running. She realized that after all it might be only her imagi-

> nation. He might have gone away to the drama, which didn't usually close before three in the morning. She rapidly uttered the holy name of Shri Rama in order to prevent the picture of Kukanahalli Tank coming before her mind. (148)

Finally she relieved to trace him next morning in deep slumber on a bench near the tank:

> She reached the tank, not daring even once to look at the water. She found him sleeping on one of the benches that lined the bund. For just a second she wondered if it might be his corpse. She shook him vigorously, crying "Ramu!" She heaved a tremendous sigh of relief when he stirred. (148-149)

"Sweets for Angels" is the story about a man Kali who earns his living by pulling bags of rice on a lorry to a grain store of the market. Narayan abruptly begins the story telling about Kali and his two companions. Kali and his friends' home was a brick pyol attached to a locked up deserted house in Royapuram. His one fellow was Kuppan, a rickshaw puller, and other was Pachai who begged at bus stands pretending to be blind. Kuppan's wife had eloped with her lover some years ago. Pachai's family was in the village to whom he sent money-order. Kali himself was an orphan.

Kali loved children very much and looked them going to the school and admired them. The writer remarks:

> At other time he liked to sprawl on the pyol and watch little children go to a school nearby. It filled him with delight. He often remarked to Pachai, "How do these babies read so much! What is the use of wooden dummies like you and me! We cannot really count even our own earnings". He looked admiringly at the children, at their pencils, books and slates, and often thought, "I wish they had taught me how to use these. Even a tiny tot among them holds a pencil and scrawls so confidently!" The children were unaware that there was a man fervently worshipping them as he, sometimes softly walked behind them, and stood at the school gate, staring far into it. The hum emanating from that yellow building was as music to his ears. It filled him

> with a mystic joy – I call it 'mystic' purposely: it was an emotion that could not be satisfactorily explained. (33-34)

On account of pulling many sacks of grains on the previous evening the purse was bulged with coins. He concealed his money from his friends. He told them that he had pain at the shoulder so he must rest at least for half a day. At about eleven he felt hungry. After taking bath he took his midday meal and slept. He rose at about four O' clock in the afternoon. He was feeling drowsy so he went to coffee house to get rid of his drowsiness. After two cups of coffee he felt refreshed and came out. When he was paying bill at the counter, he heard the ring of school bell. When he was coming out he saw a display of sweets and edibles beside the counter. He took one seer of sweets. Its flavour was attracting him so he tasted a bit of sweets and closed his eyes in excessive joy. He desired to pick up another bit but he checked himself saying this that it was for those children.

Presently, he saw school children coming down the road talking themselves. He seized the package towards three children but they were so much lost in their talk they didn't notice him. At this he was dejected. At that time a pair of young fellow came. They were brother and sister. Kali opened and held up the package. To see the sweets, they lured and their mouth watered. Kali asked them to come on and take as much as they wanted. Children replied that their father would be angry if they ate anything outside. Kali said that he would be happy if they tell him that they had eaten good sweets. This argument of Kali encouraged the children to eat the sweets. They ate it with great delight. Presently, more children came and hemmed Kali. The package was snatched from his hand and the children shouting and attempting to get sweets. As a result traffic paused. People stood unaware of what the matter was. The child replied that bearded man gave them sweets.

Hearing this, the man misunderstood him to be a kidnapper because five children had been missing from the school and ten had died of poisoned sweets in their street. Other reason was that Kali's physical appearance was formidable. When the man failed to catch him he screamed for help and collected the people. Narayan describes the struggle between crowd and Kali in the following words:

> The children gazed on Kali from a distance and shuddered, "Oh how frightful he looks with his beard!" The result of all this talk was that a crowd was pounding and tearing at Kali, the more he resisted, the more violent they grew. They chased him from place to place. The whole city seemed to be after him now. They pushed him down and sat on his chest. He tried to ask what he had done. But nobody would let him speak. Blood trickled down and dripped on his tongue. He felt suffocated. "They will kill me if I don't get up". He heaved himself up, shot out his arm, seized a nearby stone and hit the nearest man. That relieved the congestion a little. He shot out his elbows and hit people in their faces; that gave him a little more space: he wriggled and kicked and was on his feet very soon. He fled down the road with a yelling crowd behind him. A crowd from the opposite side hemmed him in. He turned and dashed into the nearest house on his side and bolted the door. (36-37)

The dwellers of the house ran away in panic. People knocked at the door. Kali heard it from a distance. His dozen wounds were bleeding and he felt drowsy. At that time some people climbed the roof tiles and opened the street door. Kali was unaware of it. Then many people caught him and brought him out. The police came and got Kali. After two weeks Kali's two friends stood beside him in a hospital. Kuppan advised him to come back to his old pyol because people would not hurt him any more. They did it thinking him someone else. The doctors had shaved his beard and head. His other fellow Pachai suggested him to leave the children alone.

Narayan ends the story with these words of Kali: "Hereafter I'll turn and run as if a tiger chased me if I see the tiniest tot ahead at me in a street" (37).

In the short story "The White Flower" Narayan took up the theme of marriage problem from his own life. In this story Krishna a youth who was studying in the B.A. class fell in love with a girl whom he saw at the street tap. A common friend played a part of mediator. The girl's father became ready to set her marriage because she would be fourteen years old in the next month. The girl's father was satisfied with Krishna's certificates. On the other hand Krishna's parents were satisfied with girl's certificates.

One day, the girl's father came to Krishna's house. Krishna and his father welcomed him cordially. After sometime talking the girl's father gave his daughter's horoscope and demanded Krishna's horoscope. At this Krishna's father said that he had no faith in horoscopes. But girl's father clung to the ancient custom and would not agree to proceed without matching the horoscopes. He said: Marriage was a leap in the dark and it was necessary to estimate the happiness, longevity, and the health of the couple – factors which could be affected either way by combining two horoscopes, by mixing up planets, so to speak.(92) After few days girl's father came to Krishna's house and informed that:

> There was a serious flaw in Krishna's horoscope. There was Mars in the Seventh House, and it indicated a short life for the wife. He could cite any number of cases where such a flaw had been overlooked and the wife had died immediately after the marriage, and he did not propose to risk his daughter's life now. Krishna felt that stars and superstition had combined to floor him. (92)

Krishna's father consulted a great Astrologer and informed the girl's father that:

> The wife killing planet was a spent force now, though, if the boy had married five years earlier he might have had to marry again. The girl's father promised to consider this and consulted his astrologer again, who maintained that it would not be safe even to keep the two horoscopes in the same envelope. Krishna's father persisted that the wife-killer was impotent and added that to be afraid of an impotent Mars was unheard-of cowardice. The girl's father felt so himself. He was torn between the desire for this alliance and the fear of Mars, and said that he was unable to decide. Krishna's father suggested that they might resort to the usual method of dealing with such dilemmas – leav-

> ing things to God's decision. The girl's father clutched of this suggestion gratefully. (92- 93)

On Friday, early in the morning the party gathered at the temple. The priest had come and lit the oil lamp before the image of Hanuman. He asked them to call the little girl from the next house to choose the flower. A red and a white flower were taken from the garland and put it on the entrance of the sanctuary. The priest said to the girl to pick up one flower:

> The child stood there just for a second, contemplating the flowers, little realizing the immensity of the part that she was asked to play, a medium between God and man, a mouthpiece for God to say whether Krishna could marry his choice or not. The white flower was for Yes and the red flower for No. Everybody held his breath and waited, the child stooped to pick, and Krishna, unable to bear the strain, shut his eyes. When he opened them, he saw the white flower on the polished door-step of the innermost sanctuary. "He knows what is best for us", said the elders, pointing to the idol. Krishna felt stunned for a long time, and when he recovered he wished that he had it in his power to bleach all the flowers in the world. (93-94)

In this story there are autobiographical elements. Krishna is the reflection of R.K. Narayan. In the same way Narayan had fallen in love with Rajam and their horoscopes had not also matched. The story resembles to Narayan's novel *The Bachelor of Arts*. It employs the horoscope motif much in the same way as that novel.

R.K. Narayan has written various stories about children. "The Regal" is one of them. The story is about a twelve years old child Dodu who is very fond of playing cricket. But he could not find place for it. Earlier he had played with few of his friends at the home. After this he didn't play there because one day all the flower buds in the compound of the house had been destroyed. In this story Narayan has narrated skillfully how Dodu made his cricket club by his effort and struggled for finding the place for it.

Dodu met Shriram who was the son of the district judge recently posted to Mysore. He put first-class cricket idea to the minds of the boys. He had a real set and they could start with real team but place was not available for it. They made their cricket club and gave the name to it "The Regal". Being the best cricketer among them Dodu was elected captain and for giving his cricket set Shriram was made vice-captain. After this, Dodu tried to find out a place for his club. These lines show his struggle for finding the place:

> Dodu spent the next fortnight searching for a home for the Regal. Six lawyers, three merchants, a liquor contractor, and a dozen retired officials refused to lend the compounds of their houses for Dodu's use. Dodu now realized how ill-distributed the gifts of life were. However, he never took the refusals lying down. He asked one house-owner what he proposed to do with his compound, and was himself so convinced of the offensive nature of the question that he ran out without waiting for an answer; he asked another why he should not start a cricket team himself and again ran away before receiving a reply; he asked a third why he should not become a member of the Regal; he asked the fourth if he was thinking of digging a tank in the space around his bungalow. (108)

Finally Dodu found an old doctor, who touched by his request and gave the compound at the service of the Regal. Dodu offered him membership of the Regal and exempted him from paying subscription. The doctor was about fifty years old and never touched bat in his life. Dodu decided to coach him personally if he would join the Regal. He expected to be a first class cricketer soon. To see him, other doctors started to learn cricket to open the window of their room. In various ways "Lakshmi Villa" the doctor's bungalow, was an ideal cricket ground. In admiration of Dodu's club "The Regal" writer writes:

> In about six months the Regal had become a star in the cricket firmament. It was now in such excellent form that it met and defeated the Mysore players, which practiced every day at the tail-end of Viceroy Road; the Champion Club, which used the broad footpath in Vani Vilas Road; and the M.Y.R.C. (Mysore Youths' Recreation, club), which

> was a wandering team. It started out in the evening with bat and ball and played wherever space was available. Sometimes they played in the college quadrangle, sometimes in the primary school compound and sometimes in the streets. It was said that they once played at the foot of the Chamundi Hill. The Regal met the M.Y.R.C. and squashed it. The match was played in "Lakshmi Villa", and M.Y.R.C. slunk out after defeat. (109-110)

Dodu and his friends went to inform the victory to the doctor, but he only said is it so, saying this he moved away. They hoped that he would celebrate the victory with fruits, coffee and sweets. Next evening Dodu and his friends saw some new persons moving in and out of the "Lakshmi Villa". After two days when they were playing, a stranger came and asked about them. Dodu replied who he was. At this the stranger ordered him to leave the place immediately. Dodu answered that he had the permission of the master of the house to play there. Hearing this, the stranger pulled the stumps out, snatched the ball and bat and threw them into the street. He warned them if they came again, he seized their things and whipped them. Dodu started to go to the house hailing the doctor. The stranger checked him asking where he was going. In the end Dodu came to know that the stranger was the owner of the house and the doctor was tenant whom he expelled last night, and he didn't know where he was.

"Man-Hunt" is one of those funny stories of Narayan which are remarkable for their surprising ending. We often come across advertisements in newspaper about missing persons. Generally there is a reward for the person who would bring back the missing person. This story revolves around this very fact. Sankar, the central character of this story comes across such an advertisement which announced a cash prize for him who could bring a man called Gopalkrishna. There was a photograph of the missing person.

Sankar was unemployed and was searching for a job in Madras. Throughout the day he went from one place to another in search of job. Now he also started searching for the missing person. The writer describes his search:

> Before evening he had travelled in a score of trams, tramped most of the important thoroughfares in George Town, been into almost every public building from the high court down to free Reading Rooms, watched the doorways of ten coffee hotels, pulled the newspaper cutting out of his pocket a hundred times and gazed intently on a thousand faces. His last spot for the day was the beach where a vast crowd sat around the radio stand enjoying the music. At seven-thirty he suddenly realized that he had been working continuously for nine hours. His head ached from eye-strain, and he was foot-sore. He turned homeward. (96)

One day he came across the person he was looking for. Narayan gives a very humorous description of the conversation between the two. Sankar manages to stick him. Finally he sends a telegram to the father of the person to come immediately. However, when the father comes it is revealed that the person was not Gopalkrshna but his brother who has also come in his search. The confusion was created because of the wrong photograph that was published in the newspaper. The father says:

> "This is the matter, sir," said the old man. "My sight is not what it used to be, and so I suppose the wrong photo went to the paper. When I tell the paper fellows that they have printed the wrong photo they want money again to print the right one. I ask you, is it just? Is it reasonable?" (100)

"The Artist's Turn" is the story about a poor artist Krishna who would not accept anything from the greedy publisher and fault-finder who knows little about art. When Krishna was going down to the market Road Kodanda, the owner of the "Kodanda Hall, printers and publishers" hailed him and informed that his first book was one of stories of Tenali Rama and he wanted to make an illustration for its cover page. Kodanda told Krishna that their common friend Ramaswami had suggested his name. Krishna said that he would do his best for him. He said that he didn't charge from friend the same rate as he charged others. At this Kodanda replied that he would willingly payed him the highest price. He had the greatest regard for artists. He must accept it not as a payment for work, but as a token of his regard. The writer describes the scene that Krishna had to sketch:

> The publisher commissioned him to sketch the great clown Tenali Rama and his cat for the book cover. The king had presented a number of persons in his court with cats and announced a prize to the owner of the best-fed cat. Tenali Rama kept his cat starved for some days and then placed before it a pan of boiling' milk; the cat attempted to drink it and would never go near milk again. Tenali Rama demonstrated it before the king who thought that the cat was so well fed that it hated the sight of milk. Krishna had to draw this scene. He conjured up a vision and saw every detail of the picture as he walked home. He came back with a thud to earth as he remembered that he had no Indian ink at home, nor drawing nib, nor paper. And he hadn't an anna on him. (119)

Krishna borrowed rupee from his friend Ramaswami who worked in the bank. He worked after midnight and completed the picture at about one O' clock. He surveyed it with contentment. He expected that the publisher would pay him at least ten rupees. Then he would return borrowed rupee and found postage to send out some of his cartoons.

Next morning he went to the publisher and put the picture before him. The publisher took the time till the evening to study the picture. In the evening when Krishna asked if he liked the picture, the publisher seemed sad and didn't give any answer. When he was pressed he gave his opinion thus: "You have made Tenali Rama too thin; he must look more healthy. I don't know . . . but the figures are rather unsightly; they aren't like photographs." (120)

Krishna brought the picture home and destroyed it and drew another picture. He drew a handsome Tenali Rama, a handsome king and a puffed up cat. Next day, he went to show the picture to publisher who said: "I am not quite unsatisfied this time, but can't you improve the cat? You see the cat is the most important thing in the story. Can you make it face us? The other things seemed to be all right though I wish you could improve Tenali Rama too." (120)

Krishna worked on the picture that night. He scratched out the cat's head and turn it; he made Tenali Rama more handsome. But once again the publisher objected in this way: "You see you have made Tenali Rama's tuft too pointed and the servant behind the king does not look quite well, can't you remedy these?" (120) Krishna replied in affirmative studying the double chin, fat cheeks and the paunch of the publisher. He said that he would draw thoroughly new picture and brought it the next day.

Krishna drew the idealized king, the courtiers and the servants still more. He drew the most realistic cat, and a rotund clown with double chin, fat cheeks, and paunch. He gave the picture to Kodanda saying that he must not press him to accept money for it. He would let him have it only on that condition. He had done it purely for love of the work, and not at all for money. Kodanda replied that he would not force him to accept money. He liked the picture very much, specially the figure of Tenali Rama. It was perfect. He felt that he had seen the face somewhere. At this Krishna replied that many people were like him so he would use the picture. Kodanda asked Krishna to cover a few specimen pages, ready soon because he had to show them to some important persons on next Friday. On Friday Krishna drafted a letter telling about the reality of the picture:

> "I hope the block arrived in time. I am sure at this very moment you have a neat bundle of specimen copies under your arm, with the cover printed, and you are starting out to meet the important persons. I remember you said that you had seen Tenali Rama's face somewhere. I am writing to say that it was in a mirror. If you want, take up a mirror and compare now. How do you like your new role? Tell me if the important persons find out the resemblance. If you don't like the role you can destroy the block; but then you will be destroying six rupees, and won't be able to show your important persons the specimen cover. I hope this finds you in sound health." (121)

"A Night of Cyclone" is the Talkative Man story. Here the narrator is the talkative man. Narayan generally begins the Talkative Man story thus. The Talkative Man said:

> It was in Vizagapatanam that I finally got a job. A sowcar was building a mansions on the Beach Road and he gave the twenty-five rupees a month and a small house to live in. He labelled me supervisor of construction. At first the designation seemed to be vague. But I soon learnt what I was expected to do. A supervisor's job is no joke in the beginning: the contractor thinks that you are an upstart; the stone-mason has a feeling that you are an intruder; and the carpenter thinks that he is your equal in status. It is plain sailing when you have discovered your duty which consists in bullying the contractor, frightening the stone mason, and pretending to be carrying out a general scheme of retrenchment. (127)

The narrator considered himself the most blessed man in Madras presidency at that time: Blessing number one: work was easy. He generally conducted his supervision from his bed through a window. Blessing number two: his wife and he were living sweet idyll. Her temper was good in those days because she was pregnant. Blessing number three: his house was situated in the finest locality. The sea was not ten yards from his door.

One November morning he got up at about 9:30 and found it almost dark outside. The workmen were ready for going home because they thought that it was going to be a rough day. He severely ordered them to work. After some time he went through Bazar Street where everything was dull and calm. There was darkness everywhere. Everybody was terrified. The school children screamed at the top of their voices. Then one child came to the narrator and asked it was true that the world was going to end that day because their teacher had told them. When he reached at home his wife told him in terrified voice that the world was going to end. That day at about midday he found that the workmen had left the work and had gone home without his permission. His wife sat up for a moment in gloomy silence and went to bed saying that she was not feeling well. He tried to busy her mind by reading to her interesting bit from a newspaper. She listened them quietly.

At about eight in the evening her condition grew worse. She asked the narrator to light oven and cook the food. He struck fifty sticks but the firewood couldn't catch fire. He came out from the kitchen in a bad temper. He was very angry and hungry too. Then his wife reminded him that there was a little milk in the store room. When he was taking milk he thought that his wife might need it any time. He decided to fill up his stomach with any stuff that was available. He searched all the things in the store room. He put his hand into tamarind pot and quickly withdrew it with a cry. There was a big black scorpion in the pot. The sting started to effect. He jumped and cried with pain. He fell down on the floor. Describing the storm scene the narrator writes:

> Now the storm had gathered full strength. Tiles from the roof were flying off. In the best room in my house calendars and pictures were flying like missiles hither and thither. There was no place to stand in. Water was deep everywhere. The house might collapse any moment. I could have borne anything, but not the scorpion sting at that time. I waded through the water in the front room and reached my wife's room. She was wailing and moaning, writhing like a worm on her bed. I had to stand there and look on not knowing what to do. (130)

His wife asked him to bring some help. He was new to that place so he couldn't know any doctor or a person who could help him. In spite of it he went away taking an umbrella and a lantern. Half-way he stood undecided. He didn't know where anybody could be found. Then he suddenly remembered that in the same road a doctor lived. He started towards doctor's house. A lady opened a window and asked who he was. He gave her brief summary of his miserable life. The lady misunderstood him to be a ghost or a thug. He asked in soft tone if the doctor was at home. The lady told him that the doctor was away at Bombay, and wouldn't return for a month. Reaching at home he assured his wife that help would be coming. To hear this she felt relief. The wind was very strong. It crashed the kitchen and broke the window of the room. The light went out. When he was putting the window down he heard the loud, lusty cry of a newborn baby which was piercing the stormy darkness. The writer ends the story with these words of the narrator. The Talkative Man rose and hallooed, "Boy! Come here!" A giggling radiant urchin came in. The Talkative Man patted the urchin on the head and said, "Well, sir, this is the gentleman who arrived on that fine night." (132)

In this story the Talkative Man is more garrulous. He tries to pull the legs of his listeners by a fib about the birth of his son, for which he invents a frightening cyclonic background. The story is told with considerable gusto. But yet, to my mind, it is not as convincing as some of his other stories, not because of its improbability – as seen already the Talkative Man delights in the improbable – but because he is much more garrulous than he ought to be. His garrulity and his weakness for the fantastic tempt him to some overdoing in the narrative, particularly in his account of his adventure in the storm. Therefore, his trick of producing his son at the end of the story, as proof of the truth of the story does not make as successful an impact as a similar trick he uses in "The Tiger's Claw."

"Leela's Friend" is one of the touching stories by R.K. Narayan. Unlike most of his stories which are comic, this story has pathos as its characteristic note. It is the story of a servant Sidda who forms friendship with the small daughter of his master. Mr. Shivasanker was in need of a servant when Sidda came to him for a job. Soon he became indispensable for the whole family. But it was Leela, the little daughter of Mr. Shivasanker who grew quite attached to Sidda. He played with her, told her story at bed time and took her wherever he went:

> "Sidda, come and play!" Leela would cry, and Sidda had to drop any work he might be doing and run to her, as she stood in the front garden with a red ball in her hand. His company made him supremely happy. She flung the ball at him and he flung it back. And then she said, "Now throw the ball into the sky." Sidda clutched the ball, closed his eyes for a second and threw the ball up. (132-133)

With the passage of time Leela and Sidda became quite inseparable:

> Day by day she clung closer to him. She insisted upon having his company all her waking hours. She was at his side when he was working in the garden or chopping wood, and accompanied him when he was sent on errands. (134)

One day Leela's mother noticed that a gold chain Leela had been wearing was missing. It was searched for everywhere but could not be found. The suspicion fell on Sidda. The master and the mistress both agreed that he must have stolen it. The police was finally informed about it. The police inspector arrested Sidda it was then known that Sidda was an old criminal. He had been in jail half a dozen times for stealing jewellery from children. Sidda however, kept denying that he had taken away Leela's chain. The police took him away. He was beaten up but he kept saying that he had not taken the chain.

The story ends with the discovery of the chain in the house itself. The master and the mistress however have not regret for what they had done to Sidda. The story reveals the callousness we show to the poor people. The charges of theft are easily made against them. Narayan evokes pathos through this very effect.

CHAPTER – V
A HORSE AND TWO GOATS

A Horse and Two Goats is the next collection of short stories by R.K. Narayan. It was published in 1970 by Indian Thought Publications, Mysore. It contains five long short stories with illustrations by Narayan's brother R.K. Laxman. Each one of them is a finely executed part of "an admirable sequence of fiction, relaxed but profound" (Gilra, 86). In this collection Narayan left his off-beaten track i.e. the brilliant tradition of his better known stories. For some, some of these stories are inexcusably lengthy and discursive. They feel that Narayan has lost his grip over the successful narrative technique he employed in his earlier stories. Variety is the spice of life and it is not good to find fault with a great writer for not being monotonous in his themes and techniques. Even in these stories we find a rare and different kind of technique which bewitches the readers and keeps them spell-bound. Just like 'generation gap', 'communication gap' gives much scope to an imaginative writer to spin a beautiful story out of it. This communication gap depends on various factors and exists on different levels. This gap may be the result of the difference in the linguistic, physical, intellectual or spiritual levels of the characters involved. Narayan makes use of this novel narrative technique in some of his novels and short stories with an amazing success. This collection of short stories stands as a proof to Narayan's craftsmanship in employing his technique to the maximum possible limits.

The title story deals with Muni, a village peasant, and his meeting with a red man from the United States. The language barrier is responsible for confusion about a statue and a pair of goats, with hilarious results. The second story "Uncle" is a masterpiece; it slowly unfolds the mystery that teases a growing boy about his benevolent but inexplicably sinister "Uncle". "Annamalai" and "A Breath of Lucifer" deal with two simple, hardworking, faithful servants. Annamalai is an eccentric gardener who attaches himself to a reluctant master. Sam in "A Breath of Lucifer", with an autobiographical preface, is a Christian male nurse. In the end, both Annamalai and Sam, governed by their own impulses, unceremoniously leave their masters. "Seventh House", perhaps a continuation of "The White Flower" in Lawley Road, dealing in astrology and superstitions, touchingly explores a husband's tender devotion of his sick wife. Each of the five stories is a character study; all the stories are embellished with picturesque native customs. The dominant tone throughout the collection is casual understatement.

The title story of the collection "A Horse and Two Goats" is based mainly on communication gap resulting from the difference in the language of the Redman and Munni In this story an uneducated Indian goatherd thinks that the Redman wishes to buy his two goats, whereas the tourist bargains for the big clay horse in the shade of which Muni sits. Muni, a once flourishing shepherd and goatherd is now reduced to herding only two scrawny goats and is utterly dependent upon a shrewish but efficient wife for his wretched allowance of food. Narayan gives a touching description of their poverty- stricken life:

> His wife lit the domestic fire at dawn, boiled water in a mud pot, threw into it a handful of millet flour, added salt, and gave him first nourishment for the day. When he started out, she would put in his hand a packed lunch, once again the same millet cooked into a little ball, which he could swallow with a raw onion at midday. She was old but he was older and needed all the attention she could give him in order to be kept alive. (6)

Muni comes from an order of life which seems wholly to precede anything we can conceive of, an age old society, a universe in many ways as old and strange as we see in Nirad C. Chaudhuri's autobiography of an unknown Indian, priests with scimitars sacrifice goats and garlanded buffaloes to the music of drums, cymbols and gongs while worshippers smear themselves with the animals blood and pelt each other with a dough mode of blood and dust. Muni's life as it drags towards its end has nothing in it of comfort or even of consolation. The earlier happier part of his life seems like the memory of a previous birth. His cattle had been laid low by a pestilence, in Munni's view wished on him by an enemy. His wife was barren, suggesting the gods also were against him. The story deals with the events of a day when Munni happens to meet an American by the roadside where he was herding his goats. While sitting at the foot of the horse statue at the edge of the village, he is confronted with a red-faced American who has run out of petrol and wants direction to the next gas station. The man is fascinated by the statue which he supposes belongs to Muni, and wants to buy it. The story consists of two parallel lines of talk and a series of absolute cross-purposes. To the American, Muni is some kind of peasant property owner who can be treated politely and democratically and persuaded to sell his statue which can then be transported to the Unite States to decorate his living room, even if it means shifting the television and the book cases. To Muni the red faced man in khaki clothes must be a policeman or soldier who may chase him or shoot him if he starts to run. The card the foreigner presents to him must surely be an arrest warrant, but on the other hand, the cigarettes are most acceptable. Muni is under the impression that he is being questioned about a crime – there has lately been a murder in the village – but then imagines the conversation to be about his cattle which he explains to the tourist are sometimes carried off by jackals or cheetahs or thieves from the next village. The priest at the temple, he assures the American, can see in the camphor flame the face of thief, and when he is caught he would be duly punished. Muni dimly discerns that the subject of the conversation is connected with the statue of the horse. Why the American is interested in horse, of course, he cannot determine. For Muni the horse is the guardian of the village, meaning death to its adversaries:

"This is our guardian, it means death to our adversaries. At

> the end of Kali Yuga, this world and all other worlds will be destroyed, and the redeemer will come in the shape of a horse called 'Kalki'; this horse will come to life and gallop and trample down all bad men." As he spoke of bad men the figures of his shop-man and his brother-in-law assumed concrete forms in his mind, and he revelled for a moment in the predicament of the fellow under the horse's hoof: served him right for trying to set fire to his home.. . . (19-20)

While the American is wondering how he can have the statue transported, Muni's mind is hovering on visions of avatars, on Kalki, on Vishnu, who had come in the shape of a fish, or a wild boar. Muni remembers how he played the part of the goddess Laxmi in his youth when the story of avatars was staged at the full moon. The two kinds of discourse play off against one another like some totally unrelated strophc and antistrophe:

> "When we played Ramayana, they dressed me as Sita", added Muni. "A teacher came and taught us the songs for the drama and we gave him fifty rupees. He incarnated himself as Rama, and he alone could destroy Ravana, the demon with ten heads who shook all the worlds; do you know the story of Ramayana?" "I have my station wagon as you see. I can push the seat back and take the horse in if you will just lend me a hand with it."
>
> "Do you know Mahabharata? Krishna was the eighth avatar of Vishnu, incarnated to help the Five Brothers regain their kingdom. When Krishna was a baby he danced on the thousand-hooded giant serpent and trampled it to death; and then he suckled the breasts of the demoness and left flat as a disc though when she came to him her bosoms were large, like mounds of earth on the banks of a dug-up canal." He indicated two mounds with his hands. The stranger was completely mystified by the gesture. For the first time he said, "I really wonder what you are saying because your answer is crucial. We have come to the point when we should be ready to talk business."

> "When the tenth avatar comes, do you know where you and I will be?" asked the old man. "Lend me a hand and I can lift off the horse from its pedestal after picking out the joints. We can do anything if we have a basis of understanding." (22-23)

Misunderstanding is compounded by misunderstanding: the two worlds never engage, the two kinds of thought never touch. When the American flourishes a hundred rupee note Muni can only suppose he wishes to buy his two goats, but the American is only thinking that it would be polite to show some interest in the man's pets. Muni hurries home with the cash securely tucked away in the waist of his dhoti, to fulfil a life-long dream of setting up a shack at the spot where he had met the foreigner and on a gunny sack spread on the ground display fried nuts, coloured sweet and green coconut to sell to the thirsty and famished wayfarers on the highway. In the meantime the red-faced American summons help, drags the horse off its pedestal, places it on his station wagon and drives away. Hardly has Muni reached home and explained to his wife what has happened when the goats arrive back at the door:

> He muttered a great curse and seized one of the goats by its ears and shouted, "Where is that man? Don't you know you are his? Why did you come back?" The goat only wriggled in his grip. He asked the same question of the other too. The goat shook itself off. His wife glared at him and declared, "If you have thieved, the police will come tonight and break your bones. Don't involve me. I will go away to my parents." (26)

The story is told in the typical Narayan manner. It is great source of humour. The confusion created on account of the language in which the two figures Muni and the red-faced man speak with each other is pivot round which the action of this, story revolves. Muni's wife serves as a foil to other female characters of R.K. Narayan. She leads Muni by the nose. When Muni grumbles at the food stuff leaves and the drumsticks – served to him every day, his wife commented:

> You have only four teeth in your jaw, but your craving is for

> big things. All right, get the stuff for the sauce, and I will prepare it for you. After all next year you may not be alive for asking anything. (6-7)

Thus here we come across a perfect picture of an aged but nagging wife. The story provides us with a subtle and real entertainment. It is artfully told and carefully plotted.

"Uncle" is a remarkable story of character and atmosphere, dexterously built up and viewed through the eyes of a child. The mystery enveloping the uncle is left unresolved. The oblique and sinister hints of his being an impersonating doctor, murderous impostor and swindle are all swallowed up in the radiant warmth of this partly man's love for the boy whom he is rumoured to have brought as a fifteen-day-old baby in arms from Rangoon. Whether he actually pushed the boy's father off a cliff and finished his mother by giving her poisonous injections is all left mysterious and ambiguous by the author. It is also takes the reader to the world of childhood with its frightening fancies and distorting mirrors, reminiscent of *Swami and friends.* There is a small but significant and even sinister shadow over the background of "Uncle".

The story is more intense in both treatment and feeling than "A Horse and Two Goats" and while it has comic sketches, including a quite delirious passage when the small boy who tells the story is left by his uncle at a photographer's shop in order to bring back, when it should be framed, a school photograph, the general atmosphere is darker and even on occasion menacing. The boy who lives with his uncle and aunt in an old house in Vinayak Street, is doted on at home, not unreasonably happy at school – the famous Albert Mission School – and happy whether reveling in the mud, greens, slush and water of his own garden or playing in the streets outside. He has an orthodox religious upbringing. He loves the pictures of the Gods Krishna, Vishnu, Garuda, Lakshmi, which hang amid a perpetual smell of incense and flowers in the puja room. As is habitual with Narayan, we are made to see the connection between these remote legends in the immediate detail of family life. If his aunt ceased to hear him praying aloud before the gods she would shout over the hissing of the frying pan, "Why have you stopped?" (36) Then he turned to the picture of Saraswathi, the goddess of learning, as she sat on a rock with a peacock, playing the veena with one hand and turning the rosary with the other:

> I would raise my voice and say, "*Saraswati Namastubhyam*", which meant "O Goddess of learning I bow to you", or some such thing. I secretly added a personal request to this prayer. "May you help me get through my school hours without being mauled by my teacher or other boys, may I get through this day unscathed" (36)

The aunt devoted herself, as all the elderly women do in Narayan, most solicitously to the care of the boy. The uncle, who always adored him, spent his days in a curiously languid way leaning against a pillar in the hall with his eyes shut in meditation, only emerging from it to check the boy's equipment, his slate, pencil and satchel, as he left for school.

With characteristically unassertive but confident tact, Narayan deposits here and there, as the story develops, hints suggestive of a certain mysterious note in the uncle's background. An old Muslim tailor who comes to make shirts embarrasses him with his gratitude for having saved him from death while vultures circled above them, and for having carried the boy for thousands of miles, as he puts it, over the mountain passes. Or a school friend will baffle the child with stories of his uncle having impersonated someone. Or the domineering photographer and frame maker will whisper to his cronies in a sinister undertone the story of a brilliant doctor's servant who escaped from Rangoon with jewels and gold and a fifteen-day-old baby-in arms while the doctor took ill and died on the way. Narayan effectively conveys the characteristic exaggeration of the bumptious, uneducated storyteller, the dim understanding of the child, and the sense that he is left with of some particle of truth under the veils of exaggeration. When he flees in terror from the photographer's house and finally finds his way home sobbing and hungry, he is consoled by his aunt. The child lies in bed analysing and examining the charges made against his uncle, finding them flimsy and yet impressed by the dark whispers and furtive glances as he sat in the half-lit back room of the photographer's shop. He goes over to his aunt as she is sleeping on her mat at the edge of the open courtyard:

> "I whispered, "Aunt, are you awake? I want to tell you something." She encouraged me to speak. I gave her an account of Jayraj's narrative. She merely said, "Forget it. Never mention it to your uncle." "Why?" "Don't ask questions. Go back to your bed and sleep." (66)

The rest of the child's life, told in a paragraph or two, is lived on this ambiguous plane of flawed confidence. As he grows up he catches oblique references to his uncle but he ignores them. Sometimes he is prompted to ask the question, "What am I worth? What about my parents?" but he rigorously suppresses it:

> Thus I maintained the delicate fabric of our relationship till the very end of his life. After his death, I examined his records – not a shade of correspondence or account to show any connection with Burma, except the lacquered casket with a dragon on it. He had bequeathed the house and all his possessions and a small annuity in the bank to me and left my aunt in my care. (67)

This story presents the two worlds, the two levels of consciousness. Narayan takes us into the world of childhood and shows what "the distorting mirrors of adolescence" could do to reality. This mysterious story set in Malgudi presents a loving, old man whose day passes between "Munching and meditation", a lady who advises the innocent child bursting with curiosity to know whether his uncle is really "a murderous impostor" to forget what he heard from other, particularly from the photographer, Jayraj and not to ask his uncle a single question. The child followed the advice and never asked anything about his parents. In this story we enter again into Narayan's familiar enchanting world, full of life and activity. Here is a example:

> The crowd passing through the market gateway, shoppers, hawkers, beggars, dogs and stray cattle and coolies with baskets on their heads, all kind of men and women, jostling, shouting, laughing, cursing, and moving as in a mass trance. (52)

"Annamalai" is third story of the collection. It is again a character study. Annamalai is a gardener who does not know much about gardening. He has his own independent and eccentric notions about things. He is simple, naïve, unlettered, but unshakeably loyal and honest. The story has rich comic quality. The rustic life with its funny squabbles and transactions is realistically portrayed. Annamalai's bond of loan with the village tailor causes the amusing crisis in the story after fifteen years of service, when he leaves for his village to renew his bond. Annamalai's younger brother Amavasai, though physically away in the village, provides great amusement through his letters full of his problems, crisis and troubles. It is an interesting character portrayal, truly and realistically drawn with, of course, a touch of comedy.

The story begins with the arrival of the mail The mail is brought in, a postcard crammed with minute calligraphy containing a message in Tamil. This meant it came from Annamalai, or from his professional writer. The letter begins with an elaborate ritual of praise:

> At the Divine Presence of my old master, do I place with hesitancy this slight epistle for consideration. It is placed at the lotus feet of the great soul who gave me food and shelter and money in my lifetime . . . (71

It continues with a report of the excellent health and spirits of the family and of the flourishing state of his land, gardens and orchards. Abruptly it switches to the real purpose of the letter, all the beginning being simply a part of a polite code of epistle writing which has no relation to the facts:

> My purpose in addressing your honoured self just today is to inform you that I am in sore need of money. The crops have failed this year and I am without food or money. My health is poor. I am weak, decrepit, and in bed, and need money for food and medicine. My kith and kin are not able to support me; my brother Amavasai is a godly man but he is very poor and is burdened with a family of nine children and two wives, and so I beg you to treat this letter as if it were a telegram and send me money immediately ..." (72).

But there is no way the recipient can determine whether this letter really has come from Annamalai. It might be from his brother who had hit on an excellent scheme for drawing a pension in the name of his dead brother. Such is the suspicion which flits through the writer's mind. He remembers that Annamalai's last words before he retired were a grand description of his own funeral which he was looking forward to with considerable anticipation.

The body of the story consists of a cool, exact account of the relationship of Annamalai and the author. They are marked by complete assurance on the side of the peasant and a total absence of any measure of puzzlement at his master's ways, and a thoroughgoing bemused incapacity on the part of the author to grasp Annamalai's psychology, assumptions, mode of reasoning, logic or purposes. Whether trying to communicate the name of his village, its address, how one got there, he is always just beyond the grasp of the author's intelligence: "How does one get to your village?" I asked. "Buy a railway ticket, that's how", he answered . . . (75)

He cannot bear to give his name. He bows his head and mumbles. His name is matter of great delicacy which ought not to be bandied about unnecessarily. A name was something to be concealed, not blazoned forth, and he was constantly at his master to remove the name from his gate. The name, he thought, should be hung inside the house among the pictures in the hall. Annamalai was smooth and easy in his movement outside, shuffling and creaking inside. He was frightened and self-conscious in the presence of walls, books and papers. He was absolutely trustworthy, but in so mystifying a way that his master could never still his suspicions in any way. He would declare 'This is a weed' and tear it up and throw it over the wall with a curse:

"Why do you curse that poor thing?"

"It is an evil plant, sir."

"What kind of evil?"

"Oh, of several kinds. Little children who go near it will have stomach ache."

"There are no children for miles around."

"What if? It can send out its poison on the air . . ." (81)

Sometimes he would follow his master's instructions, sometimes his own inclination, but it was impossible to determine which or why. He would push a seed with his forefinger into the earth and stoop over it each morning to observe it minutely. If it sprouted he watered it twice a day but if it showed no response to his living touch he looked outraged. "This should have come up so well, but it is the Evil Eye that scorches our plants . . . I know what to do now (85). He would paint grotesque emblems on a piece of mud pot with his finger, so that visitors would be filled with revulsion and therefore the flowers would flourish. The only treatment Annamalai gave the garden was an incessant supply of water from a hundred foot long hose pipe with which he doused and drowned every leaf, and he also covered the roots with every sort of garbage and litter which he called manuring. If asked to cut the hedge or crop the plants he would not contradict the master but courteously put him off. And then one day, again equally without reason so far as the master could see, he would take a scythe and hack whatever came within his reach. Protests were answered by the statement that the more it was cut the better its growth.

When his gardening was finished he would coil up the hose and lock it away in his basement room. He bathed noisily under the rap and visited the shop at the level crossing. It was owned by the railway gate-keeper who gave out for reasons of policy that it belonged to his brother-in-law. It was here that Annamalai kept in touch with the news, which was read out by the owner to the gathering from a news sheet published by the man who had started the Truth Printing Press. He was kept in touch with his family in the village by postcards from his brother Amavasai, all beginning with a flourish of compliments and reassurances and ending with complaints and requests for something or other. The affair of his family were indescribably complicated and muddled beyond belief. For example, a shepherd had left his sheep as a pledge for a loan of ten rupees. When the lamb was born Annamalai and his brother claimed that it was theirs, thus setting of a feud, and everyday the shepherd came and created a scene, abusing and cursing the family. Another postcard brought news of the tailor and the sewing machine:

> The tailor purchased a sewing machine with the loan from Annamalai. Annamalai's brother accommodated the tailor and the machine on the pyol of his house, the tailor renewed the bond from time to time, paid the interest regularly and also a daily rent for occupying the pyol. This was a sort of gold-edged security, and Annamalai preserved the bond in the safety of a tin box in my cellar. When the time for its renewal came each year, he undertook a trip to the village and came back after a month with a fresh signature on the bond, attested by the village headman. But now the entire basis of their financial relationship was shaken. The original tailor had decamped, and the new tailor did not recognize his indebtedness, although he sat on the pyol of their house and stitched away without speaking to anyone. (99-100)

For Annamalai and the world he came from and doggedly represented, this behaviour was sensible, straightforward, only to be expected. For the author and for us whose representative he is, it speaks of a kind of existence, a mode of feeling, a tradition, which are unimaginably alien. It is, in essence, the contradiction between the member of an age-old agricultural society, the true peasant, and contemporary urban man. It makes us realize the indescribable remoteness from one another of these two orders of life, seen in all their starkness in their Indian conditions. We, like Narayan, are obsessed with flimsy and palpable things, while the solid, four-square realities of the world are really sheep and tailors and bonds, and all that they stand for and imply. The only way to exist in harmony with Annamalai and his world is to take him absolutely as he is, since to improve or enlighten him, concludes Narayan, will only exhaust the reformer and disrupt nature's design.

"A Breath of Lucifer" is the fourth story of the collection. It is outstanding in many ways. It is truly a window "into half invented world." Sam the Lucifer of the story, is conceived and portrayed in the auditory half tones of the imagination. The story is experience based and, as Narayan says in the prologue it was conceived during a period of hospitalization after an eye operation; and in a state of total black-out for nearly a week, with both eyes sealed up with a bandage. It was "my attendant whose company and conversation have inspired me to write the accompanying story" (115). The story is an artistic peep into the libido of a man whose psychological repressions get released in a state of inebriation. His imagination runs riot: "Those lovers again. These two figures! I see them. She is pouting her lips, and he is trying to chew them off, with his arm under her thigh". The fancy grows wilder as it transforms the clean and tidy hospital room into the inferno. He declared, "I was Lucifer once when I came on stage with fire in my nostrils, children screamed in the auditorium and women fainted. Lucifer has been breathing around" (114). He imagines Marie, who had crept into my bed at night", coming in the room for the night and leaving at sunrise. In his drunken generosity he offers: "You are a good officer, have her if you like" (115). Sam is never seen by the author as he goes away to Madras and writes from there for payment of his charges. The story maintains its delicate texture of ambiguity and its balance in the borderland between wakefulness and dreaminess. It is a Freudian story with a dramatic structure.

In this story Narayan appears explicitly as himself, and he has even attached a signed and dated autobiographical prologue to the story. In it he reports on his condition as a patient in a clinic after an operation for the removal of an opalescent patch from the retina of his right eye. The operation itself, he tells us, is painless and accomplished without bloodshed. But Narayan imagines the surgeon's delicate and responsible task, the concentration of his powers in his fingertips, and the hands which have to hover with the lightness of a butterfly over the patient's eye while a tiny opalescent piece is detached from the surface. The operation is followed by total immobility and the sealing up of both eyes. The disappearance of the visual world means an absolute reliance on the spoken word. What before the operation had seemed to Narayan an inhuman state, becomes one of intense and concentrated introspection. All his life he had loved rocks, monuments, ancient sculptures, and he now watches day and night immense pillars, cornices and carvings:

> Sometimes I see a goddess enthroned on a lotus seat in a corner, and not far from her is a formless slab smoothed by time, but faint etchings, possibly edicts of some ancient emperor, are still visible on it. A closer scrutiny reveals that this whole setting is not actually a corner – there is no corner, no direction, east, west, south, or north; it is a spot without our familiar spatial relationships. (104)

He finds, too, that the irritations and stresses of ordinary life strangely disappear. And he is free from elation, fury and despair. Reality is of the moment and now possesses a convincing, solid quality. This is the context in which his relationship with Sam and his rich, reverberating baritone voice develops. Sam is the male nurse although he disliked the term 'male nurse' since he thought women were useless at nursing which was essentially a man's job. It appears from remarks he lets fall that Sam had had some odd army background of a vaguely medical or surgical kind:

> He had mostly been a surgeon's man. He only spoke of incidents where he had to hold up the guts of someone until the surgeon arrived, of necks half severed, arms amputated, and all aspects of human disjointedness and pain handled without hesitancy or failure. He asserted, "My two hands and ten fingers are at the disposal of anyone who needs them in war and peace." (107)

Sam is projected as a solid, conscientious, appealing person. And yet a curious thread of ambiguity, uncertainty, incomprehension, runs all through the relationship. His vagueness about himself cannot be wholly un- selfconscious, the curious contradictions of his career, and the sudden qualifications he is pushed into when questioned, imply some cloudily suspicious patches in his life. This hinted strangeness becomes explicit in a weird experience when Sam suddenly appears in the middle of the night warning that the bathroom is on fire, crying that he was Lucifer once, that he has come to save his patient and, in fact, among delirious or drunken ravings, he gets the sick man out of his bed and takes him in increasing fear out into the open where he leaves him, telling him that the whole area is mined and that he mustn't touch anything or move an inch.

The terror of the experience, the impotence of the blind patient, the peculiar blend of benevolence and menace in Sam, are conveyed with the sparest, lightest, and surest touch.

In this story, the narrator's difficulty in understanding or reading the life of another character (in this case the nurse, Sam) is dramatized by his lack of sight. Everything he knows and can tell us about Sam comes from voices and interpretations of voices. The narrator tells us "perhaps if I could have watched his facial expressions and gestures I might have understood or interpreted his worlds differently, but in my unseeing state I had to accept literally whatever I heard" (106).

The attendant seems a miracle of helpfulness and kindness – disappearing and returning instantly with coffee, solicitous over every aspect of his patient's care. But the narrator can never get him to reveal the factual details of the stories. He asks him which war he served in or in which campaign a particular feat of bravery occurred. But he gets no factual response from him. Sam's stories operate on a level above such authenticating detail. At last, Sam's decision to celebrate both his own birthday and the removal of the patient's bandages ends in a new aspect of Sam. His scrupulous modesty disappears under the influence of alcohol, and the narrator finds himself led out of the hospital into unfamiliar surroundings, while Sam appears to have entered completely into his war fantasies, with the narrator playing the part of a wounded man.

The narrator of this story is literally at the mercy of his character and, at the end, has become a character of Sam's fantasies. And the narrator is inclined towards fantasy, too. In his blindness, he imagines himself walking through strange geological formations, pillars of rock, or mounds of cotton wool. In this story, the pattern of Narayan's narrator being a flawed reader of signs is more obvious than in other stories. The blind narrator tells us not only what he knows but the limitations of that knowledge. As readers, we must trust our guide; but that guide, we are told, can never know the full meaning of what he tells.

It is a comic story. Sam's account of his own likeness to Errol Flynn, or his congratulation of his patient for his tidy use of the

W.C. and even the disappearing drunken voice singing, "Has she got lovely cheeks? Yes, she has lovely cheeks" (115) are very funny. Yet it is also story which suggests a dark side to the situation – the "Breath of Lucifer" of the title. Where, in a story such as "Annamalai", the narrator is in control of his own life if not that of his servant, in "Breath of Lucifer" he is physically vulnerable. And imaginatively too he is vulnerable. His vision of an immense pillar in his way suggests lewd carvings to Sam, so that the characters seem to be entering into each other's nightmares – one a result of blindness, the other from drunkenness. The story reveals that there are other modes, besides the comic, in which misreading can occur where the comedy in a story such as "A Horse and Two Goats" or "Annamalai" may come from the different levels of knowledge which the reader or characters possess, "A Breath of Lucifer" recognizes that a sense of security in that knowledge (however meagre or misplaced) allows us a comic perspective. It is when we feel that matters have gone beyond our control that darker ideas impinge.

"Seventh House" is last story of the collection. This story brings us back to the familiar Indian world of horoscopes planetary influences, astrologers and priests. The opening is almost a leaf from the novel *The English Teacher* and the flower test is reminiscent of *The Painter of Signs* and the short story "The White Flower" theme is used for the second time; it has already appeared in the novel *The English Teacher*, where it represented an immediate and personal pain of the writer himself. In this story marriage takes place between a boy and a girl when the boy's horoscope indicates Mars in the Seventh House, a situation which spells disaster for the bride. The boy, who is greatly in love with the girl, persuades his family to enlist on his side much against their will, and in fact the horoscopes are manipulated and the marriage takes place. In due course the wife falls ill and nothing the doctor does. Krishna, the husband, desperate, asks advice from an old astrologer, but find in his panic that it is impossible without his wife to organize the elaborate ritual the man asks for:

Krishna was panic-stricken. How could he organize all this

> elaborate ritual (which was going to cast a great deal) when every moment and every rupee counted? Who would nurse his wife in his absence? Who would cook the ritual feast for the Brahmins? He simply would not be able to manage it unless his wife helped him. (139)

If he will not do this, the old man tells him, the only thing which will abate the malignity of Mars and neutralize the rigour of the planet is being unfaithful to his wife. He says:

> The trouble is, your love is killing your wife. If you were an indifferent husband, she could survive. The malignity of Mars might make her suffer now and then, mentally more than physically, but would not kill her. I have seen horoscopes that were the exact replica of yours and the wife lived to a ripe age. You know why? The husband was disloyal or cruel, and that in some way neutralized the rigour of the planet in the Seventh House. I see your wife's time is getting to be really bad. Before anything happens, save her. If you can bring yourself to be unfaithful to her, try that. Every man with a concubine has a wife who lives long . . . ." (139-140).

A cruel or disloyal husband lessens the jealousy of the god. Krishna ignorant of the technique of infidelity, looks for a pimp and finds that every house he approaches seems to be occupied by respectable people like lawyers, tradesmen and teachers:

> He returned the hired cycle to the shop and seven was walking up Golden Street. In his Imagination he had expected glittering females to beckon him from their balconies. The old houses had pyols, pillars, and railings, and were painted in garish colours, as the houses of prostitutes were reputed to be in former times, but the signboards on the houses indicated that the occupants were lawyers, tradesmen and teachers. (141)

He gives up and the story ends with himself returning home resigned to his fate. The irony of the situation lies in husband's futile, attempt, astrological advice, to save his wife's life by being unfaithful to her as this alone could neutralize the rigour of a malignant Mars in the Seventh House of his horoscope. The end is again left in suspense as Krishna returns home without getting an opportunity to be unfaithful to his wife, after being given a long "homily on conjugal life" by an old and well meaning jutka driver.

CHAPTER – VI
UNDER THE BANYAN TREE AND OTHER STORIES

It has been a practice with R.K. Narayan that his later collections of short stories have contained several of the stories published earlier as well. This is so with *Under the Banyan Tree and Other Stories* also. It is a superb collection of twenty-eight tales, published specifically for American readers. Several in it are drawn from earlier volumes. When the collection appeared on the American scene, glowing reviews were published in leading weeklies and periodicals. This collection further confirms Malgudi's place as a great imaginary landscape. The title story, fittingly taken from Narayan's, first collection, reaffirms story telling as a central human activity. The villagers of Somal "lived in a kind of perpetual enchantment. The enchanter was Nambi the story-teller" yet having regaled his audience for several years with his tales, Nambi spends the rest of his life in "great consummate silence."

"Nitya" is the opening story of the collection. In "Nitya" Narayan presents a fine story based on the principle of "Generation gap" Nitya a college student of twenty years, shows his unwillingness to offer his fine and well-cared hair to fulfil a vow made by his parents, when he was two years old and stricken with whooping cough and convulsions. Nitya half convinced, goes to the place of worship. When all the arrangement are made for the tonsure ceremony, he argues with his parents and priest and suddenly leaves the place and thus avoids a rape of his locks. In this story Narayan depicts the sentiments and pious feelings of the old parents and recklessness and atheistic temperament of a young man like Nitya. While the old generation respects and wishes to cling to certain custom and values, the young generation pooh poohs them.

At six on Friday morning Nitya had noticed a preparation at home for the trip. Mother packed lunch for three and filled a basket with coconut, flowers and incense for worship at the temple. They were making preparation for fulfilling a vow which they had made before twenty years. The vow was that Nitya's head would be shaved clean and his hair offered with due rites if his life was saved. Father searched the record of their promise to God. Mother too, remembered knotted coin in a piece of cloth as a reminder. That day, when father fixed a date for the trip, Nitya showed his disapproval and argued with his parents. Here are some dialogues between Nitya and his parents:

"It doesn't concern me, your twenty-year-old promise. You had no business to pawn my scalp without consulting me".
"You were only two years old then"
"You should have done it when you could handle my head as you pleased."
"But you were very sick and for a long time, too."
"I have survived, which proves that the disease died rather than me and so where is God's hand in this, if there is a God and if he is interested in my hair?"
"His parents were aghast at his manner of talk. Mother pleaded "Whatever you do, don't talk like that."
Father admonished, "Nitya you must not be blasphemous. If God had not responded to our prayers and saved your life . . ." He could not complete the sentence.
"Was it a bargain?" Nitya asked leeringly.
"Yes, replied his father. "It was indeed a bargain and there can be no going back on it."
"Very well, but the head offered for a shave was not yours. You have been carrying on negotiations with a commodity that he did not belong to you."
"It was for your welfare"
"Did I ask for it?" Nitya asked puckishly. His mother burst into tears. Father remarked with a scowl, "You talk like a sinner, cold and godless. Wonder where you inherited it from" (2).

After argument with his parents Nitya went with them. When they reached at the temple Nitya's father called up the headman. He asked the priest to open the temple. Nitya's father told him that they had to leave by the evening bus. The headman proposed him to spend the night at the rest house. When Nitya heard this he protested and said that they might both stay if they chose but he wanted to catch the bus. His parents calmed him. After some time the priest came. Narayan describes the temple priest in the following words:

> The temple priest, his forehead ablaze with sacred ash and vermilion, shoulder wrapped in a red shawl, a lanky person with a booming voice, arrived, dangling a large key in an iron hoop. After greeting the Trustee in the correct manner, he plunged straight into business, cataloguing his demands (5).

The priest sent a boy to call up the barber, Raghavan. But his house was locked, none was there. Nitya agreed to give four inches of his front lock. After sometime someone declared that Raghavan was coming up. He was panting and perspiring. He went straight to the well at the backyard because he never opened his razor box without a bath specially when he had to perform a tonsure ceremony. The barber explained that he had gone to a nearby farm for a baby's first shave. Someone asked not to play pipe at a wedding. He told him that he had jealous neighbours who created false rumours to spoil his business. Nitya's father took him by hand and sat him on the stone platform in the corridor. Nitya got himself free and said: "I agreed to give four inches of hair, it was up to you to have taken it now. You have lost the opportunity, which must be seized by the forelock" (P, 8). The priest forbade Nitya to hurt his parent's feelings, and requested to move on that platform where the barber was ready. At this Nitya retorted to the priest in these words:

> But my head is not ready. You promised to accept four inches of my hair. Now you are demanding my head itself. Have you no logic or reason? No contentment or consistency? How can God tolerate fickle minded people like

> you? Now I have changed my mind – I won't give even an inch . . ." (8-9)

Nitya's mother and father cried at the same time not to talk to the priest like that in his own temple. Nitya was angry and hungry too. His parents did not let him touch even one plantain out of the dozens offered by the villagers under the tree. When his parents were gazing at him helplessly, he abruptly left the place saying that he would wait for both of them at the bus stop.

"House Opposite" is the story of a hermit who could not concentrate on meditation on account of a prostitute who lived across the street from his opposite house. His mind was always occupied with thoughts of that lady. The story begins with the mediation of third person narrator:

> The hermit invariably shuddered when he looked out of his window. The house across the street was occupied by a shameless woman. Late in the evening, men kept coming and knocking on her door – afternoons, too, if there was a festival or holiday. Sometimes they lounged on the pyol of her house, smoking, chewing tobacco, and spitting into the gutter – committing all the sins of the world, according to the hermit who was striving to pursue a life of austerity, forswearing family, possessions, and all the comforts of life. (10)

The hermit found his single room abode with a couple of coconut tree sand a well at the backyard. The narrow street was filled with children. Sometime he summoned the children, sat them around and taught them simple moral lessons and holy verse. He had hung a few pictures of gods on the walls and made the children prostrate themselves in front of them. He woke up at four, bathed at the well and sat down on a piece of deerskin to meditate. After this he lit the charcoal stove and baked few chapattis for breakfast and lunch and cooked vegetables and greens.

One afternoon when he opened the window to sweep, he noticed that a woman was standing at her doorstep. He became angry to see her and whispered, "Get in you devil, don't stand there!" (11). She suddenly went in shutting the door. The hermit felt victorious although his command and her submission were coincidental. He shut the window and sat on the deerskin and repeating "Om, Om Rama, Jayarama. But he could not concentrate on Rama. His mind was elsewhere. After sometime he put the picture of God shiva in front of himself and recited "Om Namasivaya." His coarse voice echoed in the entire hall. His wandering thoughts were stopped for a moment. But after some time his mind was diverted to that woman. He thought she opened her door at least six times on an evening. If she slept with them all together at the same time. Then he thrashed his fist on his temples which pained but improved his concentration. At that time he heard the sound of the door of the opposite house. The hermit compared the strumpet with a serpent. In her grip everyone was destroyed. A few days ago he had seen a B. Sc. Student from Albert Mission Hostel at her door. He prayed to God Shiva to expel that woman. He thought:

> He would confront her someday and tell her to get out. He would tell her, "Oh, sinful wretch, who is spreading disease and filth like an open sewer: think of the contamination you have spread around – from middle aged tailor to B. Sc. Student. You are out to destroy mankind. Repent your sins, shave your head, cover your ample loins with sackcloth, sit at the temple gate and beg or drown yourself in Sarayu after praying for a cleaner life at least in the next birth . . ." (12-13)

Thus the thoughts of the woman were never leaving his mind. Then he remembered an ancient tale that he had heard from his guru. A strumpet was sent to heaven when she died but her slanderer a self-righteous reformer was sent to hell. The reason was that the prostitute sinned merely with her body whereas her detractor was corrupt mentally. He was troubled with the prostitute and her activities and could not meditate on anything else.

The hermit decided to leave his habitation. He packed his wicker box and went out of the house. In the twilight shadowy figures were moving. Milkman was driving his cows ahead; labourers were going with their crowbars and spades. Women with baskets were going to the market. When he stopped to take a last look at the shelter that he was leaving, he heard a mournful cry "Swamiji" from the opposite house. That lady was calling him. She had a tray filled with fruits and flowers. She put it at his feet and said in a low respective tone: "Please accept my offering. This is a day of remembrance of my mother. On this day I pray and seek a saint's blessing. Forgive me . . . ." (13). The hermit touched her tray with the tip of his fingers as a sign of acceptance and went down the street without uttering a single word.

"A Hero" is the story of a young school boy Swami who accidentally caught a thief who had hidden himself under the bench. Swami was unaware of it; he was thinking that some devil was there. Swami's father read a news of the gallantry of a village boy and asked his opinion. Swami's notions were different from his father. He argued with him. Consequently he had to accept the challenge of his father of sleeping in his office room all alone. R.K. Narayan begins the story with the news that Swami's father was reading from newspaper:

> News is to hand of the bravery of a village lad who, while returning home by the jungle path, came face to face with a tiger . . . . The paragraph described the fight the boy had with the tiger and his flight up a tree, where he stayed for half a day till some people came that way and killed the tiger (56).

Listening the news Swami did not believe that a boy could fight with a tiger. He thought that he must have been a very strong and grown up person, not at all a boy. At this his father said: "A man may have the strength of an elephant and yet be a coward: whereas another may have the strength of a straw, but if he has courage he can do anything. Courage is everything, strength and age are not important" (56). Swami argued with his father and asked: "How can it be father? Suppose I have all the courage what can I do if a tiger should attack me?" (56). At which his father asked him to prove that he had courage. He challenged him to sleep alone at that night in his office room. Swami always slept beside his granny in the passage so he expected that his father was merely joking. He tried to change the topic but his father remained firm at his decision. Swami tried to coax him but all his efforts proved to be a wild goose chase. Ultimately, Swami had to sleep alone in his father's office room. He recollected all the stories of devils and ghosts that he had heard in his life. Every moment he hoped that the devil would come up to carry him away. Swami shifted his bed under the bench. It seemed to be a much safer place. He covered himself with his blanket, fell asleep and started to see bad dreams:

> A Tiger was chasing him. His feet stuck to the ground. He desperately tried to escape but his feet would not move; the tiger was at his back, and he could hear its claws scratch the ground . . . . Scratch, scratch, and then a light thud. . . . Swami tried to open his eyes, but eyelids would not open and the nightmare continued. It threatened to continue forever. Swami groaned in despair (59).

He moved to the edge of the bench and gazed into the darkness. Something was moving down. He went near him, crept under the bench embraced it with all his power, and bit it. There was a thief who made a mournful cry. At that time Swami's father, the cook and a servant came in carrying light. Three of them caught the thief who was lying amidst the furniture with a bleeding ankle.

Next day, everyone congratulated Swami. His teacher praised him. The headmaster said that he was a true scout. The police were grateful to him for it because he had bitten one of the most infamous house-breakers of the district. The inspector advised him to join the police when he were grown up. Swami replied that he would, although he wanted to become an engine driver, a railway guard or a bus conductor. When Swami's father returned home from the club that night, he inquired about Swami. His mother replied that he was asleep. Father said: "Sleeping beside his granny again!" "No wonder he wanted to be asleep before I could return home – clever boy!" (60). At this Swami's mother said angrily to let him sleep where he liked and not to risk his life again. Father whispered: All right, molly-coddle and spoil him as much as you like. Only don't blame me afterwards . . . ." (60) Swami was hearing entire conversation of his parents under the blanket. He felt extremely relieved to hear that his father was leaving him.

In this story there is a reflection of R.K. Narayan's first novel *Swami and Friends.* The character Swami is taken from that novel who is the main character of this story.

R.K. Narayan has written many child stories. "Dodu" is one of them. The main character of this story is eight years old child, Dodu. Narayan begins the story with the introduction of Dodu who was demanding money for several things like Chinese crackers for the coming Deepavali, to buying a pen holder etc. Dodu had a great passion to collect things. He had a dealwood box in which he contained the waste- paper basket, attractive book jackets, brown wrapping paper, large envelopes, charming catalogues, and pieces of brown thread. Day by day the contents of his box enhanced. His uncle had given him a rupee of which Dodu had purchased twelve brown stamps, four green stamps, and four postcards. He wrote a placard in Kannada, STAMPS FOR SALE and hung it at the door. People purchased cheerfully these stamps and postcards. He sold his goods with a profit of three pies over each item. Only one card was left in the end, and a neighbour came to buy it. When Dodu mentioned his price he became angry. He behaved like a madman and threatened that he would report to the police. Dodu's dream of investing his rupee and getting profit was shattered.

Dodu was recollecting the lessons which he had learned from his past experience: Lesson number one was that he could not expect help or sympathy from his elders. Lesson number two: If his uncle should give him a rupee again, it was not to be wasted on foolish schemes. Buying and selling stamps was a silly idea (63). Dodu saw a pests-man who was climbing up a coconut tree. He went to him and asked how much he earned. He decided to do a business of palmyra leaf. He recollected the incident of his brother's friend who took a palmyra leaf with writings on it to some library and was paid for it. Dodu's brother told him that the director of Archaeology, Dr. Iyengar purchased from some one a historical document written on palmyra leaf, for the Mysore oriental library.

Next afternoon he made up his mind to meet Dr. Iyengar. Reaching at the library he suspected if he would be allowed to enter it. He informed the peon that he wanted to meet Dr. Iyengar. But he was very sleepy and didn't care. Dodu stepped in the building. R.K. Narayan gives the interior description of the library in the following words: "Everything looked powerful and big. All around there were stone images and stone slabs with a lot of writing on them. Many pundits wrapped in gaudy shawls were poring over long- palm- scrips" (64). Dodu asked Dr. Iyengar if he was a doctor. He was surprised to see Dodu because he was accustomed to receiving only dignified scholars and students as visitors. Dodu told Dr. Iyengar that he had heard that he paid a hundred rupees for palm leaves. He drew a few leaves from his packet and handed them to the doctor. Dr. Iyengar investigated with happiness. On one he found the figures of a jug, a nose, a horse, and the name "Dodu" in Kannada. On another leaf he found these interesting statements in Kannada: "The cow is a very tame animal. This is Rama's book". All these were copied from an old Kannada primer. The third bore on it in English: Cot. Ox. Fig. Pear. Baby. A A A A B C F G." (65)

When doctor finished reading he laughed loudly. Dodu thought that he should not laugh at him. If he did not want palm leaves he might return them. He would try to sell them to some other doctor. The doctor asked who had told him that he gave money for the leaves. Dodu answered that he had heard from his brother. Doctor said that he had brought the thing that he needed. He purchased the palm leaves and gave him all the copper coins he had in his pocket. Dodu was very happy to get four annas. The doctor asked him his father's name but he did not answer because he wanted to keep secret his business. When the doctor asked his name Dodu replied 'Ramaswami'. He told a lie, his real name was "Dodu" at home and "Lakshmana" at school. The doctor asked him if he could go home safely and instructed him to walk on the footpath because there were many motor cars on the road. Dodu bought fried groundnuts for three pies from a woman who was selling edibles and felt happy and satisfied.

In this story Narayan mildly satirizes the attitude of the elderly people towards children. By bringing in the pests-man climbing up a coconut tree and plucking out the sap found at its top, Narayan creates a typical South Indian atmosphere. Things collected by Dodu remind us of Tom Sawyer, an immortal character of Mark Twain, and his choicest treasure.

"Another Community" is the story without name of the hero. It reveals Narayan's hatred of communal riots. In the beginning of the story Narayan informs the readers that he was not going to mention caste or community. So he refers to "One Community" and "Another Community". That is why he has not given the hero of this story any name. He has left it to the readers to find out what community or section he belonged. The story is narrated by the first person narrator. Narayan gives the detail about the work and family of the hero of the story in the following words:

> He worked in an office which was concerned with insurance business. He sat at a table, checked papers and figures between noon and five p.m. everyday, and at the end of a month his pay envelope came to his hands containing one hundred rupees. He was middle- aged now, but his passage from youth to middle age was, more or less, at the same seat in his office. He lived in a little house in a lane: it had two rooms and a hall and sufficed for his wife and four children, although he felt embarrassed when a guest came. The shops were nearby, the children's school was quite close, and his wife had friends all around. (67)

He led a happy and peaceful life till the October of 1947. After this people started to speak and act like barbarians. Someone killed a group of men a thousand miles away, consequently they avenged and repeated the evil there on those around. They spoke angrily: "We must smash them who are here" – he heard people say. "They have not spared even women and children!" he heard them cry. "All right, we will teach those fellows a lesson. We will do the same here – the only language they will understand" (67- 68)

He imagined his post office fellow sitting on his right, his postman, the fellow at the betel-leaves shop, and his friend at the bank – all these belonged to another community. He had not worried about their community, they were just friends. He heard his men talking threatingly. He imagined his post office friend being hit in the street. He imagined that some ruffians of his own community were chasing his little girl. He heard that a cyclist was stabbed last evening. Police pacified the entire matter. A woman was attacked that day. They invaded girl's school and four girls were kidnapped. They said that police were useless. They must deal with these matters themselves. He became afraid of such talks. He lost the taste of his food and felt it bitter.

At night he could barely sleep. He spent the night, awaiting the howl of riotous mobs. He felt relieved when day came. Everyone talked about the coming Wednesday, the 29th of the month. No one knew why they selected that date. In his office also people talked of nothing but the 29th. On the 29th most of the shops were closed as a precaution. Children remained at home fearing of the fight. His wife forbade him to going to the office by giving him the reference of the neighbours. But he did not take up his advice and went to office. When he reached at the office he saw most of his fellows were absent. The few that came were busy in discussing the frightful possibilities of the day. He showed no interest in their talks and busied himself in work. It was past seven- thirty when he left the office. He decided to go home by a short cut way from alley. He had walked a few steps when a cyclist came and obstructed his way. He exclaimed if he could not ride carefully. The cyclist screamed that he was blind that could not see a cycle coming. He asked where his light was. At this the cyclist became furious and hit his face. A crowd gathered. Somebody shouted that he ventured to attack them in their own place. They must teach him a lesson. Somebody hit narrator's friend with a staff, someone else with his fist. His eyes dimmed, he whispered near someone:

> But I will never, never tell my uncle what has happened. I won't be responsible for starting the trouble. This city must be saved. I won't utter the word that will start the trouble, that will press the button, so to say. That'll finish up everybody, you and me together. What is it all worth? There is

> no such thing as your community or mine. We are all of this country. I and my wife and children: you and your wife and children. Let us not cut each other's throats. It doesn't matter who cuts whose: it's all the same to me. But we must not, we must not. We must not. I'll tell my uncle that I fell down the office staircase and hurt myself. He'll never know. He must not press the button.

The incident of that narrow street spread within a couple of hours all over the city. The narrator's friend would have spoken a lie and saved the city; but unluckily that saving lie was not uttered. His body was found by the police next afternoon in a trench in that alley. The police recognized him through the kerosene coupon in his breast pocket. The end of the story is very pathetic and shocked and surprised the readers.

"Like the Sun" is the next story of the collection. It is about a man Sekhar who is a teacher. He fixed a day that he would not tell a lie but absolute truth. For the whole of the day he faced many situations in which he told absolute truth. What result he found of his practicing is the theme of this story. The story begins with these words with the mediation of the third person narrator:

> Truth Sekhar reflected, is like the sun. I suppose no human being can ever look it straight in the face without blinking or being dazed. He realized that, morning till night, the essence of human relationships consisted in tempering truth so that it might not shock. This day he set apart as a unique day – at least one day in the year we must give and take absolute Truth whatever may happen. Otherwise life is not worth living. The day ahead seemed to him full of possibilities. He told no one of his experiment. It was a quiet resolve, a secret pact between him and eternity. (73)

The first situation he faced was that when his wife served him his breakfast. He showed his unwillingness whereas his wife thought that it was her masterpiece. She asked Sekhar the reason of his not eating. He simply said that it was not good.

His next test came in the common room when one of his colleagues came up and said if he heard of the death of so and so.

He was a very fine man. But Sekhar replied that he always struck him as a mean and selfish brute. At the last period when he was teaching geography for third form, he received a note from the headmaster to see him before he went home. When he went to the headmaster's room he came to know that the headmaster wanted him to hear his music. Everyone knew Sekhar's taste in music. He was one of music critics in the town. Both of them started for the headmaster's house. He warmly welcomed Sekhar as if he were a son-in-low of the house. The headmaster said him not to worry about the test papers. He will give him a week's time. Sekhar asked to make it ten days. At which the headmaster agreed. He lighted incense sticks to create the right atmosphere. A drummer and a violinist were waiting for him. The headmaster sat down between them like a professional singer. He began an alpana, and stopped to ask if it wasn't good Kalyani. Sekhar pretended as if he had not heard the question. The headmaster went on to sing a full song composed by Thyagaraja and followed it with two more. Sekhar was comparing him to frogs because he was croaking like a dozen frogs. He was shouting like a buffalo. After this, he made sounds like loose window shutters in a storm. R.K Narayan describes the effect of headmaster's singing upon Sekhar's mind and his reaction in the following words:

> The incense sticks burnt low. Sekhar's head throbbed with the medley of sounds that had assailed his ear-drums for a couple of hours now. He felt half stupefied. The headmaster had gone nearly hoarse, when he paused to ask, "Shall I go on?" Sekhar replied, "Please don't, sir, I think this will do . . . ." The headmaster looked stunned. His face was beaded with perspiration. Sekhar felt the greatest pity for him. But he felt he could not help it. No judge delivering a sentence felt more pained and helpless. Sekhar noticed that the headmaster's wife peeped in from the kitchen, with eager curiosity. The drummer and the violinist put away their burdens with an air of relief. The headmaster removed his spectacles, mopped his brow, and asked, "Now, come out with your opinion." (75)

Sekhar asked if he could give it the next day. But the headmaster insisted on giving it immediately. He asked if it was good. Sekhar replied in the negative. After this he asked if there was any use of continuing his lessons. Sekhar replied with trembling voice that it was of no use. After giving this answer he felt gloomy because he could not speak more pacifying truth. All the way home he felt worried. He thought after this his official life was not going to be smooth sailing. He was thinking about the increment and confirmation because it depended upon the headmaster's good will. He remembered Harischandra who had lost his throne, wife and child because he had spoken absolute truth.

When he reached his home, his wife served him with a gloomy face. Obviously, she was furious with him for his statement of the morning. Sekhar thought if he practiced the speaking of an absolute truth for a week, he will not be left with a single friend. Next day the headmaster summoned him and expressed his gratitude:

> "Your suggestion was useful. I have paid off the music master. No one would tell me the truth about my music all these days. Why such antics at my age! Thank you. By the way, what about those test papers?" (76).

Sekhar reminded him that he had given him ten days for correcting them. He told him that he wanted them the next day. Sitting up all night with a hundred test papers was a small price to pay for the luxury of practicing truth.

The story is remarkable in sense. R.K. Narayan used a very simple and straightforward narrative technique to narrate this story.

R.K Narayan has written many stories about dogs. "The Blind Dog" and "Attila" appeared in an earlier collection. "Chippy" is one of the delightful stories. This story is about a dog Chippy who felt jealous of another dog which his master has brought home. R.K. Narayan begins the story with the description of Chippy's early life:

> I cannot give a very clear account of Chippy's early life. All that I am in a position to say is that he was born in London, spent several months of his puppy hood in Scotland, and then came out to India with a Major and spent a

very happy summer in a hill station. He might well have stayed with the Major, seen something of Peshawar, Quetta and Delhi, and returned home with that good man, but for a silly little Pekingese. It was the pet of the Major's wife, and Chippy did not like him. (77)

One day when no one was at home Chippy enforced small and weak dog to realize that what he thought of him for remaining on a lady's lap and eating special biscuits; but the dog lost his life in the process. Chippy did not want to kill him. Major's wife became hysterical. The Major thought that Chippy had rabies. He decided to shoot him. Then an Indian friend of the Major decided to take away Chippy. Chippy lived with this gentleman for sometime and went to Mysore with the Major's friend's brother Swami.

Swami and Chippy lived in the same room in the house. They always went out together. Every evening Chippy used to go to Tennis Club with his master, waited until his master settled down a good set, after this he peacefully went out to examine all the lanes nearby. There were a number of brown dogs and black dogs. They challenged all newcomers. There was nothing to attract Chippy. The game was dull for him because one was not let him to pursuit the ball. After tennis Swami ordinarily attended some lecture or debate in the college. Chippy accompanied him. Reaching at home he had his plateful of bone and rice and then went to meet his old friends and sweethearts. He returned at night and slept under his master's cot. Chippy led a very happy and satisfied life until Swami brought into the house another dog. Chippy had no objection of another dog but he hated short dogs. It was his habit to bite all the short dogs whenever he met on the way. To see the puppy between his master's legs he grumbled. Swami kicked Chippy. He went out and lay down behind the garage. Chippy was thinking of hurting the puppy. After some time his master called him. Chippy rose and went towards him. He slowed his pace when he saw the puppy standing beside the master, held by a chain. Swami said Chippy to be friend of the newcomer. In reply Chippy moved his tail and gave an approval. The new puppy attacked every favourite place of Chippy in the house. In this respect R.K. Narayan says:

> In a short time the newcomer made himself quite at home. He invaded every favourite place of Chippy's in the house – he came and lounged under the sofa in the hall, sat at master's feet in the room, stuck to Chippy's side during the mealtime, and even slept under master's cot at night. (79)

Chippy bore his company. He passed his time in the shady spot behind the garage. Chippy possessed the honour of going out with the master because another dog was very weak and small and so he could not walk beside master's bicycle. When no one was at home Chippy bit him a little but before his master he showed that he and puppy were the best friends. Chippy went away from the house to search his luck. R.K. Narayan describes this dexterously in the following words:

> He wandered about the town, without any aim or plan till nightfall, and then went in search of a place where he could get some food and shelter. He went to the market to try his luck there. But urchins flung stones at him, and there were the old dog of the place who followed him, growling and grumbling, wherever he went. It was all most annoying. He left the market by the western gate, and strayed into the crazy lane behind it. This lane is a nest of tea and liquor shops, from which gramophones shriek into the night; the clatter of mincing meat on iron frying pans keeps the air lively. The lane has no electric lights, but gets a chequered illumination from the blinding petrol lamps hung inside the shops with their patrons seated on iron chairs and packing cases. This part of the town is unknown to the average citizen of Mysore, but Chippy was drawn there by the smell of chops sizzling on stoves. (80)

He paused at the first shop. Someone threw him a delicious bit of curry puff. Chippy found contented that he was determined to lead his life there, far away from the short dog. In about a week he had become the favourite of the place. But he was bored with this life style. He lost his hunger. He did not touch the piece thrown at him. He had a great hunger for his master's company. One morning he returned to his master's house, when he was solving his questions in mathematics. Swami watched under the table and scolded:

> "Rascal, where have you been all these days?" Chippy curved his hind half, tucked in his tail, and stood before him with bowed head. He had lost his white colour; his coat had acquired the colour of road dust, with patches of tea stains here and there. Someone had removed his thick leather collar: he was looking perfectly nude without it. (81)

Swami brought him out and unwound the garden tape on him. He informed him rubbing a piece of soap on his back that his little fellow had gone. It seemed he had been stolen and sold to him. His original master came and took him away the previous day. He said Chippy not to worry. He would get him another companion immediately. The setting of the story is in Mysore. It is artfully narrated by third person narrator.

"Uncle's Letters" traces the life of a man from birth to his eightieth birthday by means of the letters written by an uncle to his nephew but the description here to clings obstinately to conventionalities. The story is a collection of uncle's letters. The uncle writes letters to his nephew and affords us an insight into the life of an average South Indian. The story is written in epistolary form. R.K. Narayan tried only once this form in this story. It has a combination of first & second person narration. It seems that there are autobiographical elements in this story. Narayan opens the story with warm welcome of the newly nephew by his uncle. The story is divided into passages. Here is the beginning of the story:

> Little man, just a line to welcome you into this world, my newest nephew. How do you like it? It is full of glare, isn't it? You will have to get used to it. I was told that you let out a lusty cry the moment you set foot on this earth, which is a good sign, showing that you are responding properly to our conditions. You are yet a very ignorant man. I think your only interest now is the spoonful of sugar syrup that they drop on your tongue from time to time. That is all very well, young man, but there are other things to come. (82)

In the second passage uncle said that his father became very excited at his birth. He noticed a slight movement into his cradle when he peeped through the curtain. He gave a toothless smile at his father, twisted his body and blinked. He summoned his mother to show the activities of their son. But as soon as she came he changed his mood and kicked his legs and cried. His father said that he did it because he did not show proper praise of his activities by taking him up in his arms.

In the next passage uncle said that cutting one's first tooth is an awkward work. He told him that for two years he could do and think as he pleased. When he would start to walk he had to tumble down. When he tumbled down about the next house his uncle felt very sorry to see his red and inflated nose. He also said that he barely recognized him in that condition. His mother was sure that the reverberating impact of his head on the landing must have cracked his cranium.

It was borne out by his behaviour later on. Uncle asked his nephew the reason of treating the tiny girl from the next street house in the manner he had done. It was perhaps because she would not give the half orange that he had in her hand and he had finished off his. When she did not give him orange he tried to bite off a slice of her arm as a protest against her selfishness. He warned his nephew not to do such things anymore.

In another letter uncle told him that school was a thing that he could not escape. He would have to bear it for the next twelve years. He could not expect for sympathy from anyone in this matter. He was undoubtedly perplexed by the attitude of his elders at home every morning. He knew that his father tried to put up a show of great violence in order to make him feel that the school was the lesser of the two evils. He felt sympathy for him but he could do nothing. He would have to outlive the threat of his teachers, the fearful tortures of arithmetic, the ups and downs of class room relationships, its shifting alliances, treaties and battles. He had to face also the struggle of the examination hall and the results. He advised him not to fear these things. He would come through it all right.

Further the narrator informed him that he would take his degree in convocation bearing gown on his shoulders. He would be photographed also in a studio holding degree in his hand. He hoped that his nephew would not feel excessively depressed by the speech. He advised him not to worry about these things. It was customary for the celebrity who presided over the occasion to tell him what to do with himself, what to look for in life, and how to live a life of wisdom and glory. In fact he didn't pay much attention to what he said since he was full of thoughts of his own. His mother was not what she used to be, and he was her only guide. Her life was full of sad memories, but she could forget much in a new home which he could create with the help of a wife. He was earning quite well. He could properly support her.

Uncle said that fifty blue envelopes and letter paper to match, of the highest quality, with his address written on each one of them, and properly stamped, were left with his wife as he trusted. Nephew expected that she would write to him everyday of her welfare during her stay at her father's house. Uncle must warn him that not more than a tenth of the stock would be used by the party. He would for ever be on the border of dispatching a wire to demand if there was no letter. It was too much to expect a young wife to perform the feat that only professional journalists could.

It always happened that way. The right bridegroom turned up in truth like the prince charming all of a sudden when the time came. When he were in the state of feeling sad or depressed the other day about the problems of daughters uncle knew all along that life would have a nice surprise in store for him. He told him that he could guess by seeing his daughter's face what she thought of the boy. Uncle knew the boy's father & uncles. They were his class-fellow. They were his good fellow but he didn't want to prove it. Uncle probably had a suspicion that they were greedy and might ask for dowry. He suggested him to prepare for it, and not to worry about it.

In the next letter uncle told his nephew about the problems that he would have to face in their daughter's marriage. He suggested him the solution of these problems. He says:

> There is no use sighing over a pass-book at this stage. It was bound to look emasculated after you had paid the bills of the wedding ceremonies and the feasts. With all this,

> you bitterly reflect that your bridegroom's people created scenes during the grand occasion, criticizing the arrangements, presents, and so forth. Such things are a part of our social life and you are not to brood over it any more. What is a bridegroom's party for unless it is to hector the bride's. It is a warfare with its own set laws. In any case here is a tip for consolation. You can have your vengeance in your turn when you three sons (or it is going to be four?) are ready for marriage. Your eldest should be entering the market very soon, if I am not mistaken. He is a promising fellow and a lot of people have their eyes on him. (85)

In this letter uncle advises not to be irritated at these things. His eldest son spent very much and saved very little. His son persisted to take his wife to her parents' house every other month. His first son-in-law was indifferent about the marriage of his daughters and the education of his sons. He found him very busy to worry about such things. His second son-in-law had certainly taken his place as a never do-well. Nobody would come to him for guidance in any matter. Of course his general complains seemed to be that people were minding their business. He suggested leaving them alone. He would find that it made for so much more peace of mind. Uncle felt happy to know that they were going to celebrate the occasion of his seeing the one thousandth moons. It was a very important and victorious function of his eightieth birthday. He said his nephew to give his best wishes to his wife who could feel a pride on that day. On that day he would feel like a bridegroom as drums and pipes go off, and holy smoke arose and the scent flowers and incense hung in the air, and the cheerful voices of all his children and their children rang in his ears. It was the finest function one could imagine on this earth.

At the end of the letter he told two things that he felt. One is that his nephew was then of an age to observe and understand matters of life himself. Secondly, he knew that he found it difficult to hold a pen and shape out the letters, having had his own thousandth moon celebrated before eighteen years.

"The shelter" is the story without the name of the characters. There are only two characters in the story – husband

& wife. In this story R.K. Narayan describes the crises of their married life. Narayan narrates the plight of a woman who left her husband's house after quarrel with him and began to work for harijans. But after a long separation they came across in the rain. Both of them were standing under the banyan tree, the only shelter. The story is skillfully narrated by the omniscient narrator. R.K. Narayan begins the story in his typical style in the following words:

> The rain came down suddenly. The only shelter he could run to was the banyan tree on the roadside, with its huge trunk and the spreading boughs above. He watched, with detachment, the rain patter down with occasional sprays coming in his direction. He watched idly a mongrel trotting off, his coat completely wet, and a couple of buffaloes on the roadside eating cast-off banana leaves. He suddenly became aware of another person standing under the tree, beyond the curve of the tree trunk. A faint scent of flower wafted towards him, and he could not contain his curiosity; he edged along the tree trunk, and suddenly found himself face to face with her. His first reaction was to let out a loud "Oh!" and he looked miserable and confused. The lady saw him and suppressed a scream. When he had re-covered his composure, he said, "Don't worry, I will go away." It seemed a silly thing to say to one's wife after a long separation. He moved back to previous spot away from her. But presently he came back to ask, "What brought you here?" (145)

He expected that she would not reply but she answered 'rain'. At which he replied it brought him also there. He said many things but she didn't reply. He also said if he had had the slightest suspicion of its coming, he would have stayed at home or brought his umbrella. She ignored his statement outright. She might be deaf for all it mattered. He wanted to ask if her ears were affected but couldn't ask fearing that she might feel irritated.

They had had various crises in their married life. It might be anything – whether to listen to Radio Ceylon or All India radio, whether one should see an English movie or a Tamil one, whether jasmine smell might be termed too strong or otherwise, a rose could be termed gaudy or not, etc. They signed the bond of friendship before the God in Puja room that they would never quarrel hereafter. But it was broken within twenty four hours. One day they argued over the food as usual, wife threatened to leave the home and husband asked her to go away. He left the door open for a long time believing that she would return, but she didn't. He said that he didn't hope to see her again. She answered if he thought that she would drown herself. He replied yes he feared. She asked if he searched her in nearby wells, or ponds. At this husband replied that she didn't drown herself then how could she blame him for not searching her. He asked her many questions but she didn't reply any of them. She merely looked at the rain. The wind's direction abruptly changed and a gust flung a spray of water on her face. He tried to wipe her face with his handkerchief at which she screamed not to worry about her.

The branch of a tree shook a few drops on her hair. He said that she was wetting herself unnecessarily. He desired to stand where she was. She only replied he needed not worry about her. When she was looking at the rain he offered to bring an umbrella or a taxi. But she didn't answer and turned away. He said something else. There are few dialogues between them. She asked:

"Am I your toy?

"Why do you say toy? I said no such thing."

"You think you can pick me up when you like and throw me out when you feel that way. Only toys are treated thus."

"I never told you to go away, "he said.

"I am not listening to any to that again, "she said.

"I am probably dying to say how sorry I am," he began.

"May be, but go and say that to someone else.

"I have no one else to say such things to," he said.

"That is your trouble, is it?" she asked, "That doesn't interest me."

"Have you no heart?" he pleaded. "When I say I am sorry, believe me. I am changed now."

"So am I," she said. "I am not my old self now. I expect

nothing in others and I am never disappointed," she said. (147-148)

After the argument he asked her what she was doing. He told her that he heard someone that she was doing harijan work. She remained speechless. He proposed her to live together but she refused and ran away in the rain. He screamed after her to wait. He said that he would not talk but she disappeared.

R.K. Narayan ended the story with the departure of the wife. The story is feministic in nature. The decision of the wife to lead her own life without making compromises for her bread and butter shows the desire of the woman of today to live a life of her own. In Narayan's novel *The Dark Room* the wife had to return to her husband's house, but in this story she goes her own way.

"The Mute Companions" is a delightful animal story. It is remarkable how Narayan understands animals and makes them almost living characters. In this story the monkey is more impressive a character than Sami, the beggar. Sami is deaf and dumb so he could not ask for alms like other beggars. He only gurgled at the throat. He expressed all his ideas emotions and appeal by gurgling. His residence was a corner of the Town Hall veranda.

One day he saw a small monkey searching his bag in which there were a few grains of rice that he had collected on the day. Sami caught the monkey and tied a piece of cord around his waist and trained him a number of tricks. The monkey solved his food problem. He performed his tricks in front of the houses and earned for his master many things like rice, edibles and coins. The show began with the monkey saluting everyone.

The next turn was Dancer at the temple. Other monkey trainers started the tricks by asking the monkey how the woman at the temple danced. But Sami only tickled the monkey and gave a hint by the motion of eyelids. At this the monkey stood up with one hand on his waist and the other on his head and swayed his hips in the manner of that temple dancer. People were surprised how he had taught it all these tricks in spite of his dumbness.

One day Sami played the role of an angry mother-in- law of the monkey and sent her out to bring water from a deep well. After this the monkey played the role of Hanuman setting fire to capital of the Demon king: the monkey took his tail in his hand and jumped here and there. For the mother-in-law turn Sami earned stout khaki coat and from another place he got the dark turban for the same turn. In the evening he returned to the Town Hall with the monkey and lay down in the corner of the veranda embracing the monkey.

In this way they spent three years. In this duration they worked, ate and slept together. Sami avoided the people who were arrogant, aloof and inaccessible, and kept formidable dogs and servants. R.K. Narayan describes the fear of Sami for these people in these words:

> One day Sami was going up the drive of one of those big bungalows. It was only a sporting mood that made him enter the gate. Usually he avoided those big places where people were haughty, aloof, and inaccessible, and kept formidable dogs and servants. He went up hesitatingly, expecting to be shouted off any moment, when he saw a servant coming towards him. Sami held the monkey tight and turned to flee, but the servant caught up with him and poured out a volley of words. Sami indicated that he could not hear, whereupon the servant explained by signs that the master of the house wanted the monkey to be brought to his presence. (151)

He was invited to come up and hold the show on the veranda. The show was held for the exclusive pleasure of a tiny boy who lay on a couch amidst pillows, covered with a green shawl. To see the monkey perform, his face lit up with life, and he took his medicine and food without an objection.

The monkey was performing for the third time the turn of the sweet-seller balancing a tray on his head. Then he saw a dish on the table containing a slice of bread and some fruit. He suddenly attacked and seized the slice of bread. Sami became furious and tried to catch the monkey. He tumbled over the child. Someone seized him and dragged him down the veranda steps. He saw that the monkey was enjoying his slice of bread. Everyone was angry with Sami because they had just saved the tiny patient from a serious accident stubbornly designed by Sami. He tried to explain that he had no intention to hit the child but he was trying to catch the monkey. The master of the house misbehaved with Sami:

> Send him out," cried the master of the house. "He is frightening the child. This excitement won't do for him. It is going to take weeks for him to get over this shock. Take him away, the devil!" The servant pushed Sami out. He resisted. He wanted to ask, Where is my monkey? Where is my monkey? But he could only make wild gestures and gurgle, and they thought he was menacing them. They pushed him down the drive, towards the gate. He turned, and just saw his monkey sitting on the tiled roof. He fell at their feet and cringed and begged them to let him call back his monkey. (151-152)

Sami requested the monkey to come down. He looked at his master eating the slice of bread. He didn't know whether he was going to be forgiven or punished if he returned. He was not thinking of returning and enjoyed his freedom. Day after day Sami waited at his corner in the Town Hall expecting that his monkey would come back to him. Sami stood at the gate of the bungalow staring at ventilator, the roofs and the trees. Sami requested the master of the house to tell him what had happened to the monkey. But they replied that they didn't know. Sami believed that after it had gone through the ventilator it seized and kept in the house. After waiting for weeks he lost hope. He decided to live on alms which was his old business. Here the story ends.

"At the Portal" is the story about a couple of squirrels. One is mother and other is ten days old inexperienced youth. The story is narrated by the third person narrator. The narrator missed the meeting of a certain committee that evening. It was quitely unintentional to see the activities of the squirrels to miss the meeting. In this story R.K. Narayan deftly described how the mother instructed the youth to reach their porthole which was about a height of two feet. Their home was on the other side of the university wall. Perhaps the youth was on his second day's outing. The narrator gave a slight description of his physical appearance: "The young squirrel had an excessively long bushy tail out of all proportion to his short tiny body, and moved jerkily" (153). The mother expected to be followed. She jumped down on the other side and disappeared. But the trouble was that the youth was not able to follow her. He stood and expected for a miracle to happen and carry him on the other side of the wall. Then the mother returned and asked still there. The young one said that he couldn't follow her. She climbed so high that he couldn't reach that place. At this the mother said that it was not really so high. Saying this she vanished again.

The little squirrel made useless effort to imitate his mother. Mother thought that everyone could run about as she did. She reappeared and asked him to come home. The mother was very anxious because the sun was about to set and they had to go home immediately. She advised again: "Take a deep breath like this. You need not hop up right from zero as I do, though you would do it soon. Take a dozen paces back as I am doing" (154). The young one followed her instructions. She said to take it in a run and rise himself up as she was doing. After this she hurriedly got out of view. He lay beside the wall, and expected the return of his mother with fresh instructions. When his mother came he was so tired that he wouldn't look up. His mother scolded him. The mother apprised him that it was not a safe hour for them. R.K. Narayan described this in the following words:

> The mother grew alarmed. Dusk was falling, an owl was hooting somewhere, some unknown birds or bats were wheeling about, and the deadly crows were returning to their nests – not a safe hour. The mother stood against the wall stock- still till the enemies got out of range; the young one followed her example and stuck close to her (154).

The mother asked him to make an honest attempt. She instructed again. She went up and down a dozen times and the young one tried to imitate her but every time fell back. The young one made a few more efforts and the mother said that she couldn't be proud of him. His attitude showed that he was not serious. He didn't know that it was in fact a race with time. Darkness would be on them in a few minutes and they had to reach their home. These words showed the real anxiety of the mother:

"We ought not to be here anymore. See those school youngsters returning from the playground; they will stone us, and there is a dog barking somewhere. This is a very unsafe world. We must go away immediately". The mother again demonstrated, and the young one executed more or less a caricature of her. The mother's patience was at an end now. She appeared for the last time at the porthole and demanded, "Are you coming home or not?" (155).

The young one said to carry him as she did that day. At this the mother replied that day was not this day. If he was young enough to be rolled up and carried between her jaws, she need not to his advise. The mother said that they alone are awake and their enemies are about them. So they must go soon. The youngster replied that he couldn't. The mother did not wait to listen the full sentence. He calmly turned away on the other side and disappeared. She stopped for a moment to say that God is above. If he was destined to see the following day he would definitely see it. What could she or anyone do for him? The young one waited restlessly the foot steps of his mother. He was afraided of darkness. He made various efforts to reach the hole, he practiced all the tips his mother had given but it was in vain. He was completely tired and lay down.

Observing him the narrator felt that there was an occasion for him to request to the university authorities to decrease the height of portholes on their compound walls. He wanted to help the young one. That time he gave up all attempt, ran for the nearest tree. From this height he called his mother many times but she didn't respond to any of his call. The narrator saw by his watch and knew that that scene had gone for exactly an hour and a quarter. When the convener of the meeting saw the narrator next day, they said that he had disappointed them once again. At which the narrator said that he was busy unexpectedly.

The story is very amusing. R.K. Narayan draws the couple of squirrels as if they are the living characters. The plot is compact. There is no looseness anywhere. Narayan engages the attention of the readers till the end of the story.

"Four Rupees" is a beautiful story with Ranga's avarice for money as its theme. This story repeates *The Guide* theme on a different level. Here is a typically effective Narayan's beginning:

> Ranga was never certain what he was going to do next. He sat out of his little home in Kabir Lane, and by the time he turned the corner at Market Road, he always found some odd job coming his way. Today a very peculiar task offered itself as he sat near the Market Fountain. A servant from a bungalow in the extension was going round with a searching look in his eyes. He explained, "Our brass pot has fallen into the well. Do you know anyone who can get into the well and bring it out?" (157).

Ranga said that he must see the well first and he wouldn't take less than two rupees. The servant agreed. Ranga was amazed because he didn't expect that his offer would be accepted. It was for the first time that he was going down a well. He tried to escape but the servant wouldn't let him go. When Ranga and the servant reached at the master of the bungalow they became very happy to see Ranga. They took him to see the well first. After seeing the well Ranga demanded four rupees. After some bargaining they agreed. He had never earned four rupees in a lump so he was very happy. He said that he would come back in the evening as he had to go because he hadn't eaten his food till then. At which they took him to feed. They allowed him to rest for about half an hour and then called him to the well. He tried to make a final attempt to escape. He felt if he attempted an escape, they might pick him up bodily and dropped him into the well. He took his shirt and dhoti and called for a rope, tied its end to the cross-bar of the well and let the other end down into the well. He climbed the wall, slid down the rope and stretched out his legs to reach the foot hold out into the side- wall. He was hesitating in going down. Then they increased his labour by a few annas. When he said if he didn't come up again, to inform his wife, they burst into a laugh at hearing this. At last he found the brass pot. Coming from the well he lay flat on the ground for an hour. When he awoke they said that he was a good fellow. They would summon him again if anything was dropped into the well. They asked about his residence but he refused to tell anything. He demanded his wages. They gave him four rupees and four annas. At this he argued to give four rupees and twelve annas. They became furious and said that there was no limit to his greed. When Ranga went home he had to face the ill-temper of his wife. R.K. Narayan describes this in these words:

> When Ranga went home, his wife and mother-in- law were, as usual, at the door. On seeing him his wife snarled "It is seven O' clock. When am I to buy the things and cook the food ? You think I am born to slave. It will be a fine lesson if you are made to do without a meal tonight . . . ." He flourished his four rupees and four annas. "Four rupees! Are you sure you didn't steal it?" He explained, showing his bruises on his elbows and knees. They just laughed and replied, "Never knew you to go near a well; more likely you have been in scrape and pulled the money out of somebody's pocket . . . ." (160).

"Flavour of Coconut" is one of the slighter pieces in the collection. It is the story of a trapped mouse and a boy's response to it. What makes the story interesting is the way Narayan recounts it. For quite sometime in the beginning of the story it is not clear that the story is about the trial of a criminal:

> It was a formidable gathering of accusers. People seemed only too ready to pick up and throw just another pebble at one who was already down. The walls of the prison were hemming him in, the bars seemed to be fixed in molten lead. This was both a dock and a prison. The trial was summary, because the times were dangerous. The distinction between prison and dock was a luxury for other prisoners – not for this dangerous creature. He looked up at the faces around, possibly for a sign of hope. The judge, grey-haired and bespectacled, would not betray anything in his face. His mind seemed to be preoccupied with some unfinished work; he looked as though he had been interrupted while doing some more worthwhile job. He had a pen over his ear; any moment he might snatch it and dash

> off the death sentence. He looked at the prisoner coldly. It was impossible to guess what he had on his mind. Of course, not to be unfair, he looked quite dignified and authoritative and anxious. But he seemed at the same time unduly eager not to displease the prosecution. Though left to himself he seemed to be the sort of judge who would unlock the fetters and cry to the prisoner: "Get out, and let me not catch you again" – But that was just a wishful fancy in the prisoner's fevered mind. It was impossible to guess how a judge would act. The jury looked too grim and behaved queerly. Sometimes they too joined the prosecution vociferously – a most irregular procedure. It was impossible to say who was the prosecutor and who the jury. It looked as though the whole thing was going to be settled by the prosecution alone without so much as a word of defence. (161)

Finally it is decided that the mouse has to be killed. A servant would take the cage out and drown the mouse in water. The small child who has been given the task of calling the servant is hesitant. He does not want the mouse to be killed. He has a desire to open the trap and let the mouse escape. His elder brother is watching him so he cannot do so. The servant comes and picks up the trap. At first the boy does not want to see the sad sight, but he is overcome by his curiosity and so follows the servant out:

> He knew that the servant was coming to take the trap to the execution yard, and wondered for a second whether he should not run away from this sad spectacle, but he was overcome with a morbid curiosity, and followed the servant mutely as the rat trap was picked up and taken out. (165)

"Half A Rupee Worth" is another story of the collection. The central character in this story is Subbiah, a grain merchant, born and brought up to be one, who lives among and for his bags of rice. When the war comes and brings in its wake food rationing, it does not take Subbiah long to master the art of making money out of the needs of the hungry. Corrupt and corrupting, Subbiah does not ignore even the smallest opportunity of adding to his wealth. It is over such a deal, for a mere half a rupee worth of rice, that he meets his death. In this story Narayan directly introduced Subbiah and his work. Here is the beginning of the story:

> Subbiah sold rice at the market gate. In his shop you found, heaped in wicker baskets, all varieties: from pebbly coarse rice to Delhi Samba, white as jasmine and slender as a needle. His shop was stuffy and dark but he loved every inch of it. He loved the smell of gunny sack, of rice and husk, and he loved the warm feel of rice cascading into his baskets freshly arriving from the mill. Through good times and bad he flourished. There were days of drought when paddy didn't come up and the rice mills were silenced, when people looked hollow-eyed and half dead. But even then he never closed his shop. If he didn't find stuff for twenty baskets, he scoured the countryside and filled at least two baskets, and sold them. There were times when the harvest was so rich he could hardly accept a quarter of the grain that was offered, when it seemed a fool's business to be selling rice. If you sold rice all day and night you could not hope for a profit of even fifty rupees. They called it "depression in the trade." (175)

But Subbiah survived all ups and downs. He had served as a sort of unpaid shop assistant, when his father sat at the desk and counted cash. That time Subbiah was not interested in the rice bags which were at the shop. He desired for the crowded streets, cinemas, football matches, and wrestling tournaments, which he only glimpsed through the crowded shop door. But his father trained him in this way that he thought nothing except rice and the market. When his father died he took charge of the shop that nobody saw the difference. Most of the people thought that Subbiah's father was still there counting cash.

Business increased. Subbiah kept five cows and buffaloes at home, whose milk, curds and butter, he and his wife and five children consumed day and night and became rotund and balloon like. He purchased a few acres of land in a nearby village. He used to go there once in six months to survey his possessions to make sure that they were unharmed. He used to give money at an excessive rate of interest and acquired dozens of houses and their rent increased his savings bank account every month. He became a very wealthy man. He admitted his children to a school, and appointed a tutor to teach them at home. He adorned his wife with gold ornaments and dressed her in Benares silk. He added on to his house two more storey and several halls and painted all the walls with a thick blue oil paint, and covered them with hundreds of pictures of the gods in gold coloured frames.

Whole of the day he sat near his iron safe and kept money into it. It was an entirely satisfying and tranquil condition. It seemed no cause why it should not go on everlastingly. The same set of activities and interests, going on and on, money collected and rice coming in and going out, and then one or the other of his sons to gain his shape and appearance and continue the family business. It seemed, for all practical purposes, a region beyond life, death and change. It might have been so but for the war. It frightened him. It seemed at first to be the end of all things. But after the first shock was over, it seemed not so bad after all. His profits heaped up as never before. Saigon and Burma wanted rice and it meant the stock's worth was in gold. Number of people assembled into his shop all hours. He purchased several godowns and dozen more villages. He adorned his wife and daughter with more gold and enhanced his own girth.

War seemed, on the whole, a very beneficial force- till food control came in. for the first time in his life he was perplexed and worried. He couldn't see how anyone had the right to say what he should sell and for how much. He howled day and night to a set of his admiring friends and assistants. He thought that Government didn't know of his business and became very happy which is clear from these words:

> "Sircar, what do they know of this business? Let them content themselves with tax-collection, catching thieves, and putting up drains. What do they know of the rice business?" He felt happy when heard someone say, "The Food Department is a hoax. The Government are making a mess of things." He agreed heartily and implored, "Can't some edu-

> cated person like you represent to the Government? It's disgraceful." (177)

He soon found that he could still survive but only needed a new dress to go under. By waiting before official, and seeing people, and filling up forms, he was soon allowed to continue his business as a Fair Price Grain Depot. Following words showed his unhappiness for the scheme:

> He groaned unhappily when he learnt that he had to surrender all the rice his peasants laboriously cultivated in his village fields. The whole thing seemed to him atrocious. "They have to fix the price for my produce! They have to give me permission to take what I myself produce!" The scheme seemed to him tyrannical. But he accepted the position without much outward protest. (177)

But his cunning brain was already at work. He slept for a short while and lost the taste for food. All night his mind was occupied with the problem. At last he solved the problem. He said to himself:

> I still have my rice in the fields, and I still have the bags in my godown. If I can't use my wits and keep my hands on these I might as well perish. After all, what does the Government want? To have things in nice shape on paper- that they shall have. (177)

The main action of the story takes place when a man comes to his shop to buy rice. Subbiah had just closed his shop but the man was desperate for rice. He said that the member of his family had not eaten for the whole day. So he had come out to find some rice for them. He had gone to other shop but he had failed to buy rice. Finally he had come to Subbiah's shop. Subbiah did not want be bothered any more. The man pleaded to him to give him rice. He had half rupee with him for which he wanted a seer of rice. Subbiah agreed to give him only half a seer. The man had no option. He agreed to it. Subbiah took the money from him and asked him to wait for him. The man waited for a long time but Subbiah did not return. Finally, when it became very late the man went to Subbiah's house. He had not reached his house either. His wife became worried. When both of them went to Subbiah's secret godown they found it bolted from inside. They had to break open the door. Inside the godown Subbiah was lying under a heap of rice bags. He had died when the bags fell on him. Thus he lost his life for half a rupee. The story is a fine example of Narayan's comic vision of life. A man may think himself to be a very smart but in the end the mysterious ways of God outsmart him.

"The Antidote" is the story of a film actor Gopal. He would do nothing disagreeable on his birthday because Astrologers had told him that he might not see that birthday. When Gopal reached at the set he had no idea what he had to do or why because the director was not in the habit of narrating the story to anyone. The director instructed Gopal about the scene in this way:

> "When that telephone rings, pick it up with your left hand and say . . . remember that you are not to clutch the telephone so desperately, hold it gently, and don't pay any attention to it until it has given three clear rings. A habitual telephone-user will never be in a hurry to take the receiver."(181)

The director ordered him to be natural. He told him that there was only action, no dialogue for that shot. Gopal was very happy to hear this because he thought that he could go home early. He further instructed Gopal that his last word was 'hello'. He had to stop for a moment, let the telephone drop from his hands, fell back in his chair, and let his head roll to the side ever so lightly. Gopal asked curiously "why". The director replied because he had heard shocking news on the phone. Gopal asked again if that news made him faint. The director replied "no" he had to die on hearing it, on account of his heart failing. When Gopal desired to change the story the director became furious and asked the reason of talking unreasonable things. Then Gopal told him that was his birthday. At which the director wished him. Gopal told him his problem in detail:

> "Rather a peculiar birthday", explained Gopal. "This is my forty-ninth birthday. Astrologers have often told me that I might not see this birthday, and if I lived to see this day I should have nothing more to worry about. . . . I have lived

in secret terror of this day all my life. Whenever I saw my wife and children I used to be racked with the thought that I should probably be leaving them orphans. I came late today because we held some propitiatory rites at home for the planets, and we celebrated my survival this day with a feast. My astrologers have suggested that I do nothing unpleasant today, sir. I wish to treat it as a very auspicious day, sir" (183-184).

The director was impressed and ordered his assistant to bring the story writer. The story writer refused to change the story. Gopal said: "People generally like to see happy things on the screen, sir. I have seen the public turn away from the pictures which present scenes of death" (184). At this the boss replied, "You are wrong". He turned to the writer and said, "Formerly no doubt the public liked to see only happy stuff. Today is different. I have statistics. Pictures with tragic incident have grossed thirty percent more than happy stories, if you take the figures of the last six months. (184-185)

At last, the director asked Gopal if he would be ready to go through that scene the next day. Gopal replied with relief that he would do whatever he might order the next day – even the funeral. At that time the assistant came and informed that they had to do that scene that day. They were not getting that floor the next day because the other unit wanted it for the palace set. Finally, Gopal became ready to die. Narayan ends the story in his typical vein of humour:

> Lights were on. The camera was ready to shoot. The director howled "Action". Gopal dropped the telephone. His head fell back and rolled slightly to the side. Scores of persons were gazing on his dying with satisfaction. But before the director cried, "Cut" Gopal did something which he hoped would pass unnoticed. Though he was supposed to be dead, he shook his head slightly, opened his right eye, and winked at the camera, which he hoped would act as an antidote to the inauspicious role he was doing. (185-186)

"Under the Banyan Tree" is the last story of the collection. It is an idyll of pastoral life. The story takes us into the old pastoral world of peace and tranquility inhabited by selfless, sober, sympathetic, cooperative people. The atmosphere of the story is strange yet beautiful. The charm of the story lies in the remoteness of the setting. Narayan introduces the village Somal where the story took place. Nambi is the leading character of the story. He entertained the villagers by telling stories. He was illiterate and the written words were mystery to him, but he could make up a story in his mind within one month. It took ten days to narrate him a story. If anyone asked him his age he referred to an ancient famine or an invasion or the building of a bridge. His home was the little temple which was at the very end of the village. No one could say how he became the owner of the temple. The temple was a very small structure with a stone image of Shakti in the sanctum. The front part of the temple was Nambi's residence. He spent most of the day in the shade of the banyan which spread out its branches in front of the temple. The villagers provided him food and clothes. On Friday evening people gathered at the temple to perform worship. Nambi lit a score of mud lamps and arranged them around the entrance of the temple. He decorated the image with flowers and acted like the priest and offered to the goddess fruits and flowers given by the villagers.

At night Nambi had a story to tell. So he lit a lamp and put it in a niche in the trunk of the banyan tree. It was the signal for villagers to listen his story. When they returned home in the evening they saw this, and told their wives that the story teller was calling them. As the moon went behind the hillock men, women and children assembled under the banyan tree. Nambi would not appear till then. He would be sitting in the sanctum before the Goddess, with his eyes close in deep meditation. He came with his forehead smeared with ash and vermilion. He took his seat on a stone platform in front of the temple. He began the story with the question:

> "A thousand years ago, a stone's throw in that direction, what do you think there was? It was not the weed covered waste it is now, for donkey to roll in. it was not the ash-pit it is now. It was the capital of the king . . . ." The king would be Dasaratha, Vikramaditya, Asoka or anyone that came into the old man's head; the capital was called Kapila, Kridapura or anything. (189)

Thus Nambi went on non-stop for three hours. He described brilliant durbar hall where a hundred vassal kings, ministers, and subjects sat. In another part of the palace all the musicians in the world gathered and sang. Nambi sang most of the songs over again to his audience. He narrated in detail the pictures and trophies that hung on the walls of the palace. Story-building was on an epic scale. The first day hardly conveyed the setting of the tale, and audience till then had no idea who was coming into the story. When the moon went behind the trees of Mempi Forest Nambi stopped the story. He suddenly rose and went to sleep.

After two or three days the light in the niche would again be seen throughout the bright half of the month. The villagers laughed with Nambi, they wept with him, they loved intensely heroes, cursed the villains and expressed grief or pain when the conspirator had his success. They prayed to the God for happy ending. On the last day of the story the entire crowd went into the sanctum and prostrated before the Goddess. When the next moon peeped over the hillock Nambi had another story. He never repeated the same sort of story. It had gone on for several years. One moon he lit the lamp in the tree. The audience came. He took his seat and started the story. "... When king Vikramaditya lived, his minister was . . ." He stopped and could not get above it. He began the story again with the freshness. There was the king . . ." He repeated it again and again and then his words drew into a vague mumbling. He could not understand what had happened. He stammered and looked so miserable that his audience asked him to take rest. He told them to wait a moment, he will tell the story. The audience waited patiently. Nambi sat gazing at the ground, bending his head in thought. It was first time he realized that he was old. He felt that he would never be able to control his thoughts or express them in a convincing manner. When he looked up he found that everyone had gone except his friend Mari, the goldsmith.

Next day, he lit the lamp in the niche. The people gathered under the banyan tree sincerely. Nambi had spent the entire day in meditation. He had been praying to the Goddess not to leave him.

He started the story, and went on non-stop for an hour. But after few minutes he felt dried up. He faltered. The audience went to their home without uttering a single word. After two days he had another instalment of the story and that also ended within few minutes. The crowd dwindled. Fewer persons took note of the lamp in the niche. These persons came out of a sense of duty. Nambi realized that there was no use in extending the struggle. He told the story to a speedy and premature end. He knew what was happening. He asked the Goddess why she had struck him mute. He closed himself in the sanctum. He did not eat any food and spent the most part of the day sitting in meditation.

The next moon peeped over the hillock. Nambi lit the lamp in the niche. When the villagers returned home, they saw the lamp, but only a few came. He inquired about the others and said he would not tell the story that day nor the next day until the entire village came there. He told that was a powerful story and everyone must hear it. Next day he went to the village street to declare that he had a most wonderful tale to tell that night, and requested not to miss it. This personal appeal had a great effect upon the villagers. As a result a huge crowd assembled at night under the banyan tree. They were happy that the story teller had regained his power. Nambi came out of the temple and said:

> It is the mother who gives the gifts; and it is she who takes away the gifts. Nambi is a dotard. He speaks when the Mother has anything to say. He is struck dumb when she has nothing to say. But what is the use of the jasmine when it has lost its scent? What is the lamp for when all the oil is gone? Goddess be thanked . . . These are my last words on this earth; and this is my greatest story. (191)

After saying these words he went into the sanctum. He sat there with his eyes closed. They asked if he was not going to tell them a story. He opened his eyes and shook his head. He indicated by his gesture that he had spoken his last words. After this he lived for a few more years, but never told a story.

CHAPTER – VII
CONCLUSION

Man has been telling stories for thousands of years. Indeed telling stories and listening to them must be as old as language itself. The short story as a literary form in English is however, quite recent. The short story is a convenient substitute for novel for it offers on a smaller scale and in a brief manner the same pleasures that the novel does. In 1842, the American writer, Edgar Allen Poe had offered a definition of the short story, which is still valid. He said it was "A short prose narrative requiring from half an hour to one or two hours in its perusal." It generally depicts a single incident in a forcible way leaving a strong impression on the minds of the readers. Plot, characterization and structure are combined to create a short story.

R.K. Narayan is the foremost Indian English writer of today. As a serious artist, his greatest preoccupation is to study man in his surrounding atmosphere. As a novelist and short story writer of international fame, he delineates his characters quite interestingly in the panorama of Malgudi life. The protagonist is imparted sufficient liberty to play his life-role under different environmental conditions, and the author observes him silently counting his success or failures. This preoccupation with his human characters has been repeatedly asserted by the author: "My main concern", he declares, "is with human character – a central character from whose point of view the world is seen and who tries to get over a difficult situation or succumbs to it or fights it in his own setting. (Dwivedi, 169)

Unlike Mulk Raj Anand, Narayan's artistic view does not emphasis primarily the social and political aspects of life; rather he focuses his attention on character and personality. The basis of his characters is mutual human relationship. Narayan himself has said, "I value human relationship very much, very intensely. It makes one's existence worthwhile – human relationship in any and every form, whether at home or outside. I think I have expressed this philosophy in my work successfully." (Dwivedi, 169) From the very commencement of his literary career, Narayan has employed ceaselessly the technique of irony which makes his characters and situations interesting and consequently imparts sufficient pleasure to the minds of his readers.

The setting of all the novels and short stories of Narayan is in the imaginary small town of Malgudi in South India – a place representing the world in miniature. "It is better for a writer to know a great part of the world remarkably little", says Hardy in his Note Books. (Dwivedi, 169) Narayan's fiction satisfies the truth of this statement. All the novels and short stories of Narayan are imbued with what D.H. Lawrence has called "the spirit of place."

As a creative artist, much of the finest achievement of Narayan has been in the comic rather than the tragic mode. The short stories of Narayan are readable due to their quality of finish and the role played by irony in them. He is an embodiment of the comic spirit, and the eccentricities of his characters are quite fascinating. He treats his characters deftly and deceptively. We find almost no satirical portrayal of his characters in his works; where satire is expected, we find mild comedy instead. Even serious hypocrites are portrayed with considerable sympathy. He is an artist who does not want a change in the world and sets out to show as it is. "Why take life too seriously?" asks R.K. Narayan, and says: "Mine is an unserious attitude to life." It is clear that the other side of life – spiritual and redemptive – is to be taken seriously. His works are pregnant with the Universal theme of 'failure and identity.' His heroes aspire for easy success with little effort and consequently look ridiculous to readers.

Narayan's ironic vision of life is due to the fact that he is fully aware of the irremediable incongruities with which life is constantly confronting us. In his early novels & short stories, Narayan uses irony as a means to amuse his readers. But later on, his ironic technique has been directed in different directions. In his masterpieces Narayan has advanced a few steps ahead, and in them this technique develops into a vision of life. "It is of the nature of irony", says Hillaire Belloc, "that it should avenge the truth . . . . Irony . . . . has this quality about it, that, like some fiery sword, it cannot be used with any propriety save in God's purpose." (Dwivedi, 171)

The short stories of Narayan are remarkable more for their workmanship and finish than for the quality of the reading of life they offer, and one of the chief reasons for this is the limited role played by irony in them, though a persistent ironic note is, by and large, their distinguishing feature. These stories belong to the native Indian soil and are redolent of its culture. They mainly depict the south Indian life and clearly express his view of the world and those who live in it. Simple but fascinating plot lively characterization, strict economy of narration and beautiful simplicity of language are some of the most outstanding features of these stories. They serve as a good introduction to the foreigner who wants to acquire knowledge of Indian life.

Malgudi Days is the first collection of short stories of R.K. Narayan. It was published in 1942. There are eight stories in this collection – "Naga", "Selvi", "Second opinion", "Cat Within", "The Edge" "God and the Cobbler", "Hungry Child", and "Emden." "Naga" describes the plight of a boy more than ten years old whose father, a snake charmer, has abandoned him leaving him a snake enfeebled by age to impress the street crowds. This story brings out effectively the pathos in the life of the little boy. Contrasted with the cruel behaviour of the father is the humane relationship between the boy and the snake. The second story "Selvi" is about a well known singer Selvi. Her husband Mohan interferes in his carrier. He is presented as a selfish and self-centered man. For him money is more important than any other thing. In a way the story reminds us of R.K. Narayan's novel *The Guide*. In that novel Raju who was behind making Rosie, a famous dancer also tried to control her life in the same way. Rossie became fed up with Raju's commercial attitude as Selvi is with Mohan's in this story. "Second Opinion" deals with the character Sambu who refuses to marry his mother's cousin's daughter. But when he comes to know that his mother would not live long from his family doctor Kishen he agrees to marry. He decides to take a second opinion on his mother's condition from doctor Natwar, a cardiologist and neurosurgeon. Sambu takes a sigh of great relief when doctor Natwar tells him that there is nothing wrong with his mother. Knowing this he again refuses to marry because he is afraid of losing his independence. In this story Sambu's self centered individualism gets a proper focus. He does not want to take responsibility of marriage on his shoulders. "Cat Within" deals the theme of superstitions and blind belief in ghost. It is a typical example of Narayan's humour. The description of the exorcist in the story reminds us of the astrologer in the short story "An Astrologer's Day." "The Edge" is remarkable in the sense that it reflects a particular feature of India's socio-political situation at a particular time – something which Narayan does not usually do. The story was obviously written during the period of emergency in the mid- 1970s. At that time the family planning programme of the Government of India – was going in full swing. Unfortunately, the medical officers and the other employees engaged in this work adopted both fair and foul means to achieve their goal. People particularly from the lower section of society were lured by the promise of money and gift to undergo family planning operation. This is what happens to Ranga the central character in the story. "God and the Cobbler" is the story of a cobbler and a hippie. In the seventies hippie from America were quite a common sight. They were young men and women who had left their country in search of spiritual happiness and peace. In this story Narayan depicts one such hippie. He comes to the cobbler to get his sandal mended. In "Hungry Child" R.K. Narayan also takes up the clue from the earlier novel *The Painter of Signs*. The central character of that novel, Raman is also the central character of this story. The story is about a lost child in a fair whom Raman meets. Narayan describes the activities of the lost child. "Emden" deals with reminiscence of the past life of an old man, Rao whose age is between ninety and one hundred and five.

Narayan's collection of short stories, *An Astrologer's Day and Other Stories* was published in 1947. In the title story "An Astrologer's Day" a town astrologer meets a client and reads his past correctly, saying that a man had knifed him in a village brawl years ago. He tells the man that the person who knifed him is dead and adds that he sees once again great danger in his life if he goes away from home. The story ends with the shock of the discovery that the astrologer was himself the person who knifed that man and then the irony of both his reading of the past and his advice to his client is brought home. In "Missing Mail" an altruistic postman conceals the news of a near relative's death from a family in order that a wedding, which for certain urgent reasons cannot be postponed, can take place on the appointed day. The bride's father comes to know the truth only at the end. "The Doctor's word" deals the character Dr. Raman who is very straightforward and truthful in dealing with his patients. He treats his friend who is suffering from heart attack. He tells a lie to his friend by giving him the hope of survival. This creates a great confidence in the mind of his friend, and he eventually recovers. The doctor himself gets surprised and says how he has survived this attack will be puzzle to him all his life. In "Gateman's Gift", an illiterate watchman receives a registered letter and assumes the worst ('only lawyers send registered letters') so much so that he goes mad, and his sanity is restored only on learning that the letter contained a cheque presented to him by his boss. "The Blind Dog" is a rather simplistic presentation of canine affection, which offers no variation on a common place theme. "Attila" presents another dog story, who accidentally catches the man with whom it was friendly and the man is traced as a thief. In "Fellow Feeling", a typical scene in a crowded train compartment is turned into a hilarious situation. Rajam Iyer picks up the quarrel with a brawny fellow- passenger but outwits him in a casual and clever manner. "The Roman Image" is spun around an image with an arm an eye, the nose, and the mouth missing. It was accidentally discovered by the Talkative Man in the river Sarayu. It was identified by the learned doctor (the archaeologist) as the image of Tiberius II, a Roman Emperor. The joke here is that it is neither a Roman image nor has Tiberius II ever existed, but it is that of a dwarpalaka of a nearby village temple. In "The Watchman" the girl considered herself to be a burden on his step mother. She lost her mother when she was five years old, and her father had died a few years ago. She did not want to live on anybody's charity. She had lost hope of getting a scholarship and someone was coming to have a look at her. She felt that she had no home and wanted to plunge herself into a watery grave.

"The Tiger's Claw" describes Talkative Man's supposed encounter with a tiger, alone and bare-handed, in a remote village. "The Performing Child" is the story of a little girl whose parents hope to make Rs.10, 000 out of her when her talent for dancing attracts a couple of film makers. But when the latter suggests that she should wear a frock and let her hair down, she just disappears, causing a scare. The parents have no idea where she might have gone, mother gets hysterical, father is helpless, until they locate her in the dhobi (washerman's) linen basket and pull her out in a swoon. That puts an end to the child's film career. In "Father's Help", which is a "Swami" story, young Swami armed with his father's letter of complaint against the teacher Samuel addressed to the head master deliberately courts punishment at Samuel's hands, hoping to have his revenge at the end of the day when he would hand over the letter to the head master. His hopes are suddenly frustrated when he comes to know that the headmaster is on leave that day and hence the letter has to be given to his assistant – viz., Samuel himself. Crime and Punishment" is the story of a poor teacher, ambitious parents and a naughty child with below-average ability. For only thirty rupees a month, the teacher patiently puts up with the lectures on child psychology delivered almost everyday by the educated parents. This story is comparable to Narayan's novel *The Financial Expert*. "Iswaran" is a psychological study of the behaviour of a diffident boy who is mocked by others. He gets unexpected brilliant success at the intermediate examination. This rouses his feelings to a fever pitch. The boy jumps into the Sarayu and dies. Whether it is an act of suicide or an accidental death due to frenzy of exuberance is something very difficult for us to say. Narayan, as we have already seen, is against suicide. "Evening Gift" is the story about a confirmed drunkard who employs a companion to check his drinking after nine in the evening and take him home to safety. Sankar who has the burden of paying off a substantial family debt takes up this job. One night, he is dismissed from his service by his master while in his drunken state – with an advance salary for four months. Sankar is quite delighted to be off, for after all, keeping an incorrigible drunkard company is no pleasant task. He accepts the money, decides to get back to his village, and the next morning is seen doing some shopping buying things for his mother, his sister, and the small child at home. But then, even as he is about to leave the place, he is arrested by the police on the charge of robbing his master taking advantage of his weakness. "The Snake Song" is Talkative Man story. In this story he tells the readers about his two strange encounters on a certain night: first with an unseen Sadhu who curses him that his music is at end for having refused him both food and music; next soon after mendicant's departure, with a black cobra which is apparently drawn to the place by the compelling power of his music. The latter is the startling and mysterious and forms the climax of the story. "A Snake in the Grass" is another snake story. On a worm afternoon when the dwellers of the bungalow are at their short sleep, a cyclist tells that big cobra has got into their compound. Narayan describes deftly how the whole family tried his best to get rid of cobra. In "An Accident" a car which for no conceivable reason suddenly stalls is set right by a fellow who turns up from nowhere, gives out his name as Arul Doss, and is later identified with a driver of the same name who had died in a car accident a month earlier at that very place. This is like any other ghost story. But in "Old Man of the Temple" and "Old Bones", the ghost of persons long dead enter the body of the living – a driver in the first instance, a young boy in the second – and the living thereupon talk and act exactly as the dead would have. The middle-aged driver talks with the accents, the pipes and trebles of an old, old man; and the twelve-year old Raju, provoked, takes his massive uncle roughly by the neck and flings him out of the room. In "Such Perfection" a sculptor Soma who makes a too perfect image of Nataraj later ascribes the devastation of this imperfect world to this very image. Narayan's description of the cataclysm is superb. In "Career" Ramu, a frustrated servant fall in love with a girl from Hyderabad, squanders his master's money and ruins his credulous master completely. "Forty five a month" tells the story of a poor clerk working for years and years on forty rupees a month. He resolves one day to take up his little girl to the cinema, which he can do only if he leaves his office on the stroke of 5, not keep working there till 7 or 8 at night as has become his habit. "Dasi the Bridegroom" is a touching tale of an ugly and mentally retarded young man Dasi. He falls a victim to a heartless joke of the people that Bamini Bai, charming film star from Madras was his wife and she had arrived in town. What he gets from her is a slap in the face for calling himself his "Bridegroom." He ultimately explodes in a fury of anger and ends in a mental hospital. "Out of Business" is a story of a man Rama Rao who works in a gramophone company as the Malgudi agent, loses his job because the owner of the company meets death due to a crash. Rao's financial condition deteriorates and his family is thrown into utter poverty. This stringency forces him to make an attempt for suicide. He lies across the railway lines, but fortunately is saved due to the late running of the train. In "The Axe" an old gardener, who is fondly attached to a sprawling houses loses his job when the ownership changes. The new owner is determined not to afford space for gardening. One day, one of the sons of his old master comes asks Velan, the gardener, to go back home because the house has been sold to a company. Moreover, the company is not interested in maintaining a garden. The gardener then hears the sound of an axe, and finds four men engaged in hacking the old margosa tree; he expresses his reactions because he has planted the tree and loves it as a child. Hurriedly he quits the place before the tree is demolished. We find a verisimilitude in "The Cherry Orchard" of Chekhov, but Narayan has avoided the challenge of his tragic theme in this story. In "Engine Trouble" the talkative man tries to make a story out of the fantastic idea of winning a road engine for a prize, and its consequences. In fact he makes a comic adaptation and elaboration of the familiar proverb about gifting an elephant to poor man. It gives him an opportunity to satirize incidentally municipalities and municipal administration. "All avoidable Talk" deals the character Shastri whom his astrologer friend has advised to avoid all avoidable talk the next day. Shastri follows his friend's advice. "Fruition at Forty" offers little more than the somewhat trite reflections of an office clerk on his fortieth birth- day."

Narayan's next collection of short stories is *Lawley Road and Other Stories*. It was published in 1956. It comprised twenty eight tales out of which fourteen have been reprinted from the previous collections. In this collection, as in most of his fiction Narayan is concerned more with character than with plot. He notes that he discovers "a story when a personality passes through a crisis of spirit or circumstances", but some stories present flashes of significant moments in characters lived without any dramatic circumstances; others simply show "a pattern of existence brought to view." Many of the pieces in this collection have a reportorial quality – there are sketches and vignettes, character studies and anecdotes. The title story of the collection is delightful. Named after a typical thorough fare in the fictitious city of Malgudi, the story recounts how Kabir Lane is named as Lawley Road. This story seems at first to be a mere variation of "Engine Trouble." Instead of road engine we have here an equally improbable object, a huge statue of molten lead, which the narrator gets free of cost from the Malgudi Municipality. The two stories have more or less the same pattern of development, and rely on fantasy for much of their effect. And in both there is a good deal of satire. Perhaps "Lawley Road" is the most satirical of the Talkative Man's stories and rouses good humoured laughter at many of the lapses, commissions and ommisions of Municipal Councilors and petty local politicians. But the Talkative Man is too good a man to be a pungent and indignant satirist. As a short story "Lawley Road" is much better organized. The statue of Sir Fredrick Lawley is no mere curiosity like the road engine, but becomes the centre of attention for all Malgudians whose strong patriotic passions are roused by it. Therefore "Lawley Road" is much more convincing than "Engine Trouble", through based on an equally improbable situation. The narrator of this story is one of Narayan's most engaging recurring characters, whom the people of Malgudi have nicknamed, "The Talkative Man" or TM for short, who lends distance and historicity to the story. In another strong story "The Martyr's Corner", the focus is on a humble seller of bondas, dosais, and chapattis rather than on the violent action. It is the character of the vendor – his dreary and drab life and his attitude toward existence that holds the interest of the reader. The story is about a street vendor who used to sell edible items in the evening. This story is one of those stories of Narayan which end on a serious note. It also deals with the little ironies of life, but the irony in this story takes away all happiness from the life of the hero of this story.

"Trail of the Green Blazer" is the story of a pickpocket Raju who cunningly picks the purse of a man in the Green Blazer. He takes away the cash from it, and before he tries to throw the purse away, he finds a toy balloon tucked inside it. His heart is filled with filial affection and pity for the child whom it is meant and decides at last to put the purse back in the blazer's pocket and is caught red-handed. This story is a good example of Narayan's use of irony. Life is full of contradiction and this is what the story conveys to us in a typical Narayan's way. The pickpocket was successful so far he was a professional devoid of human sentiments. As soon as he became sentimental he was caught. "Wife's Holiday" presents Kannan, the gambler, as a deceiving guardian who taking advantage of his wife and child's temporary absence smashes the little money-box and takes away all the coins. He returns home losing all the money, meets his family and apprehends the consequences. The absence of irony makes the story pointless. There are also a number of stories where a child's feelings or reactions are in focus. In "A Shadow" a boy's sorrow for his dead film-star father is lightly suggested in a mixture of his pride and enthusiasm, his longing to see his father's last film, his delighted recognition of details in it which remind him of their real-life relationship. It is not until the end. When the lights go up, that he realizes the finality of his parting from his father. The boy's emotions are set off by the different expression of his mother's mourning, the unbearable pain she suffers on seeing her husband on the screen.

There are some stories about simple minded adults with an innocent love for children. One of them is "Sweets for Angels" in which Kali still thinks of himself as an urchin "although to the outside world he appeared six feet tall." He is looking forward to the pleasure of offering sweets to the school children he admires and delights in seeing. His generous offer is misunderstood as an attempt at kidnapping and he is exposed to severe mob violence. Another case is "A Willing Slave" with the Ayah who so completely enters the games and fantasies of her protégés that she renews her own infancy with each child of a large family. "Leela's Friend" is also a story demonstrating the devoted and childish adult who is a little girl's best friend and compassion but is harshly and unfairly treated by her parents and society in general.

In "Mother and Son", Ramu, an unemployed and unmarried youth quarreled with his mother, abandoned his home and did not return at night. His mother, with her usual fears and anxieties, apprehended that he has gone and drowned himself in the water, but is finally relieved to trace him next morning in deep slumber on a bench near the tank. "The White Flower" is a mild satire on the superstitions and blind belief in astrology. In this story there are autobiographical elements. Krishna is the reflection of R.K. Narayan. In the same way Narayan had fallen in love with Rajam and their horoscopes had not also matched. The story resembles to Narayan's novel *The Bachelor of Arts*. It employs the horoscope motif much in the same way as that novel.

Narayan has written various stories about children. "The Regal" is one of them. The story is about a twelve years old child Dodu who is very fond of playing cricket. But he could not find place for it. Earlier he had played with few of his friends at the home. After this he didn't play there because one day all the flower buds in the compound of the house had been destroyed. In this story Narayan has narrated skillfully how Dodu made his cricket club by his effort and struggled for finding the place for it. "Man-Hunt" is one of those funny stories of Narayan which are remarkable for their surprising ending. We often come across advertisements in newspaper about missing person. Generally there is a reward for the person who would bring back the missing person. This story revolves around this very fact. Sankar, the central character of this story comes across such an advertisement which announced a cash prize for him who could bring a man called Gopalkrishna. There was a photograph of the missing person. "The Artist's Turn" is the story about a poor artist Krishna who does not accept anything from the greedy publisher and fault-finder who knows little about art. "A Night of Cyclone" is Talkative Man story. In this story storm is described in a superb manner.

Narayan's collection of short stories, *A Horse and Two Goats* was published in 1970. It contains five long stories. Each one of them is a finely executed part of an admirable sequence of fiction, relaxed but profound. The title story deals with Munni, a village peasant, and his meeting with a red man from the United States. Munni thinks that the red man wishes to buy his two goats, whereas he bargains for the big clay horse in the shade of which Munni sits. The language barrier is responsible for confusion about a statue and a pair of goats, with hilarious results. The second story "Uncle" is a masterpiece; it slowly unfolds the mystery that tease a growing boy about his benevolent but inexplicably sinister uncle. It also takes the reader to the world of childhood with its frightening fancies and distorting mirrors, reminiscent of Narayan's novel *Swami and Friends*. "Annamalai" and "A Breath of Lucifer" deals with two simple, hardworking faithful servants. Annamalai is an eccentric gardener who attaches himself to a reluctant master. Sam in "A Breath of Lucifer" with an autobiographical preface is a Christian male nurse. In the end, both Annamalai and Sam, governed by their own impulses, unceremoniously leave their masters. "Seventh House" dealing an astrologer and superstitions, touchingly explores a husband's tender devotion to his sick wife. Each one of the five stories is a character study; all the stories are embellished with picturesque native custom. The dominant tone throughout the collection is casual, understated.

The next collection of short stories, *Under the Banyan Tree and Other Stories* was published in 1985. The title story, fittingly taken from Narayan's first collection, reaffirms story telling as a central human activity. The villagers of Somal "lived in a kind of perpetual enchantment. The enchanter was Nambi the story-teller." Yet having regaled his audience for several years with his tales, Nambi spends the rest of his life in "Great Consummate Silence." In "Nitya" Narayan presents a fine story based on the principle of "Generation Gap." Nitya a college student of twenty years shows his unwillingness to offer his fine and well-cared hair to fulfil a vow made by his parents, when he was two years old and stricken with whooping cough and convulsions. Nitya half convinced, goes to the place of worship. When all the arrangement are made for the tonsure ceremony, he argues with his parents and priest and suddenly leaves the place and thus avoids a rape of his locks. "House Opposite" is the story of a hermit who could not concentrate on meditation on account of a prostitute who lived across the street from his opposite house. His mind was always occupied with thoughts of that lady. "A Hero" is the story of a young school boy Swami who accidentally caught a thief who had hidden himself under the bench, and become a hero among his school friends. In this story there is a reflection of R.K. Narayan's first novel *Swami and friends*. The character Swami is taken from that novel who is the main character of this story. "Dodu" is another story about a child Dodu. In this story Narayan mildly satirize the attitude of the elderly people towards the child. By bringing in the Pests-Man climbing up a coconut tree and plucking out the sap found at its top, Narayan creates a typical South Indian atmosphere. Things collected by Dodu reminds us of Tom Sawyer, an immortal character of Mark Twain, and his choicest treasure. "Another Community" is a moving story of a martyr at the bloody altar of communal blood bath – one of the rare stories of Narayan with a topical theme. It reveales Narayan's hatred of communal riots. "Like the Sun" is the story about a man Sankar who is a teacher and fixed a day that he would not tell a lie but absolute truth. Whole of the day he faced many situations in which he told absolute truth. What result he found of his practicing truth, in this story Narayan describes this very skillfully. "Chippy" is a very delightful story about a dog Chippy who felt jealous of another dog which his master has brought home.

"Uncle's Letters" traces the life of a man from birth to his eightieth birthday by means of the letter written by an uncle to his nephew but the description here to clings obstinately to conventionalities. The story is a collection of uncle's letters; uncle writes letters to his nephew and affords us an insight into the life of an average South Indian. The story is written in epistolary form. Narayan tried only once this form in this story. "The shelter" deals the plight of a woman who left his husband's house and began to work for harijan. "The Mute Companions" is a delightful animal story. It deals monkey. Sami, the deaf and dumb beggar found the money searching his bag. Sami caught it and taught him several tricks to perform in the street. One day he went to perform before some big house and there his monkey disappeared and never found. Perhaps the owner of the house had caught him. Sami had to depend again upon alms. "At the Portal" is another animal story. It deals a couple of squirrels one is mother and other is ten days old inexperienced youth. In this story Narayan described how mother squirrel teaching her young one to climb up a wall, while the youth has its own fears and anxieties. "Four Rupees" is a beautiful story with Ranga's avarice for money as its theme. This story repeats *The Guide* theme on a different level. "Flavour of Coconut" is the story of a trapped mouse and a boy's response to it. For quite sometime in the beginning of the story it is not clear that the story is about a mouse. We get the impression that it is about the trial of a criminal. "Half a Rupee Worth" is the story about Subbiah, a grain merchant, born and brought up to be one, who lives among and for his bags of rice. When the war comes and brings in its wake food rationing, it does not take Subbiah long to master the art of making money out of the needs of the hungry. Corrupt and corrupting Subbiah does not ignore even the smallest opportunity of adding to his wealth. It is over such a deal, for a mere half a rupee worth of rice, that he meets his death. "The Antidote" deals a film actor Gopal who would do nothing disagreeable on his birthday because astrologers had told him that he might not see that birthday so he denied the director to do the dead scene on his birth day. He desired to change the story of the film but director refused. At last he had to do the dead scene. Though he was supposed to be dead, he shook his head slightly, opened his right eye, and winked at the camera, which, he hoped would act as an antidote to the inauspicious role he was doing.

Narayan's novels are set in Malgudi but Malgudi is not the locale of all his short stories. Sometimes the action takes place in Mysore, sometimes in Banglore, Madras, Kritam and other places. In his stories, Narayan has depicted familiar situations and explored ways of life with which he was intimate. But the people here represent humanity at large and hence Narayan's short stories have universal appeal. Some of Narayan's short stories contain parallel characters.

Several of Narayan's characters are illiterate. Characters like Doctor Raman form an exception. As Frank O' Connor says: "The short story has never had a hero what it has instead is a submerged population group." (O' Connor Frank 18) Narayan also has his own waifs. He presents poor artists, neglected working, peddlers, astrologers, beggars, rickshaw pullers, lock repairers, servants and attendants and other homeless, helpless persons. What Narayan says for the vendor in "The Martyr's Corner" is applicable to him also. His custom was drawn from the population swarming the pavement. Quite a number of his stories are character studies, "a glint of mankind." The characters are both believable and likeable. Narayan loves them all and it is this that illumines them.

Narayan's minor characters are more assertive than any of his major characters. In the brief precious moments allowed to them they act their part exceedingly well. With the deft strokes of a clever artist, Narayan creates living and breathing characters which haunt our memory long after we have finished reading his stories. Narayan's major characters can be divided into three or four categories as under:

We meet idealists like Sekhar ("Like the Sun"); Doctor Raman ("The Doctor's Word"); Soma ("Such Perfection"); Gopal ("The Antidote"); Kutti ("The Performing Child"); Krishna ("The Artist's Turn") etc. These characters are self-willed or wayward. Sekhar would not tell a lie on the day devoted to the practice of truth, though his vow drives him into a corner. Doctor Raman has developed a blunt truthfulness. He does not believe that agreeable words ever save life. It is none of his business to provide an "unnecessary dope" when Nature would tell the truth presently. Soma, the sculptor, would not maim the image of God though perfection infuriates nature. Krishna, the poor artist, would not accept anything from the greedy publisher and fault-finder who knows little about art. Kutti hates the "cinema men" and would not dance or sing for any film. Gopal would do nothing disagreeable on his birthday. He would at least shake his head and open his right eye though he has to play the part of a dead man.

We come across practical people like the astrologer ("An Astrologer's Day"); Thanappa, the postman ("Missing Mail"); the Priest ("The White Flower"); and the watchman in a story, titled, "The Watchman." The astrologer accepts Guru Nayak's challenge without being intimidated, names his antagonist, takes him into confidence, inspires faith in his knowledge of astrology and makes the antagonist flee homeward by employing a clever trick. Thanappa, the postman, does not deliver a letter and a telegram to Ramanujam. For he knows that the marriage of Ramanujam's daughter must not be postponed under any circumstances. It was only after Kamakhi's marriage that Ramanujam learnt about the sad demise of his uncle. Krishna wanted to marry the girl whom he loved. But the horoscopes did not match. The priest asked a child to pick up one flower out of the two presented to her and to put it or the door-step of the sanctuary. The girl picked up the white flower which stood for God's permission for the wedding.

In Narayan's short stories there are sentimental characters like Govind Singh ("The Gateman's Gift"); Iswaran ("Iswaran"); Sankar ("The Evening Gift"); and the girl in ("The Watchman") also play their part in Narayan's short stories. Govind Singh does not follow the advice of the people to open the registered letter that he has received and to read the contents. Iswaran presumes that he has failed at the intermediate examination and behaves like a desperado. He hates the idea of going to the Senate Hall to know his examination result. Sankar does not tell his employer a word about his problem but leaves the wealthy drunkard at the moment when Sankar's company was badly required. A police complaint was lodged and Sankar who "felt sick of his profession of perpetual cajoling and bullying" the wealthy drunkard, got into hot water.

The girl in The Watchman considered herself to be a burden. She did not want to live on anybody's charity. She had lost hope of getting a scholarship and someone was coming to have a look at her. She felt she had no home and wanted to plunge herself into a watery grave.

Another category of R.K. Narayan's characters is household servants. Household servants in Narayan's fiction are broadly speaking, honest, hard working and sincere but rather simple to a fault. Ramu ("A Career"), a frustrated servant fall in love with a girl from Hyderabad, squanders his master's money and ruins his credulous master completely. We have already seen how Annamalai and Sam the Christian male nurse leave their masters in the lurch. The beggars that we come across in short stories are as a rule, cheats. Pachai, the blind beggar in "Sweets for Angels" is not really blind. Narayan has heroes; no heroines. His female characters are passive and unimpressive. Rare exceptions like Bamini Bai in "Dasi the Bridegroom" only prove the rule. Many of his female characters are like those of Dickens. Narayan hardly cares to mention them by their names. He does not assign to them any important role. They do not have independent existence. Yet they all bear some feminine traits. Children in his stories are playful, innocent, intelligent, resourceful, and mischievous. They are against conventional discipline and hence often ill-treated by superior parental or educated authority.

Narayan's short stories, unlike his novels, are usually either not mentioned at all or dismissed as by-products, not to be taken seriously. The author himself may be said to cultivate such a view expressed in the following way in his introduction to his latest collection of short stories:

> I enjoy writing a short story. Unlike the novel, which emerges from relevant, minutely worked-out detail, the short story can be brought into existence through a mere suggestion of detail, the focus being kept on a central idea or climax (Shrinath, 184).

Narayan has written more than ninety short stories. Most of them first appeared in The Hindu or other periodicals, among them Narayan's own short-lived quarterly, Indian Thought. They have subsequently been published in book form, the later collections always printing varying selections from the earlier ones together with some new material. The original conditions of publication determined the size of the stories – they tend to be very short. In later years when the author has not had to think of the newspaper format he has been able to expand at leisure, which is the most immediately striking difference to be noticed in the last few collections. In the earlier stages we may suspect that the demands on his time as a journalist may also occasionally have had a hampering effect.

When Narayan's stories have received any attention at all from literary critics there has mostly been a brief account of the content and, possibly, a classification according to subject matter, such as stories dealing with children, animals or ghosts, with social or economic problem, with ironical, pathetic or humorous situations. In these stories, we find a single stroke of irony. In some of his stories, irony works like a linked chain, causing laughter at every moment. Tragic irony does not appeal to Narayan so much as comic irony. He softens the seriousness of tragedy with a comic effect unlike his novels; the finer artistic resources of Narayan leading to the comic exposure of eccentricity do not find full expression in his short stories. Almost all the short stories of Narayan are built around either situation or character. But whenever he discards these props and tries his hand at a different kind of short story, all his attempts prove abortive. All the short stories of Narayan have got a clear-cut technique, and he subscribes to the idea of the well-made short story. They are compact and neatly structured. Narayan's fiction and stories are example of the harmony of style with subject. The beginning and the end of Narayan's well-made short story are very important, and like O. Henry, Narayan tackles them very efficiently. Narayan's stories may begin in diverse ways, but they endeavour carefully what H.E. Bates, referring to O. Henry, describes as "an instant contact between reader and writer" (Bates, H.E, 63). No doubt, Narayan is greatly influenced by O. Henry, especially in his technique of the trick finale. In all his stories where irony plays a major role, whether it is comic or tragic in nature, the ending surprises the reader.

As a short story-writer, Narayan's real strength as a stylist lies in his strong ironic sense. On the other hand, he obviously "lacks the flair for the imaginative and the passion for the profundities which Raja Rao offers or the kind of verbal exuberance and hearty gusto characteristic of Mulk Raj Anand" (Naik, 137). The influence of journalism on the style of Narayan cannot be neglected – both the virtues and sins of journalistic writing are evident in his works. But at his best, Narayan "succeeds in turning his very limitations into artistic assets" (Naik, 137). Regarding his style in narration, Narayan seems to be at his strongest. He is quite competent in the presentation of his dialogue, while the limitations of his style "are betrayed when he tries to indulge in imaginative scene-painting, his descriptions of places usually being workmanlike, rather than evocative" (Naik 138).

No doubt, Narayan has written quite a good number of short stories, but unfortunately none of his short stories deserves the rank of universally acknowledged masterpieces. In this regard his stories are inferior to those of Mulk Raj Anand (e.g., his "Birth" and "The Lost Child") or to those of Raja Rao (e.g., "Javni" and "The Policeman and the Rose").

Narayan began his career as a short-story writer and obviously he could not free himself from the influence of the magazine story which carries a limited purpose to amuse the reader. Naturally, he failed to develop his talent much beyond that. The thematic range of Narayan's short stories is limited, though he has portrayed a great variety of characters drawn from the lower and middle strata of society. This variety is not matched by a corresponding thematic richness and the result is that the reader finds a "general lack of social, political and even existential awareness and urgent emotional involvement" (Naik, 104) in Narayan's short stories.

Lastly, Narayan's limited thematic range and lack of richness in experience and imagination, which are vital ingredients of great short stories, do not impart him a superior rank among the great short-story writers of the world.

BIBLIOGRAPHY

Primary Sources

Short story collections by R.K. Narayan

Malgudi Days. Mysore: Indian Thought Publications, 1986, originally published, 1941.

An Astrologer's Day and Other Stories. Mysore: Indian Thought Publications, 1968. First published in London: Eyre and Spottiswoode, 1947.

Lawley Road and Other Stories. Delhi: Orient Paperbacks 1982. Originally published, 1950.

A Horse and Two Goats. Mysore: Indian Thought Publications, 1982. First published in New York: Viking, 1970.

Under the Banyan Tree and Other Stories. Madras: Indian Thought Publications. First Indian Edition 1992, reprint 2001. First Published in Great Britain in 1985 by William Heinemann Ltd., and in the US by Viking Penguin Inc.

Novels by R.K. Narayan

Swami and Friends. Mysore: Indian Thought Publications, 1983. First Published in London: Hamish Hamilton 1935.

The Bachelor of Arts. Mysore: Indian Thought Publications 1985. First Published in London: Nelson 1937.

The Dark Room. Mysore: Indian Thought Publications, 1986. First Published in London: Macmillan, 1938.

The English Teacher. Mysore: Indian Thought Publications, 1985. First Published in London: Eyre and Spottiswoode, 1946.

Mr. Sampath. Mysore: Indian Thought Publications, 1985. First Published in London: Hamish Hamilton 1949.

The Financial Expert. Mysore: Indian Thought Publications, 1984. First Published in London: Methuen, 1952.

Waiting for the Mahatma. Mysore: Indian Thought Publications, 1984. First published in London: Methuen, 1955.

The Guide. Mysore: Indian Thought Publications, 1984. First Published in New York: Viking, 1958.

The Man-Eater of Malgudi. Delhi: Hind 1979. First Published in London: Heinemann, 1962.

The Vendor of Sweets. Mysore: Indian Thought Publications, 1981. First Published in London: The Bodley Head Ltd. 1967.

The Painter of Signs. London: Penguin, 1985. First Published in New York: Viking, 1976.

A Tiger for Malgudi. Mysore: Indian Thought Publications, 1983. First Published in London: William Heinemann, 1983.

Talkative Man. Mysore: Indian Thought Publication, 1986.

The World of Nagraj. Mysore: Indian Thought Publications, 1990. First Published in London: William Heinemann, 1990.

Grandmother's Tale. Mysore: Indian Thought Publications, 1992.

Retold Legends by R.K. Narayan

Gods, Demons and Others (Tales from ancient Indian epics). Delhi: Hind, 1979. First Published in London: Heinemann, 1965.

The Ramayana. Mysore: Indian Thought Publications, 1973.

The Mahabharata. Mysore: Indian Thought Publications, 1979. First Published in New York: Viking, 1978.

Other Works by R.K. Narayan

Reluctant Guru. New Delhi: Orient Paperbacks, 1974. Originally Published 1964.

My Dateless Diary. Delhi: Orient Paperbacks, 1969.

My Days:A *Memoir*. Mysore: Indian Thought Publications, 1975. First Published in New York: Viking, 1974.

A Writer's Nightmare: Selected Essays 1958-1988. Penguin Books, 1988.

A Story- Teller's World: *Stories, Essays, Sketches*. Penguin Books, 1989.

Salt & Sawdust: *Stories and Table Talk*. Penguin Books, 1993.

The Writerly Life: *Selected Non-Fiction* ed. S. Krishnan. New Delhi: Viking, 2001.

Secondary Sources

Amur, G.S. *Indian Readings in Commonwealth Literature*. New Delhi: Sterling, 1985.

Batia, Aban T. and Mathur, P.S. ed. *Twenty Short Stories*. Delhi: Oxford University Press, 1976.

Bhagwat, S. Goyal. *R. K. Narayan's India: Myth & Reality*, New Delhi: Sarup & Sons, 1993.

________________ *A Critical Spectrum*. Meerut: Salabh Book House, 1982.

Biswal, Jayant.K. *A Critical Study of the Novels of R.K. Narayan.* New Delhi: Nirmal, 1987.

Bhatanagar, M.K. *New Insights into The Novels of R.K. Narayan.* New Delhi: Atlantic Publishers and Distributors, 2002.

Budholia, O.P. *Critical Essays on Indian English Literature.* Jaipur: Book Enclave, 2003.

Bates, H. E. The Modern Short Story in English. London, 1941.

Dwivedi, A. N. *Studies in Contemporary Indian English Short Story.* Delhi: B. R. Publishing, 1991.

Dhawan, R.K. *Commonwealth Fiction.* New Delhi: Classical, 1988.

Dodiya, Jaydipsinh. (edited) *Perspectives on Indian English Fiction.* New Delhi: Dominant, 2002.

Gilra, Shiv.K. *R.K. Narayan – His World and His Art.* Meerut: Saru, 1984.

Gupta, G.S. Balarama. *Indian English Literature: Some Forays.* New Delhi: Anmol, 2003.

Hudson, H. *An Introduction to the study of Literature.* New Delhi: Kalyani Publishers, 2000.

Holmstrom, Lakshmi. *The Novels of R.K. Narayan.* Calcutta: Writers Workshop, 1973.

Hariprasanna, A. *The World of Malgudi: A Study of R.K. Narayan's Novels.* New Delhi: Prestige Books, 1994.

Iyenger, K.R. Shrinivasa. *Indian Writing in English.* New Delhi: Sterling, 1985.

Karnani, Chetan. *Eminent Indian English Writers: An Assessment.* Delhi: Rawat, 2001.

Kumar, Gajendra. *Indian English Literature: A New Perspective.* New Delhi: Sarup, 2001.

Kumar, Gajendra and Ojha, Uday Shankar(edited). *Indian English Fiction: Readings and Reflection.* New Delhi: Sarup & sons, 2003.

Longman, Valerie Shaw. *The Short Story: A Critical Introduction.* London: 1983.

Mc. Leod, A.L. ed. *R.K. Narayan: Critical perspectives.* New Delhi: Sterling Publishers Pvt. Ltd., 1994.

May, E. Charles. *Critical Survey of Short Fiction Second Revised Edition.* California: Salem Press, 2001.

Maheshwari, Vinod Kumar (Edited). *Perspectives on Indian English Literature.* New Delhi: Atlantic, 2002.

Mukherjee, Meenakshi. *The Twice Born Fiction: Themes and Techniques of the Indian Novel in English.* New Delhi: Arnold-Heinemann, 1974.

Mehta, P.P. *Indo-Anglian Fiction: An Assessment.* Bareilly: Prakash Book Depot, 1968.

Nair, N. Gopalkrishnan. *Contemporary Indian English Literature. The Short Stories of Manjeri Isvaran: A Study in Themes and Techniques.* New Delhi: Prestige Book, 1996.

Naik, M.K. *The Ironic Vision: A Study of the fiction of R.K. Narayan.* Jalandhar: ABS Publications, 2001.

__________ *A History of Indian English Literature.* New Delhi: Sahitya Academi, 1982 (1989, 92, 96, 97, 99).

__________ *The Indian English short story- A Representative Anthology.* New Delhi: Arnold Heinemann, First Published, 1984.

__________ *Twentieth Century Indian English Fiction.* Delhi: Pencraft International, First Edition 2004.

__________ *Dimensions of Indian English Literature.* New Delhi: Sterling, 1984.

Naik, M.K. and Shymala. A Narayan: Indian English Literature. Delhi: Pencraft International, 2004.

Narasimhaiah, C.D. "Indian Writing in English- An Introduction." The journal of commonwealth Literature, vol.5, July 1968.

Naik, M.K. *Indian English Literature 1980-2000: A Critical Survey.* New Delhi: Pencraft International, 2001.

Naikar, Basavaraj (edited). *Indian English Literature.* New Delhi: Atlantic, 2002.

__________ (edited) *Indian English Literature: Vol.* V. New Delhi: Atlantic, 2004.

O, Connor Frank. The Lonely Voice. Macmillan.

Pontes, Hilda. *R.K. Narayan: Man and Writer A Bibliography of Ezekiel, Nissim.* (ed) *Indian Writing in English.* New Delhi: Concept, 1983.

Prasad, Amar Nath. (ed) *Critical Response to R.K. Narayan.* New Delhi: Sarup & Sons, 2003.

Prasad, Amar Nath. *Critical Essays: Indian Writing in English.* New Delhi: Sarup, 2003.

Phillips, David Scott. Perceiving India through the works of R.K. Narayan, Mulk Raj Anand and Raja Rao. New Delhi: Sterling, 1986.

Parmeshwaran, Uma. A Study of Representative Indo- English Novelists. New Delhi: Vikas, 1976.

Ram, Atma. *Indo-English Writers Series-3 Perspectives on R.K. Narayan*. Ghaziabad: Vimal Prakashan, First edition, 1981.

Rao, Ranga. *Makers of Indian Literature R.K. Narayan*. New Delhi: Sahitya Academi, First Published 2004.

Ramakrishna, D. *Critical Essays on Indian English Writing*. New Delhi: Atlantic, 2005.

Subramanyam, Ka Naa. *Modern Indian Short stories: Volume Three*. New Delhi: Secretary Indian Council for Cultural Relations, 1977.

Sundaram, P.S. *R.K. Narayan*. New Delhi: Arnold Heinemann, 1973.

___________ *R.K. Narayan as a Novelist*. Delhi: B.R. Publishing Corporation, 1988.

___________ *"Malgudi: the World of R.K. Narayan." The Indian P.E.N.*, vol.43,nos. 1-2, 1977.

Sinha, U.P. *Patterns of Myth and Reality: A Study in R.K. Narayan's Novels*. Delhi: Sandarabh Publishers, 1988.

Singh, Pramod Kumar. *The Novels of R.K. Narayan*: A Critical Evaluation. New Delhi: Atlantic Publisher, 1999.

_________________ *Five Contemporary Indian Novelists. (An Anthology of Critical Studies on Mulk Raj Anand, Raja Rao, R.K. Narayan, Kamala Markandaya and Bhabani Bhattacharya)*. Jaipur: Book Enclave, 2001.

Singh, R.A. *Critical Essays on R.K. Narayan's Novels*. Jaipur: Book Enclave, 2002.

Shrivastva, Ramesh K. *Six Indian Novelists in English*. Amritsar: Guru Nanak Dev University, 1987.

Sinha, Krishna Nandan, ed. *Indian Writing in English*. New Delhi: Heritage, 1979.

Surendran, K.V. *Indian English Fiction: New Perspectives*. New Delhi: Sarup & Sons, 2002.

Indian Literature in English: New Perspectives. New Delhi: Sarup & Sons, 2002.

Shahane, V.A. Kushwant Singh. New York: Twayne publishers Inc., 1972.

Venugopal, C.V. The Indian Short Story in English (A Survey) Bareilly Prakash Book Depot, First Edition, 1976.

Vyaghreshwarudu. B. *Themes and Techniques in R.K. Narayan's Short Stories. New Insights into the novels of R.K. Narayan*. Edited by M.K. Bhatnagar, New Delhi: Atlantic Publishers and Distributors, 2002.

Verma, M.R. and Sharma A.K. (edited) *Reflections on Indian English Fiction*. New Delhi: Atlantic, 2004.

Walsh, William. *R.K. Narayan: A Critical Appreciation*. New Delhi: Allied Publishers Pvt. Ltd. First Published in Great Britain 1982, First Indian reprint 1983.

Williams, H.M. *Studies in Modern Indian Fiction in English*. Calcutta: Writers Workshop, 1973.

Walsh, William. *Indian Literature in English*. London: Longman, 1990.

Williams, H.M. Indo-Anglian Literature 1800-1970: A Survey, Madras: Orient Longman, 1976.

Westbrook, P.D. "The Short Stories of R.K. Narayan" The Journal of Commonwealth Literature 5. July 1968.

Journals

The Literary Criterion (Mysore), December, 2000.

The Journal of South Asian Literature (Asian Studies center, Michigan State University), Summer 2001.

The Journal of Indian Writing in English (Gulbarga), January, 1985.

Indian Literature (New Delhi), December, 1988. *New Quest* (Pune), July-August, 2000.

The Indian Literary Review (New Delhi), September-October, 2002.

Commonwealth Quarterly (Mysore), Special Issue on Indian-English Women Writers, December, 1978.

Littcrit (Trivandrum), June, 1982.

Journal of Literature and Aethetics (Quilon), April-September, 1982.

The literary Criterion, December, 1983.

Ariel (University of Calgary, Canada), October, 1985.

The Literary Criterion, December, 1983

Littcrit, (Trivandrum), 1998.

Littcrit, (Trivandrum), 1990.

Indian Literature, (New Delhi), 2002.

Indian Literature, (New Delhi), 2001.

The Quest (Ranchi), December, 2000.

Encounter: Journal of Policy Research and Developmental.

Initiatives (Delhi), July-August 2000.